Geogirl

by

Kelly Rysten

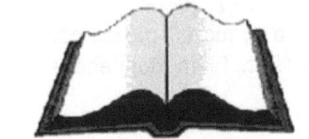

CCB Publishing
British Columbia, Canada

Geogirl

Copyright ©2014 by Kelly Rysten
ISBN-13   978-1-77143-150-7
First Edition

Library and Archives Canada Cataloguing in Publication
Rysten, Kelly, 1960-, author
Geogirl / by Kelly Rysten. -- First edition.
Issued in print and electronic formats.
ISBN 978-1-77143-150-7 (pbk.).--ISBN 978-1-77143-151-4 (pdf)
Additional cataloguing data available from Library and Archives Canada

Cover artwork by Kelly Rysten: www.kellyrysten.com

Cache In Trash Out and Geocaching are trademarks and Travel Bug is a registered trademark of Groundspeak, Inc. Used with permission.

Publisher: CCB Publishing
              British Columbia, Canada
              www.ccbpublishing.com

This book is dedicated to more than a million people. It's to all those who hide caches in interesting places, create odd containers, and share their little known favorite quirky things around the world with the rest of us. How would I know about the giant cow at the California/Nevada border, about how mining was done in the early 1920's, or where to buy the best pizza in a town of 30 without geocachers pointing the way through their little, hidden containers? How would I know that a pool a hundred feet down from a wire platform was the home to a fish that only lives in that one pool? I followed a geocache description there! I even sat in a fake electric chair, just because of geocachers.

Then there's the finders, the people who search through rain, snow, sleet and hail in the dark of night and then post interesting stories about their adventures... and misadventures.

I can't leave out the geocachers at Groundspeak Inc., owners of geocaching.com, and all the reviewers, the lackeys who travel from event to event, and Signal the Frog who attends mega events just to say "hi!" or rather... wave hi. Signal doesn't speak. I've discovered Signal. Have you? Or the can of beans... have you discovered the can of beans?

Anyway... here's to all you geocachers who walk, ride, paddle and fly to find elusive boxes hidden in weird places and keep the hobby, obsession, addiction alive.

And finally to my husband, best friend and geocaching buddy TSPI who goes with me on almost every hunt. May we find more lookout towers, weird little fish, and tunnels of mice. Maybe someday we will actually see a bat! So many tunnels, so few bats.

Cache on!

Other books by Kelly Rysten

Kelly Rysten is also the author of the Cassidy Callahan Adventure Novels. Cassidy Callahan is a young woman who grew up on a quarter horse ranch. Given free run of the local hills she developed an eye for tracking, and with the help of Detective Rusty Michaels, she joined the local search and rescue team to track lost hikers. Unfortunately she is also a terrible trouble magnet, and her job brings her into contact with more trouble than the police can keep her out of. One adventure follows another as Cassidy tracks her way from one mishap to another.

The books are:

Triple Trouble
Published 2009 – ISBN 978-1-926585-41-3

Car Trouble
Published 2010 – ISBN 978-1-926918-03-7

A Cache of Trouble
Published 2011 – ISBN 978-1-926918-87-7

A Double Dose of Trouble
Published 2012 – ISBN 978-1-77143-025-8

A Shot of Trouble
Published 2013 – ISBN 978-1-77143-107-1

Chapter 1

What do you do when you're in college, school's about to get out for the summer, you're up at two a.m. the night before a final, and a friend comes into the university library and says, "You're going to think I'm crazy, but there's this HUGE geocaching contest and the winner gets to take somebody on a four day cruise to the Bahamas."

Well, I can tell you what I did. I tried to think of how to study exponential equations and set up a coffee IV drip at the same time. When I realized I had no coffee, no needles or tubing or a bag to put coffee in I began trying to figure out how to get Twiggy to get me some.

Most people would hear a name like Twiggy and immediately think of the skinniest girl they knew and take off about twenty pounds. Twiggy was thin, but he wasn't that skinny. He mostly got his name from being all elbows and knees. He was like one of those bugs that look like a walking stick. He was good at coming up with harebrained schemes and running out for coffee. Or vodka. But I'd never had vodka and tonight called for coffee, so I rubbed my eyes and said, "Coffeeeee," in a desperate sounding voice.

He just stood there, arms folded across his chest and said, "You're pitiful."

"Thank you, now go away, or at least help me with this problem. I don't see how they got from point A to point 62B to the negative 7th."

"You're still pitiful. Let me see."

He took my book and my page of incorrect notes and squinted at it.

"How many weeks did you sleep through class?" he asked.

"I don't sleep in class. I don't even sleep at night!"

"You, dearie, need help. You need to take a week off as soon as school gets out and go with me to find little boxes hidden in weird places. After your mind is clear of the sheer numbness of college classes you can think about changing your major again."

"I change it every semester, but it doesn't help the classes get any easier. It just means I know how to talk about anything from astrophysics to art in the seventeenth century."

"That might be a useful skill," he said. "Did you know there is a spot on Mercury that looks like the Mona Lisa?"

"Wrong century. That was the sixteenth century."

He closed my book and held out his hand. "Coffee, or sleep. You need one or the other. Do you want to hear about the contest or not?"

"I don't want to flunk my final."

"What's your average?" he asked.

"Three point seven, but I…"

"The final won't bring you up to an A and flunking it won't lower it to a C so forget about point A and point 62B to the negative 7th."

Just the fact that he could remember my gibberish proved he was smarter than me. I staggered after him hoping he was going to the nearest coffee shop. I tripped over a student who had fallen asleep with his face in a book and his legs stretched across the walkway. Taking an exam with a crick in your neck is a bad way to start off a day of finals.

"I can't go with you on this contest," I said. "My mom expects me home for my sister's birthday. It's her sweet sixteen and I'm supposed to do her hair."

"Hair shmair. She's going to have hair whether you do it or not, right?"

"Right."

"So, she's a big girl now. Let her do something daring like dye it blue and cut it like a rock star."

"Do you really think my mom would let her do that? My mom who wears dresses to the grocery store, who goes on a date so she can make out with my dad without 'exposing' the kids?"

"Okay, you're right. When is your sister's birthday?"

"The middle of July."

"Perfect! We have to finish the contest by July tenth anyway!"

My given name is Gwendolyn Amelia Brody, but this being a university full of eccentric and brainy people, they have to make an acronym out of everything, so my friends took GAB and decided I was to be Gabby from then on. Well, Twiggy did that. I can't say I have a lot of friends.

Twiggy's real name is Tony, not Anthony. It really is Tony. He is named after Tony Hawke, the snowboarder. So, let's see if I remember this right. Tony Van Yancy. The name Van came from Van Morrison. So you can see Twiggy's background is a little different from mine. His parents got divorced when he was four and his dad tried making a living racing cars but he sunk more money into cars than he ever won. Next he tried being a golf pro but ended up running the shop at the local golf course. He wore Bermuda shorts and polo shirts. He had tried going to college just like Twiggy but he majored in booze and drugs, so he strongly discouraged Twiggy from following in his footsteps.

My parents are proper. That's about the best description I can think of, which is really strange because in Creative Writing 101 I was the one who liked making up fictional, fanciful creatures and filling my stories with things the reader couldn't even imagine. So I only got a C. Luckily this story only contains real creatures. Or maybe that isn't lucky. Maybe what's lucky is that we survived.

I had been geocaching a few times with Twiggy. I thought it was fun and somewhat adventurous. To think there are containers hidden all around us and normal people walk by them all the time without knowing they are there is kind of mysterious. I felt like I was part of a secret society because I knew that the knot in the tree outside the Biology classroom concealed a little box hidden in it and if you reach up and in a little bit you can find it, but only if you know it's there. Geocachers carry a mystery with them everywhere they go!

"I want a large Super Charged Caffeine Torpedo," I said to the barista. The barista at the campus coffee shop was used to working nights during finals week. The Super Charged Caffeine Torpedo was so named because it would explode in your brain and cause massive damage, or at least keep you awake long enough to study. University students have a way of over naming just about anything.

"One shot or two?" she asked. She looked just like my sister would if she did what Twiggy said and cut her hair like a rock star and dyed it blue, except my sister was a little pudgy. My mom wasn't sure what to do with Meredith.

"One... no make it two," I said.

"Are you sure?" Twiggy asked. "You still need to sleep, you know."

"I'll sleep on Thursday," I said.

"Whipped cream?" she asked.

I looked down at my muffin top.

"No, just the caffeine please."

Twiggy didn't order coffee. He ordered a huge cookie. Sugar might help, too, I thought but then remembered my muffin top.

"So what's this contest?" I asked. "Are you seriously going to do it?"

"Yeah! My dad's got a fishing trip lined up and he said he'd leave the key under the eaves. He'll never know if I'm there or not. I don't really care about a cruise, but just think... geocaching an island overseas! Dang! I've never been on an island except when Dopey dared me to swim the lake at the park. All I found over there was tons of goose droppings. It made me glad the only way back was another swim."

"Geocaching in the Bahamas does sound adventurous," I admitted. "What makes you think you can win?"

"Because," he said, "I have the best geocaching partner."

"Oh cool! Who's going with you?"

"Uh... you?" he said hopefully.

"There's *no way* my mom would let me do that. Where is it? Where will we stay? What time will I get to sleep at night? Is there drinking, drugs, speeding, kissing or anything beyond holding hands involved? Those are all questions I have to have an answer for to get permission to go with you."

"Gabby, you're over eighteen. You're over twenty-one. You are old enough to do whatever you want."

"But I am not old enough to be disrespectful and do something that would send my parents into a worried, heart wrenching wait for their precious child to return from a wild fling with an irresponsible boy. My mom makes out with my dad on dates. She knows what cars are for."

"It's a wonder they had four kids."

"Twig! What a thing to say!"

"Well, it's true isn't it?"

"No! Well... I admit they are a little strict."

"A little? You're the only student I know who has to keep a chart proving they brushed their teeth every night. You don't even lie on it! You could just as easily sign the little box even if you don't brush your teeth."

"That would be lying."

Twiggy and I had this conversation often. It wasn't that he was a chronic liar or anything, it's just that his parents didn't keep track of him as carefully, and to be honest he could really use somebody to keep him from doing things he'd be sorry for later, which gave me an idea.

Chapter 2

I got a B on my final. In the classes I liked better I got A's just barely. I was a good student, but I wasn't destined for greatness.

"Hello?" my mom said when she answered the land line. I sure wish my parents would come up to speed with technology.

"Hi, Mom!" I said. "I did pretty good on my grades."

"That's wonderful, honey. Your dad and I are so proud of you."

Akk! She could sure pour it on thick.

"Thanks, Mom. Hey, I need some advice."

"Of course, honey, that's what mothers are for."

"I have this friend. We do this fun hobby together. And well, Twiggy has this bright idea to enter a contest. It involves this hobby, but it also involves some travel. I worry that Twiggy will fall asleep at the wheel or something and we're really the best of friends. We study together and hang out at the coffee shop. If you had a friend who just wanted to do something a tiny bit adventurous don't you think you should go along to, like, make sure they didn't fall off a cliff or get a speeding ticket or fall asleep and run off the road? We have so many similar interests. I can crank up the car stereo and do impromptu karaoke to keep us awake. I'll even teach Twiggy some hymns if I can go. It would just mean being a little late coming home from college, but I'd be there for Meredith's birthday." There, I thought that covered most of her questions.

"What is this hobby?" she asked.

"It's called geocaching!" I said brightly. "We look for hidden treasures."

"Like time capsules?" she asked.

"Yeah!" I said only lying a little, teensy bit. They were time capsules of a sort. They just represented a time very recent.

"Where are these time capsules?" she asked.

"Oh, all over the place! There's a few right here on campus! There are a few thousand of them in town."

"Really!"

"Yeah!"

"And where will this travel take you?" she asked.

"I don't know! That's half the fun! You see we go online and they have a treasure map." I felt a little guilty leading her on about the treasure or time capsule idea. The treasure was worthless and the time capsule was only half true. But she could understand the idea of looking on a treasure map for a time capsule. "The map gives us the coordinates to find the capsule."

"The coordinates?"

"Yeah! The longitude and latitude. We load the coordinates into Twiggy's GPS and it leads us to the capsules."

"Wow, you are learning a thing or two at college."

"Yeah, did you know the coordinates are broken down into degrees, minutes and seconds? We're given the coordinates down to three decimal places which is about three feet, so there is no way to get lost!" I crossed my fingers hoping she would believe me. I wasn't quite sure if it was that close but it could be.

"And this Twiggy, is she usually a responsible student?"

"Oh! Yeah! Better grades than me!" Without studying, I added mentally. "We study together a lot and I'm sure my grades have improved."

"When will you be home?"

"The eleventh!" I said. As long as I had answers and sounded excited maybe I could sway her.

"That's a long time. Where will you be staying?"

"We'll get reservations. I still have enough money for a night or two. Maybe Twiggy's parents will let us have a slumber party at their house."

My parents were so, so, so traditional. I had to think traditionally when I talked to my mom about things like this.

"Is there any partying involved? Any drinking?"

"Coffee, tea and soda."

"Drugs?"

"Only Tylenol if we drink too much coffee."

"Sex?"

"With Twiggy?" I asked.

"With anybody!" she almost gasped.

"Mom! What kind of a girl do you think I am?"

"I'll think…"

"Thanks Mom! Oh I just knew you'd see it my way! I'll be home in time to help Meredith get ready for her sweet sixteen! I can't wait to tell Twiggy!"

And I hung up. They sure didn't know what a schemer of a kid they raised.

Chapter 3

Bam, bam, bam! I pounded on Twiggy's dorm room door.

There was the sound of a chair sliding and stocking feet kicking things out of the way as someone came to the door. The door opened and there stood Skippy. Skippy was Twiggy's roommate. He was a cross between an Old English Sheepdog and a giraffe. He was tall and thin but his hair was light blonde, fine and long. With all those qualities it tended to fly out from his head so he looked like a young, tall Albert Einstein. Or maybe he was a cross between Einstein and Stretch Armstrong.

"Is Twiggy here?" I asked.

"He's in the shower," he said.

"Oh," I said looking down the hall. I wasn't allowed in the men's shower room. "Can you tell him I was looking for him? And tell him I'll wait for a little while at Holey Moley?"

"What's that supposed to mean?" he asked.

"He'll know where to go," I said.

"Okay. You sure seem excited about something."

"Don't tell him that. I'll just wait until I reach a stopping point in my book."

"Okay."

Holey Moley was the name of the geocache in the knot hole of the tree and the tree made a good reading spot. The only problem with reading there was that if a geocacher came looking for the cache they would think they couldn't. Geocachers are not supposed to search for a geocache in the presence of non geocachers. If they do, they are not supposed to be obvious about it. They call people who don't geocache muggles and if muggles were to see a geocacher geocaching they might think we were doing something suspicious and call the police. The police don't like to find what they called "suspicious packages" because they have to evacuate buildings, call the bomb squad and blow up perfectly harmless containers that only held a small notepad and a few toys. It was kind of a waste of time and resources. So when I read at Holey Moley I watched for geocachers and if anybody eyed the tree disappointedly I would wave them over and tell them I was a geocacher and then they could look. And even though I had only found ten caches I still felt like I was a real geocacher, because I had an account and a geocaching name and knew how many finds I had. That made it official.

My geocaching name is Grabby Gabby, which my roommate somehow made into something crude and sexual but really it just meant that I "made the grab" when Twiggy and I went geocaching. I don't know why I always found them before he did. He had much more experience at finding geocaches, but I still managed to find them first. I was beginning to think he really found them first but he wanted me to feel like I was doing well so he let me find them first. Holey Moley was the only one he found first and it was because he was taller. I could reach in the hole if I really stretched and stood on my tiptoes, but he didn't even have to stand on his toes.

I settled down with my book and fingered the pages. Hmm, I only had about a hundred pages to go to the end of the book. Maybe I would wait a little longer than I told Skippy. Then I spent several minutes wondering why Skippy needed a nick name, too. I decided if he was anyone else's roommate we would just call him Jake, but he was Twiggy's roommate and Twiggy was the one constantly assigning nicknames to people. I wondered how Skippy got his name. It wasn't a derivative from his real name. Then I remembered that Skippy's family lived along a river and his dad had a motorboat and a sailboat. They used the motorboat for quick trips to the store and they sailed the sailboat out to the ocean and visited ports up and down the east coast. Maybe Twiggy considered Skippy a junior skipper? For a smart guy Twiggy sure could be immature.

I was maybe fifty pages into my book when Twiggy walked down the sidewalk in my direction. He walked like Ichabod Crane and he had large feet so it was easy to recognize him amongst the other students. They all looked very relieved that classes were almost at an end. Some of them carried boxes of belongings. I needed to think about packing up, too.

"Guess what!" I said.

"You didn't really flunk your final and the coffee really did explode in your brain and you've lost ten million brain cells and you're in need of a second brain. Well, here I am!"

"I got my mom to not say no!" I exclaimed.

He thought about that for a second. "But she didn't say yes?"

"No, she didn't say yes, but she didn't say no and I said I'd be there for the party."

"What does that amount to in your family's language?" he asked.

"It means… I guess we better start planning!"

He wrapped his arms around me and lifted me clear off my feet, right there in the middle of the crowded sidewalk!

Ten minutes later we were back at the coffee shop.

"Okay, when is inspection?" he asked.

"The day after tomorrow."

"Are you packed up?"

"No!"

"You better start packing."

"I need boxes. It's amazing how much stuff one person can accumulate in one semester!"

"What are you going to do with it after you pack it up? You're not going home."

"Oh shoot! I forgot!"

"My stuff fits in my car. If it doesn't, I send a box on ahead and catch up with it later."

"I think my mom would freak if my belongings landed on the doorstep via UPS."

"So what are you going to do?"

"I don't know!"

"How much money do you have?"

"Maybe a couple hundred."

"We could rent a storage space for the summer. If your stuff fits in your car and my stuff fits in my car then one storage unit ought to hold all of it."

"What about the car?"

He frowned. Maybe we hadn't quite thought this out enough.

"Well, we have to crawl before we can walk. So let's crawl down to the store and get some boxes. We'll pack up and research storage units."

"What's going on?" asked my roommate, Sarah Culverson.

"Nothing," I said.

"Something's different about you. You're trying not to smile. You're *humming* as you pack!"

"I'm just glad to have finals over," I said.

"You've never been happy enough to suppress grins and hum before."

"Then maybe I need to get out more."

"Hmm," she said. "Is your family going on a vacation together?"

"No, but my mom has a big party planned for Meredith's birthday."

"That's so cool that your parents celebrate your Sweet Sixteen."

"I guess."

She huffed, frustrated that she was being left out of something that meant more to me than school ending or my sister's birthday.

"Hey!" I said. "How did you get through the semester without getting a nick name from Twiggy?"

"I refused," she said. "He tried to nick name me Pluto and I said, 'no way!' Then I just didn't respond unless he called me Sarah."

"You could have chosen what you want him to call you," I suggested.

"I wanted to be called Sarah."

Maybe Sarah was my parent's kid and not me.

"Why did he choose Pluto?" I asked.

"Because I used to wear my hair in a French braid around the side of my head and he thought it stuck out like Pluto's ears."

I tried to remember, but I couldn't recall how Sarah wore her hair at the beginning of the semester. I did agree that Pluto was a lousy nick name.

She got up and walked over to me. "So spit it out," she said. "What are you so happy about?"

"You really want to know?"

"Naaaahhh, I keep asking you because I don't want to know."

"I'm going on a geocaching road trip with Twiggy!" I said. I couldn't help but smile. I was going on a road trip!

"With a guy??" Sarah said.

"He's not a guy. He's my best friend!"

"Just in case you didn't notice," she said a bit sarcastically. "Twiggy… Ooo I hate nicknames. Tony is very much male. He walks like a guy. He talks like a guy. He drinks beer like a guy. He reacts to you like a guy."

"He does?"

"Yes, he does, and do you know what males think about when they go on a road trip with a female?"

"Geocaching?"

"Sex!"

"Twiggy respects me enough to know we are just friends."

"You… are… blind. Or ignorant."

"Okay! I think it'll be fun. He'll teach me all about geocaching. I will double my find count! Wow, can you imagine? Twenty finds!"

"How many does Tony have?"

"Last time I looked he had over two thousand."

"And you think twenty is a lot?"

"He's been geocaching for years. I've only been doing it for one busy semester."

"Wow," Sarah said. "I thought you were going to get married at forty and never have kids and travel the world with your rich husband and now it looks like you're here for your MRS degree!"

"I'm going geocaching! With a friend! I am not getting married. I am not having sex. I admit I don't really want to wait until I'm forty to get married but I am not interested in Twiggy. We're just friends who enjoy the same hobby."

"And developing new ones all the time," she muttered.

The next morning my cell phone blipped and I looked at the caller ID. Twiggy!

"Hey! I did it. I found a storage unit where the first month is free! We have to sign up for three months but if we split the cost I think we can do it."

"Cool! I'm almost packed!"

"Remember you need hiking shoes. Remember your jacket."

"It's summer! It's sweltering outside."

"Okay, do what you want. Just be prepared to hear I told you so when you freeze."

"Where are we going?"

"Wherever the contest takes us."

I wasn't sure what that might mean. So far I'd found the geocache in the tree on campus, a little magnetic key hider near the library, and a couple on lampposts. I told Twiggy we could skip those from now on. Those were so embarrassing. The cache was hidden under a square cover and no matter how careful we were it made a horrific screeching noise and everybody around looked to see where the noise came from only to see two people poking around underneath the lamppost skirt. I didn't even know it was called a skirt and I was a little embarrassed when Twiggy called it a skirt lifter. I couldn't think of any reason to bring a jacket to go geocaching.

"I'll come for a load of boxes in a couple of hours and we can plan our strategy over lunch. I'll buy."

"I've got enough for fast food," I said.

"It's okay. I got it."

When I answered my door two hours later, Twiggy stood there in shorts, a muscle shirt, and sandals. Thankfully, he wasn't wearing socks. However, with his Ichabod Crane walk he looked like his legs were trying to escape the shorts. And he was smiling like a fool.

"You're sure about this?" he asked.

"Of course!" I said. "I'm really excited about it!"

"Then let me see those boxes," he said. "Moving man at your service."

"Did you get a close parking place?" I asked.

"As close as possible. In other words... no. But don't worry about it. We'll have it done before you know it."

"I'll go ask about using the dolly," I said. Each wing of the dorm had a dorm supervisor and the sup had a dolly that we could borrow. It was sometimes hard to get my hands on it, but it was worth asking about. It would move three or four boxes compared to lugging the boxes out one by one.

"After you ask Mavis for the dolly, I want you to sort. Keep your clothes, bedding and toiletries. I'll put the rest in storage."

"All my clothes?"

"Yeah. We don't know how often we will be able to do laundry. Boy Scout motto, always be prepared. Works well for geocachers, too."

I didn't really know what I needed to be prepared for. So far geocaching had been a relaxing, yet interesting pastime; something to make a walk across campus more interesting.

We had to carry several boxes to Twiggy's car but then the dolly was left at my dorm room door and I stacked the remaining boxes on it.

"You're sure you saved anything you might need?" Twiggy asked.

"Yeah."

"And you have good shoes and a jacket?"

"If I must."

He nodded and pushed the cart out to the wheelchair ramp.

Good byes in a girls' dorm were so uncomfortable.

"So... you'll write?" Sarah sniffled.

"Yeah, and I'll even remember that you collect stamps and I'll send postcards, too."

Sniff, "Thanks! You're like a sister to me!"

"And I'll see you next semester, too."

"Call."

"You, too."

"Ohh! I can't believe it is over!" she cried.

Twiggy walked up, this time dressed in jeans and a geocaching t-shirt. I didn't even know they made geocaching t-shirts.

"Take care of my new sister!" Sarah cried.

Twiggy didn't understand the tears at all. Actually, neither did I. It was just a summer. No big deal. My sights were set on the road trip. I wasn't very well travelled and the prospect of seeing new places was more enticing than winning the contest. Sarah gave me a tight hug with more promises to write and call. Twiggy and I tried to look sorry for Sarah's sake, but we eagerly squeezed into his Toyota and drove to the storage unit. I helped him unload and when we were through we were tired but one step closer to adventure.

One reason I didn't have many friends was that I was content to stay home. When I lived with my parents I read a lot. I fussed over my room, rearranging the furniture and the things on the walls. I would go places if somebody asked me to, and I usually had a good time when I did, but I wasn't inclined to go by myself. In high school I was asked out a lot but boys were mostly worried about my over protective father. So I guess I was at least attractive. I had wavy brown hair that I had to control in the wind. I was fair skinned so I was constantly nagged to wear sunscreen. I did not put on a dress to go to the store. My mom seemed to understand that kids these days were not as refined as kids when she was growing up. So my jeans were acceptable if I wanted to go shopping with a woman who looked like a lawyer or a pastor's wife. To me dresses were uncomfortable. I was a comfy person. A snuggle down in flannel blankets with the dog kind of person. So Twiggy's geocaching contest sounded wildly adventurous to me even if all we did was go from parking lot to parking lot looking for magnetic hide-a-keys and peanut butter jars placed in the landscaping.

At the storage facility we had to shell out big bucks for... space. I wasn't used to spending money just to have a space to put things in, but if it meant going geocaching or not going geocaching I decided I had to make the sacrifice, so when we were through there I didn't mind so much that Twiggy was buying my lunch. We sat at Donner's, which was known for their chicken fried steak, and squinted at the screen of Twiggy's laptop. Donner's was near the university and they didn't mind students coming in and nursing a cup of coffee all night while they studied or read. The only disadvantage to Donner's was that they also didn't mind if the students played the jukebox and the jukebox had internet access so there was no telling what kind of garbage might blare forth from it while students were trying to nurse a cup of coffee and read a book. It was terribly unnerving to be reading a romance novel to the tune from some Swedish rock band. Sometimes they didn't even carry a tune. They just made noise. I guess college students think it makes them look cultured if they like foreign music. I heard a lot of Swedish, German, and Japanese music at Donner's. I was used to the music my parents listened to and I hardly ever heard that at the diner.

"We're right here," Twiggy said as we squinted at the geocaching map. I couldn't even recognize the city because of all the little boxes that represented caches.

"Zoom in a little," I said.

"Nah, we know where we are, the thing is we have to fill in our Fizzy Grid before we get to the event."

"Oh no!" I mockingly wailed. "I packed my Fizzy Grid. It's in the box labeled *Gwen's bookcase*."

"No you didn't. Your Fizzy Grid is online. And half your boxes were labeled Gwen's bookcase."

"I had three bookcases, a bed and a closet. What do you expect?"

He brought up my profile page and scrolled down. We came to a chart. I was good at charts. I even charted my tooth brushing routine.

"This is your grid. To fill in the Fizzy Grid we have to fill in all the combinations of terrain and difficulty ratings with a find. Right now you have mostly 1.5/1.5 caches. That's normal under your circumstances."

"Then why did you pick me as a partner? You should have picked somebody with more experience."

"It not about the numbers," he said. "It's the journey. That's what you haven't learned about geocaching yet. It's what you discover on the way to the caches that really makes it fun."

"Then why do we have to find all these terrain ratings and difficulty ratings?"

"We don't have to find all of them. It's just that the more we find the more likely we are to win. I think we need to give you a crash course in geocaching. We'll find some easier ones in places you aren't used to searching to mark off some of these in between difficulties before we try for a five/five."

"Oh, good. You know what they say, you can't five/five until you three/three."

"You could, but I don't think it's a good idea. I don't know about you but I'd rather find interesting caches than just ones that fill the grid. So we need to do some research. We're here. And we have five hundred miles of the good old USofA to use for a playground on the way."

He traced a highway that went from where we were to the middle of the country.

"Uh, one problem," I said. "We can't save the very hardest caches for the town the event is in. Look, there is no hard terrain in the plains."

"There could be," Twiggy said. "If they make us hike ten miles to get to it."

I frowned. "I think this will require some research."

"And you're just the girl to do it."

"Show me how the program works."

While he showed me the ins and outs of the geocaching site we ate lunch, dessert, had coffee, visited the restrooms, had another coffee, visited the restrooms, debated whether we were drinking too much coffee, argued that soda had just as much caffeine and more sugar than coffee, and then debated whether or not we should just stay for dinner. I thought I learned more sitting at Donner's than I had in my whole semester of Geography 101. I learned how to find the caches in a given area, how to sort them by when they were found, when they were placed, who placed them, who found them, who liked them, how well liked they were... I really liked the idea of searching for them by the number of favorite points. That way we could weed out the ones nobody liked and concentrate on the ones that people thought were cool, fun, interesting, or in a good location. This was research I could get my head wrapped around! It was like planning a vacation around tiny mysteries! I jumped into the search with both feet, finding all the best caches in town, then I realized I had to find the best caches in each town between Franklinburg and the event. And when I looked closer at the map I found out the caches were everywhere! How could I find the right terrain and difficulty levels at locations along our route? Twiggy showed me an advanced search that would create a list for me, but I either came up with too many caches, or too few. And I didn't know whether the caches it listed were good ones or not.

"Gabby, come up for air every once in a while," Twiggy said.

"I think I need to just do it by hand," I said. "I want to pick the best of the best. I want to explore underground and climb mountains. I want to be Sherlock Holmes searching for those itty bitty..."

"Nanos," he reminded me.

"Yeah, those itty bitty ones. And I want to find a huge one too! How big is the largest cache you've found?" I asked.

"Oh, I'm guessing it was about four feet long and a foot in diameter."

"What was it?" I asked.

"I think it was a mortar tube or something. It looked like it came from a military surplus store."

"Wow! Can we find one like that?"

"You're the planner and navigator," he said. "Which reminds me, we need to go get our wheels."

"But we have wheels," I said. "I have a car and you have a car."

"Do we really want to cram all your stuff and all my stuff into a two door sedan?"

"What are you going to do?"

"You'll see."

After dinner I got a surprise, one I wasn't quite prepared for.

"Hey man! Thanks for trading! This'll be so cool!" said a fellow student I had never met. He was talking to Twiggy and Twiggy had just traded his two door sedan for a very used, very old, Chevy van. A van? My mother would be horrified! She would say, "Do you know what men have in mind if they pick you up in a van?"

And I'd say, "Mom, I'm not stupid." Except that I really trusted Twiggy and he had a point. My clothes wouldn't even fit in his car. I looked at the olive green monstrosity and tried to think of it as a truck that holds more passengers. That idea quickly flew out the window when they flung open the sliding door and the walls were covered with zebra striped fake fur and the floor had a remnant of purple carpet laid from the back of the driver's seat to the back door of the van. At least they removed the girlie magazines, I thought.

Twiggy tossed his keys to this other man and took the keys to the ugly, olive green machine I would come to call The Cacheamolé because it was used for geocaching and it was avocado green.

"See ya in August," Twiggy said.

"Yeah, see ya," the other man said.

Twiggy tossed all our belongings into the green van, slapped me happily on the shoulder and opened the passenger's door up front so I could get in. My mom will never believe this, I thought as I climbed in.

"You traded your car *for this*?" I exclaimed.

"Just for the summer. Ned was tired of buying gas and I needed space. It was a win win situation."

"Did you tell him your car gets lousy gas mileage?"

"It depends on how you drive it."

"And how is Ned going to drive it?"

"We'll tell him that later."

"And what about this?" I asked. "We have to put gas in this thing for the summer."

"No worries."

One thing that I liked about Twiggy also irritated me to the point of frustration. He never worried about anything. Maybe I'm a realist. Maybe I inherited "proper" genes from my mom, but I thought if we were going on a 500 mile trip with several detours along the way we should make sure we would be able to pay for gas.

Chugga, chugga, chu…uuga went the van down the road and I began to smell something that I didn't want to smell. I didn't know what it was but it smelled like something in the engine was overheating. I didn't say anything, because men like to notice engine problems on their own, but I rode along wondering if we would get back to campus without catching fire. When we did reach the parking lot of my dorm Twiggy jumped out of the van, threw open the sliding door on the side and said, "Now all we have to do is make this little beauty livable!"

Little beauty?

"It looks like a giant avocado got dropped into the zebra pen at the zoo," I said.

"Aw come on. You're a girl. You can make the van into a comfy little geocaching paradise."

I thought he was nuts.

One thing there always is around a university campus when the students are going home for the summer is pillows and furniture that nobody wants to haul home. Frequently that furniture was picked up off the street anyway so it was no big loss to just leave it by a Dumpster for the incoming freshmen. Somehow with each semester of college the dorm rooms improved a little each time, unless you had parents who saw to your every need like I did. Our trip to the storage unit involved mostly boxes, because only boxes would fit into Twiggy's car. But I still had a mushroom chair and there was a futon mattress and two pillows left by the Dumpster. I thought things were going a little too smoothly when I put all our boxes of clothes around the edges of the van, spread out the futon mattress and it fit perfectly. I wasn't sure what to do with the mushroom chair but thought it couldn't hurt to be able to slouch about occasionally so I put it against one wall of the van and stepped back. The pillows were a bit big for our needs but I decided if we were roughing it then big pillows weren't much to complain about.

Chapter 4

"I'm not sure I am doing this right," I confessed to Twiggy the next morning at breakfast. I had an appointment in three hours to have my room inspected and hand the keys back over to the super.

"There is no right way or wrong way to do it," he said. "You look for the caches you want to find. You ignore the ones you don't want to find."

"But we still have a goal," I pointed out.

"That's why I put you in charge of planning. You like to keep track of details. I like to tromp around in the hills and find boxes."

"But you're asking a freshman geocacher to master a Geocaching 400 task."

"You're a smart kid. I have faith in you. I know you can do it."

"I did find some interesting ones, but nobody will say why they are so interesting. They just say things like 'good hide, very creative, wish I knew how to do this.'"

"See, you're getting the hang of it. And when we find a few of those you'll see why they made those comments."

"After I turn in my keys I think we should go find one. I need some experience to base my decisions on."

"You want to? Cool! So… which one looks interesting within a mile or two or three?"

"Hmm, they are interesting in different ways," I said sounding rather overwhelmed by all the choices I'd seen on my little laptop the previous night. "Like… look at this one. It hardly says anything in the description but the logs make it sound like we should find it. Here's a log that says, 'been around a while. Never seen a geocache like this one.' And another says. 'wish I had thought of this!' and another, 'never would have spotted this except dogwalker sniffed it out.'"

"Hmm, and twenty-nine favorite points. We should go look."

"But what about this one," I said. "It says, 'follow the trail until you get to the old bridge. Don't get your feet wet. It's hidden where the sun don't shine and you might need some sun to spot it.' That sounds kind of vague to me. People like it, but I don't see why."

He cracked a little grin that said to me that he knew this contest was working. Working on what I wasn't sure. "Maybe we should go find out," he said.

"It's four miles away."

"I bet I can drive four miles. You can drive four miles. If you can do it, I can too."

"You'll have to download the coordinates," I reminded him needlessly.

"I've got them. I've got all the geocaches in town already in my GPS. All I need is some general directions that we can get from the map so we're halfway there already."

He stuffed the last corner of his toast into his mouth and held up his hand for the ticket.

The old van chugged down the city streets, down the country roads and onto a dirt path. Just seeing the dirt path made me think I was off on an adventure. I was a city girl, raised in a proper four bedroom, two bath house, with neighbors close by, a side walk to rollerblade on, peaceful streets to ride bicycles on. We knew our neighbors and walked to school.

Trees crowded the road and Twiggy seemed to relax more the further he drove. He stopped the van in the middle of the road and got out his GPS. He clicked a few buttons and scanned a menu. He clicked down a couple of times and toggled the little joystick to the right.

"We're sitting in the middle of the road," I pointed out.

"It's okay. Nobody ever travels this road and if they do I'll let them by."

"How did it get to be a road if nobody travels it?" I asked.

His GPS displayed a map and he put the van in reverse and turned around.

"One street too early," he explained.

"This is a street?"

"Of course!"

Little did I know that in geocaching terms this street was a highway. But I couldn't really blame Twiggy. I was the one who chose the caches we looked for. I just had no inkling where they were. I chose them because they sounded fun.

Twiggy drove back to the pavement, turned right and skipped a paved road, then turned right on another dirt road. I gawked at all the lush forest plants that crowded the road. Plants even grew in between the tire ruts. It felt like we drove for miles on the dirt road but it couldn't have been miles because this place was four miles from Donner's. When Twiggy stopped the van and turned off the engine I could hear water. I looked around to see where the noise was coming from as Twiggy popped open his door and slid out.

"Ahhh, fresh air, green trees, and not a textbook in sight!" he said as he stretched. "Do you want the GPS?"

"No, I'm just along to help out and learn a thing or two about what we'll be doing the next couple of days," I answered.

"Then take the GPS. You need to learn how to use the number one tool of the trade. You can see the cache icon. The triangle is you. The line shows you which direction to walk in."

"I thought you said to look for places I would hide something," I said.

"And you did that very well, my lady. Now it's time to add a new dimension to your geocaching experience."

He handed the device to me and I looked at the screen. It was pretty self explanatory so I began walking, following the line and trying make it match up to the land I saw before me. Twiggy laughed.

"You are such a newbie! Look at you! HA hahaha!"

"I can't help it," I said. "I *am* a newbie."

"You're doing great. This is fun. How far away is it?"

I looked around on the screen for something that looked like a number that sounded reasonable but I didn't know what a reasonable number was. There were coordinates that were very recognizable. And there was 800 feet. I didn't have a good feel for how far 800 feet was so I read it off to Twiggy.

"Eight hundred?" he asked. "Which direction?"

"To our… left. I think."

"No, which direction? North, south, east, or west?"

"How should I know?"

"Look at the map. What part of the map is it on?"

"It's right there!" I said

"Okay, that is northwest of us."

He looked to see what was northwest.

"I think we can get closer driving," he said.

"How far is eight hundred feet?"

"A little hike."

"Can we take a little hike?"

He glanced again the direction the GPS was pointing.

"All right. We'll see how it goes. We can always come back for the van."

Again I began walking in the direction the green line seemed to be pointing. It didn't take long for us to be totally surrounded by hip high weeds.

"What does poison ivy look like?" I asked.

"Leaves of three, let it be," he said.

"Leaves of three at the end, or leaves of three all by themselves?" I asked.

"We'll have to look it up. It's too late to worry about it now. If it's poison ivy we're goners already."

"Do you see poison ivy often?"

"Can't say I do often. Maybe a time or two… per semester."

"Oh great."

"But I usually don't know it until it's too late."

Since there was no point in worrying about it I kept tromping through the weeds. Pretty soon the ground became rocky and weedy. I couldn't see where to place my next step. I would take a step and my foot would slide down a rock into a squishy, muddy spot.

"I'm glad I only have old shoes," I said.

Twiggy was wearing hiking boots. He wore them a lot. I think he owned three pairs of shoes: his hiking boots, sandals, and basketball shoes. He didn't play basketball. The basketball shoes he wore when he wasn't allowed to wear sandals and it was too hot for hiking boots to be comfortable. I just wished he wouldn't wear hiking boots with shorts. It looked weird. People who wore hiking boots with shorts looked like they spent their whole lives hiking. People who wore hiking boots with shorts never seemed to have new boots. Maybe that's why I thought they spent all their time hiking.

"How far is it?" Twiggy asked.

"Seven hundred and twenty two."

I could still hear water but I couldn't see it yet. The ground went up and I tripped over a rock while I was trying to watch the GPS screen.

"You can put it down and just check it every once in a while," Twiggy called over the sound of the water.

The hillside was weedy, rocky, steep and I kept slipping. I think I traveled in one spot more than I propelled myself forward and I slipped and slid and climbed my way to the top huffing and puffing and watching the triangle on the screen grow ever so slowly nearer to the cache icon.

"Whew!" I gasped near the top of the hill. "That was quite a climb!"

"Keep going. The top is just up ahead. I bet that tree right there is on top of the hill. Then we can see where we are."

"Next time tell me how far eight hundred feet is!" I said as I climbed higher.

"I told you. It's a short hike. You're the one leading us. You took the route you wanted to take."

"No I didn't! I followed the line."

"Then perhaps you should use the GPS as a guide and choose your own route."

"Now you tell m…" I looked out over the hill and a beautiful tumbling river flowed below us and a creaky old bridge was off in the distance. The road we left the van next to went around the bottom of the hill and crossed the river at the bridge.

Lesson one: use the GPS as a guide and look at the world around you. You might be able to reason things out better than a blind computer chip.

"That's a very sunny bridge," I observed. "The cache is supposed to be hidden where the sun don't shine."

"I think that means it is under the bridge somewhere," he said.

"Do cars actually drive on that bridge?" I asked. It was made of wood and it was almost one car wide. It looked terribly bumpy. I thought we might find a troll under the bridge and halfway expected three billy goats to be trotting down the road. Before we could reach the bridge, though, we had to descend the hill. I always thought that going down hills was easier than climbing them and this hill started out being easier but quickly changed when we met a long drop off. A short one I might just sit down and scoot on my bottom but this was a sheer drop of about twenty feet. That wasn't a distance I was willing to fall. We stood at the top of the precipice and looked longingly at the decrepit little bridge below.

"Follow the ridge," Twiggy said. "It'll be less rocky eventually."

"Which direction?"

"Down. If it goes down it's more likely to just join the hillside."

I turned downhill and picked my way gingerly across the top of the cliff. A squirrel ran across the road below. It found a weed that looked tasty and nibbled at it while I tried not to fall off the cliff and turn into a human avalanche. I slipped and sent a shower of rocks down the cliff. The squirrel turned around to watch the show.

"Whoa! Gabby, be careful," Twiggy said.

I must have spotted a dozen cool geocache hiding spots on that hillside: little holes in the rocks, viney roots that formed tiny, mossy caves, hollow logs and funny shaped trees.

"It's weird," I said as I crept along.

"What's weird?"

"Geocaching makes you see things weird."

"Why?"

"I see hiding places everywhere."

He laughed, "This is only your first day!"

"I know, but look! Wouldn't this hidey hole be a great spot to hide a cache?" I asked.

"Yes, it would except for one problem."

"What's that?"

"If you put one here then you'd be forcing other people to climb this hill, too."

"Oh… yeah. I guess I don't want to do that."

"You wouldn't want to maintain it either," he pointed out.

"I'm getting thirsty," I said.

"You didn't bring any water?"

"No, we just left a café, we were only going to look for one geocache, and we were only going to be eight hundred feet from the car. Why would I need water?"

"Always bring water."

"Do you have any?" I asked.

"Uh, no. We were going to look for a cache at a bridge over a river, so I didn't bother."

"Okay," I huffed. "Next time we bring water. For now we must press on."

Ten minutes later, "Now I see why you wear hiking boots."

And half an hour later we stumbled out onto the road glad it didn't have a lot of traffic on it.

"That water looks so good," I said as I limped and jogged my way to the river bank. I stripped off my tennis shoes and stuck my aching feet into the water. "Ahhh, that's better."

"I thought you said you were thirsty," Twiggy said.

"I guess my feet were thirstier than my throat."

"I wouldn't drink from this creek anyway, unless I really had to. Too many mysterious microbes."

"I'll feel better when my feet get a rest. The water's nice and cool. You should try it."

"You have ankles," he said.

"Of course I have ankles!"

"You always wear pants. You're always covered up. I just knew you had ankles under there somewhere but I'd never seen them."

"I have elbows, too!" I joked.

"Ah, but do you have shoulders? What about knees? Do you have knees?"

I splashed a little water in his direction and pulled my feet out of the river to dry them.

"The bridge is…"

"I can see the bridge. It's not far. We'd already be there if we had walked the road, or driven."

"Sorry, guess I could have chosen better," I said.

"It's okay. I liked climbing a hill with you."

I think I blushed a little. "So, are you ready to go find the geocache?" I asked as I began pulling on my socks and shoes.

"Ready when you are," he said.

I tied my shoe laces and pushed myself up, then brushed off my pants.

"To the road?"

"Yes, the road seems a good choice, now that we have climbed the hill."

"But we saw hidey holes and gnome homes and toadstools."

"Oh my!"

The old bridge was rickety, patched, and reinforced providing hundreds of gaps and ledges that could hold a geocache.

"What does the GPS say?" Twiggy asked.

"Here," I said as I handed it over. "You said when we get close we should rely on geosenses."

"That's right, but the GPS can still be helpful. It will at least pin it down to the right part of the bridge."

"How can the cache be where the sun doesn't shine if the river flows bank to bank?"

"That doesn't mean the water level was that high when they hid the cache. What's the terrain rating?"

He handed the GPS unit back to me so I could see for myself.

"Three," I read.

"So that means it takes some effort."

"We already did that climbing the hill," I point out.

"But they thought we would drive to the bridge, so you can't count the hill. We have to assume that even if we parked at the bridge there's still some effort involved in finding it."

"But how do we look for it if it's under the bridge?" I asked.

"I don't know about you, but I'm goin' swimming!" he said as he took off his hiking boots. I began looking in the weeds beside the river when he started taking off his pants. Out of the corner of my eye I noticed he was wearing boxers as he waded out into the river.

I called it a river and he called it a creek. I didn't see many rivers but to me a creek was a little trickle. This was a wide, flowing expanse of water and Twiggy was up to his hips in the cold water as he neared the bridge.

"I do declare this to be a three terrain," he said as he slipped and slid over the algae coated rocks under the water. He craned his neck trying to see the underside of the bridge and remain upright. I decided, since he had the underside covered and there were a lot of spots you could see right through it, that I would stay drier if I searched from above.

"The sun shines up there," Twiggy shouted.

"I'm using geosenses," I called back.

When I stuck my arm through a hole in the bridge he said, "Whoa, do you think that bridge is safe?"

Just then a pickup truck came bumping down the road. The driver pulled to a stop when he saw me kneeling on the bridge with my arm through the hole.

He opened his door and got out. He stood there scratching his head.

"Miss? Are you okay?" he asked.

"Yeah, just lost something. That's all," I replied.

"Maybe you oughta stay offa the bridge. It isn't entirely safe."

"Okay," I said and backed off the bridge.

The man got back in his truck and drove across. When he reached my side of the river he asked, "What did you lose?"

"Uhh…" I had to think. I just used the lost item excuse because I wasn't supposed to talk about geocaching. "Twig! What are you looking for?" I shouted down to Twiggy.

"My wallet!" He called back. "I was trying to get something out of my pocket and it slid over the side."

"You might check around the bend," the man said. "There's a log jam and it probably got caught there. Might have to take a dive though."

"Thanks!" Twiggy replied. "I was hoping it fell in the rocks."

"Y'all have a good day."

"We're trying," I said. "You have a good day, too."

After the truck left I ventured out onto the bridge again.

"If a half ton farm truck can drive over the bridge, I think I can walk on it," I said.

"Can you go get the flashlight?" Twiggy said.

"A flashlight? Why?"

"The description said we might have to bring our own light where the sun don't shine."

"Why didn't you bring it along then?" I asked.

"I did. It's in my pocket. Just pull it out and drop it to me off the bridge," he said.

I felt terribly awkward and embarrassed to be going through a man's pants. A flashlight? How would a flashlight even fit into a pocket? His wallet was safe and sound. I did find that. When I found the flashlight I wasn't sure I had found it. I expected something long and heavy but the thing I found was only a few inches square and had straps on it. It obviously was a flashlight, though, because it had little light bulbs and a switch. I jogged back to the bridge.

"Is this it?" I asked as I dangled the thing over the side.

"Yeah. Hold on. Let me wade closer." *Swoosh, swoosh, swoosh* went the water as Twiggy found a stable position beneath the flashlight. "Okay, drop it!"

I released the light and the breeze caught it. It was so light that it drifted as it fell.

"Oh shoot!" Twiggy yelled as he dove for the light. SPLASH! "OOohhh that's cold. That… is… freezing!"

"Oh, no!" I called back. "Does it still work?"

"I… I…I… I think so," he chattered. He splashed to a standing position and attempted to turn on the light while shivering. He was soaked from head to toe. "Here!" He said. "Catch!" He waited for me to acknowledge that he was throwing something and then flung the GPS up to me. I ran across the bridge to catch it and my foot went right through a rotten board. I was lucky I was young and healthy as I sunk to my knee and fell forward right in the middle of the bridge. The GPS clunked across the boards and fell off the other side. I was glad the farmer was gone as I pulled my leg out of the hole and pulled up my pants leg to assess the damage. My shin was scraped a little but I wasn't really hurt. I'd frightened Twiggy a lot more than me. He came splashing up the river bank and tender-footed it up onto the bridge.

"Are you okay?"

"Better than the bridge," I said. "Does the flashlight still work?"

"For now. Does the GPS still work?"

"I don't know. It went that way."

"Hey! You have shins, too!" he said as he gave me a hand up.

"I bet I even have calves attached to them."

We climbed down the river bank to find the GPS unit lodged between two rocks, the water lapping dangerously close.

"It already took one dunking," Twiggy said. "But they tend to be a little water resistant."

Twiggy picked up the GPS and looked at the screen.

"Isn't that just like a GPS?" he asked. "It wants new batteries."

"We hope it wants new batteries," I said. "And we hope I didn't kill it."

"It really does want new batteries. It has a 'low bat' message on it."

"Well, where was it pointing to before it took up bridge diving as a hobby?" I asked.

"You'll have to come under the bridge," he said as he strapped the flashlight onto his head.

"Oh! So that's how it goes!" I said. "That certainly looked like a strange flashlight to me."

"It's a headlamp."

"It's a geek label," I said.

He just smiled because he thought it was a compliment.

"If I go under the bridge I'll get all wet," I complained.

"A little water never hurt anybody. Besides, I'm taking you back to your room after this."

"No you're not. I'm turning in my keys, remember?"

"Oh… yeah. So what are you going to do?"

"I was going to go geocaching with you."

"Okay, well, hmm…" he said.

About this time I could hear my mother lecturing me about thinking things through before promising to go off on crazy hunts without having a plan in place, a destination in mind and funds to pay for it all.

"Let's see what we can do if we only get a little wet," he said as he dripped water all over the riverbank and my shoes. "Maybe the flashlight will help."

I sat down and took off my shoes and socks, then pulled my pants legs up as far as they would go.

"See? I do have calves," I said.

"Amazing," he said. "I never knew."

He put his arm around my shoulders and pointed the headlamp up at the underside of the bridge.

"See where the light is shining?"

"Yeah."

"That's where the GPS said ground zero was."

I always associated ground zero with the spot bombs fall but I decided it was a geocaching term I better get familiar with.

"Okay, maybe it's not too deep there," I said.

"Come around here where it's shallow," he said as he led me back into the river. The rocks were slippery and I gave up very quickly on trying to hold the ends of my pants legs up. I needed my hands to balance as I slipped and slid my way under the bridge.

"See? Isn't this fun?" Twiggy asked.

"There aren't fish in this river, are there?" I asked.

"No, of course not," he said, but I didn't believe him.

"Trout and little guppies are fine," I said. "I've even caught a trout once. But I don't like those spooky catfish. They're ugly. And they have wiggly whiskers."

He laughed, "Never fear. I will protect you from the catfish. Now where is that cache? The description said a light should reveal where it is hidden."

We heard a *clunkada, clunkada, clunk* as a vehicle drove over the bridge.

"I guess they know which parts of it will support them," I said. The car stopped and somebody got out. He clumped over the bridge until he reached the hole I'd left behind. He gazed down through the hole to the river below.

"Howdy!" he said.

"Hi!" Twiggy and I chimed back.

"Old bridge gets older every day," he said.

"Yeah, bridges do that," Twiggy said.

"Havin' fun down there?"

"Yeah, we are," Twiggy answered.

Just then the man flinched like something hurt his eyes. He jerked back and we couldn't see him when he stood up. He bent back down.

"What'cha doin' with a headlamp on?" he asked.

"Snipe hunt!" Twiggy said. "They're attracted to light!"

"Uh huh, yeah, right," the man said. "Well, y'all take care down there."

"Okay."

After the man left I said, "Snipes don't like light. You have to hunt them at night and they like bacon."

He just looked at me as if he didn't understand a word I said.

We waded around and Twiggy shined the light from every spot around ground zero that we could stand safely. My pants got soaked. The water was cold but after a while we got used to it. I was getting a stiff neck from looking up at the bridge. Then an idea hit me like a bright light in the darkness.

"Twiggy?"

"Yeah?"

"Where were you standing when you talked to that man?"

"I don't know. I wasn't paying attention. Why?"

"Well, figure it out. I think you shined the light on the cache while you were talking to him. He was talking to us just fine and then something hurt his eyes. Like a bright light appearing all of a sudden."

"We should have seen it if that happened."

"Not if it happened really fast and the reflection went through the hole."

"If the reflection went through the hole then there has to be a direct line from where that guy was standing and the cache. Go up and stand where that guy was standing. I'll walk around down here and try to line up on the hole again."

"Okay."

I waded to shore, climbed out, then climbed the bank to the side of the road and walked out onto the bridge. I looked around to be sure there were no cars and then looked for the hole my leg had gone through. I found it and waited for Twiggy to find it from underneath. I could hear the swooshing of his steps but I couldn't see him to guide him to the right spot. While I waited I felt around the hole for anything plastic, metal, or loose. I didn't know a lot about geocaching but I did know the container had to be retrievable. They didn't plan on it being found through a nonexistent hole, but I still thought maybe I could touch it if the light from the flashlight had been spotted reflecting off of it.

"I see your arm," Twiggy said from below.

"Yeah, it even has a forearm," I joked.

His swooshing zeroed in on the spot where he saw my arm.

"Okay, stand up and do whatever that other guy was doing," he said.

"He was just looking down through the hole. Walk around and look up like you are talking to me," I said.

"I *am* talking to you."

"Well, move the light around a bit and let me adjust my position."

Unfortunately, my Geometry 101 class taught me that the likelihood of finding the exact angle to spot the reflection was slim. Repeating the feat was almost impossible.

I heard tires crunching on small stones and looked up to see a police cruiser pulling up to the bridge. It stopped and an officer stepped out.

"Good morning!" he said.

"Good morning," I answered as I picked my way off the bridge.

"Hank Conrad was at the market and said there was folks on the old Miller Bridge. He was worried about you falling through or something. I just thought I ought to warn you that the bridge is old and unstable."

"Okay, well… thank you. I think we're fine. We'll be careful."

"What are you doing?"

Gulp, what was I supposed to do? I couldn't lie to an officer of the law.

"We're geocaching," I said.

"Geocaching? What's that?"

"There is a container hidden here and we have the coordinates to find it, except that our GPS ran out of power. We know it's somewhere close so we're looking for it."

"What makes you think there's a container on the old Miller Bridge?" he asked.

"Somebody hid it here and posted the coordinates online."

"And you believe them?" he asked.

"Oh yes! It's a popular hobby. People do this all over the place."

"What's in this 'container'?"

"Umm… I don't know yet. There's a log book that we sign…"

"Gabby! What are you doing? Watch for the light!" Twiggy called up from below the bridge.

"And some little things so we can trade if we want to."

"Things?"

"Yeah, like little toys, foreign coins, erasers, that kind of thing."

"Why do you do this?"

"Just 'cause it's fun."

I wasn't doing a very good job of explaining it to him. I thought I might know more about geocaching in a day or two but right now I could only tell him the very basics.

"Gabby! Where are you?"

"Who is that?" the officer asked.

"My friend. He's looking under the bridge and I'm look on top."

"Well, be careful. That bridge has rotten boards. The residents have reinforced it but there are still places a person could fall through."

"Okay, I'll watch for the reinforced spots then."

"Have fun."

"You too… stay safe," I said.

He tipped his hat as he went back to his car and I breathed a sigh of relief.

"Sorry!" I said as I found the hole again. "The police showed up!"

"What!"

"He just wanted to warn me about the bridge having rotten boards."

"Did you tell him you knew about them?"

"No, because then he would think it was even more unsafe."

"Good. Now watch for the light."

Ten minutes later, "This isn't working. Maybe the man was taller than me. Maybe I should be down there and you should be up here."

"It's worth a try. I'm getting hungry. We need to find this thing soon."

Twiggy waded to the river bank and we met half way and handed off the headlamp. I climbed down to the water again, then slip-slided my way under the bridge. Twiggy took his position above and I looked around for the spot of sky through the hole.

"I see the hole," I said. "Do you see me?"

He walked around until we were looking at each other through the hole.

"AHhhh! Catfish!" he yelled.

"Where?!" I exclaimed, then promptly jerked around, slipped, and fell waist deep in the river.

"Okay, it's gone now," he said.

"Ha, ha, very funny," I stammered as I attempted to stand. "That helped our search ever so much. The catfish swallowed the flashlight." I brought the headlamp up out of the water and tried to turn it on. "I don't think they planned on this being used on scuba dives."

"Oh shoot. Now what are we going to do?" he asked.

"I guess we will have to rough it and find it on geosenses alone."

He climbed down and we searched the underside of the bridge again but there were so many dark spaces under the bridge that there were hundreds of places to search and to reach them we had to stand on slippery rocks. I couldn't reach most of the timbers of the bridge so I gave up and began looking amongst the rocks on the bank. Then I couldn't help but remember that glint that came through the hole so I searched the top of the bridge and ended up with my arm through the hole in the bridge again. So far every car that had come through had been very slow, so I wasn't worried about being run over, just making the neighbors think I was crazy. I didn't mind being a crazy person to somebody I'd never see again. I reached, groped, probed. I found a stick and poked it around. I was just about to give up when the stick hit something metal and I heard a *clunk, tink, tunk, tuuummbbble, splash.* I yanked the stick out and lay face down trying to see what fell. All I could see was river rocks and water. I was so excited about maybe finally finding the cache that I dashed down to the river bank and saw a cracker tin with a mirror glued to one side lopsidedly floating down the river.

"Get it!" I exclaimed as I slipped over the slick rocks. "It's getting away!"

The cracker tin seemed to mock us in slow motion as it quietly floated away. Little currents would grab the corner of the mirror and make it turn lazily as we half dashed, half swam down the river. The tin had a head start.

"Slow down you crazy r..." I stepped into a fishing hole and disappeared under the surface. I came up sputtering and attempting to swim.

"Don't worry," Twiggy said. "The farmer said there was a log jam ahead. It'll get stuck there."

"Why is it floating if it's metal?" I asked.

"Because it's full of air?"

"Oh, yeah, hehe. I hope it doesn't leak."

We waded to the river bank and followed the river until we reached the log jam. Luckily it was only a small one so we were able to walk out onto a log and survey the river upstream from us. I noticed that the log was very worn, like children played at the river bank, and fished for spooky catfish and trout. Seeing the worn spots on the log made the river seem a friendlier place.

"What?" Twiggy asked.

"Nothing. I was just noticing that people like this river. They come down here a lot. It's like a member of their family that has been running near their houses for longer than they can remember and I like it. I really like it. Thank you for bringing me here."

"Even after you got dunked in the creek?"

"Yeah."

"I didn't bring you here. The cache did. Look, there it is."

We walked the log closer to where the tin was floating. We had to use a long stick to get the tin around a snag, but we eventually plucked it from the creek.

"You open it," he said. "The first few caches are always more fun to open. Let's see what's in it."

I pried and pulled, but the lid was really tight. I guess that was good. Had it been loose it might have leaked and sunk. Twiggy pried the lid off and handed it to me. I opened the mysterious box and looked inside. It was damp. Moisture clung to the bag the logbook was in, but the log was dry inside its baggie. The rest of the contents were a different story.

"I think we better take this to the river bank where we can spread things out and let them dry."

We sat on a little grassy spot and dumped out the contents, then sorted and dried them as much as we could. We had to throw away a card and some stickers that were too wet and worn out to be any good. I found a little purple bendy rabbit, a squished penny, a kid's meal toy of a colorful parrot, and a bottle opener. There was also an odd tag attached to a jointed metal moose.

"What's this?" I asked as I held it up for Twiggy's inspection.

"Oh cool! That's a Travel Bug... or one of its cousins. Let me see." I handed him the tag. "We're going on the road so we should take it."

"Why?"

"Because it wants to travel."

"How do you know? Did you ask it?"

"We can ask it when we get online again. If it wants to stay in the area we can always drop it off locally."

"You make it sound like the Travel Bug has an opinion about this," I pointed out.

"It does! Though we need to read the site and see what it wants to do. If it is trying to go east we should drop it off in another cache. But if it wants to go west we should take it and log it at the caches we find."

I was deciding I knew absolutely nothing about geocaching when he said, "Good find!" That kind of made up for my confusion about what a Travel Bug might be. How could a bug be a moose?

"Do I get to trade?" I asked.

"Sure, if you see something you like. What did you bring to put in?"

"I... uh, rats. I don't have anything."

"Is there something you'd like?" he asked.

"Well... I was thinking the bendy rabbit matched that green monster van we are using. Maybe he wants to go along."

"Okay, here," he said and pulled a keychain from our university out of his pocket.

"But that's yours!" I said. "I don't want you to give up something of yours."

"I worked at the bookstore when the semester started. I got them cheap. I bought them to put in caches. So… add it and take the rabbit."

"It's probably been here since Easter. It needs rescuing."

"Now you're talking like inanimate objects have an opinion about what happens to them."

We signed the log Team Twiggy, since it was Twiggy who was determined to win the trip.

"I'm hungry. I say we rehide this thing and go back to town," he said.

"But we're soaking wet. We have no place to change. We… we don't have a shower! Or a bathroom! What are we going to do?"

"First things first. The cache needs rehiding at ground zero, where the sun don't shine. Where did you find it?"

"I don't know. I was poking through the hole with a stick and I knocked it loose. So I really found it floating in the river."

"Gabby, this is not a river. This is a creek."

"Okay, well, I found it floating in the creek."

He turned the cracker tin this way and that.

"We know the mirror is meant to catch the light of a flashlight from below the bridge, so I say we find a spot at ground zero where the cache will be somewhat out of view, but where a flashlight beam might hit the mirror and when we log the cache we tell the CO what we did."

"CO?"

"Cache owner."

"Oh. Okay."

"If he wants to check on it he can."

We put all the contents back into the cracker tin, making sure the log book was securely wrapped in the little Ziploc bag. If it was going to take regular dunkings in the creek it needed that baggie. Twiggy gave me a hand up and stood there for a moment as if he wasn't quite ready to go back.

"Was that worth a favorite point?" he asked.

"I don't know. I think it would be better if the creek was lower and we had a working flashlight."

"But did you have fun?"

I kind of got the impression he was asking a bigger question. So I kept him waiting a moment.

"Yeah, that was fun."

"Even with the soaking wet search and the steep hill and falling and dancing away from catfish?"

"There wasn't really a catfish, was there?"

"No, I hope you'll forgive me."

"It was fun even after all that," I said. "And I even got a bendy rabbit."

"I'm glad," he said with a firm shoulder hug.

Chapter 5

"Morrison the Moving Moose," Twiggy read from the website at lunch. "It wants to travel overseas."

"Well, if you win that trip you'll be going overseas," I pointed out.

He hesitated before he said, "We shouldn't hang onto it that long. It should be dropped off in a week or two unless we're nearly finished traveling. It shouldn't stay in one place very long."

"Why?"

"Because Travel Bugs are sent out into the geocaching world to travel. It's not nice to keep them a long time."

"Do you think we should drop it off at the airport or the train station?"

"Nah, Morrison can travel with us for a little while. Oh, and surprisingly, he likes blue M&Ms."

"Let me see that," I said.

I read the web page and, sure enough, it said he liked to eat blue M&Ms.

"I get the brown ones," I said.

"To match your eyes," he said.

"Uh, I guess, though I just like the brown ones. You can have the other colors. If we have to buy M&Ms and he gets the blue ones and I take the brown ones that ought to leave enough for you."

"Maybe."

"Too bad there are no purple ones for the rabbit."

After lunch we went to the nearest convenience store and bought a package of M&Ms. We took a picture of Morrison sitting on the dash of the van with his blue M&Ms. Then we shared the rest of the package.

"Whatcha doing for dinner tonight?" Twiggy asked.

"I don't know, considering I am basically homeless."

"Hey, you are not homeless. I'm here. You're not going to go hungry."

"I know. It's just sort of humbling not knowing when I will ever see a shower again, or where my next meal will come from."

"No worries. Repeat."

"No... worries."

"It'll be all right."

"Okay."

We spent the afternoon in the university library downloading caches from the geocaching website. We sat shoulder to shoulder laughing at odd cache descriptions and the stories people had written when they logged the cache finds. Then we had fun writing the tale of our find at the bridge, making sure to note that the cache was safe and sound despite its trip down the river.

My mom would have been horrified to see me eating fast food on a futon mattress hunched over a computer, parked next to a business that advertised free wifi. It was cozy. Stinky and gaudy and cozy. It felt like a campout in a zebra striped blanket fort. And when night fell and we couldn't really do anything because of the darkness we lay side by side wondering what was going to happen.

Would he come on to me? I could imagine the lecture from my mom. I didn't need to hear it. I thought Twiggy respected me enough to not push, but I knew the subject would come up eventually, and how would I respond? How did I feel about spending the night with a guy? No, a man. I might still feel like a lost little kid but we were both old enough to be called man and woman. And it was only natural that eventually we would have to relate to each other as a man and a woman instead of BFF. Just the acronym sounded high schoolish and immature. BFF. Who ever knew if any friend was a best friend forever? My friends from high school had sworn to stay in contact. After three semesters of college, where were they? I didn't know. Friendships were something I enjoyed at the time and didn't hold onto tightly.

"Gabby, I won't bite. And I won't force you to do anything you don't want to."

Lethal words. And step one in the cycle. If I scooted over that would be step two. Gulp. Maybe talking would make him feel better.

"I know." Stupid, stupid, stupid. That is an insult to a man. And it's not true. "I mean… Twig… I think this is a process."

He turned on his side and propped himself up on his elbow.

"I'm sorry we're stuck out on the street in the van."

"That's not a problem. I knew we'd be doing this occasionally."

"At least trust me enough to relax."

"Okay."

Five minutes ticked by and he sighed. "You can start trusting me now."

"I've never slept with a friend before."

He laughed.

"I've never slept in the same bed with anybody, not even my parents when I was little. They said kids needed space just like parents and they always sent me back to bed. I went to a camp once where we all slept together on the floor in sleeping bags. That's the closest I've ever been to… to this."

"I tell you what. I won't do anything in bed that I haven't done out of bed. How far have we gone out of bed?"

"Uh, shoulder hugs, sitting close."

"And I tied your shoe once. Don't forget that. Your knee was sore and you didn't want to bend it. I tied your shoe. I almost saw your ankle that time, too."

I smiled in the dark.

"I didn't know my mom very well, but one thing she always told me," he said. "Is the best ones are worth the wait. It means you have pride and grit and stand up for what you know is right. And I want it to be right for you. So you don't have to worry."

I scooted closer. And I tried to relax.

"I take one thing back. I might do one thing that I haven't done while we were out of bed."

"What's that?"

"Snore. I haven't heard complaints but I can't promise not to."

"No worries."

"Atta girl."

Chapter 6

That first night didn't go very well. I had hoped our easygoing friendship would follow us day and night. I took that as a hint that Twiggy might be a little more serious about actually having a real relationship than I was. It wasn't that I didn't like Twiggy. It was that he didn't act like a person who had girl friends and relationships. He was one of the gang, with everybody he met. He would help anybody tie their shoe and handed out shoulder hugs to anybody for any reason. I even saw him hug a girl in line at the coffee shop who was happy to get a ten percent discount on Pink Ribbon Day. If you wore a pink ribbon to the coffee shop you got a discount and part of your purchase went to cancer research. She didn't have enough money for the large coffee without the discount and she just had enough with it. She clapped her hands and clasped her coffee like it as a real treat and Twiggy high fived her and gave her a hug. So I didn't read a lot of commitment into Twiggy's shoulder hugs.

Right now I could identify with the girl who was happy to get ten percent off a cup of coffee. That was only thirty cents. Being a broke college student had its ups and downs. I was thinking it also had its looses and tights. I needed to be careful if I was going to eat and shower over the next few weeks. Laying in the van, I wasn't sure what was more important to me. After climbing around muddy river banks and taking a couple of dunkings in the creek a shower was more tempting than breakfast.

Twiggy woke to find me attempting to put makeup on in the rear view mirror of the van.

"What are you doing?"

"Attempting to make myself presentable. Is my hair still sticking straight up?" I turned my head to see but the mirror was too small to see the top of my head if I tipped my head down.

"Not quite," he said.

"I wish we had a place to plug in a curling iron. We should have traded your car for one of those new cars with electrical outlets inside."

"Do you think there is a student that would trade a car like that for my car?" he asked.

"Uh… no. I guess there were some who had a car like that but they'd want to keep it for the summer."

"Did you sleep okay?" he asked.

"It was a little chilly," I said. "But after I warmed up my spot I did okay."

"I could have helped in that department," he said. "Ready for some breakfast?"

"No, but I don't see any way to be ready."

"Coffee?"

I huffed in frustration. I looked in the mirror.

"Hair gel?" he asked.

"Hair gel builds up. It might help for one day but it's not a long term solution."

"What is a long term solution?"

"A shower in the mornings."

"I tell you what. We'll get some breakfast and some coffee and we'll hit the road where nobody will recognize us and we'll find the next cache and then we'll find a place with a shower."

"I don't want to be seen in there," I said. "Let's hit the road and find a place to eat breakfast where nobody will recognize us."

"Gabby, you look fine."

"I do not look fine! I look like I haven't showered in two days and spent the night sleeping in a van. Guys are so lucky. They can go two days without a shower and spend the night in a van and they come out of it looking perfectly normal."

"I don't know if that's a compliment or an insult."

"It's neither. It's just a fact of life. Women need showers."

"We could pretend it's Halloween." He took one look at me and changed his mind. "Okay, bad idea. Wait here while I walk down to the ATM and then we'll go someplace down the road for breakfast. Did you still want to find that Pink Panther Cache?"

"Yeah."

"It's a four/five."

"I know. And that's supposed to be really difficult."

"Yeah."

"Harder than the bridge."

"Yeah, but one man's two is another man's five."

"Okay, we'll look at it again over breakfast."

He walked down the street and I went back to trying to get my hair to stay down. I finally resorted to the hair gel. When he came back he was talking on his cell phone and stuffing his wallet into his pocket.

"Ready?"

"Yeah, what do you think this Pink Panther Cache really is?" I asked.

"I don't remember the description. We'll go over it again at breakfast."

"What if we can't find an internet connection?"

"Then we go by the one on the GPS."

"Maybe we should eat breakfast here where we know we will have one. We can line up the day's geocaching before we take off."

"Okay."

"Just point out people I know so I can hide."

I looked at the menu, weighing all the options. I could get an entire breakfast for the price of the latte but it was the latte that I craved.

"What are you getting?" Twiggy asked.

"Shh, I'm sending out distress signals."

"What kind of distress signals?"

"I'm hoping a latte down the street hears my pleas and comes to my rescue."

"Ah, I see. And if it doesn't?"

"Then I'm having the special of the day."

"That's just a two egg breakfast."

"Then I'll half the order. Will they half a two egg breakfast for me?"

"Why are you scrimping?"

"Because I don't eat much in the morning and because I don't want to have to ask my mom for more money."

"Your mom's the financier of the family?"

"No, not really. She is just the telephone answerer."

"And if you were to talk to your dad?"

"He would be more willing to send some and less likely to tell my mom he did."

"Well, if you need to call home let me know. I can get you through to your dad."

"There's only one problem with that," I said.

"What?"

"They don't know… um… they don't know…"

His eye brow went up a tad.

"I didn't tell them you were a guy. They think I'm trying to help a girl friend get home without falling asleep at the wheel and then visiting her family for a few days before I come home."

"So, I learn something new. You know how to work one over your parents."

"Do you think they would let me go if they knew?"

"No."

"Where does your dad think you are?" I asked.

"No worries. He thinks I'm on my way home but he thinks I'll stop in every town along the way, find a party to crash and get drunk every night. He knows I'll show up eventually."

"Doesn't he worry about you if he thinks that's the kind of lifestyle you live?"

"Eh, he figures he survived it. It must be what sons do after school gets out."

"But you don't want to party your way home?"

"I tried it once. If you crash a party you don't know anybody. You can get free booze but the hangover isn't worth it."

"This must be boring to you."

"Boring? No. Today we get to find a Pink Panther Cache. What's boring about that?"

"What do we have to do to find it?" I asked.

"I don't know. It's going to take a hike. We have to earn that five terrain rating."

"At least we are used to walking from one end of campus to the other between classes."

"It's going to be a twenty minute drive to the next town."

"Cool! Morrison will be happy to see a different cache."

On the way to the Pink Panther Cache Twiggy drove through the Coffee Caboose, which is a little coffee to-go shop housed in a real caboose. Since trains don't use cabooses anymore the orphaned train cars have been put to use in every little town in the area. One of them is even painted yellow, has a periscope attached and goes by The Yellow SUBmarine.

"Hold on," Twiggy said as he pulled up under the big willow tree standing beside the Coffee Caboose. "You might as well get this one while we're here. Look under the steps and there's a black hide a key stuck to the underside."

"It's no fair if you tell me!" I said.

"Just hop out and sign it. It's one more smiley."

"What's it rated?"

"Just a one/one but every smiley counts."

I felt very self conscious as I went over to the steps and began feeling around underneath. I had to get down on hands and knees and look before I spotted it. I signed the log and replaced the cache, then jogged back to the van.

"Find it?" Twiggy asked.

"Yup."

"When you go to log it, remember it's called Caboose's Caboose."

"Okay." I had to think about that one before I realized it was on the back end of the caboose.

We hit the road and put in twenty miles before we turned on our newly charged GPS and navigated to a parking spot. This time we did bring water.

Twiggy had a book pack full of all kinds of geocaching things, including more of the little keychains from school. He also had a zippered pouch of what he called tools of the trade. I'd seen inside it and there were all kinds of little metal tools. I'd just have to see what kind of tools geocaching required. He also carried extra baggies, pens and little plastic containers. He seemed to be prepared for just about any geocache hunt.

It was a hot day but there were plenty of tall, shady trees and the trail looked well marked and well traveled. The sign said, "Lookout Tower .7, Kendall Remote Camp 3, Timberland Trail 4.5".

"Look out, here we come," Twiggy said.

"Is that where the Pink Panther is hiding?" I asked.

"That's what I am guessing since the GPS says the cache is half a mile away."

"But the sign says seven tenths."

"The GPS tells us the distance as the crow flies. I think we learned from our last hunt that we should follow the trail and it obviously has some twists and turns in it."

"I've got my walking feet! We brought water! Let's go!"

We found that Twiggy and I have different hiking styles. The trail was very different from our hill climb the previous day. While we were looking for the cache on the bridge we were uncertain and just following the line on the GPS screen. This time we knew to follow the trail and the path was wide, firm and scenic. I was excited and when I get excited I have energy. We would start a conversation and I would hurry further and further ahead until it became hard to talk, then something would catch my attention and I'd look at tracks, or watch a bird, or notice squirrels playing in the canopy. Twiggy walked a slow and steady pace and caught up with me just in time for the bird to fly away or my curiosity to wear off and then off I would go again. So on the flats our conversation had a sort of yoyo effect. When the trail turned and began a steady uphill climb Twiggy's steady pace kept up and my flightiness slowed down and I trudged along next to him. I became very grateful for the shade and stopped frequently to catch my breath and drink some water.

"Do you ever see wildlife besides birds on these hikes?" I asked.

"Oh yeah! I see lots of squirrels and chipmunks. If you watch the trail you might spot raccoon or possum tracks. I see deer occasionally, not that I have had a lot of time to go hiking. This is the first chance I've gotten in a long time because school kept me so busy."

"Busy? You didn't look busy when I saw you."

"You saw me the few times that I wasn't busy."

"You mean you study, too?"

"You've seen me study."

"You didn't look like you were studying. When I study I look like I am going to have a brain implosion. You... must look like you are just reading a book."

"Don't you mean explosion?"

"No, it definitely feels like an implosion."

"So what does an implosion feel like?"

"Like the sides of my head are just going to cave in and my brain is going to shrivel up and die from sheer trivialness."

"Trivialness? What do you find trivial about your classes?"

"Like Forestry 101," I said.

"What are you doing taking a forestry class?"

"I thought I might like to be a ranger," I answered. "I like the forest. It's friendly."

"Okay, so what did you think was trivial about the forestry class?"

"Well... like plant densities and different kinds of forest canopies."

"Gabby, what do you think forest management involves?"

"Uh... well... the only time I've seen forest rangers they were telling campers where the best trails were, or leading nature hikes."

"And you think that's all rangers do? You don't need a degree to point out trails on a map to people."

"I know, that's why I thought getting my degree in forestry might be easy and I might enjoy the job."

He just shook his head that I could be so naïve. "Who puts out a fire if the forest is burning?"

"Firemen."

"And who do you think the firemen work for?"

"The fire department."

"Some of them do, but many of them work for the Forest Service. Who stocks the outhouses?"

"Rangers, I suppose. At least the ones who manage the campgrounds."

"And who maintains the roads and trails."

"Okay! So they don't just point out trails to people. What does plant density have to do with any of that?"

"The forest is an ecosystem. You did learn what an ecosystem is, didn't you?"

"Yes, I learned that way back in Biology 101."

"The forest service is in charge of this ecosystem and every part of it depends on a different climate to survive. Every plant that lives here is in balance with the nature around it..." he launched into a detailed lecture and I swore I was back in class again except that class wasn't nearly this strenuous.

"So do you see why forest rangers have to know about the different plants and where they live within the forest they are in charge of?"

"So forestry was going to get complicated, too?" I asked.

"If you stay in school long enough to get a degree any subject is going to get complicated."

"Maybe I should be an artist. What's complicated about art?"

"I suppose you will have to take Art 102 to find out," he said sarcastically.

"People like you make me feel sooo, stupid," I said with a touch of frustration in my voice.

"Hey!" He said and stopped right in the middle of the trail. "I… do not… have… stupid friends. If I thought you had even an ounce of stupidity in your little finger I would be outa here."

He jumped on me so suddenly I didn't think about what he was saying. I only knew I was being scolded and it took me by surprise and all I could do was react. I have to say my reaction wasn't the best. My eyes teared up and I counted to four before I decided I better hike… fast.

"Gabby!" he said as he jogged a little to catch up. "Do you think our friendship was accidental? You think we're out here just because I needed a partner for a contest? No! We're out here because I chose *you*. There's nobody I would rather hike with, nobody I'd rather ride with, nobody who I'd take pictures of a silly mooses and M&Ms with. You'll figure out what you want to do with your life. Just don't think it's going to be easy. Every major you choose will eventually get very detailed and complex or they wouldn't have to teach it at a university."

"What about geocaching? Does it get detailed and complex, too?"

"Not enough to worry you. You will decide how complex you want to make it and you'll settle at a level you are comfortable with."

I held up my little finger.

"Nope, not even a little stupid," he said and kissed it gently.

"Do you think it can find a Pink Panther Cache?" I asked.

"We'll just have to see."

"I wish we could find all the caches in these shady woods. I love all the ferns and moss covered roots and twisty branches. It's a forest with character. Golly, this trail is steep."

"The lookout tower is on top of the mountain so it's bound to be uphill."

"Oh yeah. One time I saw a tube of little plastic dragons and I thought it would be cool to put them in caches."

"It would. I bet the other geocachers would like finding little plastic dragons."

"But if I had them I'd be tempted to put them in all these little caves along the trail."

"What caves?"

"Look!" I said stopping at a random place on the trail.

This forest was so full of interesting trees that any place had a tiny dragon cave by the side of the trail. I led him to a twisted, old tree, its roots covered with spongy, green moss. The roots were a tangled mass and glistened with dampness in the little bit of sunlight that broke through the canopy. "Can't you imagine a tiny dragon living in a little cave like this?" I placed a rock on the mossy opening where a dragon might stand surveying the broad trail at his front door.

"I have to admit I never thought of them like that," he said. "But if I was a tiny dragon I might choose this forest to live in. That's one thing I can count on with you. Your imagination always keeps things interesting."

"The two headed red dragon would live in this cave," I declared.

As we neared the top of the mountain the hillsides became very rocky and the forest was more open. The lookout tower stood over the surrounding forest like a protective old guardian. It was an abandoned fire lookout tower, so it was a wooden structure surrounded by a metal catwalk and metal steps spiraling up to a room at the very top.

"Okay, where is the cache?" I asked.

The GPS led us to the corner of the tower. We looked up through the springed steel to the room above.

"Up we go?" I asked.

"Unless it's right here, but I don't think so. There's no way to hide a regular sized container right here."

"Yes, there is, if these boards are loose."

We tested the boards but they were all too tight.

"Does it say anything about it being magnetic?" I asked.

"It's too big to be magnetic. They posted a picture of the original cache and it is an ammo can full of fake jewels. At least it was when it was new. It's probably got regular swag in it now."

"Why would it be full of fake jewels, other than the fact that they would make okay swag?"

"Did you see the original Pink Panther movie?"

"That came out before I was born."

"Me, too, but my dad likes old movies. The Pink Panther in the movie was a jewel."

"So it's named the Pink Panther Cache because of the contents?"

"I think so."

"So now it should be called the cheap swag cache?"

"I don't know. We need to find it and see."

There was a gate across the metal stairs but it wasn't locked and there were no signs warning us to stay out. As we climbed up we watched the wall beside us for nooks and crannies where a cache could be hidden out of sight. It didn't take us long to reach the top of the stairs and our way was blocked by a metal grate. It was heavy, because it had to be built sturdy enough for a person to walk on. It appeared to be built so that the ranger on duty would come up the stairs, lift the hatch and then close it behind him so once he was in the tower he could walk all the way around the room watching for smoke or flames. Twiggy lifted the grate and I snuck through, then I held it up while he climbed through the gap.

"Wow! I can see for miles!" I said as I gazed out over the forest. "How far can you see?" I asked Twiggy.

"I can see for miles, too," he pointed out with a hint of humor in his voice.

The door to the lookout had the glass broken out of it but the door knob still worked. I turned the doorknob and pushed but the door didn't move.

"Try pulling. They would want a ranger to be able to push his way out."

Glass and broken boards littered the floor of the room at the top.

"Why do people have to tear up a place just because it's been left alone a while?" I asked.

"I don't know. If it wasn't such a long hike we could clean it up a bit but that's a long way to carry some of this stuff."

"Where does the GPS say to look?"

"It won't work very well through the roof. I say we just look around."

There were plenty of places to hide a geocache. There was about thirty feet of cupboards with a workbench top to them. Some of the doors were broken off and many swung crookedly. I looked in each one. There was one curious cupboard that was tall and narrow. The shelves had slats. Some of the shelves were missing and the bottom one had a chunk out of one corner.

"Do you know what that is?" Twiggy asked.

"No. I was trying to guess. If it didn't have these weird shelves I'd think it was a broom closet."

"It's the refrigerator."

"The... na uh! It can't be. There's nothing in there to cool stuff."

"The shelves have gaps so the air will flow. Look up. I bet it's got a chimney sort of thing. And if you look down I bet it is a shaft that goes all the way to the ground. They put blocks of ice in the bottom and the air flow brought the cool air up through the shelves. I am beginning to see why this is the Pink Panther Cache though. After I thought about all the doors opening in different directions it is just like the opening of the cartoon show."

This was especially true when we lifted the bottom shelf of the old refrigerator and realized the cache was at the bottom of the shaft where the ice would be placed. I mentally went through all the doors and which direction they opened. The gate was left, the hatch up, the door in the refrigerator right, the shelf up. We had to go to the bottom and see what opened at the bottom to make an ice block shaped opening. So... push the door out, lift the grate up, descend the stairs, push the gate out, yes this was beginning to feel more and more like a Pink Panther cartoon. We searched the bottom of the lookout tower until we found a metal door, but it was locked.

"Shoot," I said. "Now what?"

"Never fear," Twiggy said. "There's usually a combination in the hint or description."

He brought up the hint and it said "elevator."

"Well, I think we have the right idea," he said. "We thought it was in a shaft. But what about a combination?"

He switched to the description. We found a story about hiding the cache and being confronted by a cranky...

"Uh, Twiggy? What's that?" I asked.

Lumbering up the side of the mountain was a big, brown form. It was slow and it wasn't coming our direction so we only got glimpses of it.

"I don't know. Let me read the description. Let me know if it gets closer."

He squinted at the screen.

"Want me to try?" I asked.

"If you want. It says they got up early in the morning to take a hike and they got to the tower. Then they got chased up by a..."

"Bear," I said.

"Yeah and they had never seen a bear before so they were very excited about seeing a bear..."

"No, Twiggy, I mean that thing over there is a bear."

"It is? Oh fuck. Sorry."

"Maybe we can get to the cache from above? Or maybe the bear isn't interested."

"You read the description, while I watch the bear." He handed me the GPS and I read the story on the little screen. "Quick, read quick," Twiggy said a little nervously.

"I did. There is no combination. But... here's something we can try. The story does have numbers," I pointed out. "We just have to figure out how they apply to our situation." I read, "'It was the crack of dawn and the clock blinked six o'clock.' So where is six o'clock on the combination lock? It'll be straight down from the zero." He twirled the spinner a few times to clear it, then found the number opposite the zero. "Then it goes into all the problems they had reaching the parking spot. Wow, a flat tire and ..."

"Gabby, just find the next number so we can get out of here."

"So they didn't reach the tower until nine. What number is at nine o'clock?"

"I don't know it could be one of three of four. The lines are so close together. So find the last one while I experiment."

"Their little boy tripped and broke his finger. Aww, poor kid."

"Gabby, the bear is getting closer."

"Then there was a bear that chased them up the stairs and hung around for an hour. So I wonder if an hour represents the one o'clock position? But it does say they didn't get home from hiding the cache until eight o'clock that night. That must include a trip to urgent care... Maybe they hid more than..."

"Uh, Gabby, go up the stairs."

"Why?"

"Yah! Yah bear! Go away!"

He sat there at the door clearly bothered by the nearness of... Yikes! The bear! Oh it was so cool! A bear! Right there on the hillside with us!

"Try six o'clock, nine o'clock, eight o'clock."

"Hurry, hurry," he muttered to himself as I watched the bear.

"Don't hurry or you'll mess up. Take your time and think."

"Nine..."

He fiddled with the lock as the bear noticed it had company.

"Oh shoot, oh shoot."

"Oh look! Little ones!" I exclaimed excitedly.

The bear stood up and sniffed the air.

"Gabby, go upstairs. The bear will stop at the grate."

"It's not worried about us. It's just here for a snack. There must be berries out there or something. You don't have any snacks in the pack do you?"

He fiddled faster and the bear wandered closer, sniffed the air again.

I heard the snap of a lock unlocking and the rattle of the metal door opening.

"Quick! Get the cache!" I bent down to retrieve the cache and he stood up to get out of my way. "Yah! Yah bear! Back! Back I say!"

The bear was making conversational noises and walking toward us. I had heard somewhere that bears could run very fast for short distances.

"Gabby! Get in! Get in now! Now! Ahhhh!" He shoved me gently toward the opening where the ice was added to the refrigerator. I glanced over my shoulder, saw the bear galloping our direction. I crawled in, realized

Twiggy was crawling in, too, and stood up. We stood nose to nose. There was just enough space for two thin people to stand, but our feet were still exposed to the bear's reach. The metal door banged as the bear tried to see inside.

"Can you climb the shaft?" Twiggy asked.

"How?"

"Push out with your hands and your feet. It's called a chimney climb."

"Not with the cache," I said.

The cache was beside me. I didn't want to let it go and have the bear get it.

"I wanted to get closer to you, but this isn't exactly what I had in mind," he said. "Try climbing. I can do it but I don't want to leave you here."

"How?"

"Push out. Like this. Then while your hands are bearing your weight bring your feet up. Push out. Raise your hands. Push out. Just keep pushing outward and upward until you get to the shelf in the refrigerator. Push it up with your head and push the door open."

"You're kidding, right?"

"No!"

"O… kay. What if I fall on you?"

"You won't. I know you can do it. If Santa Claus can do it you can, too. Push out. Now pick up your feet. Are you slipping?"

"No, wow, I never did this before."

"So while you are stable bring your feet up. Push out. Got it?"

"Uh, I think so."

I tried to copy Twiggy's actions and it worked slowly. I heard the bang of the metal door at the bottom and tried to climb faster.

"I took archery for PE!" I muttered as I climbed. "Why didn't I take refrigerator climbing?"

"Let go with your hands and find a higher spot."

I couldn't believe it! I was climbing a refrigerator!

"This is so weird," I said. "This is going to make a great log on the cache page."

"Just keep climbing. When you get to the tower I'll follow."

"Okay, too bad we can't get pictures of this." My voice started echoing in the enclosed space but there wasn't enough space for a proper echo so it just sounded hollow.

The shaft seemed longer than the stairs but I thought that was because I was taking smaller steps and doing something new. If I was used to climbing refrigerators it would go a lot quicker.

"Ooo, ouch!" I said as I bumped my head on the underside of the bottom shelf. "I think I made it!"

I had to push out with my feet and wrestle the shelf. It didn't move easily. I tried banging on it and it popped loose.

"Fore!" I yelled as it slid down the shaft. "Shelf attack!" *Whack!*

"Ouch!"

"Sorry, I tried to warn you. Are you okay?"

"Yeah, I think so. It just surprised me."

I bumped my head on the next shelf too, but I thought I had enough space to crawl out of the refrigerator. I was glad the door was not like a modern refrigerator. The door was more like a cupboard door and swung open easily. It took some squirming to get through the opening but finally I stood up once more inside the lookout tower.

"Okay! I made it!" I yelled down the shaft.

"All right, coming up," called Twiggy.

Bang, bang, bang went the door as the bear tried to reach Twiggy's feet. It didn't sound like an angry attack, but it was too close for comfort. I ran out onto the catwalk and looked down. The bear noticed movement above and paced below. In the distance I could see two bear cubs alternately eating and batting at each other. I didn't know if they were playing or irritating each other. Probably both.

It didn't take Twiggy long to climb the shaft but he had a harder time climbing out the door. When he stood up he found me grinning ear to ear pointing out to the catwalk. One cub dashed away from the other then turned around and invited a new attack.

"There's bears!" I said excitedly. "Can we take a picture? It'll be great to post it on the log!"

"Hold on," he said. "Let me get the pack and the cache."

He untied a rope attached to his belt loop, then went back to the refrigerator and pulled his pack up the shaft.

"It does have a little food in it," he explained.

When he had the pack in hand he unzipped it and pulled the cache out.

Clang! Cloong! The bear was trying to open the grate.

Twiggy pulled the lock out of his pack and carefully used it to lock the grate closed.

"At what point do we ask for help?" I asked.

"I don't know. What about you? How long are you willing to be stuck up here?"

"She'll get bored and leave, then we can hike back to the van."

We sat on the floor of the watchtower and looked through the contents of the ammunition container. I still was not so entrenched in the hobby that I called it an ammo can. There were still a few of the big, plastic fake jewels, but the geocachers before us had traded for most of them and the rest of the contents were typical of all the other caches I had found: Three fake jewels, a Matchbox car, a little girls' bracelet, a stubby screwdriver, a business card for an auto shop, two erasers, and a plastic lizard. I signed the log with an additional note, "We saw bears!"

"I think we should trade for a jewel. It's the one thing that will remind us of the cache."

"Okay, sounds good to me. I don't usually take things anymore. Just looking for them is the fun part."

"Even if you get chased up refrigerators by protective mother bears?"

"Yeah, though I wish you'd heed my warnings faster."

"I was more excited to see bears than I was afraid of them attacking."

"If an animal has young, weighs four times as much as you and has sharp teeth and claws, I suggest not taking any chances."

"Can I still take a few pictures?"

"From up here," he said.

"All right!"

I was so excited. I had never seen a wild bear, much less taken a picture of one.

"Stand right here," I said. "Let's see if I can get a picture of you and a bear at the same time."

I really couldn't. The angles were all wrong. I could see the bear below the catwalk but in a picture there would be no way to tell. I tried sitting on the rail but Twiggy gave me worried looks instead of smiling. The best picture I could get showed a worried Twiggy with the rump of the bear sticking out behind the edge of the catwalk.

"Okay, my turn," said Twiggy. "I want a picture in the watchtower. Sit on the counter. Here, we want the cache in the picture, too. Okay, turn a little bit."

He looked past me to the forest below.

"Okay, look at me. Smile. Smile! Come on I want to see it in your eyes. I like happy eyes... Thank you." He pressed the shutter release. "Do you want to see it?"

"Okay!"

He showed me the picture and then we clicked further to see the picture I took of him.

"Maybe I need to take Photography 101."

"It might help if I hadn't been worried about you falling over the rail into the jaws of the bear."

"Okay, then... let me take a different one. Show the camera how to climb out of a refrigerator shaft."

The bears were very content to hang around under the watchtower all day. We ate little cupcakes, granola and drank two pints of water we had packed. We lowered the cache back down the shaft on a rope so we wouldn't have to spend time replacing it on the ground. We could just close the door, snap on the lock and take off quickly for the van. We unlocked the grate. We checked the ground for bears. Time after time they were still there, just quietly laying about in the berry patch. We caught a couple of glimpses of the cubs. I even got a pretty good picture of them. If I was going to continue geocaching I was definitely going to have to get a better camera. And a GPS. Finally, as the light was failing, we couldn't see any bears. Maybe they had gone to wherever bears go to sleep. We crept down the stairs only to be met by mama bear walking out of the woods toward us.

"This is ridiculous. She isn't scared of us. Bears are supposed to take off running if you threaten them," Twiggy said.

"Maybe they are braver when they have cubs."

"I don't want to spend the night here. We have no sleeping bags. The windows are open to the elements. It's summer, but it's still going to get cold."

"I'm willing to risk it if you are. Maybe if they see us leaving they'll let us go."

"Do you have any experience with bears?"

"No. Do you?"

"No. But I've seen online videos of bear encounters."

"Yup, they always run away."

"Except for that one guy who got mauled and ended up losing his leg."

"It wasn't this bear that did it. The rangers got that bear."

"So…"

We crept down the stairs again. Twiggy insisted on going first. He stood there in a fighting stance daring the bear to come close.

"What do you think?" he whispered. "Are they gone?"

"I don't know."

"Whatever you do, don't run toward the van. The tower is better protection."

"Right."

We walked toward the trail gawking around like two little kids in a haunted house. The light was dim and we really only decided to try the trail because we thought the bear had gone home and we had the head lamp. We just passed the first bushes and had started to relax when there was a *snuff* and a *whuff* from the brush and we both jumped and dashed back to the lookout tower. Twiggy was nice enough to let me jump over the gate first and we stopped at the grate huffing and puffing. It was twice as heavy this time and we ended up back in the office room sitting there collecting our thoughts and giving our confidence the little boost it needed to spend a night in the tower.

"So, which side of the bed do you want this time?" Twiggy asked.

"The linoleum. The wood is too hard."

"You got it. Gabby... I'm sorry I got you into this. If you would rather I take you home..."

"No! No. I want to keep going. I don't know how we can ever win the contest only finding one cache a day, but I do want to try. If I go home I'll read books and listen to music and wish I could be doing something outside. But there won't be anywhere to go and... here there is. There is always somewhere to go and something to do. I saw a bear today! That is so cool! And I found tiny dragon houses in the tree roots. I was really hoping for a shower but seeing a bear was worth it. I can't wait to see what we find next!"

We ended up spooning that night. We started out just laying there side by side, shivering in the night. Tired and hungry but unable to sleep, we finally found a little warmth curling up together. Twiggy was surprised, but grateful, when I finally scooted over and he put his arms around me trying to conserve the little bit of warmth we had. We woke up often, still shivering. One of the times I woke up in the night I could hear howling in the distance.

"Can you hear that?" I whispered in case he was asleep.

"Coyotes," he said.

"Or wolves?"

"I don't know. I've never seen either in these mountains."

"Maybe I do want to be a forest ranger after all."

Dawn colored the sky very early in the morning atop the mountain. I had bed head again and no mirror or brush to help my attempts at taming it.

"It's not bed head if you sleep on the floor. Then it's floor head."

"We're lucky we got chased back. We almost left without locking up the cache again."

"Oh yeah."

We took a look around the watchtower and didn't see bears anywhere so we descended the stairs once more and checked on the cache before locking it up safe and sound.

"Take a picture of the tower so we will remember it always," I said as we found the trail again. He turned around and lined up the camera for the picture.

"You too," he said. "Stand next to that rock and you'll be framed right."

And so we had our second adventure captured in pixels, and we hiked down the mountain to the awful green van. Home sweet home.

"That thing is so ugly," I said as we approached it. "But it sure is good to see it again."

"I agree one hundred percent."

"What do geocachers call their cars?"

"Usually geomobiles or cachemobiles."

"With this avocado green van I think it looks more like guacamole than a cachemobile. Maybe it's a cacheamolé."

"I don't know, but it's the pits," he joked.

"There's enough dirt in it to grow an avocado tree."

"I'm starving and talking about Mexican food isn't helping. Let's go eat."

"It's a deal."

We were so hungry that I didn't even think about my hair. I don't know what the other customers thought when they saw us at the closest café. We looked like drifters, which I guess we were, temporarily. But we were very hungry, happy drifters with a goal in mind.

"Insane Asylum is next," I announced after three quarters of a huge burger had been devoured.

"Oh man, are you sure? We just lived through a bear encounter and you want to find Insane Asylum?"

"It's got a good rating. We need all the good ratings we can get."

"You mean difficult ratings. Would you allow me to define difficult?"

"We found the Pink Panther Cache, didn't we? And that one was supposed to be harder."

"It was harder. We got trapped by a bear and spent a freezing night on the mountain. I'd say we earned that one."

"Well, maybe I'm crazy, but I want to find Insane Asylum."

"Okay, you're the boss."

"And after that I want a real shower."

Chapter 7

I wanted to find Insane Asylum because I had seen the pictures. It was at the ruins of an old asylum and the walls looked spooky, like they could tell stories people didn't want to hear. It looked like the wind didn't whisper through the empty widows, it screamed like a banshee, and when it was still you could hear ghost stories on the breezes as they stirred the ashes of some long forgotten time.

Bumping along in the van I was beginning to think the van had once belonged to a resident at the asylum. The zebra striped walls and the purple shag floor looked like someone had decorated it after a bad dream.

"Turn left in about half a mile," I said to Twiggy.

"Who puts an insane asylum way out here in the sticks?" he asked.

"Somebody who doesn't want the residents bothering the neighbors."

"There haven't been insane asylums in use for years."

"That's why there's only ruins left."

"I think you're crazy to want to go here."

"Okay. So leave me at the asylum," I said. "I'll find my way home."

"Aw Gabby, I was just kidding. I wouldn't leave you behind and I don't think you're crazy. So far you've done an amazing job of choosing good caches. You know they are not all this interesting. There are some that I won't even stop at."

"Like the lamp post ones?"

"And guardrail caches. Who wants to look for a geocache with cars zipping past at fifty miles an hour? Guardrails are there to keep drivers on the road. They are nice and unobtrusive. You add a geocacher to the scene and they just become a distraction."

"I've never found a guardrail cache. Are they hard?"

"They are either very easy or very tricky. Frustrating either way."

The road ran along a farmer's field and then wandered away and over another creek. I had no idea the area I had spent four semesters in had so much running water. This bridge was sturdier than the last one we had seen. After it crossed the bridge, the road ascended the side of a hill and came out on top. A tall structure made the hill look bigger than it was. Twiggy checked his GPS.

"Still a tenth of a mile."

However, a tenth of a mile brought us up behind the building. It looked like it was made of river rock and parts of the walls had fallen down over time. Cracks spider-webbed between the rocks looking like an accident waiting to happen.

"Caches are usually not placed inside ruins," Twiggy said. "Too many muggles explore places like this and they could find it by accident."

"Can we explore it just like the muggles do?" I asked.

"Sure. Let's find the cache first."

He parked the van next to the building and we carefully stepped around the debris that seems to be around any abandoned building.

"It sure is a pretty place to send crazy people," I said.

"I doubt if most of them were crazy. Back then people were considered crazy if they were different. Some had physical problems, some mental, some were just hard to get along with. It was a place to send people to get rid of them."

"That's sad."

"I know a few people I wouldn't mind sending to an institution," he said jokingly.

"So, where's the cache?"

"I've had a few people overhear me talk geocaching and they think I'm crazy."

"Only because it has its own vocabulary and they don't understand what you're talking about. Do you remember me asking you what you were talking about? That's what prompted you to show me what geocaching was."

"I do," he said with a grin. "And you found your very first geocache that day."

"After searching and being laughed at for half an hour."

"I wasn't laughing at you. I was laughing with you. It was just so fun sharing my hobby with someone new. I was so glad you enjoyed it."

"It's weird how something can be so frustrating and enjoyable at the same time."

"It's that *aha!* moment when you finally spot it. It just erases all the frustration."

"Well, not all of it, but enough of it."

"Here, you take the GPS. I want to see you walk like a duck again."

"A duck? I walk like a duck?"

"Only when you're trying to read the screen and look for a geocache at the same time. It'll wear off with time."

"That's good. So what kind of a duck do I look like?"

"A peeking duck."

"What kind is that?"

"The kind that peeks around looking for geocaches. But if you're talking about a Peking Duck it's the white ones."

Once again we began poking around in brush and trees looking for any place that we thought a cache could be hidden in. The GPS led us to a copse of trees, then to the corner of the asylum, than back to the trees.

"Okay, you're relying too heavily on the GPS. Time to let those excellent geosenses go to work." He took the GPS back and said, "Look for a beacon."

I looked around the ruins thinking he had seen the cache and was giving me a hint, while he followed the map deeper into the woods. I didn't see any lights on the ruins and wondered if they even had electricity out here in the days when the asylum was operational.

"Where are you going?" I called out.

"Looking for beacons," he said. "They usually signify a good hiding spot."

"Way out there?" I asked. Then I remembered a beacon was anything that stood out, like a hollow tree or a pile of rocks. I felt a little silly looking for spotlights on the building. "Where have you looked already?"

"It doesn't matter. I might have missed it."

I followed Twiggy as he hunted for the cache. I probably looked in all the same places he already searched. I knew to look for piles of rocks or sticks, but what about piles of pinecones? I unpiled the pinecones to find... a bare spot amongst the ferns.

"I found it!" I heard from behind the brush ahead of me. When I got closer Twiggy said, "See if you can spot it."

When I had walked around and around it without finding it he added. "It's about two feet long, an inch and a half around and brown."

I began noticing there was a bush made up of many small branches clustered together and I assumed the cache was one of them. When he saw that I had the right idea he reached into the bush and pulled one of the "branches" out. It was a piece of plastic pipe with caps on both ends. We sat in the grass while he unscrewed the cap and dumped out the contents. I snapped up the log book to sign it, noticing several pieces of sidewalk chalk.

"What's all that for?" I asked as I opened the log. The front page of the log book had a picture. It showed the floor of the asylum and the floor was littered with chalk outlines of people.

"Add yours to the asylum," said a note in the log book.

I showed the picture to Twiggy.

"Cool! I wonder how many outlines there are in there now."

I signed the log book and we packaged up the cache and replaced it, then took one of the pieces of chalk with us as we explored the ruins.

"And so we enter the dreaded asylum of DOOOMMMMM!" Twiggy said in an evil voice as we stepped through the doorway.

Light streamed through the broken windows illuminating three chalk outlines on the floor. There had been many more in the past, but the roof was missing and water had filtered through cracks and washed away many of the chalk outlines. Some of the outlines looked more like chalky pools. Geocachers had become creative and outlined different poses. It reminded me a little of a movie I had to watch in history class of the erupting of Pompeii and how they found people in the act of doing some very typical things when they met their demise.

"Let's do one of two people handing a geocache to each other," I said.

"Okay. I'll trace you and you can trace me," he said.

Hmm, I wasn't sure I wanted to be traced but there was no polite way to refuse. I handed him the chalk and sat on the floor.

"Lie down and put your arms out like you're handing your sister a present on Christmas day," he said. "On your side might work better. Feet apart so we get more of an outline." He positioned my hand so a geocache could be drawn in it. "There, that's good. Stay like that." He began tracing around me and I tried not to be too uncomfortable when he reached sensitive areas. That reminded me that I was going to have to trace around him next. He might have taken a little longer to trace around some spots but he was polite. After I got up we drew a box in my chalk drawing hand and Twiggy put a GX symbol on the side of the box.

"It looks like a first aid kit now," I said.

"Okay, let's see," he said as he attempted to position himself correctly in relation to where my chalk outline was.

"Right hand a little bit up," I instructed. "Okay. Now you can do whatever you want."

I started at his hand and worked my way around trying not to smear any of the other chalk outlines.

"I wonder if this makes us residents," he joked. "If you outline somebody in an asylum, does it steal a little bit of their soul?"

"That's silly."

"I need to sneeze."

"No don't sneeze! You might mess up the lin…" *BAM! Splat!*

Twiggy was on top of me in an instant shielding me from harm.

"Where are you… CRAZY PEOPLE? Whar the tarnation are you hiding? Good for nothin' trespassers!"

"We're not trespassers!" Twiggy yelled "We're just exploring the ruins!"

"Damn people think they can go anywhere they please. This is MY land!"

"Sir… Uh… if you'll put the gun down we'll be out of here." *BAM!*

"He's not putting the gun down," he muttered to me.

Little pieces of the ceiling rained down on the chalk outlines. It must have been a shotgun.

"He's not shooting at us. Maybe he's just trying to scare us away."

"It's working, except I'm too scared to move."

An old man prowled the ruins. He seemed to feel his way forward and he walked bleary eyed.

"He can't see well," I whispered.

"Then what's he doing carting a gun around?!" Twiggy whispered into my ear.

"Shotguns are good for people who can't see well. It sprays out so you hit a wide area."

"How did you learn about shotguns?"

"I watch the History Channel. Get off me. Let's run for the stairs. He might not even know we're moving until we're out of range."

"No. A shot gun can shoot a long ways. They use them for hunting birds! We're bigger than birds and closer, too."

"But he's mostly shooting up. He'll miss."

The man was following the wall like he needed a reference point muttering about trespassers and crazy people and the government spying on innocent citizens. I began to think he had lived too close to the asylum for too long. Twiggy watched him.

"Okay. I think you're right," he barely whispered as he slid off of me. "On the count of three." He waited while I got ready to run. "One, two…" he stole a glance to make sure the old man was still acting feeble. "Three!"

We dashed to the stairs and when we reached them we realized only half of them still existed.

"Wow," I whispered as I carefully picked my way up the broken steps. "I should major in geocaching. So far I've really moved up in the world while geocaching."

"Shhh."

"Watch towers, asylums… what will it be next?"

"Quick! He's coming!" he whispered.

We reached the landing and peeked over the wall to the floor below.

"Harhar, har," the old man laughed grimly as he followed the wall toward the stairs.

"He can't see us when he gets close to the stairway," I said. "So when he disappears from view make a run for it."

"Okay… ready?"

We couldn't run because some of the stairs were so deteriorated we could see through them. We had to find the most stable boards we could. The second floor was almost as bad as the stairs. Pools of water had rotted the floor and caused it to sag. There were gaping holes giving us glimpses into the spidery world of the floor boards. We had to inch along the edges of the walls.

"Gabby! There are no stairs at the end of the hall!" Twiggy said.

"Who builds an asylum without emergency exits?" I whispered urgently.

"It was built before building codes," he said. "And they didn't want people to be able to get out."

"Well, we want to get out!"

Thunk... thunk...

"He's reached the stairs!" I whispered.

"Quick! This way! There are too many rooms for him to search. We'll find one at the end and buy some time."

"He'll never make it down this hall," I said. "He'll fall through!"

"I have a hunch he's done this many times."

"Then where does he stash his victims?"

"This way, we can do this."

"I know you're in here CRAZY PEOPLE! QUIT haunting my property!"

"He's nuts," I whispered.

"Appropriate, huh?"

"I don't want to find the next geocache," I whispered.

"Why?"

"It's called Snake Pit."

"Watch out for exposed nails," he said as he led the way down the hall. He turned at a doorway and we entered a small room. The window was broken out and iron bars dangled from a single bolt. We went back to the hall and entered the next room. It didn't have a window. The next one had a window but no glass and no iron bars.

Thunk... thunk...

"I say we climb out the window and use the iron bars to get us closer to the ground and drop from there," I said.

"You're crazy!"

"Do you have a better idea?" I asked.

"No."

We went back to the room with the iron hanging down. If we could hang on, it would give us an added three feet. I thought I could dangle and drop from a second story window. It was going to hurt but I thought I could make it down and then run to the van.

"Do you want to go first?" I asked.

"And leave you up here with the crazy man? No way!"

"So you want me to go first?"

"And have you fall to your doom? No way!"

"Well, one of us has to go first," I pointed out. "The man is slow. You go ahead."

"Oh shoot, oh shoot," he said.

"We don't want to think about shooting. Just go!"

He put a leg through the window. He stomped on the iron bars a few times to make sure they were stable enough to support his weight, then he felt his way out onto the iron frame and looked down. He let his legs down and grasped the iron bars tightly.

Thunk... thunk... went the old man's steps on the hollow floor. *Creeeeak... Thump....*

I watched as he used his hands to work his way to the end of the iron bars. *Crack!*

"Twiggy! The sill is breaking! Let go! Let go! Find a place to land and..."

The wood split and I couldn't look as the iron bars peeled loose. Then there was a mighty *clannnngg* as the bars hit the ground below.

"Twiggy! Are you okay?" I shouted out the window.

There was no answer so I stuck my head out the window. The iron bars were not on top of Twiggy, of that I could be thankful, but he sat there trying to figure out if he had survived.

"Now how am I going to get down?" I asked.

Going out the window didn't look safe anymore. I rushed to the doorway and looked down the hall. The old man was going door to door. He still had the gun. I waited. I knew all the rooms we had gone into could be inspected with just a glance, but maybe the rooms on the other side of the hall were different. The man was dressed in ragged jeans and old shoes. His shirt was worn thin and only half tucked in. His hair was in disarray and his beard was a week old. His eyes looked cloudy, and he walked with an unsteady step. I examined the path I would have to take to get past him.

"Gabby!" Twiggy called from outside.

I rushed to the window.

"I'm okay," I said. "I'm planning a way out. Wait for me by the door."

I went back to the doorway and glanced down the hall to find the old man. When he stuck his head into a room I dashed to the next room and ducked inside. Doorway to doorway I snuck down the hall. I thought I had made it when I was caught. The man turned suddenly and said, "Thar you are! I don't take kindly to people thinkin' they can go wherever they please."

I ran toward the stairs and stumbled all the way to the landing with the *thunk, thunk* of the man's steps following quicker than I thought possible.

"Come back here! Trespasser!" *BAM!*

I found my feet and stumbled down the bottom half of the stairs. I sprinted to the doors right over all the chalk outlines. Twiggy waited for me like I told him to, but he clasped me in a hug. I was so scared all I could do was hug him back.

"Oh, Gabby, please don't scare me like that again," he said as he clasped me tightly. "I didn't know what you could do. I wanted to go back…"

"It's okay. I'm glad you didn't. Are you okay?"

"I think so. But if I wasn't it wouldn't matter. When I thought of you trapped in there I forgot all about any scrapes or bruises I might have picked up. Are you okay?"

"Yeah, not even scrapes or bruises."

"Can you walk okay?"

"Yeah, how about you?"

"Let's get out of here. The crazy man can keep his asylum."

As we started up the van we could see the old man leaning out an upstairs window yelling something out across the hillside.

Chapter 8

Later we stopped at a pizza place in the next town. Being poor college students we were used to finding a cheap meal. We drove to a budget motel and looked for their rack of tourist brochures. Sometimes next to the brochures there were coupons for local eateries. Mom and pop pizza places were famous for their specials. We could usually count on splitting a two topping pizza for less than ten dollars. The motel did not disappoint. We found coupons and little mini menus for several places in town, but the pizza place was close by.

Twiggy bent over his laptop and read his log to me, "We found the cleverly cammoed container but the special effects were a bit over the top. Beware the insane, shotgun toting, zombie farmer. He guards the asylum and chased us up the rotten stairs. I had to jump out a second story window to escape. My life flashed before my eyes. Grabby Gabby had to sneak past the loony while he was searching the rooms for us and I thought she was a goner! Luckily she's faster than a half blind old man. What a weird experience, but we did get the smiley! TFTA, thanks for the adventure, I think."

"Gee thanks," I said. "I didn't have to run I just had to have good timing."

"The next cache we go look for has got to be safer," Twiggy declared. "No Snake Pits."

"Okay. Safe. Hmm. I suppose it also has to have a high difficulty level so we get a better score on the contest," I said. "Why are you picking off your pineapple? You only have two toppings there."

"You chose pineapple. I chose pepperoni."

"If you didn't like pineapple why did you order a pizza with pineapple on it?"

"We each chose one. I wanted you to have what you like."

"Then can I have your pineapple?"

He began placing his pineapple bits on my slice of pizza as I looked over my list of potential cache finds.

"Okay," I finally said. "Here's one in town. It's a one and a half/ four. It's in a city park. You can't get much safer that that without sacrificing difficulty points."

"Sure, we can try that one. This is a cute little town. I wouldn't mind seeing more of it."

"Somehow I thought being in a contest would be more intense than this. I thought we'd be on the run all day, every day."

"We haven't had much time to rush," he said. "We've found and gotten out of every predicament as fast as we could. We have to eat."

"Well, a cache at a park shouldn't take very long."

"And I promised you a shower today."

"Oh, yay! That would be great!"

"In fact, that motel where we got the coupons looked like they had vacancies."

"And it looked cheap. I mean affordable."

"No, it looked cheap."

"That's okay, as long as the shower works."

I should have thought before I spoke. As it turned out the motel had very tiny rooms. The room was so small that only a double bed and a dresser fit inside. A TV perched on the dresser and a trash can sat inside the tiny bathroom. But it did have a shower.

I went out to the van to find a box of appropriate clothes and my makeup and toiletries bag. I was glad I had bought this bag for showering at the dorms. It was big enough to hold my shampoo, conditioner, styling tools, makeup, towel and shower wrap.

"There's a couple of caches down the road. I'll go find those so you can have some privacy," Twiggy said as I entered the room.

"But... are they hard to find?" I asked. I thought we were in this geocaching thing together.

"I doubt it, but it's something to do," he answered.

"Okay," I said, though I was a little put out. I wanted to find those caches, too.

I couldn't really ask to tag along since he was giving me time to shower without feeling any pressure from him.

The shower was glorious. The showerhead didn't work well and the water spit and sputtered but just standing in the warm stream with steam filling the bathroom was like heaven to me. I debated. Should I splurge and use the fancy shower gel my mom had given me or save it and use the little shower soap? I opened the little bar of soap and smelled it. It had a nasty chemical odor to it so I set it on the soap dish and pulled out the shower gel. Ahhh, cherry blossom. Just the smell of it made the steam feel pink and brought spring back. I took my time shampooing and washing and just enjoying the spray. I shaved my legs and rinsed slowly, then I blow dried my hair, styling a little as I went. I looked in the mirror and surprised myself. I seemed more mature looking, but I couldn't figure out how that could be. I felt more grown up, too. I still had the medium length dark hair, still had a sprinkling of freckles. My mother had always said it meant I was kissed by the sun. Maybe facing a bear and a crazy gunman had changed my attitude and it showed in my bearing. I stood a little taller to see if it helped. Hmm. Maybe if I spent some time in front of the makeup mirror I'd feel better.

I turned on the clock radio, found my little cosmetics bag and applied a little foundation, then blush. The foundation helped a lot to make me look older. It covered some of the freckles. I wondered why I bothered putting makeup on if all we were going to do is drive to a little park, find a geocache and then eat dinner, but then I thought that as long as I was going to feel clean and presentable I might as well do it right. I was just finishing up with the makeup when there was a light knock at the door and then the beep of a key card.

"Can I come in?" Twiggy asked.

It suddenly occurred to me that I was only wearing a towel.

"Uh, yeah, I guess," I said feeling half naked. "I'll be ready to go in a few minutes."

He climbed onto the bed and sat there cross-legged, then got up and looked for the TV remote. I pulled the flaps of the box open and sorted through clothes until I found a pair of underwear, jeans and a t-shirt. Twiggy tried hard not to watch but he wasn't succeeding.

"Why do you wear makeup?" he asked.

"It makes a girl feel pretty."

"Why? You're pretty without it."

"Why do you shave in the morning?" I asked.

"Because it bugs me to have whiskers that rub. I can hear them brush against my shirt."

"Oh. A little shadow looks good on you. A beard might too. But not one of those long flowy ones."

He rubbed his chin. He had a little more than a shadow after two days.

"You like guys with beards?"

"Sometimes. It depends on the guy."

I took my clothes into the bathroom and put them on.

"Okay, your turn," I said. "Did you find it?"

"Find what? Oh, um, yeah…"

"Can I try to find one while you're showering?" I asked.

"I guess," he said and handed me the GPS unit.

"Cool! Maybe I can figure this thing out and find one all by myself! How much time do you need?"

"Fifteen minutes?"

"Okay."

First I had to go outside. I knew the GPS wouldn't work very well indoors. I walked around the parking lot waiting for the GPS to find a signal. When it bleeped I pressed buttons until I found the map. If Twiggy had found some caches nearby then they would show up on the map. When I didn't see any cache icons on the first map I clicked back and found a screen that displayed a list. Hmm, the closest cache on the list has four tenths of a mile away. I did a little math and decided if I didn't get distracted that I could walk down there and back in half an hour and Twiggy had said it was an easy find, so off I went. The day was hot but I felt refreshed after my shower so I walked at a pleasant pace for a while before checking the GPS and adjusting my course. I found out pretty quick that four tenths of a mile on the GPS didn't equal four tenths of a mile on foot. I walked two blocks and then came to a maintenance yard and to walk around it took me a block out of my way. On the other side of the maintenance yard was a cemetery and the cache appeared to be on the other side of the cemetery. There was a funeral going on and I didn't want to disturb the mourners so I walked a big circle around them. After I went past the funeral I came to a pond. It was a pretty pond, with trees leaning over the water and koi that followed me hoping for a handout. This was a large, old cemetery and it had areas that were much older. There was a section of almost tomb sized graves, acres of headstones and some flat grave markers. The flat markers were much more recent. The cache, it seemed, was in an older part of the cemetery. The grounds changed from flat, well groomed, park-like surroundings to little undulating hills and trees crowded the outside edges of the cemetery. It was peaceful, in a rather too-quiet way. Occasionally I would see graves in between long established trees and imagined caskets and roots entwined forever. I began pushing my way through undergrowth, still seeing grave stones poking up out of the weeds. I decided a hint wouldn't hurt so I clicked through the screens to find the hint, but it didn't help much.

"Standing in plain sight," it said.

I guessed that I would have to be right on top of the cache to see it. This was a strange cemetery. It was almost as if this part of it was forgotten and from a lost time in the town's history. At last I reached a grouping of trees with a metal fence around it. I read the headstones and all the graves inside the fence were of family members. Old sun-bleached silk flowers poked out of ancient vases that were part of the headstones. Somebody did not forget these people, though it had been years since the flowers had been replaced.

The GPS said the cache was within ten feet of me. So it had to be somewhere in this little group of graves, or in the trees above. The trunks of the trees were not gnarly and there were no hollows to hide a cache in. Maybe it was hanging in the branches? I hoped not.

Right about then I noticed that nobody had visited this place in weeks. The area didn't look the least bit trampled and I knew that when Twiggy and I geocached we left a lot of foot prints behind. Twiggy hadn't found this cache. So where had he gone? He wouldn't have walked farther than this during my shower. I dismissed the thought. I had a geocache to find. I glanced around in the overhanging branches but gave up on that idea quickly. Then I examined the ground around the fence and the bases of the gravestones. Nothing. I looked further afield but the GPS kept bringing me back to the same group of gravestones.

I sat down to rest and read the description. I was certainly learning a lot about the workings of the GPS on this little hunt. Before I had mostly just followed the map and Twiggy was right there to find hints and descriptions. The description was a rambling account about the Bannock family who had come from Kentucky and headed west only to be stopped short by disease. It was a common occurrence when families traveled west and there were no doctors handy. The cache owner's family had been part of the group and his great uncle and aunt were dropped off in the next town to be raised by strangers. Family back east had traveled to find the children, and set up a proper burial spot. However the cache owner had always liked the area and came back to live in the town where the strangers had helped his aunt and uncle. He came to this cemetery often. He said the pond frequently had ducks in it and he liked the koi in the pond. All this was pleasant reading but it didn't help me find the cache. At last, at the bottom of the description it told me to look for a small container, well hidden. It was only big enough for a rolled up log so I was to bring my own pen. Oh shoot! I didn't have a pen! I couldn't sign the log even if I found it! I felt like such a newbie geocacher. Twiggy always had a pen. I used to make fun of him for it, but I wouldn't anymore. The last sentence of the description said to look for "the odd one out".

I stood and looked at the graves again. They were not all the same but they were all similar. Most of them were light colored granite but one was newer and darker colored rock. Maybe that was where I should concentrate my search. I had already searched the bases of all the gravestones without crossing over the fence. I didn't think I should step over it. Fences were for keeping people out. The odd one out kept coming to mind. The odd what? The odd grave? The odd tree? I looked around at the trees and the one that came up out of the middle of the graves stood out, though it wasn't really odd. It just looked like it was friendly in an intrusive sort of way. I didn't see a cache in the branches or anywhere on the trunk for the third time. The flowers? The flowers! There were many of the old, faded, silk flowers. Was one of them different? There were roses, lilies, baby's breath, irises, all in muted tones after weathering many rainy, snowy and sunny days out in the open. The roses were red, the lilies orange, the baby's breath white, the irises lavender and blue. Whoever brought the flowers didn't have much of an eye for arrangement. They just seemed to be put into the vases and left. I ruled out all the flowers that couldn't be reached from outside the fence. That only left two gravestones on the ends of the fenced area. One was the dark rock and the other was the light rock. Flowers leaned over these graves, too, bent by the wind. Lilies. Suddenly I spotted it!

"Oh! I found it!" I exclaimed to no one at all. I was so excited to spot the odd one out that I snatched it from the vase and held it up in triumph. Taped to the wire stem was a little vial and in the vial was the log sheet. The flower that was different was a white Easter lily in amongst the orange Tiger lilies. I found it! I found it! All by myself!

I sat down and opened the vial, then pulled out the log sheet. The log was old. The dates on it went back five years. It wasn't found often. And in the winter it was hardly found at all, probably because of the snow. The names were strange and some of them I could hardly read at all. Some of the ink had run and some had just worn off. The more recent names were easier to read: Blueboy, Sir Cachealot, The Maniac Monkeys, Jeddy4, and Lady Lily who liked the cache because of the link to her name. It made me think that I should choose a creative geocaching name. Gabby Gal? No, I wasn't really very talkative. I decided I needed more experience geocaching before I chose a permanent name. I could read more log books and see what had already been chosen. I didn't see Twiggy's name on the log and the last logger had signed in three weeks ago. This seemed to be a lonely place. The thought of nobody coming here for three weeks was a little depressing, but then I thought that nobody would come here at all except the cache owner if it weren't for the cache. And there were many graves scattered amongst the trees that were never visited at all. Forgotten people. I walked around, finding several other gravesites hidden in the trees. Oliver T. Martin beside his wife Alletta 1894, Walter Kolinsky 1932, Sunshine Moonbeam 1964. A 60's baby? 1963-1964. How sad. I went on before I could dwell too long on little Sunshine. Willard Bertram Tudor 1887-1958. All these graves had an old fashioned headstone and then I came to a small rugged cross that just had Mary carved in the crossbeam. Mary? Mary who? When? Why? Each headstone held a mystery, especially that one. What had happened to Mary? Was her family with her? I thought I better leave, but I noticed I was still carrying the Easter lily with me. All these graves with no visitors and no flowers. As I went back to the replace the cache I touched each headstone with the flower. It might be old and frayed and had to go back to its hiding place but these people had been visited today. These few people were remembered in some small way. I replaced the flower in the vase and realized I had been gone a lot longer than I planned and I still had a walk ahead of me. I headed back to the motel feeling downcast and triumphant at the same time. I realized I'd been gone a little too long when I spotted Twiggy standing by the pond gazing out over the cemetery. He trotted over when he saw me walking across the grass, making sure I didn't step on any markers.

"There you are! Are you okay?" he asked.

"I found it!" I said. "How did you find me?"

"I looked up the nearest cache on the laptop. Gabby... I'm sorry. I really didn't find a cache while you were showering."

"I know. But it's a nice cache and I didn't have a pen. Can we sign the log?"

"You went geocaching? And you didn't even bring a pen?" he teased.

"No, but I was hoping you'd come back with me. It's a neat spot and a good hide. It took me a long time!"

"Your first solo find?" he asked.

"Yeah! And it was a hard one!"

"What's the rating?"

"Uh, I don't know, let me check," I said as I clicked back through the screens. He smiled as he saw me navigate through the screens with ease.

"Time to get you your own GPS," he said.

"I can't afford one. How much do they cost?"

"That one was only a couple hundred, but the fancier ones are more."

"Oh. See? I can't afford one. It's only a 1.5/1.5! It sure felt like a 3/1.5 to me."

"They'll get easier with practice. Are you okay? You seem a little down. I thought finding a cache all by yourself would have been really exciting."

"It was, except... I'll show you."

"You didn't find another dead bird, did you?" he asked "I remember the first time I was with you and you spotted a dead bird on campus. You almost cried!"

"Maybe I'm growing up a little. I didn't find a dead bird, but... I'll show you."

"A cemetery isn't the most cheerful place to go geocaching," he pointed out.

"It's sort of cool and sort of sad and sort of... I'll show you."

He laughed, "Okay, so show me already."

"You have to find it. It's up that way though," I said and pointed in the general direction. "I'm kind of glad it's out here away from where the funerals are likely to be held. No muggles."

"You're even talking like a real geocacher," he said. "You're not mad at me?"

"No, why?"

"I was just giving you some space so you wouldn't feel pressured. I called my dad."

"That's good! He's probably glad to hear from you," I said.

"Actually, I was asking him if we should continue with this contest," he confessed.

"Why would we quit?" I asked.

"Gwen, I was really scared for you," he said. "Maybe these hard caches are not a good way to start out. Nobody ever starts out by looking for the really tough ones. They look for big easy ones in safe places."

"So I'm still weird. That's okay. We're building stories!"

"Stories?"

"Before school got out and we started geocaching the most exciting thing I had to talk about was missing the bus when I had to be at an afternoon class in ten minutes. Now I can say I've been trapped in a lookout tower by a bear and shot at by a crazy man."

"And that's a good thing?" he asked.

"Yes... no... oh look! It's over where you see that fence. Now you're on your own. If I can find it, you can find it."

It took him two minutes to find the cache. I huffed disappointedly.

"I've found this kind before," he said. "See? You just need practice."

"You didn't even read the hint!" I said.

"Geocachers just automatically look for the different thing in amongst a bunch of same things. It'll become second nature to you one of these days. You did well to find this one! A lot of newbies would DNF one like this several times before they found it. We need to take a picture of your first real find. Here, hold the flower."

I stuck the flower over my ear and he snapped a picture of me standing in front of the graves. Then he took one of me signing the log. Of course he brought a pen.

"Thanks," I told him as I handed the log back. "I feel better already."

He signed the log, rolled it up and stuck it back into the little vial, then added the lily to the flowers in the vase.

"Good job! High five!"

I gave him a high five and dragged him through the woods.

"There are graves all over back here," I explained. "Look, Sunshine Moonbeam. I wonder what she would have become if she had grown up. I picture a person working in a plant nursery."

"You've got such an imagination. I suppose there are fairytale creatures that live in this cemetery, too."

"Of course! But I haven't seen one yet. Cemetery creatures usually come out at night."

"Vampires?"

"Ick, no. In my imagination the creatures are friendly, even if they live in a cemetery."

"I should have guessed that."

"Look at this one," I said leading him to Mary's grave. "I guess this is the one that made me sad."

He looked down at the rugged cross.

"Well, look at it this way," he said. "She represents all the Marys that have gone on. Anybody who ever loved a Mary will remember her when they see this cross."

"I guess," I said, though the number of people who would ever see this cross was rather small.

"Let's go find a micro cache in a park."

"Okay."

He had driven the van to the cemetery so we didn't have to walk back to the motel.

"You really walked all this way, just to find a cache?" he asked as we climbed into the van.

"Yeah, it was a nice walk until I got to the maintenance yard. That wasn't exactly scenic. But the cemetery was cool. I liked seeing the fish, and the graveyard was interesting. I learned not to trust distances on the GPS, though. That was more than four tenths of a mile."

"No kidding."

"What did your dad say about quitting the contest?" I asked.

"He said, 'Quit being a wimp. And choose your adventures carefully.'"

"I guess we can do that," I said.

He drove through the quaint streets lined with old houses and tall trees. In the fall the streets would be yellow, covered with a blanket of leaves.

"I bet you like the vine covered houses," Twiggy said.

"Yes, though Sarah says vines are a pain to deal with. They even work their way into attics and garages if there is a crack they can grow through. Why do pretty things always prove to be problematic?"

"What about you? Are you going to prove to be problematic?"

"I hope not."

"You've already worked your way into my attic," he said.

I wasn't sure how to take that, although I had to admit my opinion of him was changing, too. He was beginning to lose a little bit of his dweebiness.

And I noticed he hadn't shaved. He looked rather rugged in clean jeans, a collared shirt and hiking boots. He could use a hair cut but I hoped he'd wait. We couldn't afford haircuts and I liked the way his hair was beginning to curl over his collar. Maybe I was a rebel. My father would insist Twiggy get a haircut as soon as his hair covered his ears. I really wasn't into long haired guys but at the same time there were some guys that looked better when their hair was allowed to have a life of its own. I knew what he looked like with short hair. He looked like a math teacher.

"Are you navigating, or am I?" he asked.

"Oh, I can!" I said. "I got distracted."

I took the GPS and figured out where we were on the map compared to the streets I saw going by outside.

"Go three blocks up and turn left. Then go all the way to the end of the street. There will be a street running along the side of the park but we need to turn left and then right into the little parking lot."

When we pulled into the parking lot we found out that this cache might be a little more difficult than the others for a different reason. Muggles. The fields were full of kids playing soccer and the edges of the fields were lined with parents sitting in camp chairs, guarding coolers of soda. The playground was full of younger brothers and sisters with an adult watching over the group. A fenced area was marked as a dog park and five dogs of different sizes and dispositions played fetch, or did obedience lessons in the fenced area.

"What do you do if you get to a cache location and it's like this?" I asked.

"Sometimes I just keep driving, but it can't hurt to look. There are techniques we can try but step one is getting out of the van and trying to guess where the cache might be just by the lay of the land."

After getting out and walking back and forth in the parking lot to get a bearing Twiggy said, "I think it's on the other side of all those people. I wonder if there's parking on the other side."

"There's one way to find out."

We climbed into the van and drove around the park. On the other side we found a parking lot so Twiggy pulled in and we got out again to take another reading.

"Well, I can't say we're closer but at least we're on the right side of all the people," he said. "It's that way."

We followed the side walk all the way to the end, passing shaded picnic tables and grungy charcoal grills. Right before the sidewalk ended was a large, half circle flower bed which was filled with pansies and marigolds, along with a sculpture of a small town main street scene. It was made of different colors of metal carved by a welder's torch and bolted together with sturdy nuts and bolts. It was attractive in a rustic way.

"It seems to be somewhere in his planter," Twiggy said.

"It had several favorite points," I remembered aloud. "I wonder what it was that people liked so much."

"You can give a cache a favorite point for any reason. We won't know until we find it."

I started out looking in the easy places, which included the inner side of the wall of the planter. I didn't think it would be in the bushes. Those might be pruned by landscapers. The flowers were probably replaced every year or two. That left the sculpture, but it was a big one. I was guessing it was twenty feet long. The main street include a post office, barber shop, general store, soda fountain, assayer's office, café, and an old time gas station complete with a Model T and an elderly driver. When I noticed the driver I began noticing other people in the scene. There was a woman stepping out of the general store with a bag hooked over her arm. Two men sat outside the café playing a board game. The barber stood at the door of his shop with a pair of scissors in hand. There was a mailman walking down the street with a mail pouch draped over his shoulder. All the people in the scene were pieced together from junk, but they still resembled people enough to be able to identify each person's gender and activity.

"Do you know how to make it go?" A little boy asked Twiggy.

"No. How?" he asked.

"You have to put a quarter in," the little boy said. "Do you have a quarter?"

"I might," Twiggy said.

I began searching my pockets for a quarter but I had put on clean pants and my pockets were empty. That reminded me that I better check my pockets before I did laundry. Twiggy produced a quarter and gave it to the little boy. He ran on top of the wall to the other end of the flower bed, hopped down and stuck the quarter into a machine. When he turned the meter and the quarter fell into the machine the sculpture began moving. A car drove down the street and the postman clicked down the sidewalk stopping at each door to, presumably, deliver mail. Another car drove down the street and the lights flicked on in the windows.

"It looks cool at night," the little boy said.

Ding, ding came a noise from the gas station and light flickered on the gas pump. A woman began walking a dog down the sidewalk and there were a couple of yaps when they reached the barber. As the time ran out on our quarter the postman and the woman had traded places. I could only assume another quarter would make the postman come back around and leave the woman and the dog behind the sculpture.

"Cool!" said Twiggy. "A cache on a moving sculpture makes it a favorite for me!"

It was a cute sculpture, but seeing it move didn't help us find the cache.

"Should I read the hint?" I asked.

"Not yet. I think we can do this one," he said.

"It should be in the planter," I said.

"Or sneakier. Feel everything you can reach. It won't be part of the sculpture that the artist would see, but it's there somewhere."

"Part of the sculpture? How can that be? Hundreds of people stop to look at it and half a dozen a day put a quarter in and watch it run."

Twiggy had a sneaky look to him as like he was trying to put himself in the cache owner's shoes. Where would *he* hide a cache on a moving sculpture?

The boy ran off to join his family at the soccer field so we were free to search as much as we wanted to, so Twiggy dug in his pocket and produced another quarter. He inserted it into the machine, cranked the switch and positioned himself so he could watch the workings as the figures moved. The woman and dog clicked their way down the metal sidewalk. They were out of reach so we didn't check them. However, as soon as the mailman made an appearance Twiggy stuck his finger into the mailman's mail pouch, then looked disappointed when he found nothing in there. He walked around the sculpture watching for any other parts that might come within reach from the sidewalk. When the figures stopped he put another quarter in and checked the shopping bag that the woman was carrying.

"Well, we ruled out the obvious," he said. "Time to get down to the nitty gritty."

"What's the nitty gritty?" I asked.

"We'll have to search everything within reach."

I started at one end of the flower bed and, feeling very self conscious, began examining everything I could get my hands on: plants, rocks, sprinkler heads, the undersides of the sculpture. I gently tested everything.

After about ten minutes Twiggy sat down on the grass and watched me search.

"Hey," I said. "I'm the one that needs help."

I walked over and sat beside him.

"You're cute when you're trying to figure something out," he said.

"I am not. It's frustrating trying search a flower bed without making people think I'm weird or unbalanced or something."

"You admit you're weird," he said.

"Yeah, but I don't want those parents over there to worry about the safety of their children. I'm not *that* weird."

"So, you need help?"

"Yes!"

"Would a hint help?"

"Yes! Did you find it?"

"Yes, and it's a good hide."

"Oh great, that means I'll never find it."

"It's about as big as my thumb. And it's in plain sight," he confided.

I looked around on the sculpture as much as I could from outside the flower bed.

"Gabby, you have to get nosy. You'll never find it unless you're willing to try things."

"I don't know what I'm looking for and it's a work or art. I don't want to hurt it."

"You won't hurt it. The rules are very strict about cache placement. If it would harm anything they wouldn't publish the cache."

Just then a man strode across the grass from the soccer field and sat down next to Twiggy.

"No FTF For Me," he said as he extended his hand.

"Today? Team Twiggy," Twiggy said.

"How many finds?"

"Three thousand four hundred twenty-two," he said.

"Including this one?"

"Yeah."

"What about her?"

"She's new to it."

"Ah, I see." Then he called out to me, "Check the other side."

"Geocaching 101," Twiggy said.

"This one's more like 301," the man said.

It was a little aggravating to be doing something for the first time with an audience watching. I was just glad the man seemed to be another geocacher.

"So you're not into the whole FTF race?" Twiggy said.

"Nah, there are plenty of people around here that will run out at all hours of the day or night to get an FTF. I'm not one of them. It's not a competition for me. I like the places the hobby takes me to."

"Me, too."

"Do you think the rating on this one is accurate?"

"Me? Yeah. Gabby's never seen one of these before. I suspect we're going to be here a while."

"If you're going to be in town in two weeks there's going to be an event at Moby's Fish House."

"Sorry, we're just passing through."

"We usually hide a few more caches, and have a door prize or two. We've got a group of ten that usually show up but sometimes geocachers from surrounding towns will join in. We've had as many as fifty."

"Cool, sounds like fun."

All this time I was walking around and around from one side of the flower bed to the other, but everything looked perfectly normal.

"It's disguised," the man said. "If you were a tiny geocache hiding on a metal replica of downtown, what you go disguised as?"

"A fire hydrant?" I guessed.

"You're close."

"I don't see any fire hydrants," I said.

"What *do* you see?"

"Uhh, people, doors, buildings, the dog…"

"What's it held together with?" he asked me.

"Nuts and bolts."

"And…"

"I don't know… glue?"

"Try the nuts and bolts approach."

I tried turning each of the nuts, though I couldn't imagine how you'd hide a geocache in a nut, but then I turned one and the nut and bolt both just came loose. I thought I had broken it! But the guys both smiled when I did it, so I looked at the thing I had in my hand. It looked like a bolt with a nut on it, but the nut had a magnet in it and it unscrewed to reveal a place for a log sheet inside. Wow, that was a mean trick!

"You did it!" Twiggy exclaimed and he slowly stood up and walked over to see the cache up close. "Now you see how sneaky they can be?"

"Yeah."

"It could have been done in several ways but this one is cool because you can look right at it and not know it's a cache."

"Thank you. I'm glad you like it," the man said. "Where are you off to next?"

"We're in a big geocaching contest!" I said. "We're helping Twiggy win a trip to the Bahamas!"

The man looked at Twiggy half way interested and half way skeptical.

"Uh, yeah," he said. "We're working on filling in our grid in preparation for it."

"You got the GC code for that?" the man asked.

"Yeah, in the van. Come with me and I'll write it down for you. Gabby, can you sign the log while I do that?"

"I can't get the log out," I said. "It's too tight."

"You need a tool of the trade?" Twiggy asked.

"Maybe. What do you use to get logs out?"

"Most geocachers carry tweezers, but the safety pin clipped onto the GPS does the trick."

The GPS had a strap on it and I had wondered why a pin was always dangling there. It got in the way sometimes and I wanted to remove it, but it was Twiggy's GPS so I left it there. I unfastened the safety pin and noticed it was bent at the very tip. These geocachers sure could be puzzling at times. I opened the cache and looked inside. I looked at the safety pin. I took a glance at the two men at the van. They smiled and waved. I decided I better figure out how to get a rolled up paper out of a hollow bolt before they started laughing at me. I stuck the useful end of the pin into the cache and it snagged on the paper. I thought it would rip the log but I was able to gently work the center of the roll out until I could grab it with my fingers. After that the log slid out easily. Then I had to figure out a way to flatten it out long enough to sign it. There were two pages that tried to tangle up. After a couple of tries I got the two pages to lay flat and I signed our name to the log, then I read some of the other entries and noted that this was a very popular cache. It was found every three or four days. Bojangles was the last person to find it. I imagined an older, quirky man who listened to oldies rock. Maybe he rode around in a van, too, but a VW van with original paint and fuzzy dice hanging from the mirror. It took some work to get the log rolled up tight enough to fit back into the bolt. I had to pin the safety pin back onto the strap of the GPS and hang the GPS from my wrist to roll the log as tight as it would go. When it was safely enclosed in the bolt I screwed the nut back on and put the bolt back in the spot on the sculpture where I had found it, then I stepped back to see how well it blended with the rest of the bolts. Maybe the cache was just a little too solid of a rust color, but at first glance it looked like all the others.

"You two have a great trip!" No FTF For Me said as he returned to the field. "I wish I could be there when they announce the winners."

"Thanks! Bye!" I called after him.

"You did well. I commend you," Twiggy said.

"After all the hints in the book," I said.

"Now you know how to find a magnetic bolt cache," he said. "Next time it will be easier. Let's find some dinner and look for our next target."

The little café didn't have wifi but our motel room did. I ordered soup and a half sandwich. I could tell a call home was going to be inevitable and I was putting it off as long as I could. My hesitance didn't stem from the money issue. My mom would ask me where I was and want details and I really didn't want to lie to her any more than I almost, sort of, kind of had already. My very first serious punishment that I could remember came because of a lie and I still felt it. I didn't think she would spank me again, but I would certainly feel her wrath.

"What other things are geocaches disguised as?" I asked Twiggy over lunch.

"Hmm, bolts are fairly common. I have never found, but I've heard of one that looks like chewed gum, a penny on the ground, bird houses, trash on the side of the road, dog poop, and logs. I've actually found a bird house cache and one that was made from a hollowed out log. I can't say I am eager to meet the dog poop cache."

"Why would anybody make one that looks like dog poop?"

"To make it hard to find. If you had a dozen likely hiding spots to search and you saw dog poop on the ground you'd avoid it, right?"

"Right."

"Well, imagine how hard it would be to find a cache that you'd been avoiding the whole time you were at ground zero."

"Still, it's icky. And how do you make fake dog poop?"

"Eh, there's products you can buy at any home improvement store."

"I wonder what else you could make out of stuff like that."

"I don't know, but on the road is not a good place to experiment."

"I know. How would you make a cache that looks like a penny on the ground?"

"Easy, use a penny. Remember that vial that was taped onto the flower stem?"

"Yeah."

"Well, take a vial like that and glue a penny to the lid. Then insert the vial into the ground so only the penny shows. People do that with bottle caps, too."

"I'm so broke, I'd pick up a penny. What if somebody picks up a penny and there's a cache glued to it?"

"You don't leave those where people are likely to be picking up pennies."

"It's weird that a beacon can be a big old tree and a penny on the ground," I said.

He just shrugged like it was perfectly reasonable in geocaching.

That night was awkward again. The room only had a double bed and a dresser in it.

"Which side do you want?" Twiggy asked.

"It doesn't matter."

"Well, are you an edge sleeper?"

"No, not really."

"Are you a side sleeper?"

"Usually."

"Which side do you sleep on?"

"My left."

"Okay then you get the left side of the bed so we won't be breathing in each other's faces."

"Okay."

"Or you can have the right so we will."

"Twig, just climb in. I'll find a spot."

He climbed in on the left side, so I climbed in on the right. We lay there side by side until I needed to turn onto my left side and then I was facing him. Did he plan it this way?

"Gabby?"

"Uh huh?"

"Do we have to stay friends forever?"

Oh golly, I wasn't prepared for that!

"What do you mean?"

"I mean, if we're supposed to be friends, that's fine, I can live with that. But what if maybe we were meant to be more than friends?"

Gulp.

"Do you want to be more than friends?" I asked, a little fearful about the answer, especially on short notice, in bed.

"I'd like to. I just don't know if you could think of me the way I think of you."

"What do you think it will take to find out?"

"I don't know, but it feels like a cliff before me, and I don't want to be like Wiley Coyote and run off it and then find nothing there. But I don't want you to run away like the Road Runner either."

"So you want to eat me for lunch?" I joked and then realized how it could be taken. I hoped he couldn't see my embarrassment in the dark.

"I just want you to be comfortable with me. Every time we even hint at the subject you tighten up. Are you really that much against being close to a guy?"

"Me? No. I kissed a boy once, in high school."

"And... what happened?"

"I fell off the cliff like Wiley Coyote."

"What's that supposed to mean?"

"It fell flat. And my mom asked me about it. And she wasn't pleased."

"You're letting your parents dictate what you do?"

"No, yeah, I mean no…"

"What if you just scoot over and let me put my arms around you. What would be so terrible about that?"

I could see that cliff. I knew what it felt like to be out in space and I didn't want to make the choice of falling, or frantically grabbing for a life line. And I didn't really know which was which. I knew I was a prude. I knew eventually I'd have to take the plunge. Would there be hard rock, followed by an anvil? Would there be a river and I'd be washed away to new adventure? I didn't know! I was twenty-two years old. Half my high school class had lost their virginity in high school. I was like an old maid compared to them. I was… like… my mother! Noooooo!

I felt so mixed up that I scooted closer. I put my head on his shoulder. And I cried a little.

"I'm sorry," he said, but I didn't scoot away, and we slept like that.

Chapter 9

The next cache we needed to find had to be a good long ways down the highway if we were going to make any progress toward the event. The website allowed us to search for caches based on difficulty and terrain but a difficulty four, terrain four cache wasn't exactly commonplace. The easiest one to get to on our route was ten miles off the highway and it was called Bird's Eye View. The drive along the highway was fun. I'd never been away from my family, just doing things with a friend. All my activities while I was growing up were strictly monitored. Just going to a movie with friends was an ordeal for me. Half an hour after the movie ended my parents were checking up on me. It made me wonder why I hadn't received at least a couple of calls since school ended. Were they actually trusting me for once?

We turned off the highway onto another paved road that seemed to lead to houses way off in the countryside. Ranches perhaps, or farms. The area was very rural and we occasionally saw cows grazing in amongst brushy trees. This wasn't a forest, but it looked like it could become a forest with a little more water. The cows had plenty of room to graze. Every half mile or so we would pass a row of mailboxes posted all in a row. If the residents took the local paper there was also a yellow newspaper box nailed to the same post as the mailbox.

The road turned and followed a fence and when the fence ended the brush became thicker. Very soon after the private property ended we began seeing little piles of junk beside the road. The junk seemed to irritate Twiggy. He didn't say anything but I could tell he disapproved of the careless dumping. The further we drove the bigger the piles became and we drove over boards and carpet remnants. We even saw a boat and a hot tub dumped back there. Why couldn't people take their trash to the local dump?

The road deteriorated and as it got bumpier we found less trash. The van seemed to handle the rough road well, but we had to hang on to keep from getting jostled about.

"I hope the cache is not up there," Twiggy said.

I couldn't see where he was pointing but I hoped it wasn't, too. If Twiggy didn't want to go up there it might be a long climb.

Half a mile later the road ended. It had a loop on the end and it looked like people had camped nearby. Each tree that offered shade in the summer had a fire ring nearby. There were a lot of droppings from cattle or horses and this looked like a wonderful place to go for a trail ride. Twiggy stopped the van and looked again at the GPS.

"It's over a mile away and this is as close as we can get," he said.

"Well, it's rated a four. I guess we have to work for this one, too," I answered.

"We should dig through the boxes and find what food and water we can."

All we found was three bottles of water, bought only because we learned a partial lesson on our hill climbing hike, and junk food. We couldn't buy fruits, vegetables and meat because it wouldn't keep, so everything we found was very processed, very salty and probably very bad for us, but it would fill our stomachs if we ended up on the trail longer than we expected.

"What about this?" I asked as I held up a half package of beef jerky.

"Did you buy it?"

"No."

"I didn't either. That means we don't know how long it's been sliding around on the floor of this van. I'm not eating it."

I pinched the bag. The jerky felt hard as rocks.

"We need to trash it next time we find a garbage can so we won't keep finding it over and over."

We packed the junk food and water into the geocaching pack and took out most of the gear to lessen the weight. There was only one cache up there so there was no use bringing more gear than we needed to fix one cache.

"A little over a mile," he said. "I suggest we read all we can about it before we leave. I don't want to hike all the way up there unless I think we have all the resources we can get."

"Okay."

We read the description, which didn't help much. The cache owner just said that he loved this trail and the view from the top. He did not recommend hiking it in the winter or right after a rain storm. The cache was a medium size "with plenty of goodies for the kids". The logs said things like, "Wow, quite a hike! I sure got my exercise!" and "Great views all the way up. Thanks for bringing us here." That didn't help much either.

"Well, it sounds like we can just follow the trail most of the way there," Twiggy said.

"What's the hint say?"

I don't know why I liked reading the hints. It was kind of like cheating a little but nobody ever knew if you used the hint or not. I liked decoding the hint on the web page but the GPS decoded them for us.

"Think like a bird," is what the hint said.

"Well, it seems safe enough," I said. "No indications of bears or crazy people. We shouldn't get questioned by the police. I'm ready!"

"How's your staminameter?"

"Full speed ahead!"

We should have paid more attention to the sky. We were not even a quarter mile up the trail when the sky became gray and ominous. When the mist started, the hike was actually pleasant. We sang, "I'm hiiiiiking in the rain, oh I'm hiiiking in the rain. I must be insane to be hiiiking in the rain." We were not insane yet, but another quarter mile down the trail it was raining like crazy and we were soaked to the skin. We ran to the nearest tree and huddled underneath it. This was when the thunder and lightning started.

"You know, lightning hits trees," Twiggy pointed out.

"And it hits high spots like mountains," I added.

"So being under a tree on the highest point around might not be the smartest thing to do."

"Right. So what do you suggest?"

Crash! RRRRRuuummmmbbbble, rumble, rumble, rumble.

"Make a run for it?"

"Which direction? Toward the cache or the van?"

"I don't know!"

Crash! Ca....rash!

"Are you scared?" he asked.

"No! Just s-s-soaking wet."

"I had to put the GPS in the pack."

"It's okay we can hike for a while without it. The trail's plain."

We hiked as quickly as we could, following the trail. When conditions allowed we even jogged a little with rain pounding down, lightning hitting the mountains around us and thunder shaking the ground beneath our feet.

"Okay, stop," Twiggy finally said. "We better check our position."

We found a little shelter under a scrubby tree. There were several tall trees around so we felt safer under the little tree even though it didn't keep much rain off. At least we could see enough to read the screen and the GPS didn't get soaked.

"Oh shoot!" he said. "We over shot the cache!"

"How far!"

"Four hundred feet."

"How could we do that?"

"We were in a hurry."

"Does the GPS work in a lightning storm?" I asked. We were practically shouting over the pounding of the rain and the booming, rumbling, grumbling clouds that felt as if they were just overhead.

"Look on the bright side," he said. "No snakes!"

"Yeah, they're all holed up under rocks and trees like us."

"And to answer your question, not very well."

"Oh, then how are we going to find the cache?"

"It should get us within a hundred feet or so."

"And how many hiding places are there within a hundred feet of the cache?"

"Statistically speaking? Thousands."

"What about geocachingly speaking?"

"Fifty? A hundred?"

"Oh, that's all," I said sarcastically.

"Technically any place could be a hiding place, but that's not likely. Geocachers think out their hides and that helps narrow the choices down."

"I wonder how long this storm might last."

"You said you love rain," he reminded me.

It is true. I do love rain. During the school year I was the student strolling to class in the rain while all the others rushed from place to place in raincoats and holding umbrellas.

"I do, as long as I can still function in it. This is borderline."

"It's freezing!"

"Yeah it's a bit nippy."

"Okay, judging by the GPS the cache should be over by that hollow tree."

A bit nippy. I was trying very hard not to tense up and shiver. It might be summer but it felt like winter in those soaking wet clothes. I tromped toward the tree.

"If I was a bird I would like to sit up on that branch and survey the valley below," Twiggy said.

"You mean that lightning rod?" I asked. "That tree has been hit before."

"Lightning never hits the exact same spot twice."

"Maybe not, but it might miss by a couple of centimeters."

"I think that tree has got to be the beacon that the hint refers to."

"I think so, too! But it's pouring out there. They told us not to do this in the rain and the tree is on the side of a hill. It's going to be slick!"

"I know. Wait here," he said. He dashed out into the rain and he practically disappeared behind a wall of water. Oh shoot, I thought. I came along so he wouldn't do stupid things and now what do I do when he decides to do stupid things? I sit under a tree and wait. A minute ticked by, or rather it flowed by. Everything seemed to be flowing. The rain. The mud. The common sense. They all seemed to be flowing down the mountainside. I dashed out into the rain determined to find the cache and end this foolishness. How could we even sign the log in this downpour? And once it was wet the whole cache would be damp.

It was easy to find Twiggy. I just headed for the suicide tree.

"I think we should be able to choose the emoticon for our finds," I said when I caught up to him. "This one would have a shocked expression."

"It's not at the base of the tree," he said. "It's not in the bushes around it. It's got to be up there! See that hole?"

"That one seven feet off the ground?" I asked.

"Yeah!"

"No, they wouldn't put it there. No normal person could reach it and climbing this tree would be dangerous. One fall and you'd end up at the bottom of the mountain!"

"There was a log here," he explained. "But it went over the side when I checked it for caches. I think it was left here to stand on and reach in the hole."

"Oh great!"

"Let me boost you up. You can take a quick look."

CaBASSHHHH! The lightning struck a hill nearby.

"You... are... insane!"

"Lightning isn't going to strike in three seconds. On the count of three." I put my foot into his hand. "One... Two..."

CRASSSHHHH ruuuummmmmble rummmbbbble, rummmble.

"You were saying?"

"Three!" He lifted me up. I stuck my hand into the hole and... thank goodness the cache was there. He lowered me back down.

"Bingo!" He said triumphantly.

"How are we going to sign it?" I asked.

You might be an overly dedicated geocacher when you use your own body to shelter a simple piece of paper in an electrical storm just to keep the paper dry.

"I say we go pot luck on the swag," he said.

"What's that?"

"Just grab one. I'll toss in a keychain. We replace the cache and make a run for it!"

"Okay!"

I pulled out the first thing in the cache that my fingers felt. He tossed in a keychain and the log book, screwed the lid down tight, then we did the one, two, three, boost maneuver again and I replaced the container.

"Don't run downhill!" Twiggy warned me. "Dang this is wet!"

The trail back was slick with mud and we ended up sliding as much as we hiked. While I was hiking I managed to stave off the cold but as soon as we got back to the van the icy rain seemed to chill me clear down to my bones.

"Dry clothes," Twiggy said.

"We can't even look for dry clothes without soaking the mattress."

"Doesn't matter. We need to get you as dry and we can."

"One of the boxes has towels in it."

I was so cold I didn't even care about stripping down in the van and even submitted to a rough toweling off. When we were as dry as we thought we could get we burrowed under the covers and huddled together shivering.

"Relax," Twiggy said. "Come here, conserve your warmth and try to relax."

It took a long time for the shivering to stop, but after a while hunger overruled the urge to shiver.

"That's better," he said. "Look, the windows are all steamy. You'd think... uh, never mind what people would think."

"I think the rain is letting up."

"Looks like it. I almost wish it would start up again."

It was beginning to feel comfy all snuggled up under the blankets. Too bad it smelled like an old van with damp mud smeared inside.

"We need to find some lunch. That granola bar just did not fill me up for some reason."

"Okay, so... dry clothes. I'll find them so you can stay warm. What box would they be in?"

"The one by the door so it would be easy to sort through at stops."

"That's smart."

"There's blue jeans that are lined with flannel," I said. "My mom thought they'd be good for long winter treks across campus."

"This is summer."

"I know and I'll probably roast once I get dry, but for now toasty sounds comfortable. And there's a blue top I like. And socks. I don't care what socks as long as they are dry."

He shifted around trying to find my clothes in my box, trying to figure out my packing and my sense of organization without making a mess of things, and I was thinking, "Hey, he's in pretty good shape. If he'd wear clothes that played up his strengths he'd be really handsome."

"Twiggy, wait," I said. "Choose what you want me to wear."

"Really?"

"Yeah. I might put on a jacket for a while, but I'm curious. I see you differently than you see yourself. Maybe you see me differently, too."

It was funny watching his different expressions as he held up my clothes. It was a little embarrassing having him go through my boxes of personal belongings, but I learned a lot.

"I wish I could remember what this looks like on," he said.

He put the flannel lined jeans back immediately and pulled out ones that were more fitted and had fancy stitching on the pockets. He pulled out a top that was made of lace and his eyebrows went up. He looked to me, then back at the top.

"I usually wear a spaghetti strapped top underneath that," I said.

"Have I seen it?"

"I don't know. I guess not. I usually save it for a night out on the town and that didn't happen very often."

"Did it happen ever?"

"Yeah, usually Sarah and I would go with the two girls in the next room down. They liked karaoke, so we'd all go to a bar and I'd order soda with a cherry in it so it would look like I was drinking and I'd watch the girls sing."

"You didn't go hard core and order a Shirley Temple?" he joked.

"No, that costs more. Plus I like the cola taste better than the lemon lime."

"Have you ever been drunk?"

"Yes, and I never want to do it again."

"Why?"

"I was six and I didn't know what alcohol was and I downed a whole martini all at one time. I was so sick. A lot of fun for about an hour, but ugghh, no."

"You've never been to a party?"

"Not the kind you're referring to."

"What if I wanted to take you to one?"

"Then you'd probably be disappointed because I would sip on a soda and eat finger food and talk. What do you do at parties?"

"Sip on anything liquid, eat junk food and talk louder and louder and yell at some game on the TV that I don't even care about."

"And that's fun?"

"Eventually. Here, try this," he said handing me the fitted jeans, the lace top and my summer pajama top. "What?"

"Nothing. I'll wear that, if it's really what you want me to wear. I just hardly ever mix my PJs and my day clothes."

"Your... how was I supposed to know? You said spaghetti straps. I looked for spaghetti straps. It was better than a t-shirt or a blouse. Hey, a guy can hope, right? The lace is..."

"Yes?"

"I tell you what. If I don't have to answer that question, you can pick mine, too."

I couldn't believe it. I was stuck in a smelly van in a rain storm while looking for silly boxes hidden in the woods and my... my friend wanted me to choose his clothes for him in some male/female communication of some kind. I wasn't sure what kind, but, I could play along, since we didn't have much choice about being stuck in the van. I already knew which of his shirts I liked. It was a simple shirt, made out of t-shirt material. The dark blue over the shoulders made his shoulders look broader and the main body of it was an outdoorsy brown. It made him look like a rugby player.

"Why that?" he asked. "I haven't worn that in months."

"Not since March. I know dark colors are supposed to be for winter but you look better in them."

"I do?"

"It helps a girl... people see your eyes."

"So?"

"Twiggy, trust me. Those white collared striped shirts make you look like..."

"A geek?"

"And the calculator can go into a backpack pocket."

"I need that."

"To walk across campus? To eat lunch? I'm not even going to start on the cell phone. Most guys have a cell phone in their pocket."

"If I am working on an algorithm I might have to try a calculation or two. What's wrong with that?"

"Nothing. Nothing at all. What would you think if I walked around with... paint brushes sticking out of my pocket and I had to paint a picture in line at the coffee shop? Would that be weird?"

"Yes."

"So what's the difference between me painting a picture in a coffee shop and you working on your algorithm?"

"So the white shirts have got to go?"

"No, of course not. I just like this shirt because you look better in it. More like a geocacher and less like a CS major who can't stop programming."

"Can I take that to mean you'd rather date a geocacher than a programmer?"

"Twiggy, no, sheesh! You're reading too much into this. I like you just as much no matter what you wear. I like you, not your clothes, or hobby, or college major."

I was saved from the topic for a while because the sun broke through the clouds prompting us to hurry and dress while we had time. We tried to change clothes in the van but everything was so wet that it did little good. We threw one of the floor mats into the mud and dressed standing on that. I tried not to think about Twiggy watching very move I made. Twiggy put an end to my embarrassment as soon as he took his turn on the mat.

"Uh, Gabby, we have problems," he said.

I didn't even need to ask what kind. If it was that obvious just from standing on the mat I thought I could figure it out so I stepped around the van and saw that we had a very flat tire on the passenger's side of the van.

"Do you know what this means?" I asked.

"Yeah, we have a lot of hard work ahead of us."

"No kidding. We have to empty the van."

"Where are we going to put stuff? We're surrounded by mud!"

"Well, there's that rock," I suggested.

"All right, sturdier boxes on the bottom, lighter boxes on top."

"What about the mattress?"

"Climb up to the roof and see how wet it is. Use one of the used towels if it's too puddly. Then we will slide the mattress on top."

So there we were at the foot of a mountain, in a muddy turnaround, piling up boxes on a round rock. I eventually dried off the roof of the van enough to slide the mattress up there. Twiggy began looking for tools. He found a jack and he placed it under the van, then began pumping the handle until it was firmly in place. He was bent over, looking at the jack when he said, "Oh, shoot."

"What?"

"No spare."

"Who drives around without a spare tire?"

"Poor college students."

"Now what are we going to do?"

Just then a gust of wind went by and our tower of boxes fell off the rock and into the mud with a slight splash. I didn't know whether to laugh or cry.

"Does your friend have roadside assistance?" I asked.

"If he doesn't have a spare, do you think he can afford roadside assistance?"

"No, I guess not."

"Neither can we."

We stood there staring at the flat tire, willing it to self inflate. It didn't do it.

"There's an often used geocaching technique that we can put to use now," Twiggy said.

"What's that?"

"Phone a friend."

"No matter who you call they are not going to have a spare tire for an outdated van."

"No, but they might have something we don't, a telephone book."

You know you're with a geek when they use their cell phone to call a friend; that friend uses their tablet computer to find a garage in another town; then he doesn't just write the number in the dust on the van, he inputs the number into his address book on his cell phone, calls the garage, gives the operator our longitude and latitude off his GPS receiver, hires a guy to come out with a tow truck, and makes a note of the estimated time of arrival in his cell phone so he will be alerted when the mechanic is near.

"You're not going to calculate the ETA on your scientific calculator?" I teased.

"Why would I do that? He told me when he'd be here."

We began restacking boxes but it was soon obvious a trip to a Laundromat was the next task on the list, provided we had wheels.

"Insidious mud," Twiggy grumbled.

"If we have to spend an afternoon in the Laundromat we can kiss this contest goodbye."

"Not necessarily," he said.

"Twiggy, we are not by any stretch of the imagination hard core geocachers. We might be going for some tough ones but there are geocachers willing to climb the highest mountain and swim the deepest ocean to win bragging rights at the next event. We cannot compete with those people."

"So you want to give up?"

"No, I just want to continue without mishaps stalling us every time we turn around."

"We could skip doing laundry and geocache naked," he suggested.

"We'd get arrested," I said.

"Would you?" he asked.

"No, or, at least, not yet. How am I supposed to know what I might be able to talk myself into in a few years? Two years ago I wouldn't have even done this."

It took the mechanic over an hour to figure out how to locate us. He had nothing to guide him except a highlighted dot on a map of the area.

"Wow, how'd you kids get way back here?" he greeted us on arrival.

"Our GPS led us here," Twiggy said.

"Never trust 'em," the tow truck driver said.

"It did get us where we wanted to go. We just drove over trash to get here and something in the road punctured our tire."

"And we haven't got a spare," I added.

The tow truck driver looked like he could push the van out of the woods by himself if he had to. His name patch said "Doug" and the shirt it hung on was grease stained and untucked. His Dickies were too long and the hems were frayed. He walked around the van with a grease stained clipboard.

"Uh huh... zebra stripes? Really?"

"The van's not ours," I added. "We borrowed it."

"Nineteen eighty-three Chevy. Still runs?"

"Yeah," said Twiggy.

"Uh huh... well, I hate to break it to you kids but you got a couple of nails in your tire and one through the side wall. What'd you do, take a nice scenic drive through the dump?"

"Almost," Twiggy said.

"If it was just the two the tire would be fixable. As it is you're going to have to replace it. I can take her in for you."

"How much?" Twiggy asked.

"A hundred sixty dollars for the tow job. The tires... it depends on what you choose. I'd say a good pair will run you a couple hundred."

"Dollars?" I asked.

"No, finger nail clippin's. Yes, dollars."

Three hundred sixty dollars, a trip to the Laundromat, another night in a motel. This was not looking good.

"How much have you got?" I asked Twiggy.

He opened up his wallet. "Do you take a card?" he asked.

"At the station," the tow truck driver answered.

"All right, tow it in."

"Are you insane?" I asked. "A hundred sixty dollars just to have the van towed to town?"

"What else are we going to do? Give us ten minutes to load it back up," Twiggy said.

"You'll want to call a friend to come get you," the tow truck driver said.

"What?!"

"You got a problem with that?"

"Well... yeah! We're from out of town. The semester just ended. All our friends are in Franklinburg or gone home for the summer."

"Where are you from?"

"South Dakota," said Twiggy.

"I'm not supposed to, but I'll let you ride in the cab to the station. After that you're on your own."

The tow truck driver went to work lining up his truck and getting the chains arranged right while Twiggy and I figured out how to get the mattress off the roof and into the van without letting it touch the ground. We quickly loaded the muddy boxes. By the time we were finished the futon mattress was in a sorry state.

"What were you trying to do out here?"

"We were looking for a geocache," Twiggy said.

"Did you find it?"

"Yeah, in the rain."

"Damn overzealous kids. Did you know this is called Lightning Ridge?"

"No, but we could have guessed."

"We were sitting in the office taking bets on whether it was too wet to start a fire up here."

"I think it was too wet," Twiggy said.

The cab of the truck smelled like cigar smoke. It was illegal for the tow truck driver to give us a ride because there was only one seat belt for the passenger's seat, but Twiggy and I squished together and attempted to buckle the seatbelt over both of us.

"Now isn't this cozy?" Twiggy asked as he put his arm around me. I had to admit it was more comfortable that way. I'm afraid I wasn't thinking about the coziness of the ride. I was wondering if I had enough money in my pocket to wash all my clothes again. My finances didn't improve when Twiggy used up the last of his savings on two tires. I never considered the fact that tires are bought in pairs.

The owner of the garage was just pulling down the doors and locking up when the tow truck driver pulled up. Doug's boss folded his arms over his chest and glared at Doug in disapproval as we slid down from the cab.

"I couldn't leave them up there and they're from out of state," Doug explained.

Since Doug's boss had probably given an illegal ride or two to stranded motorists he relented but said, "My wife's got dinner on. I can get to it first thing in the morning."

"Can you point us toward the nearest motel with a vacancy?" Twiggy asked.

"There's a nice bed and breakfast..." the tow truck driver began and quickly cut off. "Three lights down. Turn right. You'll see it."

"The bed and breakfast?" I asked.

"No, uh, your... other choice."

It wasn't as bad as I feared. It was actually better than the last place. I was beat by the time we packed up a few belongings into the geocaching pack and hiked to the hotel. We flopped with a tired, but relieved sigh on the bed. Another double. But at least we had a table and wifi and we could log our one find for the day.

"Is geocaching always like this?" I asked.

"No, hardly ever," Twiggy said. "Usually we find a cache in a bush and we go on our way."

"I wonder what we are doing wrong."

"By the way," he said. "What did you end up pulling out of that cache?"

"I don't know. I stuffed it my pocket. It was too wet to worry about one piece of swag."

"Well, what is it?" he asked.

"I don't know. My pants are with the dirty clothes in the van."

I showered first, thankful for the little bottles of shampoo. I decided I should take whatever was left over so I could put off buying shampoo later. I crawled into bed before my hair was dry, knowing I'd wake up with a terrible case of bed head but I was too tired to care. Then when Twiggy came to bed I was too tired to think and snuggled into position, my head on his shoulder. I woke up in the night on the other side of the bed, but I could have sworn we had laid there cuddled up and comfortable for a while.

"Thank you," he said in the morning when I got up to shower my weird hair into normalcy again.

"For what?" I asked.

"For trusting me. For being you. For being you and accepting me all at once."

I went back and sat on the bed. "You're really serious about this, aren't you?"

"You have no idea," he said.

I crawled back into bed to think. I tried to think about what I wanted in a guy and I came up blank. Oh sure, there were all the things my dad would ask. Do you have a job? What are your plans? But I knew the answers to those questions. Twiggy had a part time job, during school. He had plans to graduate and search for an engineering position on the ground floor of some company that needed a programmer. It all sounded well and good. But what did I really want? I wasn't sure what my dad wanted and what I wanted were the same thing. I wanted... something more. I wanted to see the world. It didn't matter if it was hitch hiking across the country or flying to Africa. I just wanted to get out there and experience a little slice of life and I felt like I was doing that. Despite all the setbacks, I really felt like I was finding a little slice of life that I wouldn't have experienced if I had gone home to do my sister's hair for a party.

I snuggled closer.

"Hold me," I said. "Just hold me."

Chapter 10

That day was not the most exciting one of my life. We hiked back to the garage where the van sat with two new tires. I wanted to kick them, but knew it wouldn't do any good. We got directions to a coin laundry near a burger joint.

"Okay, there's a method to this," I said as we stood in front of the washing machines. "This one is for whites, this one is for colors and this one is for permanent press."

"Why?"

"Because you have to wash them separately or bad things happen."

"Ooooo. Like what?"

"Like you get wrinkles in your permanent press, color in your whites and bleach in your colors. All those are bad."

"Gabby, I've never done that before. It doesn't matter."

"Okay, then, you do your laundry over there and I'll do my laundry over here. I sort. You can have wrinkly colored laundry if you want to."

He scratched his head but began sorting his clothes into the three washing machines.

"What about white permanent press? Does it go in the white one or the permanent press one?"

"Permanent press. Your shirts are old enough that the color won't run much."

We had to use a fourth machine because the one we were putting colors in got too full.

"Did you ever find the swag you pulled out of that cache?" Twiggy asked.

"Oh shoot! No!" I said and began unpacking the washer with colors in it. I had to search the pockets of three pairs of jeans before I finally found a pair with a little lump in the pocket. I stuck my hand in and pulled out... a lucky rabbit's foot.

"Ugh! I've been walking around with a rabbit's *foot* in my pocket. Gross!" I said.

"Yeah, but just think how bad yesterday might have been without it."

"It sure isn't a very lucky rabbit's foot," I said.

"It wasn't even lucky for the rabbit."

We fed the change machine, put our quarters in the washing machines and went to the burger place in search of breakfast. They didn't have much on their breakfast menu, but at least it was cheap.

Half an hour later we switched the laundry to the dryers and then tried to get enough of a signal to look at the geocaching map.

"What caches do you have in your GPS?" I asked.

"Not very many for this area."

"Even if it's within a few miles we should be able to drive there, find the cache, and drive back before the clothes are dry."

"Okay, let's see." He turned on his GPS and waited for it to boot up. "One. I only see one close enough."

"Okay, so what is it?"

He clicked to the description.

"Well, it doesn't look too interesting, but it's still a smiley."

We left the Laundromat and attempted to drive to the cache, but the area was full of dead end streets and we had to turn around time after time.

"This town is a maze," I said.

"No kidding, but that's half the fun. I kind of like seeing how people live in different towns. All the houses are small. The lots are large. The people grow fruit. They all have dogs and cats. Small town America."

"It is kind of interesting," I admitted. "I keep expecting to see a lemonade stand. But if I did see one I'd be tempted to ask the kids for a loan instead of buying a glass of lemonade."

"Your finances are that tight?"

"I could hear the quarters crying for help as I pushed them into the washing machine. They wanted to pay for something more worthwhile than making a machine jiggle."

Twiggy turned the van down yet another dead end street but this one had a little parking area at the end and beyond the parking area was a little park.

"I didn't invite you along so I could break your bank," he said. "You've done more than your share. So only pay for things you want."

"I can't do that. That would be like... like a date or something."

"Define a date."

We parked and eyed the park for muggles. It was a quiet day and we didn't see any so we opened the door and slid out of the van.

"A date is when you arrange a time and an activity and then you go do it and the person who invites the other person pays for the activity."

"Okay. So. Would you help me fold clothes and go out to lunch with me today?" he asked.

"You want to turn today into a date?" I replied.

"No, I want to turn the whole week into a date, but folding clothes and eating lunch comes first."

I couldn't deny it anymore. My best friend had other intentions. I should either accept his invitation and the role of girl friend or I should call my parents and figure out how to go home. To stay would just lead him on and I didn't want to do that. Or did I? I was so confused.

"Can I be totally honest with you?" I asked.

"Yes, I hope you will be."

"I don't believe that, but since you stated it I can hope what I say won't hurt you."

His look made me think that what I was going to say just might hurt him, but I wasn't sure what it was I was going to say, so I jumped off that proverbial cliff and ran in mid air for a few sentences.

"If I have sex before marriage I am going to be disowned. I am not going to have sex with you until I am ready for either marriage or disownment. If you're willing to accept that stand, then we're on the right track. But I am not ready for marriage. And neither are you. We both have huge financial considerations before we can decide anything and the middle of college isn't the... what?"

"I know that."

I quit running in midair and I wasn't sure if I was falling or not.

"Gabby, you're so afraid of the forbidden S word that you run away. Can't you relax enough to just come along with me and see what the day brings?" He stopped and he turned to me. "All I want right now is an occasional... this." He wrapped his arms around me and pulled me tight. "And maybe later, we can think about... this." He put his fingers gently beneath my chin and tilted my head up. Then he kissed me. My second kiss. And it was like the first one. But I didn't want it to be. "Relax. Just go with it." Then he kissed me again. "That's better. You'll learn. Listen to your heart and your lips will reflect what's in there." He took my hand and led me into the park. "Now let's find that cache. It should be easier than the others we looked for."

The park was small, so it was only a short walk to where the cache was hidden. I began to worry about the clothes sitting in dryers that had run out of time. In the dorms it was a major infraction of the unstated rules to take up machines after the cycle had ended. There were so many people trying to use a few machines and there was a five minute rule. If you left and were not back five minutes after the cycle ended the next person had a right to take your clothes out, toss them in a cart and use your machine, no matter what the state of your clothes were. I learned very quickly to keep tabs on my machines. It wasn't unusual to find three loads of damp laundry piled all together in the cart and then there was confusion about who owned what.

"You take the GPS," Twiggy said. "I've got some ideas to check out and I don't need the GPS for that."

Since Twiggy had some ideas I took the time to read the hint and description. It was only a two/one cache. Anybody should be able to find this one. It was a small one, but we'd found small ones before.

"Tricky, I almost gave up on this one," one of the logs read.

"How could I miss this? All I can say is it is good at sitting quietly in a bush," said another.

"My five year old spotted it easily. His first real find!" said a third.

Reading the description and logs told me a lot. It had the easiest terrain rating, which meant it was wheelchair accessible, providing a wheelchair could go through park grass. A five year old child spotted it easily. So it was low, within reach of a wheelchair bound person or a child. Now I knew to ignore the canopy of the trees and anything directly on the ground.

We walked around a playground, the swings swaying gently, but empty in the breeze. Beyond the play ground was a copse of trees. The neighborhood surrounded the park and each house had a walled backyard. There were bushes separating the yards from the park. Twiggy headed for the trees and I headed for the bushes.

"Over there? Really?" Twiggy asked.

I read the distance off the screen of the GPS. "Twenty-three feet. But I think it's down low because of the logs and the rating."

"Hey! You're learning! What did you read that makes you go to the bushes?"

"It's only a one."

"And what does that mean?"

I sighed. "I'm tired of pop quizzes. A one terrain means it can be reached and retrieved from a wheelchair. So that restricts the hide to somewhere between a foot and six feet off the ground. But it was retrieved by a little boy so that means it's probably between one and five feet. Wow, that shaves a whole foot off the area."

"Still, that's good thinking. I'll make a geocacher out of you yet."

Searching bushes was not my favorite part of geocaching. I tried the visual approach first. I scanned the branches looking for anything that looked like it was out of place. I found a lot of trash. Sometimes Twiggy and I would pull out a plastic bag, fill it up with trash and throw it away later. I was told this was being a good geocacher citizen and was referred to as CITO. Cache In Trash Out. I especially liked to do that in little parks because it made a distinct difference right away and I felt good about helping the park be a fun place to go. I followed Twiggy until I could unzip and pull a bag out of the pack. I waved it in the wind to open it up and then began picking up candy wrappers, paper cups, chip bags, beer bottles, bottle caps, a pill bottle, a muddy pony tail holder... on and on I gathered trash keeping a sharp eye out for the cache. We looked and looked some more. Twiggy moved to the trees but I knew the cache wasn't going to be up high.

"Our laundry is sitting in a dryer wrinkling to death and there's an angry customer willing the machine to spit it out," I said.

"I hate DNFs."

"I know. We can come back after we fold the laundry."

We walked dejectedly back to the van, the bag clunking as I walked. I dropped it behind the seat and climbed in. When we got back to the Laundromat I pulled out the bag and it hit the side of the van and clunked and rattled again. I tossed the bag into the trash can just inside the door of the Laundromat and it didn't clunk, because the can was full of little soap boxes, lint, dryer sheets and holey socks. The dryers had stopped running but there were no irate customers waiting for us. I stuck more quarters in the permanent press dryer and let it tumble again while we folded the other loads.

"Why do we have to fold all these clothes?" Twiggy asked.

"Because it minimizes the wrinkles."

"Who cares about a few wrinkles?"

"Me."

I folded mine and his and stacked his so my favorite shirts and pants would be on the top. When all the laundry was folded we looked at the box situation. It was pretty sad. The boxes had dried out but they were no longer sturdy. I collapsed a box and stuffed it into the trash can and it hit the bag of trash I had dropped in there earlier. The sound was just a bit odd and that was when I remembered the medicine bottle.

"What are you doing?" Twiggy asked when he saw me burrowing in the trash.

"Checking something. I think..." I opened the trash bag and pulled out cups and wrappers until I found the bottle. "I think I threw away the cache!" I pulled out the bottle and shook it hopefully.

Twiggy looked around taking a muggle count, then he grinned.

"Open it!"

"We need to fold the permanent press."

"It'll only take a minute."

"Oh, okay." We took the cache to one of the folding tables and dumped it out. Inside was a washer, a nut, a little pop up toy, a domino, a small coin from Germany, and a little, decorative metal disk.

"Hey! A pathtag! You struck it rich! These are hard to find!"

"What is it?"

"It's like a little geocoin. See the hole? That lets you put it on a key ring or necklace. Lots of people collect them. What's the picture on it?"

It had a wave and a surfer and said *CAgoofyfoot* on it.

"Cool! It's from a geocacher all the way from the west coast!"

I was puzzled by it. I'd never seen one before. I traded for it so I'd have it handy while I thought about what made these little metal tags so popular, yet hard to find. I signed the log and we set the cache aside so we could hide it again after the clothes were all packed away. As we folded I asked Twiggy about pathtags.

"What are they? And why are they hard to find if they are so popular?"

"They are kind of expensive and each geocacher designs and buys their own custom tags."

"You mean this guy designed his own tag and had it made for him?"

"Yeah."

"How much is expensive?"

"Well, you usually order them in batches of fifty to two hundred depending on how involved you are in the hobby. I haven't priced them but I bet it's over a hundred dollars."

"Wow, no wonder they are hard to find. I want to keep this one, since it was my first."

"Just don't get any ideas of attending some school in California."

"Okay. You know this contest is in jeopardy if we spend many days doing laundry and looking for two/one caches in parks."

"Hey, it was a cute park."

"It was. And we need to go back there. We don't want to steal a cache."

We loaded the permanent press into the van, I made sure I had the cache, and we drove back to the park. About half way to the park a police car pulled in behind us and followed us the rest of the way to the park.

"What's up with the cop?" Twiggy asked.

"I don't know. Maybe he is looking for a nice quiet place to fill in reports," I suggested.

"That's what doughnut shops are for," he said. We opened our doors and slid out.

The police car pulled up behind the van and the officer leapt out of his squad car.

"Freeze right where you are," the officer said.

"Uh, excuse me officer, we haven't done anything wrong," Twiggy began but he got a very official looking glare and the officer acted like he might draw his weapon if we did anything questionable.

"I have a report that you were heard talking about stealing some cash."

"No," I said. "We didn't want to *accidentally* steal a cache. C-A-C-H-E. Cache. We were looking for a geocache and I was picking up trash and I accidentally CITOed the cache so we were..." I'd done it. I'd slipped into geospeak. And the officer was totally lost. Twiggy thought it was great, like a geocaching milestone or something. I began again. "When geocachers look for a cache, a container hidden specifically for them to find, they pick up trash and clean up the area, too. When I was picking up trash I thought the cache container was trash so I stuck it in my trash bag. You can go back to the Laundromat and see the rest of the trash. I can even itemize it for you if you want. And this," I said producing the pill bottle, "is a geocache. We are just returning it to its rightful place."

He didn't like the fact that the cache was a pill bottle. He was used to finding pills in pill bottles and they were not always the pills on the label.

"What's in it?" he asked.

"A log book. We always sign the log. Then there are little tradeable items. If I remember right this one now has a washer, a nut, a little pop up toy, a domino, a foreign coin, and a keychain in it."

"Open it up."

I opened the bottle and poured the contents out into my hand.

"This is the cache, and this is the cash," Twiggy said as he plucked the coin from my hand. "Coins are left in caches a lot."

"Where did you find it?" the officer asked.

"In the bushes at the back of the park. We'll use our GPS to find the right spot and hide it better so only geocachers can find it."

"Open up the van," the officer requested. Actually he was being polite, if a bit too thorough. "I'll need to see your license and registration."

"The van is not ours. We swapped cars with a buddy so we could geocache for a few weeks."

"Just open it up."

Twiggy produced all the requested documents and the officer wasn't pleased that all Twiggy's information matched the registration.

"Did you know this registration expires next week?" the officer asked.

"No. Oh shoot. I'll call and see if I can get the new sticker."

Finally the officer said, "Sorry for detaining you. The person who called has been a trusted citizen of this town for more than fifty years."

"It's okay," Twiggy said.

"Let's see about this geo-cache," he said.

Half way across the park the LOWBAT message flashed onto the screen of the GPS.

"I think we can get enough of a reading to find ground zero," Twiggy said as we hurried to the back of the park.

I jogged ahead because I had a rough idea of where I had picked up the cache. I reached the spot and began looking around for hiding places.

"It has to be within reach, but out of sight," I told the officer as the two men caught up with me.

"Ground zero's over here, Gabby," Twiggy said.

"But I found it over here."

"We still have to replace it at the coordinates. That's where the GPS is going to lead people so that's where the cache belongs."

"I guess that makes sense."

We began looking around where the GPS pointed us.

"Just find a spot out of sight," Twiggy told me. "we'll post how we found it, about the trip to the Laundromat and how we replaced it. If the cache owner wants to make sure it's in the right spot he'll come look."

"But I know it was supposed to be in a specific spot or it wouldn't have this hole in the lid."

"Good catch!" Twiggy said. "You're beginning to think like a geocacher. Maybe there was a wire and it was hooked on a branch."

"Oh! Oh! I know! Look for a wire or something silver!"

"Why?"

"Remember? There's a nut and a washer in it! I bet it had a bolt or something through the hole and it worked loose over time!"

It took a lot of searching but we finally found an S hook with an eyebolt connected to it.

"Bingo!" Twiggy said. "Now all we have to do is tighten the bolt again and hang it back up."

"Are there many of you geocachers out there?" the officer asked.

"No, not really," Twiggy answered.

"Are they all looking for random bottles in parks?"

"No, there's different kinds. This is just a little one."

"Maybe I need to learn more about this hobby," the officer said.

"That would be cool," Twiggy told him.

"You kids have a good day and stay out of trouble," he said, then left us to our geocaching.

"We will," I called to his retreating back.

Twiggy slid the eyebolt through the hole in the lid and put the nut on. One of the tools he carried in his geocaching pack was a device that had several tools on it and he was able to use the pliers on it to hold the nut still while he tightened the eyebolt as much as possible.

"So, miss inspector, do you think it's tight enough?"

I tried to loosen it but it held tight.

"You're a cache repair man," I said.

We hung the cache back up and he gave me a playful snack on the shoulder as we walked back to the van.

"We have to find another hard one or we'll have no hope of winning," I said.

"Okay, onward and cacheward!"

Chapter 11

Twiggy stopped at a gas station on the outskirts of the next town.

"Did you find a new one to look for?"

"Yeah! But it's very different from any we've found yet. It's a five/one."

"Ahh, a challenge!"

"Is the one terrain too easy?"

"No, any challenging cache is worth adding to the count."

"One thing I don't like about it, people complain that it's muggly."

"That probably contributes to the difficulty level. You have to retrieve it without people noticing."

"I don't know if I want to do that."

"Aw come on, we can at least go look at it."

"We can look at it but I'm not exactly miss invisibility."

"You don't have to be invisible. You just have to be inconspicuous."

"Did the station let you fill up this time?" I asked.

"No, it shut off at seventy-five dollars again, but it will get us to the cache."

We took a complicated route to find the area the cache was hidden in. We ended up circling around and around a small downtown area.

"It appears to be in front of that building," I said.

"Yeah, looks that way to me."

"The logs are right. People everywhere."

"Where can we park? It's all metered and I don't even see any open spaces."

Three blocks outside the downtown area we found a parking spot in front of somebody's house. We wouldn't be gone long so we left the van there.

"These little towns are getting cuter and cuter," I said. "The sidewalk is brick. The police station looks like a house. The post office only has one counter. The mailman walks his route."

"When you grow up, would you rather live in a little town or a city?"

"I don't know. I'm used to the conveniences of cities. I don't know how I'd shop in a town with one small grocery store and a mom and pop dress shop. But cities don't do things like this," I said as we walked under hanging planters of flowers.

"I think the cache was to the right and then down a block and a half."

"I think so, too."

We turned the corner and found wide bricked sidewalks and open fronted restaurants. I scanned the street and saw that the next block, too, had a row of restaurants. Tables lined the sidewalk and it appeared the area was a social gathering place. We made one pass with Twiggy holding the GPS. We passed the cache and kept going, found a bench and I took the GPS.

"I'm not sure," he said. "And there's so many folks walking around I don't want to take the time to search."

"And it's a five. How many times can we walk past a spot without making people suspicious?"

"I don't know. It depends on if it's the same people or different ones."

We walked back down the street while I watched the GPS.

"Oh shoot," I said as we walked past ground zero. "The only thing over there is a bank machine!"

"That's what I thought, too."

"Well, if there's one thing people do at an ATM it's stand there for a minute and figure out banking problems. I need money. I'll use the machine while you search."

"But one thing ATMs have is security cameras."

"Ooo, you're right. Maybe small town ATMs are not as secure. Cameras cost money and they might not want to monitor every ATM in town. I'll use the ATM and you tie your shoe so you can look around."

We walked over to the machine and I took my time finding my bank card. I looked at the machine for a slot to slide my card into but it was taped over.

"This is one weird machine," I said. "I thought it was out of order but it's just plain weird."

"Why?"

"Well, look at this. The slot has tape over it. If it was out of order it should display it on the screen. But even the screen is blank."

Twiggy tapped the screen. It didn't do anything but the machine rocked as if it was too light.

"It isn't real," he said. This seemed to give him a little confidence and he looked around for security cameras. "The only problem is we can't claim a find without signing the log."

"You mean this machine *is* the cache?" I asked.

"I think so," he said casting a glance back at the sidewalk. A woman was standing there watching us. "Come on. We need to think about this. We'll come back later."

As we walked back to the busy sidewalk Twiggy told the woman, "It didn't work for us, but it's your turn."

Unfortunately the whole time we were in the downtown area the restaurants got busier and busier. As the sun set and music began drifting over the shoppers and diners, the area took on more of a party atmosphere.

"Hey, I can blend in here," Twiggy said. "I'll buy. Let's go join the crowd!"

"We're here on business," I said.

"Relax. We're doing great. What do you want for dinner? I like the looks of that microbrewery. Have you ever tried local beers? They're distinctive and it's fun tasting different brews."

"I've had a martini. Once."

"Oh yeah. You do have your ID, right?"

"Yeah, but…"

"And you're legal drinking age."

"Yeah, but…"

"Are you afraid of what one beer might do to you?"

"No, but, maybe I should be."

"They usually have good food too. Let's go!"

We went to the microbrewery and waited in line for a table.

"How many in your party?" a woman asked. She was wearing shorts and a tight t-shirt that advertised the restaurant. The picture on the front showed a mountain man on a hilltop holding up a bottle of beer. There were snow capped mountains right across her own.

"Two," Twiggy answered.

She led us to a tall table. I had to climb up onto the stool. The inside of the restaurant was decorated in used brick and there were posters of bottles of beer all over the walls. Flags were stapled to the ceiling. There was an elk head over the fireplace and a jackalope over the bar. As I looked around I discovered more stuffed animals. There was an armadillo on a shelf with the liquor bottles and an antelope trophy hanging above the other end of the bar. It wasn't until I went to the restrooms to freshen up a bit that I noticed a bear climbing a telephone pole in a back corner of the brewery. When I got back to the table the waitress was just leaving.

"Water," Twiggy pointed out. "And a taster tray on the way."

"A taster tray of what?"

"Beer!"

"Twig…"

"Don't worry! They are all only three ounces each. A sip is not going to kill you."

"What if it turns out I don't like beer?"

"Then there's more for me! I recommend starting with the lighter colored ones."

"Why?"

"The darker ones are richer, and they can be more bitter." When the tray was set down on our table he chose one of the little glasses, held it up, and swished it a little. He set it down. He picked up another, swished it, smelled it. He picked up a third one and swished it, held it up to eye level and gazed through it watching the bubbles move. He set it down and picked up the second one. "Try this one."

I took the little, round glass from him, gave him a questioning look and took a sip. It tasted... like I don't know what. I hope I didn't make a face at it, but I think I did based on his smile. I took another sip. It was a little better, but still not something I could think about enjoying.

"You're funny, you know that?"

"Yeah, I know."

"What do you think of it?"

"What's it supposed to taste like?"

"Beer! Here try this one. You'll see why I started you out with the lighter one."

I sipped it and this time I did make a face.

"You don't like it?"

"Ugh, no, not that one."

He took the little glass from me and drank it down.

"Ahhhhh, it's been a while."

"How much is too much?" I asked.

"Six three ounce glasses? I could drink all of them and not get a buzz."

I wasn't so sure about that. I didn't want him to drink all those and then drive. So I decided it was my moral responsibility to give it my best try. I picked up the first one I had tried and took a bigger sip. I was definitely not a natural born beer drinker. I decided maybe sipping wasn't the way beer was meant to be drunk. I took a bigger swallow. Ugh! Why did people drink this stuff?

The waitress came back to take our order and I hadn't even had a chance to think about food.

"You go first," I told Twiggy. "I haven't found a menu yet."

"It's written on the blackboard over the bar," he said.

"Okay, order slow, and I'll find something."

It took him about twenty seconds to give the waitress his order which included a larger beer. I threw a mental dart at the menu and it landed a few inches from the blackened salmon, so I ordered that.

"Wow, you're going all out," Twiggy said.

"Why? What did I do?"

"Nothing. I'm glad to see you getting something you like."

I looked back at the menu and realized I'd ordered a twenty-five dollar dinner. I was shocked and I almost apologized but knew Twiggy wouldn't want me to. I made a mental note to read the menu very carefully before the waitress could show up next time. I went back to the beer. If Twiggy had his own beer I didn't want him to drink all these, too. Maybe if I held my breath.

When the first sample was gone and I reached for the second Twiggy said, "So you like it?"

"Not yet," I said. "What is it?"

"Hops. I like this one," he said. "It's smoother but it still has a nice hoppy taste to it. It's not as bitter as some dark beers are. Want to try it?"

"I'll save that one for you, since you like it."

"I've got another one coming," he said.

"We need to start thinking about this geocache," I reminded him. "Before we are unable to walk to it. We left the van in front of those people's house thinking we'd be gone ten minutes and now it's been nearly an hour. We still need to eat, find the cache and walk back."

I managed to drink two of the little glasses of beer and didn't want to think about trying to drink the darker ones.

"Don't they have anything to drink that tastes like normal food?" I asked.

"Okay, so you're not into beer. If you like sweet I suggest a hurricane. That's a nice tame drink. If you like sour maybe you'd like a margarita. They're mixed drinks. A hurricane usually has pineapple, maybe a little mango or orange juice and a touch of rum. A margarita has a lemon or lime base and tequila."

When the waitress came back he ordered me a hurricane and I had to admit it was very good. A nice starter drink, I think is what Twiggy called it. The salmon was good. I'd never had salmon before. I wasn't sure I'd ever have it again at twenty-five dollars a plate.

"So if that machine over there is not a real bank machine how do we get the geocache out of it?" I asked.

"Well, first we have to wait for a lot of people to clear out. And they aren't going to do that any time soon. I suggest after we eat we find a place to stay, then come back and see if things are winding down."

Two of the restaurants had live bands playing and it was confusing having oldies rock coming in one ear and light jazz in the other. We were closer to the rock band so I tried to focus on the rock music. However, the night was just heating up. It might be a while before we could approach the ATM again.

Unfortunately, a hurricane tastes so much like juice that it's easy to drink one fast. When the waitress asked me if I wanted another one Twiggy said yes.

"Maybe the keypad is electronically rigged so when you put in the right pin number it opens up."

"That would be one high tech cache, but I suppose it is possible."

"Maybe it's a magnetic hide-a-key placed just out of sight."

"Then why use a fake ATM? They could just use a real one."

"Maybe… it's not the machine at all. Maybe the machine is a decoy."

"A red herring."

"I thought a herring was a fish."

"It is, and it's a decoy geocache."

"Why would anybody have a decoy geocache?"

"To make it more frustrating."

"They don't need to make geocaching more frustrating. It's already frustrating. It's just that finally finding the cache overcomes the frustration."

The salmon had some kind of Cajun seasoning on it and I ended up drinking the second hurricane to help calm down the spiciness of the dish. I wished I knew what seasonings were on the vegetables because someday I might have to learn how to cook. My mother had tried to teach me a time or two and I could make a grilled cheese sandwich and fry an omelet, but I had a lot to learn.

"How long do you think it'll take before we can even get close to the machine?" I asked.

"Hours. Last call is 2 a.m."

"Then we have time to try something new!" I said.

Twiggy looked kind of leery of me trying something new after two little beers and two hurricanes, but he was willing to go along and see what it was. We paid for our dinner and drinks and walked out into the street.

"Have you ever done the twist?" I asked him.

"Leave it to you to know how to twist," he said. "When was that dance popular?"

"I don't know. My parents taught me."

"I suppose you swing dance, too."

"Only to big band music. But you can twist to anything."

"You really want to pay the cover charge to go in there?" he asked.

"Why go in? We can hear the music perfectly fine a block away."

He gazed up and down the street. Young people were walking and chatting and stopping to talk to people eating on the patios.

"Shit," he said. "I'll never see these people again in my life. Who cares what they think?"

We found a spot near the restaurant with the band playing and I showed him how to twist. He had seen it on old movies, of course, but he was still amused to see it in this day and age in the middle of a sidewalk while we were trying to geocache. He hesitantly tried to copy me and we were soon laughing at each other. I wasn't good at Twisting even when I was sober. I didn't feel drunk but I sure couldn't balance as well as I did when my parents taught me the dance. Twiggy looked absolutely silly doing the Twist. His knees and elbows went this way and that as he tried to keep time with the music. I lost track of the music in an effort to remain upright. It didn't take long for other people to start staring. After we began laughing at each other people thought it looked like fun and they tried it, too. Those who just liked dancing chose other dances, some of which my parents definitely would not have approved of, and people were dancing all over the sidewalks. Pedestrians had to cross the street to continue walking to their destinations.

"How long until 2 a.m.?" I asked.

"Three more hours."

"We can't stay here that long. I'll pass out."

"Let's find a nearby motel and take a nap. We can set an alarm and come back later."

"Okay."

We left all the dancing people behind and walked to the van, but by the time we found it I was feeling very fuzzy headed and I had developed a headache that was trying to take over any logical thinking.

"Let's just sleep here," I said. "My head is going to explode. I don't think we should be driving and we have the mattress in back. I know I'll miss my shower but right now I don't care."

"If you're feeling that bad you might need a bathroom real quick," he said. "We won't go far."

He seemed to be experienced at finding motels. Each town appeared to have an area near the city limits sign that had motels right off the first exit. Older motels could be found around town but the town limits was a good place to look for a room at most hours of the day or night.

I waited in the van while he booked a room.

"Okay, easy does it," he said when he opened the van door and helped me down. He threw a few things into one of my boxes and carried it upstairs. I followed him willing the lights to suddenly go out. He opened the door and I flopped down on the bed, curled up on my side, and covered my eyes.

"No, no, not yet," he said. He put down the box, rummaged around in it and then went to the rest room. I heard the water running and he came back with some pain relievers and a plastic cup of water.

"Up," he said. "Take this."

"Why do I have to stand up to do this?" I asked as he began pulling the covers back. When the bed was open he took the glass, sat me back down and took off my shoes. "Sleep on this side. The bathroom is right there," he said pointing.

"I think I can find the bathroom," I said as if it should be obvious finding a bathroom wasn't the most difficult feat in the world.

"You might need it faster than you think. Try to get to sleep."

"No problem," I said as I flopped down on the bed again.

I would have been out like a light, except that something wouldn't let me. Twiggy wasn't sleeping. He undressed except for a t-shirt and underwear. Then he snuggled up to me, but he wasn't sleeping. He was intentionally staying awake and occasionally he would run his hand up and down my arm. It was distracting.

"Relax," he said quietly. "I'm right here."

"I know, but you're not sleeping. Why aren't you sleeping?"

"I…" he thought for a moment. "I'm sorry, Gabby, that I did this to you."

"No worries. Just go to sleep. When is the alarm set for?"

"Two-thirty."

"Arg, okay. Sleep."

"If you feel too bad at two-thirty we can skip it."

"Okay, now get a little sleep."

He was quiet but his hand continued to occasionally caress my arm. Right before I fell asleep his arm wrapped around me and his fingers fiddled with the buttons on my shirt.

Like Twiggy expected it didn't take me long to need a bathroom and I stumbled bleary eyed into the room, did my business in the dark and stumbled back. I noticed that Twiggy was not in bed, or anywhere else in the room. My head was still pounding so I went back to bed and fell asleep. He gently woke me up at two-thirty.

"Gabby? Gabby? Do you want to go give it a try?"

"Ooohh man. Why two-thirty?"

"Never mind. I'll let you sleep."

"No, it's okay. The mission comes first, right?"

"It doesn't have to."

"Whatsa mission worth if you don't have a little misery invested in it?" I asked as I rolled out of bed.

"Are you sure you're okay?" he asked.

"I'll survive."

"I've got a flashlight but hopefully we won't have to use it. If the cops question us don't slur."

"Okay. Am I slurring now?"

"Not as much as I expected. How's your head?"

"It still hurts but it's better than it was two hours ago."

"Good. Here, shoes."

I put my shoes on, but any movement at all caused my head to throb. Hopefully this find would be quicker than I thought it would.

"Read the whole description before we leave. All the hints, logs, everything. It might be hard to do when we get there."

"Right."

It was easy to drive downtown and all the parking places were empty. Twiggy pulled in and put the van in park. He grinned. "Ready for a cache withdrawal?"

"Ready."

I tried to move as little as possible as I followed Twiggy over to the ATM. We had to turn on the flashlight to get our bearings.

"Do you think a PIN will open it?"

"Remember the description said to look around and we'd find everything we needed."

"Great, so we get to look like bank robbers sneaking around a bank machine."

First we looked at the machine itself. It was obviously the geocache because on the back side of it was a big green sticker proclaiming it to be a geocache.

"Well, we're in the right spot. Now to open it."

We began punching in random PINs and hitting enter, but it was obvious the electronics in the machine were not working. Next we found a door with a fancy combination lock on it.

"Ever broken into a safe before?" Twiggy asked.

"No."

"Me neither."

"We need numbers."

"They said look around and we'd find what we needed."

"Okay so look around for any one or two digit numbers that stand out to you."

We had to turn on the flashlight to look for clues and when we did we heard human voices. They sounded like they were down the street so we continued searching for numbers.

"There's an 8!" I said.

"Good find. I wonder if the letters mean anything."

"I don't know but the 8 is different than the letters."

"This is the 2050 block of Stater Street. Maybe the fact that it is stating something means the 20 and 50 are in the combination."

We ended up finding more numbers than we needed. In the end we had 08, 20, 50, XI, XLV, and VII.

"The roman numerals are just plain foreign in this setting. I'm ruling out the 20 and 50 as part of the natural surroundings." Then he started mumbling to himself. "Just think geocaching, forget about computer languages. No octal or hexadecimal or binary or twinary."

"What's twinary?" I asked.

"Nothing. I just made it up. Okay, let's try 07, 11, and 45. The Roman numerals are bound to be the right ones."

He tried 07, 11, 45, then 11, 07, 45, then 45, 07, 11.

"If this is a real combination lock from a real bank it might have four numbers," I said.

"I can't even get three to work."

"Of course not, if four are needed. Hold on, I'm trying online."

"Now who's the geek?"

It was slow going but we finally found a video that showed how to open a bank vault and it did indeed require four numbers.

"But before you pull out all your hair worried about the nearly infinite number of combinations that are possible I'm wondering if there was a clue in the description. Didn't it say something about the little ones following the big ones? If that's true then we have to follow the instructions in the video but use the numbers in reverse order."

It still took a few tries because the lock was touchy. We had to spin the dial so many times before we turned it back to the first number and then go around twice before going back to the second number. I don't know how bankers ever get money out of the safe if it was that hard to figure out. Finally we heard a slight click and Twiggy tried moving the latch and it worked! I clapped enthusiastically for him. Even that hurt my head. Twiggy opened the door and inside were about a dozen spiders.

"Aieeee!" I cried backing away from the ATM.

Twiggy gingerly pulled out the container and tossed it on the ground scattering spiders everywhere. We took the plastic shoe box further along the wall to be more out of sight and farther from the spiders.

"We did it! We got the cache!" I said excitedly. "Wow! Travel Bugs galore!"

"People must think this is a pretty safe cache since you need to be an experienced geocacher to get to the box."

"We should take a few. I'll drop them in caches when I go home."

"Okay, which ones do you want?"

"I'll take the Drama Queen one. Meredith will like that one. And... the one that has the teddy bear on it. I'll have to find a big cache to put that one in. Maybe I can get my family interested in finding it."

We signed the log and traded for some of the trinkets. I ended up with a key chain from the micro brewery. In spite of my joy at finding the cache I really felt like I should go back to the motel and sleep as long as I could. So we closed the box, put it back into its spidery home, closed the door and spun the dial.

"We got the cache! We found it!" I said as we headed back toward the van. As soon as we stepped back onto the street I was yanked backwards and a knife was pressed to my throat.

"Hand over the cash or the girl gets it," a rough voice said behind me.

"We don't have any cash!" Twiggy said.

"You think I'm deaf? I heard you plain as day say that you got the cash," the punk said.

"We really need a better word for cache," I said.

"Shut up! Don't make a move! He knows what I want," the crook growled as he jerked me around.

Twiggy reached into his pocket and brought out a small wad of bills.

"Don't give it to him!" I said. "We need that!"

My head was pounding and my stomach was roiling with the tension and violence of the situation. I could feel myself turning green.

"Let her go and you can have it all," Twiggy said.

"Toss it on the ground," the man ordered.

"Come get it," Twiggy taunted.

What was he doing?!

"Toss it on the ground or the knife goes in," the mugger sneered.

Just then the contents of my stomach suddenly reached escape velocity. My head was pounding so painfully that I couldn't focus and my stomach was roiling.

Twiggy tossed the bills on the ground and the man let me go. He stepped forward just as I lost it and a stream of hurricane, beer, and salmon hit the man in the back as he reached down to pick up the money.

"Ugh!" the thug said in mild shock at the mess all over his backside.

"Gabby! Run!" Twiggy shouted as the man bent to retrieve the money. He hit the mugger over the head with the flashlight and kicked him in the face as he was going down. "Run!"

I staggered away toward the van but I didn't get far before I retched again. When my stomach was relieved of its contents I felt much better. Even my head settled down a little. It took Twiggy a few minutes to catch up to me but he came running up behind, unlocked the van and made sure I got in before running around to the other side. He started up the van, threw it into gear, and drove down the street punching 911.

"Man down in front of the Bittercreek Steakhouse," he said. "Police needed quick. He tried to rob two college students." He hung up and said, "Let them figure it out. If we stick around they'll want to know what we were doing there."

"But, we needed that money," I said.

"Who says he got the money?" He pulled the bills out of his pocket. They looked a bit damp and I wasn't sure I wanted to touch any of them.

"How did you get them back?" I asked.

"I know a few things about self defense," he said smugly. "I bet he's still there when the police arrive."

He parked at the motel and we slid out of the van. I was wired from the mugging but my head still hurt. I followed Twiggy to the hall and into the elevator. As soon as we were out of the public eye he wrapped me in a hug.

"You cannot imagine how scared I was seeing you held at knife point."

"I was a little scared, too."

"Thanks for providing a distraction."

"Gee, thanks. Actually I felt too rotten to have time to be scared."

"Thanks for running when I told you to."

"I was too sick to be of much help."

"No worries. Are you okay?"

"Yeah, though I think we should get some sleep. We're going to be useless tomorrow."

"Gabby, I don't know what I would have done if that guy had hurt you."

"Let's not dwell on that. We need sleep."

"Okay," he said as he ran his hands up and down my arms. "Okay, sleep. But first a hug."

"My hero," I joked, though I really didn't know how funny it was. I hadn't seen what he did after I left.

Chapter 12

It was 3:30 before we could even think about sleeping again. Twiggy was edgy. I guess I would be, too, if I had just fought off a mugger. I don't know how long it took for us to fall asleep. At least I thought we slept, we must have because I was startled awake with a *BAM! BAMM! BAM!* "Open up! Police!"

"Twiggy!" I said but he wasn't in the room. Where could he be? Surely if he was worried about getting arrested he'd have taken me with him. And how had they found us here? Why were they pounding on the door like we had done something wrong?

I went to the door and opened it a crack.

"Yes?"

"Open the door."

"Officer, I haven't done anything wrong." How many times was I going to have to state my innocence to a police officer before this contest was over?

"We're looking for the driver of the green van parked outside."

"Did you try knocking on the green van?" I asked.

"Management said the driver of that van rented this room."

"Uh, yeah, but he isn't here right now."

"Could you tell us where he went?"

"If this is about the guy in front of the steakhouse, he mugged us. He held me at knife point and demanded all Tw... Tony's money. He almost got it, too!"

"Who is Tony? We're looking for Markus Daniel Livingston."

"Who? I don't know anybody named Markus."

"Could you come down to the station? We'd like to ask you a few questions."

"Me? Why me?"

It turned out his polite request didn't translate to "Later, when it's convenient for you, could you drop by the station for a nice chat?" It meant I could come in peacefully, without cuffs, or roughly, with cuffs. They didn't even let me put my shoes on. Where was Twiggy? I thought he was probably in the van but I didn't want to call attention to him if he'd been accused of wrong doing. Maybe I could clear this up without involving him.

I didn't know what to do. These police officers were muggles and to tell the whole story I would have to tell them about the geocache. I was so nervous. I had never drank anything alcoholic except that one accidental martini before that night, but I knew that if I admitted to drinking before the incident occurred that it would change their whole perspective and make Twiggy and I look very bad. One question led to another and I was tiptoeing around the topic as carefully as I could when a solution suddenly dawned on me.

"The knife! If you can find the knife it will prove my story is right."

"And where might we find this knife?" they asked.

"I don't know, but I'll help you find it."

"I don't think so. Do you think you can identify the man who attacked you?"

"Yes, I think so, though I never saw his face very well. He was standing behind me and when he reached for the money I ran away. So I only saw him bent over, looking at the ground."

They were leading me to another room to identify the mugger when another officer caught up to us and said, "Emerson, there's a guy out here looking for the young lady."

Just then Twiggy burst into the hallway. He said, "What are you doing here?" at the same time that I said, "Where *were* you?"

"Marcus Livingston?" one of the officers asked.

It got rather complicated with the van belonging to someone else, the mugger claiming Twiggy had assaulted him and us claiming we reacted in self defense.

"Where is the knife?" the officer finally asked.

"In the cache," Twiggy said. "It's hard enough to open that I didn't think a geocacher would open it up soon. I was going to call you and tell you about it later."

The officers all either put their hands on their hips or crossed their arms over their chests and glared at Twiggy as if he pulled a trick on them and he was going to pay. Apparently they had heard of geocaching. They didn't ask what he was talking about.

Five minutes later we were riding together in the back seat of a squad car.

"I always wondered what it's like back here," Twiggy said. "I'm glad we're back here heading *away* from the station."

"Yeah the other direction was scary."

"Why didn't you wake me up?"

"How could you sleep through it?"

"I was tired!"

"Me, too, but I heard the banging on the door. The mugger must have gotten our license plate number when we drove away. What did you do to him that he says you beat him up?"

"He had a knife!" Twiggy said. "I had nothing! How can they say it wasn't self defense?"

"We'll find the knife. That'll prove it."

"I guess I better email the CO and tell him that the police are onto his cache," Twiggy said as he led the officer to the ATM. Then he explained to the officer about the cache. "You have to download the coordinates from the website, find this spot and then find the combination to the lock from the clues around you. That's why I didn't think it would be opened soon."

"So what is the combination?"

"It's a secret that only observant geocachers would know," Twiggy said. "It's also the roman numerals around the cache entered from largest to smallest."

"We had to watch a video online to know how to open a bank safe," I added. "But when he opens it you'll see it really is a geocache."

This time Twiggy had the door open in less than a minute.

"How did you get the combination?" the officer asked.

Twiggy pointed out the Roman numerals that could be spotted around the cache. The officer scratched his head.

"I've stopped by this machine several times hoping to catch a geocacher at it so I could ask for help. I've set up a watch on the listing. I knew to look for numbers but I never thought of looking for letters."

"I owe the antique store a newspaper," Twiggy said. "I wrapped the knife in it so it would be less noticeable if the cache was opened." He took the cache out and handed it to the officer, then he brought out the knife wrapped in the daily newspaper.

"Are your prints on it?" the officer asked.

"Just on the tips of the guard."

"I have to admit we were kind of taken aback when we pulled up and there's a guy hog tied to a lamp post."

"At least they're good for something," Twiggy quipped. "The paracord slipped out of his pocket. He can keep it."

"No he can't. We've been looking for a guy who mugs people at night and leaves them tied up in the parking lots in back of the businesses. We're just lucky he met his match."

We had to go back to the station and make sure the police had our contact information before they would let us go. But when the mugger saw his knife in the hands of the police he confessed that our story was true. It was up to the police to convict him of the other robberies in the area.

Chapter 13

Stopping at that ATM cost us a bundle. By the time the police let us go it was past our check out time and so we had to pay late fees. We packed up and drove out of town just to put the experience behind us. We did, however, give the ATM cache a favorite point.

One strange thing that geocaching does to perfectly normal people is it makes FREE WIFI signs jump out at you. Since we were on the road the only chance we had to look for more caches and log our finds was when we had a connection to the internet. Finding meals and an internet connection was a double bonus even though it made older couples glare at us for eating out, but hardly communicating with each other. We did communicate. We even had a common hobby to talk about. But to the casual observer it looked like two kids on a date who barely acknowledged the existence of each other.

"No extra muggly places," I said as we were searching for a new cache to find. "And don't order me a second hurricane ever again."

"You were kind of fun there for a while," he said.

"I was?"

"I never twisted before. You said your parents were old fashioned but I never expected them to be *that* old fashioned."

"It's good exercise," I said.

"Provided you can still stand up. I guess if you can twist you must not be too shnockered."

"I don't know, that headache was awful. I don't want to do that again."

"Here's one that looks pretty safe. There is one building close by but it's a four difficulty."

"What kind of a building?" I asked.

"Let's look at the satellite image. Maybe that will give us some clues." He clicked a link and waited for the map to change to the satellite image. He clicked to zoom in. "What is that? Gabby, can you figure out what that is? The building is here. It looks like a house, except there are lots of cars parked at it as if it's a business. But the cache is in the corner of the little parking area. On a big red thing."

"A fire truck?"

"Could be."

"Look at the logs. Maybe they say something."

"Uh oh. DNF, DNF, DNF, third try and still no luck. I don't know why I keep coming back to this place. There are twice as many DNFs as there are finds. It's that one occasional find that gives me hope there is a real cache here," Twiggy said as he read the logs. "I am the cache owner. I assure you the cache is there. Use your geosenses and feel around."

"Sounds interesting. But it sounds like an interesting waste of time."

"Yeah," he said disappointedly.

"We can look if you want to," I offered.

"I always did like fire engines."

"Then let's go look."

"Maybe business will be slow."

"It doesn't sound like it matters a whole lot if someone is there or not. It's the cache itself that is hard to spot. Nobody seems to find it on their first visit."

"Maybe we'll luck out and find it and drive all the other geocachers who haven't found it crazy."

Before we could find Seeing Red we had to drive through miles of country roads. I had never seen so many cows before in all my life. I never knew corn plants grew taller than I did or that horses didn't really eat hay, they eat alfalfa and alfalfa is stemmy and leafy, not at all like what I thought hay was. I found out that what I thought was hay was actually straw. Guess I'm not much of a country girl. The road narrowed from four lanes to two. The shoulder of the road narrowed until there was nothing but woods next to the road. If we got another flat tire we'd have to drive a ways to find a spot wide enough to pull off. It was pretty and I couldn't help but look for deer. I was a little afraid of seeing one, though, because the tree line came nearly up to the road.

"I love these little blue highways," Twiggy said. "This is what geocaching is all about. Discovering new places, however small they may be. Just a road going nowhere that I never would have seen."

We passed a few houses and I expected to see hillbillies rocking in rickety old chairs out on their porches. I knew it was silly to think that, but when the fire truck appeared ahead and we pulled into the tiny parking lot I thought we had landed in Hicksville. The building appeared to be a little general store. I would usually call it a corner market, but there was no corner and no town, just a few houses, the store, fire truck and miles more of roads leading to more green places that I had never heard of or dreamed about.

"Look at this old thing!" Twiggy said. "I wonder if they'll let me sit in it."

It was a fire truck for sure, though the red paint had faded in the sun. It was so old that the ladders were made of wood.

Twiggy sighed, "All right, to work. A micro on a fire truck."

There are just too many little hiding places on a fire truck, especially a fifty year old fire truck with the engine showing and the hoses deteriorating in the weather. The GPS put the cache at the front end of the truck but the coordinates and our GPS could be off putting the whole fire truck as a possible hiding spot. After a quick search I began a methodical search, but I gave up on the methodical approach quickly. I could search for hours and never make it past the engine.

"This is impossible!" I said with an exasperated huff. I looked up and there was a man sitting in a rickety old chair on the porch of the store. "Muggle alert," I mumbled to Twiggy.

"Heyall!" the man said. "Aint had a geo catcher here for a week! I thought y'all had given up the hobby!"

Twiggy's head popped up from behind the truck. "You know about the cache?" he asked.

"May I recommend to you that y'all go inside and order the fireman's special. Won't cost a lot but it might pay off, if ya know what I mean."

"Uh, no. What's a fireman's special?" Twiggy asked as he walked around the truck and up to the porch. "Tony Yancy," he said extending his hand in greeting.

"Ernie Crabtree," the man said.

"It's good to meet you Mr. Crabtree. Are you a geocacher?"

"No, no son, caint say that I am. Maybe you could say I'm a geocacher *watcher*. I like seeing what folks go through to find the cache on that ol' truck. I hear it's a toughie."

"It is," I admitted. "There are too many places to hide something on it!"

"This is Gwendolyn," Twiggy said.

"Ma'am," Mr. Crabtree said with a tip of his sweaty, old hat.

"What is a fireman's special?" I asked.

"It's kind of a code phrase. Means you want a clue about where the cache is. It'll earn ya a malted milkshake. Best shakes this side of the road."

I didn't see how that made it a very good shake but I was willing to see what happened if I asked for one.

"Where are we?" I asked.

"Martinsville, so named because there's more purple martins here than people."

"Never saw a purple martin. I never hope to…" Twiggy began.

"What are you doing?" I asked.

"Uh, sorry, it just pops into my head whenever I see something purple," Twiggy said.

"You are so random."

"Let's go see about that fireman's special."

"Hey Clyde!" Mr. Crabtree yelled as he got up out of his chair. "We got us some of those geo catchers! They been out there only half an hour. Does they qualify for your fireman's special?"

"Clyde's in the bathroom," a woman said. "With a book. It might be a while." When she saw us walking into the store she smoothed out the wrinkles on her apron and said, "Well, well, welcome to our little store. How may I help you?"

"This here's Glenda," Mr. Crabtree said. "She can shake 'em better'n Clyde anyhow. These folks need the fireman's special!"

"Oh, I should have guessed when I saw the GPS," she said. "Not many people come in. They mostly look and quietly disappear. Come have a seat at the counter. I'll fix you right up."

Twiggy and I were not sure about wanting a milkshake but it seemed to be part of the process of getting a hint out of the store owner so we sat down at the counter. There was a soda fountain behind it and the shelves were lined with a small assortment of canned goods, cake mixes, baking essentials and drug store staples. One corner of the store was reserved for souvenirs, most of which had purple martins painted on them. As she made our milkshakes she launched into a monologue which was worded very oddly.

"Don't let Ernie feed you a LINE. He might not know much about the cache but he's an UPRIGHT individual. Used to work for the fire department. They even had a POLE in his old station. They never used it though because they didn't polish it. It was grimy. But if it was polished up it might have worked better. They had sleeping quarters and a kitchen upstairs where they would FUEL UP but they had to find their way down stairs to get out to the fire. This town used to be twice as big until the fire of 1972. Burned half the town down. They had the old fire truck out there and a couple of bucket LINES trying to save the town. HOSES and bucket LINES couldn't save four of the buildings, though. It was tragic. But this little town stands up for itself. We help each other out. TIES THAT BIND. Neighbor to neighbor. You'd think the folks would move to other parts but we like our little crick and our one room school." She held up two wrapped straws. "Would you like one or TWO?" she asked.

"Oh, just one for me," I said.

"I'll give you two anyway. One is normal. One is what you are looking for."

Twiggy and I shrugged and opened a straw. I opened a white one with multicolored stripes. He opened a red one.

"I bet the red one blends in with the fire truck," I said.

"I never heard of hiding a cache in a drinking straw before."

After sitting in the general store drinking a chocolate malt and looking at the odd merchandise we weren't nearly as frustrated and we decided to take another look at the fire truck. Twiggy took his straw along as a reference point. We walked around the truck again trying the straw up to anything resembling a tube. There were plenty of those!

"Did you notice all the times that lady annunciated any word that had to do with tubes and lines and straws? There was probably a dozen hints in that odd story she told us. I'm sure the cache looks just like a fuel line."

It took us another half hour of searching. The plastic straw wrapped around the log had faded in the sun, but it had faded in a different way than the rest of the paint job on the old fire truck. The paint on the truck had faded to an orangish color and the straw had faded to nearly pink.

"Oh! Oh! I think I found it! Twiggy look! Is that it?"

He craned his neck to get a closer look.

"You're developing geosenses faster than anybody I've ever cached with!" he said.

"Well, is that it?"

"I think so, but how does it come out?"

We had to use the tweezers from the pack to pluck it from the engine, almost like playing the game of Operation. He held up the straw victoriously and then figured out how to get the log out. At first we thought we would have to use the safety pin and pull it out the end but one side of the straw was slit and the log came out the slit easily.

"We need to make sure the slit is on the back side when we replace it," Twiggy said. "Less water will get into it that way."

It appeared the log had been damp many times but we found a spot on the soft paper to sign our team name.

"Good work padner!" he said as I rolled the log small enough to fit back inside the straw. It wasn't an easy thing to do because the paper had been damp and dried again and it wasn't smooth anymore. It took a few tries to make it small enough.

We waved to Mr. Crabtree but then Twiggy stopped.

"Can I sit in the driver's seat?" he called toward the store.

"Go for it! Kids do it all the time!"

"All riiiiight!" Twiggy said as he clambered up into the cab of the truck. He rang the bell, looked around for the siren switch, and flipped it on. It didn't make any sound because there was no electricity but he bellowed out a siren and he pretended to drive the old truck to a fire.

"I've even seen sixty year old men do that," Mr. Crabtree said.

Chapter 14

"When we log our find we need to tell other people to go ask for the fireman's special," I said.

"You should check in with your folks," Twiggy suggested.

"What if they ask where I am?"

"Then we'll find out where we are."

"What if they make me come home?"

"They can't make you."

"I guess I didn't exactly get their permission before I went along with this."

"What did you do?"

"My mom said she would think about it and I excitedly told her thanks for saying yes and hung up."

"You should at least let them know you're all right."

"I'll call them tonight. I'll have better luck with my dad than I would with my mom."

"Gwendolyn!!!" squealed my youngest sister, Jocelyn.

"Shh, is Dad home?" I asked.

"Yeah, but you better talk fast. It's almost dinner time."

"Okay."

"DAAAAD! Telephone!" she yelled as she ran through the house.

"Hello?"

"Hi Daddy!"

"Gwen, how's my girl getting along in the big wide world?"

"Fine! I was just checking in because Twiggy thought you'd probably be worried about me by now. Everything is great, though, and I still expect to be home for Meredith's birthday."

"That's great. Who is this Twiggy? I don't think I've met her."

"Oh, they live in another dorm. That's why you didn't see them when you helped move me in."

There was a very heavy silence and I wondered what I had said wrong.

"Gwen, tell me the truth."

"I am!"

"What is Twiggy majoring in?" he asked.

"Computer Science!"

"That's great. Say, I've had a problem with my new laptop. Do you think Twiggy would have any idea what I can try to get it to connect to the internet?"

"Uh, I don't know," I said. "How can you have trouble connecting? We've found internet connections at every stop. We just watch for the signs!"

"Do you think you could put her on so I can ask?"

"Uh, no! I can't! Twiggy is…"

"Gwen, is Twiggy… male?"

It was my turn to stop in stunned silence.

"Let me talk to him," he said sternly.

Gulp. "I have to find them." I covered the phone as I said to Twiggy, "He wants to talk to you! What do we do!"

"What's wrong with that?" he asked.

"They think I'm with a girl friend! They never would have let me go if they knew you were a guy!"

"What should I do?"

"Be polite! He's already guessed."

"Okay." He took the phone. "Hello?... Yes, sir… Yes, sir... No, sir."

"You don't have to lay it on *that thick*!" I whispered.

"When you use your laptop where are you in relation to your router?... I see. Do you have any devices that might scramble the signal?" There was a long pause while my dad, presumably, listed all the electronics and electrical appliances near his work area. "Well, a fan would do it… Move the fan to a different location and see if that helps."

"He's really asking you *computer questions*?" I asked.

"Shhh," he said as he nodded yes. He took the phone and left the room, walking around outside as he talked to my father. I was sitting on pins and needles, wondering what my dad was going to do.

When he came back he handed me the phone.

"Daddy?"

"Gwendolyn… I don't know what to say. Your mother said…"

"How did you know?" I asked.

"Honey, think when you speak. Or, should I say, you've been thinking too carefully when you speak. It takes some concentration to use the word *they* instead of *he* or *she*. As soon as you said *they* I knew you were covering something up."

"Oh. Mom didn't seem to notice."

"I'll talk to her."

"No! Dad, please don't!"

"Why?"

"Because… she'll make me come home. And…"

"I won't?"

"I... Dad we're not doing anything we shouldn't. We're geocaching! We're finding hidden treasures. Today we found one on an old fire truck. What's so bad about that?"

"You told your mother you were helping a friend get home from school."

"I am! We're just geocaching our way there."

"I could demand. But I don't think demanding things of a twenty-two year old daughter is a good way to maintain a good relationship with said daughter. If I have done a lousy job of parenting then..."

"You haven't, Dad, you've been a great dad. And I won't do anything wrong. You'll see."

"Will I?"

"Yes! I'll be home in time for Meredith's birthday just like I promised."

"Be careful while you play with fire," he said.

"What's that supposed to mean?"

"Just keep it in mind."

"Okay, Dad. I'll see you soon. I love you."

"I love you, too, sweetheart. I don't want to see you get hurt."

"I know."

"Take care," he said.

"I will."

Twiggy and I stood there asking each other a hundred silent questions before he said, "If I lay a finger on his precious daughter I am dead."

"That sounds typical. Hey, it was your idea for me to call home."

"The good news is I think I got rid of his computer problem."

"Oh, good."

I held out my finger and smiled. He stuck his finger out, too, so I held my hand out palm up. He laid his finger in my hand and I curled my hand around it.

"Good, now that we have that taken care of, what do you want for dinner?"

"I feel like I need to make sure you eat right."

"That's silly. How about hot fudge sundaes for dinner?"

"Gabby... I don't want to make your dad mad."

"He'll never know what I eat for dinner."

"Still, he wouldn't let you eat ice cream for dinner."

"Ah, you don't know my dad. We've had many a midnight bowl of cereal with extra sugar on top."

"Really?"

"Yeah, in our PJs at the kitchen table crunching down cold cereal. That's his favorite snack. Well, his favorite snack that we keep around the house. He likes Honey Nut Cheerios and I like Honey Bunches of Oats. He even lets me pick out the oatmeal clusters."

"Wow, I wish my dad would let me pick out oatmeal clusters," he joked.

We ate a fairly normal dinner, but I felt bad that Twiggy was ending up paying for nearly everything. I tried to keep our budgets in mind. The soup and sandwich combo in most places was more than enough food for me and was usually affordable. I wasn't sure how many turkey club/clam chowder combos I could eat before I would start gobbling and walking sideways, though.

"At least that fire truck cache turned out to just be difficult, not dangerous," I said.

"That's the way we like them," Twiggy answered.

We turned on the laptops and began searching for a new cache.

"Difficult caches are hard to find," I said.

"That makes sense," Twiggy answered.

"No, I mean there aren't very many of them."

"That's because it's easier to hide an easy cache than it is to hide a hard one."

"So the rating is for the hide, not the find?"

"No. We need to put in some miles. The event is coming up quickly."

"Okay. That means we can look at caches further away. Maybe that will help us find a hard one to look for."

"It's getting tougher to find caches that meet all our requirements: few muggles, high difficulty, safe, interesting, fun, rough terrain, but not too rough."

"Maybe we should head off the main roads since our registration is going to expire any minute."

"Okay, we can do that. The van has a pretty high clearance. It's basically a truck frame with a box on the back."

"Have you ever done any driving on rough back roads?" I asked.

"Hell yeah! Boondocking! Haven't you ever been boondocking?"

"I went camping once. My family had a pop up tent trailer. We had to drive down a dirt road and go to the bathroom in an outhouse."

"That's not camping."

"Of course it is!"

"Camping is sleeping on the ground and eating food cooked over a campfire and watching the stars and seeing meteors shoot across the sky. It's fishing and hiking and getting away from it all. You can't get away from it all in a tent trailer!"

"Then let's do some boondocking," I suggested.

"You really want to?"

"Sure! What do you wear to go boondocking?"

"Anything you want. But you might not want to wear your best clothes. Wear something you can get dirty in."

It took about half an hour of searching before Twiggy began saying things like, "hmmm, maybe. Where does it go? Okay, zoom in. Sheesh it disappears under the canopy. Is there a road there? Oh, there it is. Wow, a mile as the crow flies is six by road. Cool!"

I peeked over my screen at him.

"Did you find something?" I asked.

He gave me a mischievous grin. "It's not a power trail, but there's caches about every quarter mile and the road winds way back in the hills. It looks like fun. The caches aren't difficult, but it is definitely off the beaten path."

"Will they help you win the contest, though?" I asked.

"Anything counts."

"How far away is it?"

"Another twenty nine miles."

"Sounds like it helps us get closer to the event, too."

"Okay," *click, click*, "Download beginning. Fifty-four caches."

"Fifty-four? How are we going to find fifty-four caches in one day?" I asked.

"No problem," he said. "We'll just do it one cache at a time. There are people who have found hundreds in a day."

"How?"

"One cache at a time."

I couldn't even imagine doubling my cache count in one day. I'd only found one or two caches in one day, and now we were going to try to find fifty-four? I prayed they were safer than the past caches we'd found and I hoped the boondocks were kind to us. It was like venturing into the bush in Australia to me. Boondocking. Geocaching. Fifty-four caches in one run. Yikes!

Chapter 15

Since we had an hour to drive while we found the dirt road in question we turned up the radio and belted out the songs we knew. It was one of my favorite memories. No matter what station we put it on Twiggy seemed to know every other song that came on and eventually I tried to find a station that he didn't know any songs on. Mexican music was finally the solution, but then I didn't know the songs either, so it was back to a familiar rock station. Mile after mile, song after song.

He had let his beard grow. It wasn't long enough to be a proper beard but it was enough for me to see what he might look like bearded. And he continued to wear darker colors and fewer math prof shirts. He was relaxing into his role and I couldn't help but think that I was learning what kind of a man he really was. He enjoyed his time outdoors looking for caches. He had watched out for me while the bear was threatening and patiently taught me how to chimney climb while the bear was pawing around near his feet. He chased me down when I'd been taken to the police station and even bought my fireman's special. He wasn't just a coffee drinking, late night study buddy, exam acing college student anymore.

"This road is really pretty," I commented.

"I never saw so many cows and sheep," he said.

"And red barns."

The road he turned on looked like somebody's long, dirt driveway. It ran along a fence around a field of grazing cows. We passed a house with kids playing out front, pushing trucks and cars around under a big shade tree. It made me wonder if they had internet out here and how we would log our finds today. It was unusual to see kids playing outside these days.

"This is a most excellent driveway," Twiggy said. "Just imagine it right after a rain and at about forty miles an hour. Mud up the wazoo! Doesn't that sound like fun?"

"Uh, I'll take your word for it," I answered.

We followed the farmer's property line through the flats, but as the road began ascending a hill we left the farmer's fields below and climbed up into some hills. We weren't far from the farmer's fence line when Twiggy found a wide spot in the road and pulled over.

"Ready for some slow power caching?" he asked.

"I guess."

"Some of these will be really easy, some a bit tougher. Let's hope there's a variety to keep things interesting."

I began to get interested in the trail of caches about the third one. We found one in a fence post, in a hollow tree, and one that was a real bird house with a fake floor.

"It's not a dragon house," I said. "But it's cute. I wonder how many birds have tried to go inside and failed."

"Should we add a little sign that says *occupied*?"

"Birds can't read."

"But they can tweet."

"Just be glad they don't yelp," I said. "We don't need the internet flooded with pictures of birdseed and bugs."

He put his arm around me. "Gabby, there's no one in the world I can joke with like I do with you. You make my heart laugh."

"You, too," I said. "I wonder what's next."

"I don't know but write down Home Tweet Home, Whoo's Looking for Me, and Pole Vault."

"Okay. Three down fifty-one to go."

"This might be a fun road if the names are any indication. The next one's called It's a Shoe-In."

"So, are we looking for a shoe or is this a particularly easy one to find?" I asked as we tromped around in knee high weeds.

"There's no telling. That's part of what makes geocaching fun."

It's a Shoe-In was just that. It was a small, metal container inside a baby shoe, inside a youth sized shoe, inside a woman's shoe, inside a man's shoe. It was quite a feat to untie each shoe and remove the shoe inside and an even bigger job putting it all back together but it was a fun cache. The man's shoe had been out in the elements and faded but each layer was more protected so the smaller shoes were more colorful. The baby shoe was a cute, pink sneaker. The metal container I would learn later was called a bison tube. We would end up finding a lot of bison tubes in our geocaching. They could be challenging because they were small, but they were a bit disappointing because they almost always contained only a log. Geocaching was still new to me and I looked forward to sorting through the contents and trading for something I could use or bring back to my sisters and brother. However, the feeling of accomplishment was greater if we had a hard time finding the cache. So sometimes the little ones were more fun. I just didn't get to trade.

The next one was hard and took us close to an hour of searching. It was called One Flew Over the Cuckoo's Nest. We looked for geocaches disguised as nests. We looked for a hidden cuckoo clock. We looked in all the usual hiding spots just in case the name had nothing to do with the way the cache was hidden. After half an hour of searching we read more about it. Since it was hidden by the same geocacher as the shoe cache we decided the name had to be a clue. We finally spotted a large nest high in a tree.

"It can't be over that," I said.

"I know tree caches exist, but that is ridiculous. The rating isn't high enough so it can't be one we have to climb to."

"That's the only thing around that even comes close to fitting in with the title."

"Then maybe…"

He began searching the base of the tree.

"What are you looking for?" I asked.

"A line of some kind. A light rope? It would have to be something that withstands the weather, and last a while."

"Why?"

"Because if it's up there it could be strung up."

"Oh! They really do that?"

"Occasionally."

I began searching the base of the tree, too. The nest was still the most likely thing around that fit with the name of the cache so I thought it had to be up there somewhere. I looked way down in the bushes because they might have tied the end to something and the branches near the base of the bushes were the only things stout enough to hold a weight. While I was searching my fingers brushed something that felt weird. It almost felt like feathers, but feathers that were not connected to a live bird anymore. I jerked my hand out and jumped back!

"What happened? Did something bite you?" Twiggy asked.

"No. It just startled me, that's all. My imagination jumped ahead of my eyes."

"So what did your imagination think it was?"

"A dead bird."

"Hmm, a dead bird would not last long out here. So what was it really?"

"I don't know. I guess I could take a second look. It's not like a dead bird can hurt me. It's just… gross."

"Want me to look?"

"I… yeah, I guess I do, if you don't mind."

"Okay, where?"

"Right down there," I said pointing to the base of the bush. "Down in the leaves a little bit."

We switched places and he reached down under the bush. I could hear the leaves move around as he searched for a possibly dead bird.

"I don't know what you found but I don't feel anything down there."

"It felt like feathers, except it was too hard to be a bird."

"Well, I declare it safe for further exploration," he said.

"O... kay."

I wasn't sure I wanted to put my hand back down there, but I knew I felt something. So when Twiggy gave up I took another look. I identified the bush I had been at before and stuck my hand into the deep dark depths, down into the leaves, and felt around. My fingers remembered the feel of object even if my mind had jumped in fright and I managed to feel the same feathery, firm object I felt before. Oh no. I found it again. What was it? I was afraid to look so I felt it a little more as my mind sorted through all the similar things I had felt like that in the past. Fortunately that list was rather short and so I wasn't afraid to look at the object, but when I tried to pull it out it was tangled in the weeds.

"I found it," I said. "Not the cache, but the thing under the bush, but it's stuck!"

He came over one more time and found the thing I was trying to pull out of the bush. He soon discovered that it was tangled up, too, so he took out his pocket knife and cut it loose.

"Gabby! Gabby, please!" he sounded frantic. There was thrashing around in the bush next to me and I couldn't figure out why. "Gabby, say something! Anything!"

"Ohhh, man! What happened?" I asked reaching for my head.

"It found you!" he exclaimed but his attitude was so mixed I still wasn't sure what happened. Usually when we found a cache we declared, "I found it!" But he had said *it* found *me*. "Are you sure you're okay?"

"No. I'm not sure of anything. What happened?"

"The dead bird is inanimate, but it was attached to a line and the line led up into the tree. It was attached on the other end to the cache, which was big and heavy and... fell when I cut the line. It was very well camouflaged. You were beaned on the head by the cache."

"Why am I under the bushes?"

"Because that's where you landed. Do you want a hand up?"

"I guess."

He gave me a hand up but I couldn't walk because I was stuck in the bush. Twiggy looked at me as if he should call 911.

"What's wrong?"

"Gabby I... Are you sure you're okay?"

"I'm still in one piece, aren't I?"

"Well, yeah, but..."

"So, help me out of this bush."

He bent the branches back so I could find a way out.

"What are we supposed to do when someone gets bashed on the head?" he asked. "What day of the week is it?"

"I don't know. I haven't known since we left school though."

"When is your birthday?"

"April Fool's Day."

"It is?"

"It doesn't help to ask me questions you don't know the answer to."

"What was your locker combination in high school?"

"Fifty-four, eleven, sixty-two."

"How many steps from your dorm room to the bathroom?"

"Twenty-four."

"Are you sure?"

"Yeah, I counted because I went there so many times in the dark."

"Lucky, you. It was all the way down the hall from my room."

"How many fingers am I holding up?"

"Three."

He decided I might live but he made me sit down to look through the contents of the cache. I put in one of our college keychains and took a crocheted bookmark. It started me thinking that I could make things to leave in caches. I'd have to think about what I could make. My sisters would like helping me. I signed the logbook and closed everything back up.

"Now how many fingers am I holding up?" Twiggy asked, but he kept changing his fingers.

"Two X squared plus one fourth?"

"And what is that?"

"I don't know. Give me some paper and a pen and there's hope of an answer."

"How do you feel?"

"Like I got hit by a container full of toys."

"Which reminds me, how are we going to put it back? I can tie a knot in the paracord but I can't get the container back up there again."

"Was the bird really a bird?" I asked.

He held up a fake bird that came from an arts and crafts store.

"Oh, so that's why it felt like feathers. Too bad we can't send him up there. We don't have to get the cache up and over the branch if we can get the other end over."

"Didn't you say you took archery in PE instead of… I don't remember what."

"Refrigerator climbing, and… yes. Why?"

"You wouldn't happen to have a bow."

"No. The school had enough for the people in class. But we could probably fashion a bow out of something else."

We scrounged around in the van but the best we could come up with was a towel. A towel?

"Okay, trial run," Twiggy said. "We put a rock into the towel and tighten it quickly."

"What?"

"Haven't you ever played water balloon volleyball?"

"Uh, no."

"Hold the corners of the towel out. I'll show you how it's done. Hold it steady. Now watch." He yanked on his corners and the rock popped up into the air. "If we do all four corners at the same time it works better. So... one... two... three... yank!" The rock went about twenty feet up into the air. "If we tip the towel we can direct the flight."

"So you want to tie the end of the cord to a rock and launch it over the branch?"

"Yeah!"

"You're nuts."

"Let's see how high we can get one to go."

From experimentation we found that we could launch a small rock close to a hundred feet, but not straight up. After getting hit in the head by the cache it didn't seem wise to launch rocks straight up, however to get a good line on the branch we had to be somewhat close to the tree. Then when we measured the paracord we found out that we just about had to be right under the tree for the cord to reach.

"Do you think a rock will go that high with a line attached to it?" I asked.

"I think a better question is where are we going to find a rock that the cord will stay attached to."

This started a search for the perfect missile: one the line could be tied to securely and one that would fly on the projected course. A small log didn't work. We could tie the cord on but it flew awkwardly. A smaller log was too light. The cord dragged it down.

"Too bad we don't get a physics lab credit or two for this," I quipped.

"This is elementary school stuff. To get a lab credit we'd have to do the math."

"Oh, then forget it. You don't suppose we could hire a squirrel," I suggested.

"No."

"What about a pipe?"

"Pipes don't grow in the woods."

"Yes they do. Look!"

I pulled out a six inch piece of pipe. It had a notch cut in one end. A notch just big enough to slip a piece of paracord through.

"Looks like the cache owner has had to fix this hide a time or two," Twiggy said smiling. "I bet he didn't bring another person and a towel."

He tied a knot in the end of the paracord and slipped the paracord through the pipe and lodged the knot into the notch in the pipe.

"Stand back," he said.

When I was standing away from the tree and watching where the pipe might fly he threw it up in the air. It didn't even come close to the branch. He tried again, harder, still without success.

"Okay, let's try the towel, but watch your head. I don't want to give you two concussions in one day."

We tried launching the pipe up over the branch but it took a lot of practice to get the right angle, velocity and height. By the time we successfully sent the pipe over the branch we were too tired to celebrate the victory. We sat at the bottom of the tree with a huff.

"We did it," Twiggy said. "I was not looking forward to emailing the CO and telling him I broke his cache."

"It still needs some tweaking but I think we can get it close to the way it was before."

After we sat and rested we began figuring out how to get the cord threaded through the bolts so the cord lay right against the trunk of the tree. We couldn't reach all of them but we threaded it through enough of them to make the cord hard to see. Then we wired the bird and the paracord to a perch in the bush so the bird would be findable, yet easily overlooked. When we stepped back we agreed that everything looked the way the cache owner had originally intended it to. There was a little bird in a bush perched as if he was watching the world go by. Only a geocacher would investigate far enough to discover the little bird's secret.

The next cache was called Dropping Like Flies. I couldn't imagine what the cache owner could possibly have done to make a cache of dead flies, but he'd done it. It was very odd and puzzling. At the coordinates we found a little child's fishing pole and on the end of the line was a magnet. We stood there with the little fishing pole in hand thinking, now what? We looked around for someplace to go fishing. We had to read the hint, which said, "rock fishing". There was a pile of rocks so we lowered the fishing pole until the magnet went into a gap. We pulled it out and two plastic flies were attached. Twiggy grinned.

"What is this guy going to make us do next?" he asked.

Again and again we lowered the magnet into the rocks and it always came up with plastic flies with little magnets glued to them.

"One of these holes has got to have a plastic bottle or a magnetic nano in it," he said, but it took a lot of fishing to finally pull it out.

"I hope lots of kids find this one," I said as I signed the log.

"We can write in our log that it was fun and kids would enjoy it so parents will be more likely to bring their kids along."

We scattered the flies around on the rock pile and made sure they fell down between the top rocks, then dropped the cache into one of the holes.

"Whoever laid this trail of caches has some imagination," Twiggy said. "Most geocaches are just a plastic jar hidden in a tree or bush. These odd ones are fun."

We hid the little fishing pole again and went on down the road.

The next one was not as inventive but at least it was easy. It was called Pipe Down and it was in a pipe that was bent over on its side.

Between Pipe Down and Off the Record it began misting. It was rather pleasant driving through the misty woods.

"Do you mind hunting in the rain?" Twiggy asked when we closed in on the next cache.

"Not this rain. I hope it doesn't start pouring though."

"Do you have a rain coat?"

"I'm the one who strolls to class in the rain, remember?"

"I take that as a no."

"If this cache is off the record does that mean we can't log it?" I asked.

The cache was a little metal box screwed to an old vinyl record. I had never heard of the song before.

"I think it should have been called Off the Charts," I said.

"Just because you never heard of it doesn't mean it wasn't popular. After all, if it's on a record it was a song from before you were born anyway."

"Uh, yeah, the date on the record is 1975. So why is it called Off the Record if the cache is on the record?"

"Because you have to take it off the record to sign it? I think you are over thinking this hobby a bit. The name is just a pun. It's not supposed to be taken literally."

"Off the Record is an idiom. It's not a pun."

He sighed. Okay, so maybe I was over thinking the names a little too much.

We came to another fence line. I wasn't exactly pleased about the fence. Fences meant property lines and property lines meant people.

"Oh look!" I said. "A horse!"

"It's not a horse. It's ground zero."

"On a horse?"

"The name of the cache is Don't Look a Gift Horse in the Mouth."

Just then the rain started pattering down steadily.

"I know I'm not supposed to look a gift horse in the mouth, but I am not grateful for this gift of rain," Twiggy said.

"Aw, come on, what do you think makes this forest so green?" I asked.

"So, are you ready to look the gift horse over?" he asked.

"Sure, it's not quite pouring. We won't get too wet."

We got out and walked over to the horse, but we couldn't look at him very thoroughly because he was looking over the fence and one rule of geocaching is that caches are not suppose to be on private property. The horse himself was private property, but his mouth was accessible from public lands so we walked over and said hi to the horse. He didn't answer.

"It says don't look in his mouth. So what do we do?"

"Sometimes a title just refers to something close by."

"So," I said to the horse. "Are you the gift horse? I've heard of a Tooth Fairy and an Easter Bunny. Do you hide gifts?"

The horse didn't answer.

"The Easter Bunny never answered me either," Twiggy said.

"What *did* he say?" I asked, but he just wriggled his nose at me.

"That's what they all say," I replied.

"The Tooth Fairy always wrote 'thanks' on the envelope of money she left, though," he said.

"My Tooth Fairy wrote poetry," I said.

"Oh?"

"Uh, yeah, lousy poetry, like it was made up in ten seconds while she was leaving my money."

"Do you remember any of them?"

"Hmm, let me see. 'Your tooth was loose, and so I came, to give you nickels, and a dime.'"

"That's terrible."

"I told you. How about, 'You pulled it out, now do not pout, I have some money but not a lout.'"

"How could you stand it?"

"It was funny," I admitted. "My sisters and brother liked to hear them. Since I was the oldest it was all new and exciting and they had something to look forward to. But I think even they got tired of the lousy poems."

"I guess your mom and dad were trying really hard to be original."

"I guess proper tooth fairies try to be creative."

While we talked we were looking around the horse for a container.

"The hint says 'just hoof it.'"

"That just means to walk to it."

"Not with a horse statue. It's bound to be a little one down by the hoof."

The hoof of the horse was just reachable from outside of the fence. There was a box with a bolt on top by the left front hoof and the right back hoof, but there was another box by the right front hoof without a bolt. The box was painted the same colors as the other boxes, but there was no bolt. Twiggy reached under the fence and the box without a bolt came free. He pried off the lid and looked inside. He pulled out a piece of paper.

"May you win the lottery." He pulled out another. "May you be FTF for every cache."

"What are you doing?" I asked.

He pulled out another one. "Good health." He pulled out the log book and read the first page. "We're supposed to write a gift on a page of the note pad and add it to the cache as swag."

"Oh, hmm, I don't know what I would write for another geocacher. May all your coordinates be true?"

"Here," he said and handed me a page. Then he ripped one out for himself. I wrote my gift on the piece of paper and stuck it in the cache. He sat down and puzzled about his gift and then scribbled a quick note.

"What did you write?" I asked when he stuffed it into the box.

He handed me the cache and I plucked out the first paper. It said, "May you see dragon houses under each tree."

"That's the gift you'd like to give other geocachers?" I asked.

"It's a gift you gave to me," he said. "And I treasure it."

Chapter 16

The next cache was at a horse statue, too. I guess the ranch behind the fence had more than one way in. One gate had a reddish horse. That was the Gift Horse. The other gate had a very dark, chocolate brown horse and the cache was called The Dark Horse. The swag in the cache was black chess pieces from a cheap chess set. Some geocachers had traded for the pieces and left typical swag but enough chess pieces remained for us to see it started out with only chess pieces in the cache. Predictably we didn't find a black knight in the cache. The two knights had probably been the first ones chosen.

"Do you want to trade?" Twiggy asked as the rain dripped down his hair and into his face.

"No, though I feel like a pawn in this game."

After The Dark Horse the road ran right along the ranch fence and there wasn't any place to hide a cache for half a mile or so. The rain continued in a relentless light drizzle and the road began to get muddy. Twiggy thought the mud was wonderful fun to drive in. He splashed through the puddles and I imagined the back end of the van changing from avocado green to a muck brown.

"What are we going to do for dinner?" I asked. "We're a long way from town now."

"I hate to turn around. These caches have been safer than most of the ones so far and they've been interesting, too."

"I know. What do we have for food in the back?"

"Chips, two warm sodas, week old beef jerky and a half a package of M&Ms."

"We still have the M&Ms?"

"The Travel Bug has to eat, too, you know."

"What's the name of the next cache?"

"It's Anybody's Call."

"What is?"

"The name of the cache."

"Nah uh, we cannot call it anything we want. It has a title what is it?"

"It's Anybody's Call."

"Somebody had to name it," I declared.

"Gabby, drop it, okay?"

"What if it's fragile?"

We pulled up to ground zero and we saw the cache before we even opened the van door. The cache was an old fashioned rotary dial payphone attached to a good, sturdy railroad tie fence post.

"I want a picture of this one. Pretend you're calling somebody," I said.

"Take it quick. We don't want the camera to get wet."

"This is so cool! I've never seen a telephone like this. How old is it?"

"I don't know. I've used one a time or two though."

"Where?"

"Belle Fourche, South Dakota."

"Isn't that where the contest ends?" I asked.

"Yes, and it happens to be my home town and the geographical center of the United States."

"You came from the town at the center of the country?" I asked.

"Yeah. Why? What's so weird about that? I know several people who are from there."

"I guess you do," I admitted. "So, who do you think is the most likely to win the contest?"

"I don't know. That's your call."

"Mine? Why?"

"I, uh… I wonder how to get the cache out of this telephone," he said.

"If we can get the cache out of an ATM we can figure out this phone," I answered.

He checked for change but there was no container inside. He picked up the receiver and unscrewed the ear piece, then the mouth piece. He put the receiver back together. The next obvious place to look was the metal plate where the serviceman emptied the money from the phone, but it required a key. We stepped back and thought about the problem at hand, the telephone standing there on the post waiting for nobody to make a call, the receiver dangling from its cord and swaying gently in the breeze.

"Maybe there is a key hidden somewhere," I suggested.

"Could be," he said, "though the description should tell us if there is."

He absentmindedly hung up the receiver as he turned to search the nearby hiding places for a key, but when he hung up the phone the bottom of the phone box lowered about three inches and inside was a small, black, metal box.

"Wow, coolio!" said Twiggy. He removed the black box and shook it. It rattled like it had quite a bit of swag in it. When we opened it up there were wires, switches, computer chips, connectors and a dead cell phone. "It looks like people don't trade because they think it's a theme cache," he said.

"Or they don't have a use for a switch."

"Neither do we."

"But the telephone is cool," I pointed out. I signed the log before it could get wet. "I want to add something so people will start trading other stuff."

"We should read the description. If it really is a themed cache then we shouldn't divert from its theme. Let's see... no, it doesn't say anything about a theme. Go ahead and add something if it fits."

Unfortunately we only had the keychains to add.

"Where can I get different swag?" I asked. "We need more than just keychains. A kid doesn't want a college keychain. Maybe an adult, but..."

"You don't like my swag?" he asked.

"Well, I do, but I like a little variety, too. We see things that little girls and boys would like. We should get some little toys."

"That's going to cost us."

"And we need to finish this road," I said as I dropped another keychain into the black box.

Halfway to the next cache we had to splash through a wide puddle. Twiggy thought it was great fun. He took a good run at the puddle and water sprayed up above the widows until the van began slowly sliding to a stop in the middle of the puddle. He hit the gas and the tires spun but the van didn't go anywhere.

"Stay in the van," he told me. "I got this covered."

"Yeah, covered with mud," I said.

He opened the van door and all I could see below us was murky water. He hesitated before hopping out and splashing through the puddle. He waded around the van checking over the situation, but there wasn't much to check out. It looked the same from all angles.

"Can you drive the van?" he shouted.

"Sure!" I said, though I had never driven a van before. I moved over to the driver's seat, turned the key and eased off the brake. I hit the gas a little.

"Whoa! Hold on!" Twiggy yelled.

I waited until I heard an, "Okay, I'm ready!"

I tried the gas again and heard the tires spin uselessly. The van slid through the mud about three feet and I watched the rear view mirror as Twiggy slowly slid out of view. His feet had slid in the mud more than the van had and he splashed face first into the puddle. He stood up completely drenched in muddy water.

"Are we there yet?" I asked.

He splashed around to the driver's side window so I rolled it down.

"Are you okay in there?" he asked.

"Yeah!"

"Good, because I don't think we're going anywhere soon. Normally I have a few tricks to try but it involves there being less water."

"I hate to inform you," I said. "But there isn't going to be less water for at least a day."

"So what do you suggest?"

"I don't know. All my solutions require dry roads."

"We could call for help."

"Help costs money, something we have very little of right now."

"We have to eat," he pointed out.

"So you suggest we walk back to town in the rain to eat dinner?"

"That doesn't even come close to sounding like fun."

"It's bound to be several miles."

"We could hike back to that ranch and see if they have a truck and a tow strap."

"We can't ask them to come out in this rain just to pull us out of a puddle," I insisted.

"We can offer to buy some produce from them. They had trees. Maybe they had a fruit stand out on the highway. At least it's something to eat."

I looked uncertainly at the constant rain and thought about walking back to the ranch.

"Let's wait out the rain."

"Do you really want me to climb in there like this?" he asked.

"It's your buddy's van," I pointed out.

"I'm going to hike to the ranch," he declared.

"Well, you're not going alone," I said.

He folded his arms across his chest.

"I promised your dad I would take good care of you."

"Okay," I said as I opened the van door and looked down into the muck.

"No, Gabby, stay there. I'll go get help."

"From a crazy, shotgun toting rancher?" I asked.

"If they are crazy, shot gun toting ranchers I don't want you along."

"If you're going, I'm going."

"Grab a bottle of water," he said.

"In the rain? We couldn't die of thirst if we tried!"

"I'll carry it."

I found a bottle of water and climbed out into the five inch deep mud puddle. It was slick and I slipped and slid my way to the edge of the puddle, trying not to fall in.

"No wonder the tires just spin," I said.

On the way to the ranch we talked.

"Will we get to finish geocaching this road?"

"Not if my stomach has a vote," he replied.

"Rats. They were funny ones and now we'll have to put miles in again."

"We'll bookmark the road and come back to it someday."

"Will we? School will take over. We'll never be in this part of the country again."

"We won't?" he asked.

"I'll be at my parents' house, you'll be... I guess with your dad. What do you do over the summer?"

"Work."

"How come you're not working now?"

"I've got something more important to do."

"You really think you can win this contest?"

"I hope so, but we can't be sure."

"That's okay. I'm never sure of anything these days. I think it goes along with college life. You think you're getting a C and surprise you get a B! Or it can work the other way around, too. One test and your grade gets flushed down the toilet. At least my whole future doesn't hang on this contest."

"Uh... yeah," he said. "Though you never know. Sometimes a little thing like a contest can have lasting consequences."

"Why is it," I asked as I splashed through yet another mud puddle. "That I am constantly glad my shoes are almost worn out?"

"Because geocaching is hard on shoes. If you're going to make a real hobby out of it you really should buy some good, sturdy hiking boots."

"I don't know if I could walk in them. They are so stiff. I'm used to shoes that bend with my feet."

"Hiking boots will, too, after you break them in."

"How long have you been wearing them?" I asked.

"Since I was about ten, when my dad and I decided to do more than wallow in our situation. We decided there was more to life than one woman and began getting out more. We bought camping supplies and fishing rods. Eventually we figured out that our tennis shoes just were not going to keep up with our active lifestyle and we switched to boots."

"What's it like growing up without a mother?"

"It's... dang, I wish I knew. I mean I do know. It's just that... I think it's different for everybody. At first we were angry. Then we tried to turn it into a bachelor's life sort of deal. That worked until Dad saw me turning into a bachelor before my time. Then he decided I needed more than a bachelor buddy and decided to be a family again. That's when we tried the camping and eventually geocaching."

"Do you wish you had a mom?"

"Gabby... you can't go back. You can't know if it would have been better any other way. People do things to you and you just make the best of it. I can't blame dad for how things turned out. He did the best he knew how.

So, no, I don't really wish I had a mom. I wish I could erase the angry years and just live like they didn't happen."

"Sorry," I said. "I didn't mean to get off on such a serious topic."

"It's okay. It's not a serious topic unless you make it one. So, what was it like growing up with two sisters and a brother in the house?"

"Chaotic."

"Would you go back and change it?"

I was glad he asked it in a lighthearted manner. I just smiled because he'd proven to me that you can't go back and what would you change if you could? We are dropped into this world to live a life and we can only live it to the best of our abilities.

"I'm glad you found geocaching," I told him. "I think that was a positive change."

"You think so?"

"Yeah. And I'm glad you told me about it."

"You are?"

"Yeah."

"I'm glad you're glad."

"I'd even be glad if this rain would stop."

"Mabel! There's two drowned rats standing on the doorstep!" yelled the rancher who answered the door.

"Sweep 'em off with the broom! Or step on 'em!"

"Not that kind!" yelled the rancher.

"Well then what in tarnation... oh! What are y'all doing standing out there in the rain! Come on in!" yelled Mabel.

"I uh, I don't want to get mud on your floor, or drip on your carpet," I said as I slipped off my shoes. Twiggy had a little rougher time getting his boots off.

"This here's a farm," Mabel said. "If mud will hurt anything in this house it's ruint already. Farms is where they grow mud in the off season."

"Our van got stuck down the road from here. We were wondering if anybody had a tow rope to help point us toward town again," Twiggy said.

Mabel had been in the act of untying her apron and putting it away, but she walked over to us with it still in her hand and looked us up and down.

"You ain't had a lick to eat today, have you?" she asked.

"Well, we did have breakfast," Twiggy began. "But..."

"I knew it! Come on in. We can fix you up some grub. Can't let you starve on our property. No, siree!"

"I'm sure we'll be fine," I began but Twiggy glared at me.

"I think I got some good old fashioned ham 'n' beans and cornbread. That oughta stick to your ribs."

"That's good cornbread," the rancher said. "Ask her for some homemade peach preserves, too."

They didn't even have a microwave. Mabel spooned some ham 'n' beans into a sauce pan and heated it up on the stove. It was an old stove that she had to light with a match. It was a monstrous white and black affair and the oven looked like something out of Hansel and Gretel. Everything in the kitchen looked like it was from another era. It was freshly painted and carefully cleaned but as old as the house, which I took to be the original building.

The house had wooden siding and a big porch in front. Wisteria grew in lavender cascades across the front of the porch and I felt like I stepped back in time. The kitchen only reinforced that feeling. There was a pie on the window still and the kitchen smelled like a bakery. I caught the aroma of yeast, as if she had been making homemade bread, but also of something sweet.

"So, who are you and where are you from?" Mabel asked.

"I'm Tony and this is Gwen," Twiggy said. "We're students in Franklinburg."

"Ah, I see. So what brings you to our neck of the woods?"

"Geocaching," Twiggy said.

"Did you find the two out front?" she asked.

"Yes! We did! And we were going to find more but then we got stuck in the mud."

"You should wait out the storm. You two must be freezing!" Mabel said.

"It's summer. We'll be okay," Twiggy replied.

"Bertha needs to get out," the man said. "We'll take 'er down once you get some vittles and we'll pull your car out, no problem."

Mabel continued, "A friend of ours put the caches out front. We'd never heard of geocaching, but he explained it to us and asked if he could put them down at the front gates, said it might be entertaining to watch folks lookin'. If we see em out there, which doesn't happen too often, we want to coach 'em along. No! It's not over there it's over thataway! And if they see us, oh my! You'd think they was going to jail or something. Heaven forbid they might get caught," she laughed.

"Yeah, we're like that, too," I said.

My stomach was growling loudly by the time the ham and beans were warmed through.

"Mabel's got to feed everybody who comes over. Doesn't matter who they are. If they've eaten they get dessert, if they haven't eaten there's plenty to share. If it's not already in the works it can be warmed up perty darn quick."

"Dessert?" Twiggy said.

As college students our idea of dessert was a pastry from the snack machine. Or, if we were extremely lucky one of the girls would make chocolate chip cookies in the dorm kitchen and share. I'd taken cookies to Twiggy's dorm a time or two but real, homemade dessert was one of the most sought after things in college life, probably even more so than a good grade, or knowing we had a test aced. I remembered getting a care package from home. I had fourteen girls gathered around me as I opened the mysterious treasure before me. My mother had layered cookies in between clothing to protect the cookies from becoming nothing but crumbs. I opened the box and discovered... fuzzy socks! Although we all enjoyed new fuzzy socks there was a sigh of disappointment. I took the socks out and discovered... snickerdoodles! Now I have to hand it to my mom. She knew snickerdoodles was not my favorite cookie but the girls were so thankful that I shared my snickerdoodles that they happily took those. A few of the girls even went back to their rooms. Then there was a sweater, scarf and gloves. When those were removed I found a layer of sugar cookies. Then a new shower wrap. My mom placed the double chocolate chip cookies and the brownies in the very bottom and by the time I reached the bottom of the box only Sarah and I were left. I managed to make a lot of friends and still keep my favorite snacks for myself. I took some over to Twiggy and Skippy and rationed the rest for the next few weeks, only allowing myself one brownie or two chocolate chip cookies per day until they started going stale.

"Oh, my, would you look at the boy!" Mabel said. "You look like you need pie in the worst way!"

Mabel put a large piece of peach pie into a bowl and added a large dollop of ice cream, then she left it next to the pot on the stove until the ice cream began to melt. Twiggy was drooling. I thought, when she set the pie down in front of us, that there would be no way we'd eat ham and beans after a large piece of pie and ice cream. I admit I only ate a little lunch after the dessert but Twiggy managed to polish off pie, ice cream, and a large bowl of beans. Mabel sat and watched Twiggy eat and seemed content that she did her part in saving him from total starvation.

Gradually we began hearing a loud rumble outside, but it wasn't thunder. It was the sound of a large engine.

"Oh dear," Mabel said. "She needs a tune up. I can tell by how the windows shake."

The windows were indeed shaking and we could feel the rumble through the wooden floor of the old house, too.

It turned out Bertha was an enormous green tractor. She towered over the porch when we went outside to see what the rancher had in mind.

"Let her warm up a bit," the rancher shouted over the rumble of the engine. "She ain't seen work in weeks, not since I dragged the orchard. Snapped a few branches off in the process. Guess I ought to go do some trimmin'. Always something gotta be done. Gotta drag the orchard so the water flows right. If it don't we get all our peaches in one part of the orchard and not the dry part. Shoulda used little Moe but Bertha needs to work every once in a while, too. All good machinery likes a workout now and again."

I noticed there was only one seat in the cab of the tractor.

"How are we going to get back to the van?" I asked Twiggy.

"I guess we get to hike," he said.

"Never you mind," the rancher said. "The grandkids pile on this thing and go for rides through the fields. If you can hang on tight, we'll make it."

I couldn't see any place to sit except in the driver's seat.

"You climb up here," he pointed out to Twiggy. "See that bar? Sit beside the seat and hang onto there. Ma'am? You see him? What he's doin'? Jus' climb up the other side and hold on tight. Bertha lurches a bit but you sit tight and hold on we'll find your car on down the road."

"Thank you Mabel!" I yelled and waved as the tractor began moving. "You make the best peach pie!"

She just waved as Bertha's wheels churned through the mud of their driveway and carried us toward the road.

"As long as the sheriff don't swing by we'll be fine," the rancher said. "He don't like the idea of folks fallin' off and gettin' run over."

"I don't blame him," Twiggy said.

A tan farm dog trotted after the tractor until he noticed it raining, then he squinted into the drizzle and retreated to the porch.

"Hey," Twiggy called to me. "Just one more thing I've done because of geocaching. I never rode a tractor before."

"You know how to drive?" the rancher asked.

Twiggy looked at the configuration and said, "Not this."

"All right, just thought I'd check. Can't do much wrong on this here road. I'd even let JR have a try on this road and he's only twelve. A big twelve."

Twiggy watched the rancher's movements, the coordination between hands and feet, and by the time we reached the place where the van was stuck he thought he had an understanding of the workings of the big tractor.

The rain had settled down to a fine sprinkle. I felt like I'd be damp for a week after this little geocache hunt.

"Which way are you headed?" the rancher yelled over the roar of Bertha.

"How bad is the road likely to get if we continue on?" Twiggy yelled back.

"Eh… if the rain don't get worse you oughta be okay. The road widens a bit where folks have driven around the puddles. If you follow their example you should be able to get through."

"And where is through?"

"Dickens."

"Is there a motel there?"

"Maybe, maybe not. Hard to tell. Sally never seems to know the why or where for when she gets booked up but likes it when she does. She a can use the money. She's got little ones in school and growing like weeds in the spring."

"To Dickens then," Twiggy said.

The rancher hopped down from the tractor and slogged through the mud to the front of the van. He wrapped a chain around a bracket that held the bumper onto the van and he attached the other end to the back of the tractor.

"Can I try it?" Twiggy asked.

"You sure you want to?" the rancher asked.

"Hell yeah!" Twiggy said.

"Okay, it's your wheels," he said. "Ain't no way you can hurt Bertha but you might oughta go easy. Easy does it, or you're likely to do some damage to the frame there if you're not careful."

"Really?" Twiggy asked. "I can drive her?"

"I didn't say you could. I said you could try."

"All right!"

Twiggy scrambled up into the driver's seat and looked over the controls eagerly. Boys and their toys. Would he ever grow up?

"Like this?" He asked as he made artificial shifting movements.

"Oughta work. Now nice and easy. She's a might touchy. You tell her to go an' she'll for sure go. Them big tires on the back weren't made for piddly little lawn mowing jobs. They were made to haul ass."

It was a little ironic when Twiggy shifted the tractor into gear and quickly ripped off the van's bumper. He hauled ass all right. He hauled it right off the van, across the road, and up a hill!

"Boy, I told you to take it easy! Well, I'm glad you did it and not me. Your van's going to need some work though. Police won't take kindly to your bumper being wired in place so's you have the proper ID on your vehicle."

I didn't think now was the right time to bring up the fact that the van wasn't ours and the registration was expired. The rancher slogged over to the van and gazed underneath.

"Yup, you're going to need a welder. Only one welder in Dickens and that's Charlie Mosely. Tell him I sent you."

"I'm afraid we didn't get your name," I said.

"Gib Collins. Short for Gilbert, but folks around here call me Gib. Put her in reverse and ease her down the hill," Gib shouted to Twiggy.

I thought Twiggy should ease *himself* down the hill and leave the tractor driving to Gib. I heard a grinding noise and then the tractor began rolling backwards.

"Hit the brakes! Hit the brakes!" Gib hollered. "Easy, boy, easy!"

He went easy alright. He easily went over the bumper, through the puddle and over the other side of the road.

"Forwards is easier," Twiggy said. He pulled the tractor onto the road again and jumped out happily proclaiming, "Your turn!"

Gib grumbled all the way to the chain where he detached the useless bumper and looked for a new spot to connect it to.

"Now you need a bumper but the nearest Chevy dealership is fifty miles away. Might oughta look at some junk yards. It would be cheaper."

The bumper reminded me of a cartoon character when it freezes in surprise in mid air, but it didn't as much when Twiggy opened up the van and tossed the muddy bumper onto the futon mattress. I wanted to say, "Hey! I might have to sleep on that tonight," but I thought Gib might get the wrong idea.

I stood back while Gib expertly maneuvered the large tractor in the narrow dirt road and dragged the van to higher ground pointed toward Dickens.

"Can I pay you for your time and gas?" Twiggy asked Gib when the van was on safe ground again.

"No, siree, we don't take money for helping folks around here. All I ask is that you do the same for the next person that needs a helping hand."

"Will do and thank you," he said. "Thanks for trusting Bertha to my inexperienced hands."

"Too bad tractors can't talk. I bet she'd like to tell little Moe all about you."

"Tell Mabel she makes the best ham 'n' beans and peach pie I ever had," Twiggy said.

"I guess that means I raise the best peaches you ever had, too."

"Yes sir."

"Ya'll enjoy the rest of your trip. Be careful and go around the puddles. You go through them and they're likely to swallow you whole."

"Okay."

He climbed back into the driver's seat and laughed as he pointed Bertha down the road toward home.

"That really was good peach pie," I said to Twiggy.

"Yeah."

"I need to find some of that sugar topping she had on the crust. It was like sugar but the crystals were bigger."

"Sugar is sugar."

"But hers was better."

"If you make a pie I get a piece."

"Of course. But I've never made a pie."

"Maybe someday you will."

"So…" I said. "Are we going for the next cache?"

"We don't have much time left in the day, but… why not?"

"Daylight might not be needed for this one. It's called Bats in My Belfry."

"Oh, great, this better not be like Insane Asylum!"

Chapter 17

We sat at the bottom of the hill debating.

"We're going to need light," Twiggy said.

"Agreed."

"How much light do we have between us?"

"Well we each have our cheap, regulation, dorm variety flashlight in case of emergencies," I said.

"I wonder if the head lamp works again. This is what they were made for."

We crawled into the back of the van and Twiggy searched for the headlamp hoping it had dried out enough to work. He opened the battery compartment and made sure it was dry and replaced the batteries. I noticed Twiggy had an unusually large supply of batteries. I tried to remember the last thing I put batteries in but I couldn't think of anything. Maybe my clock radio, so it wouldn't forget the time in a power outage. He blew into the battery compartment, stuck in the batteries and switched it on. He shook it a little and the light came on.

"Okay, you take this one. I'll use the headlamp. It pays to have both anyway. A flashlight you can shine wherever you want, not just where you turn your head."

We slid out of the van into the muddy road and looked for a path through the woods that might lead us three hundred feet.

"Ready padner?" Twiggy asked.

"Yeah, but… where?"

I followed Twiggy as he pushed his way through the brush.

"Don't you just love bushwhacking?" he said a bit sarcastically.

"It depends. There's bushwhacking and then there's impenetrable forest."

"I think we can get through. Sometimes a cache gets hidden and the person who hid it doesn't realize that the little bushes that were there two years ago are now trees and the little weeds are now bushes. It can work the other way around, too, though. I've found caches that were hidden in a bush and the bush died years ago."

"What happens to a cache when its hiding place dies?"

"Usually the geocachers will find a new place close by, or pile rocks or sticks on top of it."

"Why are we looking for Bats in My Belfry?"

"It's got a three terrain rating."

"Don't crazy people have bats in their belfry?"

"Yeah."

"This isn't like Insane Asylum, is it?"

"Doesn't look like it."

"I don't see any belfries though."

"It might just be a play on words. Maybe the cache itself is a bat."

"How would they do that?"

"I don't know," he said as he forged ahead. I was glad he was parting the branches for me. If I was ahead I might not see a way through all the plants. He stopped at a hill. Oh, no, not another hill. "How are you at rock climbing?" He asked.

"I don't know. I haven't climbed many rocks. Is it hard?"

"Doesn't look too difficult," he said. "Just be careful."

"Why are we climbing rocks?"

"See that dark spot right up there?"

"No, you're in the way."

We traded places and he pointed it out to me again.

"I think that's where we're going," he said.

"That's not a belfry," I said worriedly.

"No, but we might find bats there," he said.

"*You* might find bats there. I'm *not* finding bats there. Bats are creepy. Bats are... flying mice and even mice are creepy."

"Oh come on, where's your sense of adventure?"

"Right here out in the open with trees all around and a nice pattering of rain."

"I bet it's a cool dragon house," he said to tempt me further.

"Oh... arggghhh..." Why did he have to say that? He knew I'd have to check out anything halfway resembling a dragon house. "Up there?"

"Yup. Up."

"O...kaaaay."

It wasn't very high as far as cliffs go, but it was a bit of a height if one were to fall on the way up.

"You go first so I can help you if you need it," Twiggy said.

"No, you first and check for bats."

"You go first. If there are bats up there they are in the dark back part of the cave. They won't bother you."

"You go first so I can see how it's done."

"Gabby," he said a little bit exasperated. "Are you really that afraid of the bats?"

"Afraid? No! Creeped out and heebie jeebied maybe, but not afraid."

"What's the difference?"

"It's a matter of degrees," I said matter of factly. "I am afraid of things that could kill me. I'm creeped out by things that can't hurt me."

"Okay, wait down here and I'll see how difficult the climb is. If I think you will need help I'll climb back down and help you. If I think you can make it easily I'll go in and check for bats. Is that fair?"

"I guess."

I could see how the headlamp was better for rock climbing as I stood at the bottom of the rock trying to figure out how I was going to climb with my flashlight in hand. I finally stuffed it into my pocket so I could use both hands, but it stuck out awkwardly and I was afraid I'd lose it on the climb up. The climb didn't look too scary as I watched Twiggy scramble up the rock, but when it came to be my turn I looked for a way up the rock and it didn't seem to have any place to grab hold of it and it was too steep to just walk up.

"You okay down there?" Twiggy asked.

"I think so. You made it look so easy."

"It's not a difficult climb. Do you want me to come down and help you?"

"No," I said unwilling to admit defeat so quickly. "I'll figure it out."

I put my foot on the rock and it slid right off. Somehow I expected to be able to see little bumps and bulges that I could use to climb on but with the rock all wet everything looked the same to me. I wasn't very experienced at rock climbing but a little piece of my brain said rock climbing and rain did not mix. Some little word from Physics 101 came to mind: friction. You want friction when you climb rocks and it was a rather low friction day. I tried again and had a little bit better luck but I worried that I'd get half way up and then the rock would get worse.

Twiggy stuck his head out of the cave entrance.

"You need hiking boots. If you had them you would be up here already."

"Why?"

"They've got more traction than a Jeep tire."

"I'll start saving my pennies," I said. "In the mean time I keep trying to slide off this rock and I don't want to land in that bush down there. It looks prickly."

"Give me your hand," he said.

"I can't reach."

"It's not much farther. Two more steps, then reach up."

"I don't want to make you fall."

"Don't worry. The bats have hold of my leg."

"If the bats really have hold of your leg I'm not going in the cave."

"I was just kidding. They are just hanging upside down napping the day away."

"Really?"

"Actually, I haven't looked. I thought you'd want to explore the cave with me."

"I tell you what, I'll keep climbing and you read the logs and see if people complained about bats."

"Okay. If you need a hand just yell... before you fall."

He sat in the cave opening where he could spring to my aid if I needed it and he clicked through the menus until he found the logs from the previous finders.

"'What a great adventure for the kids. They had never seen a bat cave before. Had to leave the missus outside because there was no room in the cave for a dad, two kids and mom. Or maybe she planned it that way. The kids had a ball.' No mention of bats."

"I say the mom stayed out because she was scared of the bats," I said.

"It doesn't say that. Let's see... 'CacheCzar and I found this one. Easy hike and climb but you need a flashlight.' That doesn't help much." Then, "'Oh my goodness you never saw a geocacher move so fast! First of all I'm a bit claustrophobic. Add the bats and... well... our group found the cache but the courageous Geo Eagle Scout was the brave signer of the log.'"

"So somebody did find bats," I said.

"Yeah, but that was months ago. This one is not found often."

"What does the most recent one say?"

"TFTC."

"Like that tells us anything."

I hooked a hand over the rock beside Twiggy and held on while I found a foothold.

"There you are!" he said brightly. "Give me your hand."

"I think it's better if I figure this out myself," I said. "Scoot over so I have room to work."

He scooted further into the cave and I dragged myself over the ledge.

"I told you you could do it," he said.

"You're right, though, I do need shoes with better tread," I said as I gazed past him into the cave beyond. "That's a bat cave? It looks like a big hole in the rock to me."

"What do you think a cave is?" he asked.

"It doesn't look too scary. And it's dry. Let's go look!"

I crawled past him and tried to stand up. The cave was too low for standing but it was high enough to walk down if I crouched low.

"Do you want me to go first... in case of bats?" Twiggy said.

I examined the ceiling of the cave. No bats.

"I think they're gone," I said. "I don't see any signs of bats."

"Okay, just remember they'll be in the dark part of the cave."

I pulled the flashlight out of my pocket and turned it on even though the cave still had plenty of light. I wanted to see those bats before they saw me.

"Look out, dragons," Twiggy said. "She's got a flashlight and she knows how to use it!"

We crept down the tunnel careful not to hit our head on the rocks. The light faded quickly, until blackness surrounded us. I looked behind me to make sure the light was still there, even though we hadn't gone far. The light from Twiggy's headlamp shined over my head and made the ceiling come alive with gold glitter.

"It is a dragon cave!" I said. "Look!"

"Gold. But not enough of it to make hauling it out worthwhile."

"You mean this is a mine? Not a cave?" I asked.

"Could be."

"Who would dig a mine way up here?" I asked.

"Someone who wanted to get rich? It's got to be a mine. If it's a cave it sure is straight. Besides, you never know what kind of a structure they might have built at the entrance. It could have fallen down and been hauled away years ago."

"For a mine, it sure is small. Maybe this is a dwarf's mine. Don't dwarves mine for diamonds?"

"Only in fantasy worlds," Twiggy answered.

"Oh. Dragons collect diamonds, too," I said.

"Only in fantasy worlds."

"Maybe this is the gateway to a fantasy world."

"And maybe it's a mine full of bats with a plastic peanut butter jar under a rock."

"I haven't seen a bat yet. What do bats look like when they are napping in the dark?"

"I don't know. I've only seen them flying around at night."

Every little nook and cranny of the mine jumped out at me in the light of my flashlight beam and the gold in the walls shimmered and twinkled like a million tiny gold stars on a rough background of rugged rock. A shadow crossed the twinkling of the gold flecks and I jumped, thinking a moving bat had created the shadow.

"The cache isn't going to be on the roof," Twiggy reminded me.

"But the bats will be," I reminded him.

A dark, hollow spot appeared overhead and I stopped to shine the light up inside.

"What is it?" Twiggy asked.

"Just a hole."

"Is the cache up there? That would be sneaky."

"I don't see it."

"You probably wouldn't. If a cache owner is smart they put a cache out of sight, or disguise it really, really well."

"It's not a large hole, but if a bat came along just now I might try to chimney climb it," I admitted.

He laughed, "I'd like to see you try."

The hole was less than a foot wide so I had to admit it would be funny to see me try.

"Stick your hand up there and feel around. You have to get used to touching things if you're going to get into geocaching."

I shined my flashlight up into the hole and it seemed safe so I stuck my hand up there and felt...

"Whoa! Whoa Gabby! Take it easy!" Twiggy said as I thrashed around shaking my hand and attempting to get past him to exit the tunnel. "What happened?"

"Is it on me? Is it on me?" I asked.

"What? All I know is you stuck your hand up into the hole and turned into an Olympic gymnast. How did you do a pirouette without even standing up?"

"Spiderwebs!" I exclaimed.

He laughed and stuck his own hand up there.

"Why are there spider webs?" I asked. "Bats eat insects!"

"It's not up there," he declared. "Spider webs are everywhere. You might consider getting used to them."

"It's not the webs I worry about. Spiders use them to catch their food. I don't want to meet any hungry spiders or their leftovers."

"We'll add a stick to our pack. You use it to clear away spiderwebs. Okay?"

"Okay. The cache must be that way," I said pointing down the tunnel.

The geocache turned out to be a gold ammunition box sitting where there used to be a pile of rocks. It looked like the rocks had slid off over time because they surrounded the box except for one flat rock that was underneath it. Twiggy sat on the ground beside the box, reached over and picked it up.

"Oh, look! A nest!" I said. "How cute!"

The nest consisted of a few twigs, fluffy fiber from plants and a little stuffing that looked like it came from a pillow. Leaves were caught in the stuffing but all in all it looked like a comfortable home for... something. Twiggy passed the box to me, but a movement near my head distracted me.

"What was that?" I asked.

"I don't know. You're closer to it. What is it?"

"I don't know. Hey, there's another one! On the ceiling. Is it bats?" I wondered aloud as I stooped lower. It wasn't bats. It was something so quick and light-footed that it could run right up the walls and ceiling of the cave. I shined my flashlight on one. It was tan with white under parts and big beady eyes. "It's cute!" I exclaimed. "It's…"

"Mice," Twiggy added.

"Mice?"

"Yeah. And this must be their nest. Why would they build a nest under a cache?"

"Because it's sheltered?"

The heebie jeebies were starting to creep in. I was in a cave full of… mice!

"Open the cache," I said. "Let's get out of here."

He opened the cache and handed me the log book. There was another movement above and one on the floor of the cave. Mice! I was surrounded by little micelings! I couldn't hold the flashlight and find a page of the logbook at the same time.

"I need light right here," I said.

Twiggy stood up so he could help with the light and when he did there were little scurrying movements everywhere. I felt something on my leg. On my leg!

"Oooooooohhh! Here! One's up my pants leg! Sign it! Sign it!" I screeched. I don't know how I got past him, but I was standing on the ledge outside the cave half naked, and shaking out my pants before I could even stop to figure out the logistics of it. "You stupid mouse! Where are you?" I cried as I shook my pants some more. The mouse had claws. It was probably inside my pants leg holding on for dear life. How could I know it was gone? To turn them inside out I had to put my arm down the leg hole. If I did that it might bite me! But I didn't want to squeeze the pants either. What if I squished a mouse in there? I didn't want to hurt it. I just didn't want to be anywhere near it.

There was a flash inside the tunnel. Then Twiggy's headlamp moved around as he made his way out of the cave.

"You have thighs!" he said. "I took a picture of the cache and the end of the tunnel to see if we could find any mice in the picture."

"Oh good," I said. "Just what we want. Evidence proving I don't want to go in any more caves."

"Oh, come on, Gabby, wasn't that cool?"

"This is cool," I said. "In fact it is freezing! Standing out here in the rain with no pants on wondering where the crazy rat is."

"Mice and rats are not the same thing."

"Just tell me it's gone so I can get dressed!"

"It's gone," he said without even glancing at my pants. "But you don't have to get dressed if you don't want to. We can go find one of those clothing optional caches."

"They have those?"

"Well... I haven't personally found one, but I've heard they exist."

I slid my hand down the pants leg gently squeezing as I went. I didn't feel any little bulges in the fabric.

"I think they are safe to put on again," I decided.

"Rats, I kind of liked it better the other way."

"Maybe they should call this minor mice, since they have a minor mouse problem, or miner mice, or minor miner mice. I didn't see any baby mice. Those would be minor miner mice," I said.

"I was hoping to see bats, though you made the mice almost as entertaining as the bats would have been."

I put on my pants and we slid down the rock to the van. We had to shove the bumper out of the way to have space to sit and plan our next move.

"There's no way we can find all the caches on this road today," Twiggy said.

"We can pick and choose and find a place to stay in Dickens. Avoid anything that sounds like there might be mice or bats, just for today. I might get used to the idea... eventually."

"Personally, I think we should be avoiding bears and gunmen but if it's mice and bats you want to avoid, then, well, I guess we can. Here's one that sounds safe. It's called A Dime A Dozen."

"Dimes are pretty safe," I had to admit.

He clicked to the logs and read a little just to make sure.

"Hmm, it takes people a long time but it's easy to find. I don't get it."

"Oh, those easy, time consuming ones are a dime a dozen," I said.

A Dime A Dozen was easy to find. It was a five gallon bucket. We opened it and inside it was filled to the brim with film canisters. We opened up a film canister and happily pulled out a piece of paper thinking we would sign the log and be on our way quickly. However, the paper that we pulled out had a picture of a dime on it and a note that said, "This isn't the log, keep looking." After we had opened several film canisters we decided to settle in for the long haul. Soon we were surrounded by film canisters with little notes in them.

"It's probably in the bottom corner of the bucket," Twiggy said and reached for the bottom, however when he did, he upset all the canisters on top and so the contents were even more mixed up than they had been. Some of the film canisters had little pieces of swag in them, but I couldn't trade because our key chains didn't fit into a canister.

"With my luck it'll be in the last one, no matter what order we open them in," Twiggy said. "It's like the Murphy's law of geocaching."

It wasn't in the very last canister. When we finally found the one with the log, there were about five left rattling around in the bottom of the bucket. We opened those, too, just to see if there was swag in them. One of them held a domino but the rest only had the dimes in them.

"Well, you have to admit it lived up to its name," I said. "The dimes were not dangerous and there were dozens of them."

We really wanted to find all the caches just because we couldn't imagine what some of them might consist of. What kind of a geocache would Knee Jerk Reaction be? We had to find out.

"So what's your first impression of this cache just by the title?" I asked.

"Har, har," he said. "I'm as baffled by it as you are."

"What do the logs say?"

"Hmm, they aren't supposed to post spoilers but let's see… 'Good one, the kids had a blast.' That doesn't help much."

"Well, at least it sounds fun."

He read another, "'How do you come up with these things? I'll have to remember this so I can build one.'"

"Well, it's not a five gallon bucket."

"The hint says 'too obvious for a hint.'"

Indeed it was. The cache turned out to be a tube anchored to a post. The bottom of the tube had a rounded spring-loaded thing poking out the bottom.

"Oh! I get it!" Twiggy said. He hit the rounded object on the spring with his knee and a cache popped out the top. "Cool!" he dropped the cache into the tube and tried it with his hand. He was worse than those kids had been. He tried kicking it. Any upward motion would propel the cache out of the tube. I finally had to catch it before he could so I could sign the log while he played with the cache some more.

"You're going to wear it out!" I told him.

"Did I tell you I played soccer in high school?"

"I would have guessed after seeing you at this cache."

"I bet I can get the cache out by using my head," he said.

"If you'd use your head you could just reach in and grab it," I said.

"You're no fun. Come on, try it!"

"Okay, hold on. Here's the log. I'll bop the cache out so we can put the log back in the container."

I brought my knee up and missed the tube. I tried again.

"Harder," he said when the first attempt failed. "Just… *bam!* Knock it out of there!"

"Okay."

Bam!

"Harder!"

"You have so much fun doing it. Why don't you?"

Bam! Out popped the cache. He caught it in midair.

"I'm going to log the same thing that dad did," I said. "The kid had a blast with this one."

I opened the cache and dropped the log in.

Twiggy wouldn't tell me the name of the next one. I suspected it had bats or mice in the title, though I couldn't think of another idiom that had bats or mice in it.

"Come on, I have to know what the name of it is to log it," I complained.

"It's a surprise."

"They all are even if I know the title."

"We're going to have to walk a little ways, but I expect this one to be the last one of the day."

"Darn."

"I'm getting hungry and we still have to find this town we were told was around here somewhere."

"Dickens."

"I'm having a dickens of a time remembering it."

"Just remember we need to go see Charlie in Dickens."

"You're kidding, right?"

"No. Why would I joke about that?"

Twiggy parked at a pullout a few miles down the road.

"This one's yours," he said as he handed me the GPS.

"Mine? Why mine?"

""Because you need to learn to poke around until you overcome your squeamishness."

"Squeamishness? Me?"

"Yes, you. Plus I don't think I can do this one. We'll see when we find ground zero."

I didn't like the sound of that.

"What am I not supposed to be squeamish about?" I asked squeamishly.

"Be watching for a stick," he said.

"Ewwwweeee spiders!" I said. "Why do I have to do this one? You know I hate spiders. And bats. And mice. And anything you have to fend off with a stick."

"I won't let you do anything dangerous," he said.

"Dangerous is a relative term. Anything that results in extreme squeamishness might be deemed dangerous in the right setting. What if I had run out of the cave and off the side of the hill, just from sheer squeamishness? Then it would have been dangerous."

"How are we doing?" he asked as we tromped through the woods.

"About a hundred feet to our left," I said.

It was early summer and last fall's dry leaves were still on the ground and crunched and rustled as we walked. It reminded me of fall in Franklinburg. I was the student who shuffled her feet through the leaves and stomped on particularly crunchy looking ones. I thought fall was the best time of year, not yet bone chillingly cold, but not too hot either. The colors and the holidays coming up blended to make fall the perfect time to dash through falling leaves and add pumpkin flavoring to my coffee and dig around in the closet for cushy scarves and fuzzy socks. The forest here was like campus without the sidewalks and chill.

"What are you doing?" Twiggy asked.

"Crunching leaves! They should offer a degree in leaf crunching."

"And what kind of a career could you build from a leaf crunching degree?" he asked.

"Unlandscaping!" I said. "Just give me all your leaves and I'll gladly take them off your landscaping… for a nominal fee."

"Anybody with kids would not hire you. That's what kids are for."

"Do you see any likely hiding places?"

"Yeah, I think I see it."

"From here? We're still thirty feet away."

"Well, judging by the title and what I see I think that's it," he said pointing to a large hollow log. "Did you find a stick?"

"It's in there?" I asked.

"Just my guess."

"If it's in there it's got to be by the opening."

"Let's check. But I don't think so."

"Why?" I clicked back to the description. "Not Enough Space to Swing a Cat. Down the rabbit hole you go. Can you swing a cat in here? Is it alive or dead? Only one way to find out!" It was rated a large cache, yet it was hidden in a small place. A cat? I had to agree with Twiggy that the log was the logical hiding spot, and not at the open end of it either. I began looking for a stick.

"Hello, hello, hello, hello," Twiggy said into the log like an echo.

"Can you fit?" I asked hopefully.

"I don't know."

"I think you're skinnier than me," I said.

"It's the shoulders," he said straightening up and puffing out his chest.

"It's the boobs," I said standing up and... not puffing out my chest. "It has to be big enough for an average sized person to go in. What if a big geocacher hiked all the way in here and then couldn't reach the cache?"

"That's why it's a four," he said. "They don't have varying difficulties so they have to rate it for anybody. So us skinny people get a free four while fat people get a difficult four."

I snatched a stick out of the leaves and crunched over.

"So that means you should be able to go in there just fine," I pointed out.

We stood there in a little stare down. I gazed into the log. There were probably termites in there. Spiders. Grubs. Squirrels. Mice. Splinters. Okay, I told myself, now you're just making excuses.

"Flashlight?" I asked.

He took off the pack and pulled out the headlamp.

"Oh goodie, the geek label," I said.

He stretched it and fit it around my head and smoothed down my hair so I wouldn't get headlamp hair.

"Our intrepid explorer!" he said in a low, booming, intrepid voice. "Find yonder cache, my brave young soul!"

"Maybe there's a baby dragon in there," I said hopefully.

It wasn't hard to find the cache. I used the stick to swat at a few spider webs and did my best to not look for the spiders. There was a lot of rotten wood on the floor of the log and lots of bugs climbing the walls of it. The beam of the headlamp fell on a plain plywood box. There was no lock on the top. The lid was hinged, but just sat on top of the box. The title was right. There was no space to swing a cat.

"Did you find it?" yelled Twiggy.

"Yeah! Found it!" I said as I army crawled closer.

"Can you pass it to me?" he asked.

"I... don't know... hold on." I crawled closer. I could barely lie beside the box and had to do a bit of wriggling to get my arms where they could push the lid up. The box didn't even budge when I tipped the lid so I lowered it again and gave the whole box a push. It didn't move. "No, I can't pass the cache to you. It's anchored somehow!" I opened the lid again and felt inside. I felt something irregularly shaped and plastic. I wriggled past the cache and maneuvered slowly and clumsily until I could look over the edge of the box. It was a cat. A plastic lawn ornament sort of cat. It just sat in the box. I kind of felt sorry for it, locked in a box in a log and only visited by skinny geocachers. Beside the cat was a little metal box which was easily removed. I grabbed the small box and backed out of the log.

"Well?" Twiggy said when I was back in the daylight again.

"Yup, it's in there. And there's no space to swing a cat, that's for sure."

"And?"

"You have to go see for yourself. But first, let's sign the log."

"The log? Or the log?" he asked.

I produced the little metal box.

"Oh, the log."

"But you have to put it back," I told him. "I scared away all the spiders for you. Plus you have to see where I got the log from."

We opened the little box, which I would eventually begin calling an Altoids tin, and I pulled out the log sheet. I signed the log, replaced the log sheet, closed the box and handed it to Twiggy. "Your turn."

He squatted down and looked uncertainly into the log.

"Will I fit?"

"Yeah, though you'll have to army crawl. Just crawl past the box, curl yourself around a bit and lift the lid."

"Why is there a box, if this was back there?"

"That you have to see for yourself," I said as I handed him the headlamp.

He crawled into the hole and he began chuckling about half way down the log. When he got to the end he burst out laughing. "Schrödinger's Cat!! HA, ha, ha, ha... ha! That's a good one! Ha, ha ha... favorite point for sure! Now I get the alive or dead part. My log is only going to have one word: inanimate."

"You can't. That would give it away."

When we got back to the van and Twiggy was about to open the door I asked him, "So, there's a bumper in there. Is it alive or dead?"

"It's dead," he said.

"So, to Dickens," I said. "A new bumper, dinner and a shower."

"Righto."

Chapter 18

We followed the dirt road through the hills lamenting all the funny caches we had to pass up. When the road hit pavement again there was no sign pointing to a town.

"Left is the direction we're headed so left it is," Twiggy said. "Even if Dickens isn't down here we'll come to a town eventually."

When we did reach a town it wasn't very clear where we were. This was not the main road into town. So first we saw a few farms, then a few houses. The road became less rural and the houses more numerous until the road ended at a busier road. Twiggy shrugged and turned right because there were businesses within view. He pulled into the lot of a mom and pop grocery store.

"Let's find out where we are," he said.

"And load up on junk food."

I snatched a package of Ding Dongs off the rack. I was tempted to grab three but I thought one package might beat down my gooey whipped cream craving. There was a balance of calories to deprivation. Sometimes the calories were worth it. Iced coffee! Oooo… cheesy party mix!

"Dinner," Twiggy reminded me.

"Maybe if I eat these I'll survive until dinner."

"Pizza?"

"I guess I could eat pizza."

"The checker's name is Kathy. Her sister, Casey, has a pizza place downtown. And her uncle Wilbur owns the motel three blocks from the pizza place."

"Her last name isn't Dickens is it?" I asked.

"No, she's married."

"Are we in Dickens?"

"No, Dickens was the other direction. This is Sutherly."

"Is it south of northerly?" I asked.

"Yes. Are you going to eat all those by yourself?"

"No, I'll share. Except for these. These are to soothe my gooey whipped cream craving."

At dinner we had the normal topping discussion. Twiggy is of the opinion that pizza with pineapple is not real pizza, while I like pizza of the Hawaiian variety.

"A pizza chock full of meat is not a pizza," I usually add. "All you can taste is sausage. A real pizza is a blend of flavors. You should be able to taste crust, sauce, cheese and the topping you are currently eating."

"I'll agree with that. But tasting ingredients is a matter of degrees. A meat pizza is thirty percent crust, four percent sauce, ten percent cheese and the rest is toppings so it is supposed to taste like meat."

Twiggy and I usually don't share a pizza unless we are in a mom and pop place and I can ask them to put my share of the meat on his side of the pizza and only put ham and pineapple on my side, but in that case we really aren't sharing a pizza at all, just a crust. This was one of those meals where the older people in the establishment thought Twiggy and I were the most unsocial couple they ever saw. But we had wifi and caches to log. And we would rather be logging caches than listening to the pizza argument.

I was just trying to figure out what to log for the Bats in My Belfry cache when Twiggy said, "Have you ever paddled a kayak?"

"No. Why?"

"Well, there's this one on an island in a lake."

"Wow, that sounds like fun. Is it hard to paddle a kayak?"

"No. Well, it takes a little stamina to paddle very far, but there's no hurry. Lots of people do what they call paddle caching. There will be a bunch of caches along a river and they find those just like we did the ones along the road."

"Where do we get kayaks?" I asked. "I can't afford to buy one."

"If a lake is big enough and allows boats you can sometimes rent kayaks."

"How much is that?"

"I don't know. The lake near my dad's house we just take a little motor boat along and putter out to our fishing spot. I haven't rented a kayak before."

"But you're thinking of trying it. I see that look in your eye."

"It's not the kayaking part that tempts me. I guess I'm just a sucker for a pirate themed cache on an island. Pirates are a popular theme in geocaching because people liken it to pirates and their buried treasure."

"You'd make a good pirate," I said. "Especially with the beard."

"Avast thar matey, would yer be willin' to go and seek yonder treasure with a por bloke like me?"

"We can look into it, if you can find the lake."

He just glared at me. I shot him a slightly irritated look and said, "We can search yonder island and plunder it if'n ye can attain a craft suitable to... pursue our... pursuits. Sorry, that's the best I can come up with. I wasn't raised in a pirate family."

The glance I got back said, "that's okay. At least you tried."

"The island be not our next destination," He said in a pirate voice. "We have other treasures to seek in our formidable journey."

"Oh? What's next?"

"I haven't yet decided, me bucco. I've some studyin' of the map to do firstest."

"Can you tell me that in English?"

"We won't do the lake one next. It's between here and Belle Fourche. And I don't know which one to go for next without a little research."

"And what is in Belle Fourche?" I asked.

"The event," he said.

I felt a bit disappointed that our drive was almost over. It was fun never knowing what we might find next. Every step of the trip so far had led me to new places and made me do things that I never thought I would do before, like paddle a kayak. What was it going to be like to be out on a lake in a small watercraft? I thought it would be spooky to be floating over very deep water. I imagined catfish lurking down where I couldn't see them.

When the waitress brought our pizza Twiggy asked her if there was a larger town nearby, one with shopping and cheap gas. It was getting to be time to do another load of laundry, fill up the van, fix the bumper and maybe even get a latte. That all sounded expensive to me, though I thought the latte was worth anything they wanted to charge for it. When he found out the name of this larger town it began a flurry of new internet searches.

"It's only seventeen miles away. I say we skip the mom and pop motel and drive to Washington."

"DC?"

"No, just Washington. There are probably lots of Washingtons around."

"True. Sounds like a good town to stop and do laundry."

"They probably have a nicer motel, too."

"Washing the clothes, washing the body, might was well wash the van while we are in Washington."

"Or at least get a bumper. I wonder if they have a junk yard there. Old van bumpers shouldn't be too hard to find."

The bumper issue became more important when we walked out of the pizza place and the local sheriff was writing us a ticket.

"Oh no! Please! Please don't give that to us. We just lost the bumper today and we're going to fix it tomorrow," I wailed. I couldn't help it. I just knew if we had to pay an expensive ticket it would be the end of our trip. "We have the bumper and the license plate in the van. All we need is directions to a place to have it fixed."

The officer looked down at me through reflective sunglasses. I couldn't see his eyes and I wondered if they wore that kind of sunglasses on purpose.

Twiggy put his arm around my shoulders and said, "Gabby, don't worry. I'll take care of this. Why don't you... go back inside and write a postcard to Sarah. You said you'd send her one."

I knew he was just trying to get rid of me so he could talk to the police officer without an emotional girl butting in, but he needed an emotional girl butting in. They wouldn't hesitate to write a ticket to a guy who ran over his own bumper with a tractor.

"You have the bumper?" the officer asked.

"Yes!"

"And the plates match front and back?"

"Yes!"

"License and registration."

"The van's not ours," I said. "We traded for the summer so we could..."

"Gabby, would you let me handle this."

The officer looked from me to Twiggy and back again.

"Where are you two from?"

"We're driving home from Franklinburg. We go to school there."

We got the glance back and forth again.

"And you're all right?" he asked me.

"Me? Yeah! Just pleaaaaase don't give us a ticket. We're already pinching pennies until they scream and we have to buy a new bumper and a ticket will ruin everything!"

"Gabby..."

"Open up the van."

Twiggy shot me an exasperated look and unlocked the van. He threw open the back doors. The officer looked inside at the zebra striped walls, the futon mattress and the crumpled bumper. He read the license plate and compared it to the number he had written down on his ticket pad.

"You're sure you're okay ma'am?" he asked.

"Yes, I know the van is a mess but it was like that when we traded. I know what it looks like but it's..."

"Get that bumper fixed," he said and snapped his ticket book shut.

"Oh, thank you! Thank you!" I exclaimed enthusiastically. "It's an ugly van but we'll get it fixed as soon as we can!"

"I've done crazier things than that," he said. "Just be careful out there."

"Well, I'm glad we didn't get the ticket but that cop wasn't very smart," Twiggy said. "We could have stolen the van. He should have checked us out more than that."

"Maybe he thinks nobody would willingly steal that van."

"Maybe you just have an honest face."

Chapter 19

"Bumpers? We got bumper to bumper bumpers. We got bumpers from '66 Caddies to 2013 Lamborghinis."

"Do they still make Lamborghinis?" I asked, but I only got a glare back.

"It's just a 1980 something Chevy van," Twiggy said.

"Metal bumper. They don't make 'em like they used to. How'd you bend up the old one without bashing up the van?"

"I... uh ripped it off with a tractor and then backed over it," Twiggy admitted.

"Not too bright."

"I'd never driven a tractor before."

"You're going to need more work than just buying a used bumper. Go see Charlie in Dickens."

"You don't have a shop in Washington that can do it?" Twiggy asked.

"Sure we do. But Charlie and me we go way back."

"Charlie seems to go way back with a lot of folks," I thought aloud.

"Here we go. Chevy bumper. Complete with bumper stickers. I won't charge you extra for the bumper stickers."

"Well, maybe we won't get mugged again," Twiggy said when he read: *Don't worry about the dog. Beware of owner,* and *Guarded by Smith and Wesson.* The other bumper sticker was a little ironic. It said: *Scrapaholic.* I thought the van had belonged to a couple, one a gun owner and the other a scrapbooker, but the scrapaholic bumper sticker really stood out in a scrap yard.

"When you see Charlie, tell 'im Mort sent you."

"Okay."

I walked around looking at all the old cars while Mort and Twiggy went into the office. There were cars in that junkyard I had never heard of before. It looked like people drove cars for a long time in Washington. Then when we left I couldn't help but watch the traffic wondering how old the cars on the road were. After a while I began watching for a car dealership, but I never saw one. Maybe the people who lived in Washington didn't buy a new car often because the nearest new car was in another town. Somehow that seemed unlikely, but I had yet to see a place to buy a new car.

"Charlie's place is probably closed," Twiggy said as he pulled into a small chain motel. Wow, we were going up in the motel world! I decided the

Free Wifi sign had drawn him in. "I think we should wash off some of this mud and get a good night's rest."

"A most excellent idea," I said.

"Then in the morning... uh... well, here's what I was thinking. I'm not asking you to do my work for me, but it would probably save some time if you could do laundry while I drive to Charlie's and take care of the van."

"Okay. I don't mind doing laundry. It's one hundred percent better than washing dishes. That was always my least favorite chore as a kid. I think even some of the supposedly clean clothes in the van might need washing. Besides, you don't sort. How are your clothes going to last if you don't sort?"

"You can stay at the room and do it while I get the van fixed."

"How am I going to do that? Handwash in the bathrub? I guess I've done that before when I ran out of quarters."

"No," he said as he pointed to a sign. One of the things listed was guest laundry services. That sounded expensive, but it turned out it just meant there was a little laundry room down the hall from our room. It was late by the time we rented a room and hauled the boxes in so I could sort. I took a quick shower and Twiggy fell asleep before I finished. I did a little laundry sorting before deciding Twiggy had the right idea so I slipped under the covers and turned off the light. He mumbled something, got up, changed clothes, crawled into bed and pulled up the covers.

"I wish I wasn't so tired," he said.

Another dangerous statement begging for a "Why?"

"Because," he said. "You look like an angel when you sleep. I like the smell of your hair and your carefree cheerfulness even when you're asleep. I like your eyelashes. But I can't keep my eyes open."

Chapter 20

I tried to maintain a carefree cheerfulness as I sorted laundry the next day. I woke up before Twiggy and as I sorted and waited for him to wake up, I thought: Why do I call him Twiggy? It's such a silly name and he isn't a silly man. He's warm and caring and handsome and rugged. A little outdoorsy. He likes boondocking and geocaching and wading in creeks and meat pizzas and saving the brown M&Ms for me and feeding that childish Travel Bug the blue ones. He rents a room when I want a shower even though he'd be content in the van... He doesn't even look like Ichabod Crane anymore. He looks like... Tony. He looks like a man finding his way and having a great time doing it. But he doesn't look like a Twiggy.

There wasn't a lot of sorting to do and when I finished it was still too early to start up a washing machine. If somebody rented the room next to the machine they wouldn't appreciate the noise coming through the wall early in the morning. I sat in the chair in the room, bored, then dug out a book. I sat sideways in the chair with my legs draped over the arm and read the first chapter but I couldn't shake the feeling that things were changing. I considered climbing back in bed and asking Twiggy if we could drop the nicknames but I worried about the response I would get in such an intimate setting. It was a simple question that could be misinterpreted if I asked him under the wrong conditions. So I decided to just try using his name to see what reaction I got.

Wow, I didn't know such a small change could make such a big difference.

"I have to drive to Dickens," Tony said at breakfast. "I think it's twenty miles. These mom and pop garages will usually do a small job on the spot but I don't really know how long it will take."

"Remember to tell Charlie he is very popular. I don't even remember who sent us to him anymore, but at least two people did. I'll try to get the laundry done while you're gone."

"Okay. If you get bored while the machines are running you can find a new cache to hunt for."

After breakfast he dropped me off at the motel. He walked up, let me into the room and I went to load up the laundry for the first load. Then I remembered he still had the laundry soap in the van. I dashed to the door and called to his retreating back, "Oh... Tony! I need the soap!"

You'd think the police were ordering him to freeze. He stopped. The change was more than significant in his mind. He turned and walked all the way back. If I had used the nickname I'm sure he would have said, "No problem, let's go get it." But he walked back and stood silently before me.

"What happened?" he asked.

"I don't know. I just… what are you talking about?"

"Why'd you switch to my first name?"

"I do that a lot," I lied.

"No, you don't. You took to the nickname and you've always called me Twiggy."

It was my chance to take him aside and have a heart to heart talk and tell him that my opinion of him was changing, but I couldn't. I chickened out. So I said, "I'll switch back if you want me to."

He thought for a moment, wrapped his arms around me and said into my ear, "You can call me anything you want. I'll go get the soap."

Then he walked a little taller and a little straighter as he walked back to the elevator.

When he came back with the soap he found me in the little laundry room loading two washing machines. I only sorted into piles of darks and whites, since we hadn't worn our permanent press very often on the geocaching trail. He stood in the doorway for a moment, then handed me the bottle of soap when I reached a stopping point.

"Thanks!"

"You've got a room key?"

"Yeah."

"Okay, I'll be back as soon as I can."

"Remember we have to be checked out by noon."

"Righto."

When he left I thought that if we only had an afternoon to geocache I better look locally for a new cache to hunt for. Maybe one on the way to the event would work. Maybe I could find one between here and the lake Tony had spotted in his research. We couldn't drive too far or we would use up our geocaching time. Geocaching seemed to be a delicate balance between miles and fun. Do too much geocaching and you never reached your destination. Put in the miles and you pass up some fun caches. Planning was the key.

I was glad Tony and I both had our school computers because it wasn't wise to leave washing machines running by themselves. They could get off balance and cause a ruckus, or somebody could slip in and steal your whole wardrobe. So I went to the room and retrieved my laptop and took it to the little laundry room. The room only contained two washing machines, two dryers, a wooden bench and a plastic chair. The dryer had a metal hook on the side for hanging permanent press but there was no folding table or soap dispensing machines like at the Laundromat. I tried using the laptop while sitting on the bench. It was uncomfortable so I tried scooting it out from the wall so I could sit cross legged on it, but it was bolted to the floor. The plastic chair was little better, so I ended up sitting cross legged on the floor. When I finally got settled in a position I could work in I found that having so many machines in the room disrupted my wifi signal, so I ended up back in the room again. This necessitated frequent trips to the laundry room to check the progress of the machines.

"All right. First step. Where are we and where is the lake?" I said to myself. I found a little notepad on the dresser and the address of the motel was printed on the sheets so I punched that address into the search field. I found out that the motel was on the outskirts of Washington and the town wasn't very big, even though it was considered the larger nearby town and the one people drove to for shopping. I zoomed out from the town and watched for a lake. There were a lot of lakes around but the map didn't help me find the one Tony had been looking at. I refined my search to geocaches west of Washington. It was tedious clicking each cache, reading the 1.5/1.5 rating and ruling it out, then going on to the next cache. Next I tried searching for the next town, inputting the name of it into the search field and then looking for the ones with the most favorite points. This worked better, though I had to run down the hall to the laundry room before I let myself get too wrapped up in my searching.

I tried to find geocaches that were away from towns. I was beginning to get a little too wary of my geocaching activities being seen as suspicious in nature. I wasn't sure why looking for a plastic container was a bad thing, but we'd met up with the police and been misinterpreted enough times that it was best to just avoid geocaching in public places. However, a cache caught my attention and wouldn't let it go. It had sixty-two favorite points. The down side was it was at a mall. The good thing about it was the terrain was rated a two but the difficulty was a four. How could a cache at a mall be rated a two? I thought anyplace at a mall would be wheelchair accessible making it a one. I read the description and the terrain rating became clearer. Ahhh, it wasn't *at* the mall. It was under it! Under the mall? This was sounding more and more like something from a movie. What did the underside of a mall look like? How would one even reach ground zero or know when they were near the cache? I went back and finished reading the description. We were supposed to park at the outer part of the mall parking lot and follow a sidewalk to "the opening in the earth". Then, with flashlight in hand, we were to walk a hundred and five paces from the opening. A hundred and five? That seemed a strange number. There was no way the number could really be true. I assumed that they averaged the stride of a normal adult. But what if you had a long stride like Tony or a short stride like me? Well, no matter, we only had the hundred and five paces to go by so that's what we would use. I read the logs.

"Wow, creepy, but fun. Never did this kind of cache before. TFTH."

"DNF."

"This was so cool! Me and the geodog did it and the dog got totally soaked. Luckily he's a lab and loves the water. He isn't allowed in the mall but nobody said he couldn't go under it. TFTC."

"Wear waders, had fun with this one. Recommend doing it in the summer. It's freezing in the winter. TFTC."

That last log prompted me to look for shorts. I usually had a couple of pairs at school in case I got ambitious and went to the gym. I also searched for my oldest shoes. If they were going to get soaked I wanted to soak the worst pair I had.

When Tony returned I was folding the last of the laundry and I was dressed in shorts and tennis shoes.

"Whoa! You have thighs!" He said.

"You already knew that from Miner Mice, and I suggest you wear shorts, too."

"No problem," he answered though he didn't take his eyes off my white legs.

"I know. Blinding, aren't they? But I've got a reason for wearing shorts."

Tony frequently wore shorts at school. He usually wore cargo shorts with an old rock and roll t-shirt and sandals. Franklinburg didn't have a lot of warm, sunny days until close to the end of the school year. But that didn't stop Tony from wearing shorts to class. It was possible that Tony had never seen me in shorts before. The few times I had gone to the gym were due to dessert binges with him the night before. So he saw me in pants and then I went to the gym to work off my guilt trip when he was in class the next day.

"I don't really recommend geocaching in shorts. You need protection from thorny plants and poison ivy."

"There won't be any thorny plants or poison ivy where we're going."

"Oh, really? And where are we going?"

"We're following the map on the GPS until we get to a way point and then we're following the directions in the description to find a two/four cache in another town."

"You must be pretty set on this one to wear shorts and be all ready for it."

"We'll need two working flashlights, a pen, but no swag."

"Wow, I'm impressed. You're even talking like a real geocacher."

"It's contagious," I said.

"So… do you have any further information?" he asked.

"No, you'll have to trust me on this one."

One eyebrow went up.

"And wear shoes that can get wet," I added.

He wanted to ask me more about what we were doing but he kind of enjoyed me taking the initiative and risk involved in surprising him in his predominately male hobby. So far I hadn't met any women who were geocachers so I assumed more men were into outdoor pursuits.

"I got the van fixed, though that doesn't help us get an updated registration sticker on it."

"Oh."

"Oh what?"

"Maybe we shouldn't go find this cache then," I said.

"Why?"

"It's in a town and a spot that is likely to be patrolled."

"And we're going to get wet at this highly patrolled place?"

"Possibly."

"What kind of a place is this?"

"A surprise with sixty-two favorite points."

"And it's a log only."

"Yeah."

"This doesn't sound like a cache you would choose."

"I can't help it. I am too curious."

"Well… okay. I'm willing to risk it if you are. Maybe we can park outside the highly patrolled zone. It'll probably increase the walking we do, but we started out this trip walking more than we needed to."

"Really?"

"I'll follow you anywhere you'll wear those," he said.

"Just a little more folding and packing and I'll be ready. Your shorts should be in that box," I said indicating a box that obviously contained only his clothes.

He searched in the box for his shorts. "You even fold these?" he asked as he held up a pair of shorts.

"Yes!"

"I suppose you fold underwear, too," he joked.

"Just in half."

"You're sure you want to go find a muggly, wet one?" he asked. "What's this one called?"

"I can't tell you. That would give it away." Actually the name of the cache was Journey to the Center of the Mall.

"A local swimming hole?"

"No."

"A fountain in a park?"

"No."

"What would be wet and muggly at the same time?"

"I didn't say the place was muggly. Just the place we'll be parking is muggly."

That had him even more puzzled.

"Can I take any of these boxes back out to the van?" he asked after he had changed clothes.

"Give me two minutes," I said. "You can pack up your toiletries while I am folding. I didn't know where you kept them."

"In a box? I only have one box."

"But there are multiple areas of that box. You need to be able to find it."

He went into the bathroom and came back out with his shaver and toothbrush and dropped them in his box. I folded the last shirt and then placed the piles carefully into our boxes.

"Okay, they can go out now."

He grabbed his box. I grabbed mine, and we took them to the van. A quick trip to the office to make sure they knew we were checked out by noon and we were ready to hit the road again.

"Where are we off to on this mysterious geocache hunt?" he asked.

"Shafter," I answered.

"Hmm, I don't believe I remember a town named Shafter on the highway between Belle Fourche and Franklinburg."

"Right. Well, just follow my directions," I said.

"I wish this map on the GPS would show us more roads. Right now it shows us driving in the middle of nowhere."

"When we get closer it'll show the highway. The surface streets will click in about a mile from the cache."

"You have to know where you're going before you get there?"

"Roughly."

"Okay. Hopefully it will tell me more as we go along."

"How far away is it?"

"Seventeen miles."

"Okay. On this highway?"

"We might be watching for an exit."

He wasn't sure he should trust this geocacher newbie he was traveling with, but he was glad to see me trying, so he kept driving. Part of the fun of geocaching was that even we if got lost we could find a geocache wherever we were. I was beginning to think that, unless you were in the middle of a big lake or a military installation that there would be a cache within a mile of wherever you were. I kind of doubted there would be many suspicious looking containers on, say, an Army base.

"By the way, Gabby, it doesn't matter to me and it probably is used more often than the proper term for convenience sake, but the GPS is really a GPSr."

"O... kay."

"It's a receiver, that's why they add the R."

"I thought it was a system and that's why they use an S."

"Like I said, the common term is GPS but you might run into a few picky geocachers who will insist it's a GPSr."

"Well, I wish this GPS would *receive* some more roads. The map makes it look like the town is south west of us but the highway keeps going west."

"Don't worry. We'll watch for exits and I bet the next road pops in just in time. How far off the highway is it?" he asked.

"Well, the line to the cache is about three times longer than the line from this highway to the town."

"Ah, so five miles?"

"Yeah, roughly."

"As the crow flies."

"No, as the hawk soars."

"Not the dragon?"

"Hmm, no, I think distances are shrunk for dragons. They seem to get everywhere quicker than normal creatures."

"So, are we going to another dragon house?"

"No, at least I don't think so. I doubt they would allow one to live where we are going."

"Oooo, so mysterious."

"Hey, even I don't know exactly what to expect."

Five minutes later a junction sign appeared and between the junction sign and the turnoff the new road appeared on the GPS screen.

"Yes!" I said triumphantly. "Take this exit and head south."

We could tell the town had a sizeable population when we could see a downtown area jutting up from the rest of the city. To me this booming mecca meant shopping, though I was definitely not dressed for shopping anywhere. My mother wouldn't even allow me to go to the mall dressed in shorts. She would say it was immodest. But I wasn't going to shop at the mall.

The mall we were going to was not the big downtown mall. I was grateful for that because the downtown area looked like a bustling metropolis.

"Gwen, I think you've gone off the deep end," Tony said. "You're only going to find LPCs and magnetic nanos in a place like this."

"No we won't! We need to be on the east side of the mall. Watch for a little park. The parking lot butts right up to the edge of a park."

"And the cache is at the park?"

"No, but we need to begin walking close to there. Do you think we'll get a ticket if we park at the mall?"

"It's very likely."

"Shoot. We can't afford a ticket. Especially an out of state ticket. Hey, I have an idea. Where's a notebook?"

"Why?"

"Oh shoot, I think all the notebooks are in storage. Well, any piece of paper will do."

I looked in the glove compartment and there were a lot of miscellaneous papers in there so I pulled one out, tore off the blank bottom of it and began writing, "Dear Mister Officer, sir, we know our registration is expired. The sticker is at home and we are just trying to get home from college without a ticket so we can put it on the license plate." I wrote it in flowery script so it would look like a naïve girl wrote it. Then I showed it to Tony.

"It'll never work. You'd just be drawing attention to the date on the sticker."

"But they'll give us a break, you'll see. They aren't really mean. They just have to do their job."

"Every ticket they write is money in the city's bank account. It pays their wages. They have to write tickets to get paid."

"Not to everybody they see."

"Well, we'll compromise. We'll put the note on the windshield and when he goes to put the ticket there he will see it. Then it won't draw attention to our sticker, but if they stop they will still read it. Where are we supposed to park?"

"Waaaaay on the east side."

"And where are we now?"

"On the north side."

He drove around the outside of the mall which necessitated a lot of steering wheel cranking and stopping and waiting for other cars. Most of the shoppers seemed to prefer parking on the north side of mall. So the east side of the mall had plenty of parking spaces. I wasn't sure it would the day after Thanksgiving but right now the east side of the mall was relatively quiet.

I watched the GPS screen.

"Turn right and go down to where that tree is," I instructed.

He parked and glanced over at me.

"Okay, now what?"

"Now we make sure we have flashlights and a pen."

"No worries. I stuck mine in my pockets before we left."

"Okay, well, let me find my flashlight. I need one that fits in my pocket."

"Like this?" he said as he pulled out the headlamp.

"Let's hide them as long as we can. We have some walking to do. This is just the first waypoint."

"Whooooaaa, waypoints. You're learning. How many waypoints are there?"

"Only one more. Then we have to follow directions because we can't use our GPS."

"But geocaching is a GPS based game."

"Okay, well, you're welcome to try once we pass the next waypoint."

"Lead the way my intrepid mall explorer."

"I'm not sure you should use that word. What happened last time you used it?"

"I don't remember."

I stopped on the sidewalk to see which direction the GPS said to go, but then there was only one way to go and that was to follow the sidewalk. I think I must have been walking like a duck because Twiggy was laughing at me and following at a distance. The sidewalk ended and I had to cross the street. There was a lot of traffic on the street but there was a stop light at the entrance to the mall. Across the street was the park. I crossed the street and followed the sidewalk on the other side. Then that sidewalk ended too, so I entered the park looking for a way around the fence. When the fence ended the ground sloped into a big cement drainage ditch. It was still grassy like the park, but I knew when I saw what stood at the end of the ditch that this was the opening I was looking for. I stopped and let Tony catch up.

"Whoaaaa," he said. "We're going in there?"

"See for yourself."

I handed him the GPS and it said to go sixty feet straight toward the opening.

"Coooool!"

"Don't hurry. Once we get to the opening we have to count our paces."

"How many?" he asked eagerly.

"A hundred and five. But I suggest we stop at a hundred and see if there's any beacons."

He strode forth singing, "Yo ho, yo ho, off we go playing pirate games all daaay. Treasures to seek. Underground…" he stopped and said, "I never was very good at making up songs on the fly."

We stopped at the cement.

"A hundred paces," I said hoping I didn't sound uncertain.

We both stepped onto the cement.

"One Mississippi, two Mississippi," he said.

"What are you doing? It'll take forever if you count like that."

"I was told to go slow and savor the moment."

"We're in a drainage ditch. This is a sewer system."

"It's an adventure. What's this one called?"

I thought the name would contribute to his sense of adventure so I told him, "Journey to the Center of the Mall."

He resumed counting, "twenty one, twenty two…"

"Oooh, here's the water," I said. "You did wear shoes that could get wet, right?"

"Righto, madam."

"Oh my gosh, there's things in the water!" I lifted my feet higher. "What are they?"

They were light colored, like they never saw the light of day. I began wading toward the dry part of the tunnel.

"I think they're crawdads," he said. "Good bait."

"Do they bite?"

"Through shoes? No. They might pinch a finger. Let's see."

He wiggled his fingers under the water but none of the crawdads would come near, so I felt a little safer.

"Oh shoot, I lost count."

"Me, too."

"Well, let's continue on. We can always go back and count again. We should see something at the hundred pace point. It doesn't *smell* like a sewer system."

"There are two sewer systems. The bad stuff usually has its own drainage system. If people could walk around in the bad stuff they would fence it off a lot better than this."

"So this is just water?"

"Yep. At least the crawdads think so."

It didn't take long to need the flashlights. We turned around frequently trying to guess when we had walked a hundred paces. I figured a hundred paces was more than two hundred feet.

"What do you think?" he asked.

"Just ahead."

There was a sound of rushing water and off to the side was a pipe large enough to crawl though. Water was pouring out of it and flowing into the tunnel we were walking through.

"This might be the landmark we're supposed to watch for. Let's read what's next."

"When you reach the point of no return you will see creatures in the water. Never fear, they only seek things that live in the water. The creatures know of places you never dreamt of. Walk to the right thirty paces and seek the treasure at the center of the mall."

Tony turned to his right and counted thirty paces. He entered a side tunnel, but just barely. He stopped.

"Now what?"

"It should be right here."

"What does the hint say?"

We found the hint and it said, "In the drink."

"Oh great, it's under the water," he said. "And it's a log only?"

We began wading back and forth in the water hoping our feet would feel the cache. Back and forth, back and forth. As I waded I began looking at the walls of the tunnel. Geocachers were not the only ones to come down here. There was colorful graffiti on the walls. Gaudy pictures, gang tagging, signatures. One person had painted an elaborate landscape showing a spooky church and graveyard at night. Hands groped from the graves.

"There's your pirates," I said pointing out the graveyard.

"There's something right here. Shine your light in the water."

I pointed my flashlight at Tony, then followed his arms down into the water. There was a cement lump.

"It's… heavy," he said. "Or just firmly in place."

Finally there was a sucking noise and the thing flipped over ponderously. It was only about a foot square. Once it was turned over it wasn't difficult to carry it to a dry spot on the edges of the tunnel.

The crawdads still looked spooky drifting in the water, especially the dead ones. I couldn't help but wonder if I had stepped on them.

"Shine the light here," Tony said. "Let's see what we've got here."

"It's crawdad city hall and now they are all going to pinch you for stealing their only landmark," I said.

"It's got a lock and lock in the bottom," he said as he examined the cache. "It's encased in cement to weigh it down. I thought you said it was a log only."

"That's what the description said."

"Maybe they just put a log in it because they weren't sure how watertight it was."

We signed the log wishing we had something to leave for the next geocacher, but we hadn't brought anything along. We replaced the cache with a sense of accomplishment.

"I wonder where this tunnel goes," Tony said.

"Under the mall," I answered.

"Wow, I've never been under a mall before."

"Me neither."

"Too bad there aren't any handy vents. I think it would be funny to stand at the vent and say things like, 'Thank you all for shopping at AnyMall today we'd like to tell you about a sale on corkscrews at FancyFeet.'"

"Why would a store like FancyFeet have corkscrews?"

"They wouldn't. That's the point. Just make up something silly that will leave the shoppers all standing around going, 'what in the worrrld?'"

"If you did that, security would be down here and they would fence off the end of the tunnel forever."

"I guess."

"And all the geocachers would be mad at you."

"Who…WHHOOOOO's down there," came a voice from further down the tunnel.

"Oh no, muggles? Here?" I said.

"No worries," Tony said into the tunnel. "We wandered in. We're wandering out now."

"Don't hurt me!" I recognized the voice of a girl and it came from further down the tunnel.

"We're not going to hurt you," Tony said. "Why would we do that?"

"This tunnel is haunted," the girl said. "Demons live down here. They kill children."

"Why would kids be down here?" Tony asked.

"They lurk and when you turn your back they attack. They're eeevil. I've heard the stories. I come down here and the place freaks me out but I can't help but think I might see them one day, groping from the walls of the earth like the hands from the graves."

A shiver went up my spine even though I thought the girl was crazy. Maybe the shiver went up my back *because* I thought she was crazy.

"There's no demons down here," I began but she interrupted me.

"They feed on the unaware! You better leave."

"We are," I said. "Are you okay?"

She stepped into our flashlight beams. She didn't have her own light. When I saw her I almost ran away. She was dressed in mostly black and she had her face painted with black stitches. I would expect something like that at Halloween but this was July.

"Go," she said in a distant voice. "Go before they come. If they come you'll have no chance."

"Are you coming, too?" Tony asked.

"Nooo. I'll stay. I watch... for the demon... someday I will see him... someday..."

"Let's go," I said quietly to Tony.

"Uh huh," he said. "You're sure you'll be okay by yourself?"

"I hear them! Go!"

There was a sound in the distance but it didn't sound like demons. It sounded like water.

"Let's get out of here," I repeated.

I took pictures of the graffiti on the way out hoping the pictures would capture the oddness of the hunt. I worried that the camera flash would scare the girl. I wished I could take her picture, but I thought she would object. She didn't look like she expected tourists in her demon filled tunnels. The experience left me feeling a little melancholy. Tony jumped and tagged the roof of the tunnel splashing water everywhere and probably crushing a crawdad or two.

"Wow!" He said. "You sure know how to pick 'em!"

"Yeah, that was... weird. I think she must watch too much TV."

"Or take too much of something besides TV."

"You think..."

"Yeah, I think. I hate to leave her but she seems to be in her own little world."

"What a place to live. What a *way* to live. I'm glad it's weird to me. To think it's normal for somebody else... let's get out of here."

He grinned at my naivety. Maybe he'd seen more of the world than me but I hoped people like that girl were only seen on scary TV shows.

"Where to now?" he asked when we were standing out in the daylight again.

"I don't know. I didn't expect it to be that easy."

"I say we go back to the van, dry off, maybe change shoes. Yes, we definitely need to change shoes. Then let's go to the food court and see if the mall has wifi."

"Okay. In shorts?" I asked.

"Sure, why not?"

"Uh... okay."

I could feel my mother's disapproval from two hundred miles away even though I probably saw a dozen girls in shorts skimpier than mine. I felt naked. And I was a little bit irritated with myself for feeling that way. I looked around for a woman in a dress and I saw a few but they were high fashion ladies. They looked like lawyers. How could they walk in those high heels? How did they stay looking elegant all day? Hair spray for sure and lots of it. But why dress up so much that you had to maintain perfection all day?

"What are you doing?" Tony asked.

"Trying to find my place in life," I said.

"And what are you deciding?"

"That life is a river and I am failing miserably at swimming upstream."

"What!?"

"Sorry, I think the shorts have hijacked my brain. I can't help but be self conscious and when I get self conscious I start comparing myself to everybody else and everybody else has it all together and I don't so I'm drifting downstream."

He smiled and I knew I was due for one of his famous Twiggy philosophy lessons.

"If you don't like fighting to swim upstream just relax, follow the river down, and you'll end up in the ocean where you can be anything you want."

"Fresh water fish die in the ocean," I reminded him.

"Can we look in some stores?" he asked.

"Just avoid clothing stores. I don't want to be tempted."

"By clothes?"

"Yes, it's a common problem with girls. They spot clothes from several aisles away and pretty soon they are trapped in a dressing room with an armful of things they can't afford. They try them all on anyway and they get sad because of all the things they have to put back. So it's best to just not even go in those stores."

"If you could buy anything in the whole mall what would you choose?"

"I'd get a pair of jeans and go to the restroom and change so I feel like myself again."

He sighed. "No, anything you want. What would you choose?"

"I don't know what this mall has."

"Pretend it has everything."

"I guess I would get hiking boots and a GPS so I can show up at the event and look like a real geocacher."

"You won't be judged by your appearance or whether or not you have a GPS. They will know how much of a geocacher you are by how you talk and you already proved you can talk shop with the best of them. When you told that cop you CITOed the cache I almost laughed."

"I can't help but wonder if we're walking over the cache," I said. "Hey, how did they get the coordinates for the cache if their GPS won't work down there?"

"They got the first two way points and then they plotted it out on a satellite map. They counted the steps to the turn and counted again to the hiding spot, then they plotted it out on satellite images to get the longitude and latitude. If you look at a satellite image the cache icon will appear to be on the roof of the mall."

Tony stopped walking and pretended to be listening.

"Hey!" he said. "Fancy Feet is having a sale on corkscrews!" I gave his shoulder a gentle punch and we continued down the mall looking for the food court.

"Oh, cool! They have teriyaki bowls! I haven't had one of those in ages. And lasagna! And shish k bobs! Ooo, I hate food courts."

"It doesn't sound like it to me," he pointed out.

"There is such a thing as too many choices. When you eat cafeteria food for most of the year, and then only eat at places you find on the road, selection becomes more important, but I don't know what to choose."

"Cinnamon rolls," he said.

"Cookies!"

"Ice cream. Soft serve and candy bars blended into a chunky..."

"Stop it!"

"English toffee lattes."

"They have those?"

"Irish cream lattes with whipped cream and chocolate shavings on top."

"Arg! Let me see how much money I have."

"Put that away. I may not be able to get you a new GPS receiver or hiking boots but I can get your lunch. What do you want?"

"I haven't had Asian food in ages."

"Okay, Asian it is. Let's get our food first. Then the devices can be looking for a signal while we eat."

One disadvantage to letting the devices search for a signal is all the constant checking to see if they were successful. Tony's cell phone seemed to get enough of a connection to download some caches, but the search capabilities were limited.

"I've got an idea," Tony said. "But we'll have to see if they have the right kind of store here."

"What kind?"

"Are you sure you don't need an Irish Cream latte with whipped cream and chocolate curls on top?" he asked.

"If you want one, just get one," I told him.

He huffed and sat a little more firmly in his chair. I was beginning to see that he wanted me to want one so it would give him an excuse to get his own.

I had to admit I did want one. I just didn't want him to buy me one. I wondered where his seemingly unlimited amount of cash was coming from. I was flat broke, but it was because I was at the very end of my semester's allowance. Had I gone home after school ended I wouldn't be financially strapped. I'd be eating at my parents' house and working at some fast food place near their house and gaining weight with every meal.

"Let's try your idea," I suggested. "And get the lattes for the road."

"Okay. First we have to find one of those fancy gadget stores. This mall is big enough. It should have one. Let's find a map of the mall."

There was a map between the food court and the main hallway to the mall. When we looked at the map we could see that the mall was three stories tall and they had two stores that might fit the bill. I wasn't sure what Tony had in mind, though, so I followed him to the nearest one.

We entered the gadget store and Tony started drooling. I wanted to tap him on the shoulder and remind him that we were there for a specific reason. He began looking around at all the cool gadgets and pointing out the ones that didn't really serve a useful purpose, they just looked cool. A salesman approached.

"May I help you, sir?"

"Actually, I'm looking for something to help me in my hobby. I brought the laptop into the mall hoping to get a wifi signal but it seems to be weak or nonexistent and I was wondering if there was anything I could buy that would turn my laptop into a wifi hotspot."

"Yes, sir, there sure is. What kind of a hobby do you have?"

"It's called geocaching. I'm on the road and it's kind of fun to stop and find a cache and stretch my legs, but I ran out of caches in my GPS. I really need a way to download them on the fly."

"Here you go, you just plug this into your USB port..."

"Do you think you could demonstrate it? You might want to know how to download caches in case you get other geocaching customers. Geocachers really like their gadgets."

"Well... I guess. You actually have your laptop along?"

"Yes. I brought it hoping to upload caches over lunch but I couldn't do it."

"Okay. Let's find an out of the way flat spot..."

I couldn't believe it. Just by sounding interested in the product Tony got a demonstration and gave a geocaching lesson in one fell swoop. He showed the salesman how to get the caches from the internet to the computer and the computer to the GPS and we were all set for more geocaching. Unfortunately he didn't have enough money to actually buy the gadget, but he left the salesman confident that he could help more customers with his new found knowledge and he promised to look the salesman up if he was able to purchase one in the future, so he left the salesman with hope of a sale.

"That was slick," I said as we made our way down the corridor.

"Thanks. He typed in the password and everything!"

"So did you find a cache to look for?" I asked.

"Not yet, but they are all in there. I showed him how to grab caches along a route and bingo bango bongo there they were. I'll drive, you search for a good one."

"Lattes?"

"Lattes."

Before we got our lattes, though , it occurred to me that we were in a mall and a mall might have kid friendly swag.

"Do you think they have a toy store?" I asked Tony.

"Sure."

"I want to look for little toys to put in the caches."

"A toy store isn't the place to go," he said. "Too expensive. But since we're in a city, I bet they have the ideal place."

"Where?"

"We'll find a telephone book and I'll find one. You'll see. It's the ideal spot for geocachers."

We headed for the van and stopped at the coffee cart on the way.

"Two large Irish Cream lattes with extra chocolate," Tony ordered.

"Hot or ice blended?"

"Ice blended!" said.

"Hot," said Tony.

"Cheers!" said Tony and we toasted to the next leg off our journey.

"Uh oh," I said as we neared the van and saw a yellow piece of paper on the dash next to the note.

"Uh oh is right," Twiggy echoed.

He pulled the ticket off the windshield and brightened. "Good job partner! It's just a warning!"

Tony pulled into the parking lot of a party store. A party store? Mylar balloons filled the front window. Happy Birthday! Over The Hill. Golden 50. Cartoon balloons. Birthday hat balloons, balloon sculptures...

"Why are we here?" I asked.

"You'll see," he said.

I walked the aisles of the store in wide wonder. There were tiny toys everywhere! Other people would call them party favors but to me it was an opportunity to add color and fun to the geocaches.

"Look! Angry Birds masks!"

"Remember that has to fit into a geocache," he reminded me.

"Oh, right. So, no masks."

"Think small. The smaller the swag the more caches it will fit into. And remember you have to carry these things around. Don't buy it if you don't want to pack it."

"Rats."

Forty dollars poorer I had several packages of swag for girls, boys and adults. I was in business! I couldn't afford dinner, but I could make many junior geocachers happy.

"You are not going to leave those plastic dragons in every dragon house you see," Twiggy said.

"I know. I only have six of them."

Chapter 21

It wasn't easy sorting through the caches on Tony's GPS. I couldn't see the favorite points. I had to click through the list and find one that sounded interesting, check the difficulty and terrain, read the description and the logs to see if it was worth pursuing, then look at the map to see if it was a reasonable distance from our intended route.

"How's it going?" he asked after a very quiet fifteen minutes of highway time had passed.

"Well, there are lots of caches along the road. I am having trouble finding one that interests us."

"Well, just find one close to the road five miles or so away to give the GPS time to lock on and give us a map. Then we can look for a good one while we are stopped."

"Okay."

As it turns out "near the road" is a relative thing. On the little screen you lose some of the perspective so a cache that looks near the road is actually a mile off the road. I locked onto a cache with the very original title of Exit 138. However, the cache was only named after the exit we took to get to it. The cache itself was down a frontage road. We exited, turned down the frontage road and it followed the highway for a while and then diverged from it to go down a small canyon and the cache was half a mile from the highway, but over a mile down the frontage road. We didn't mind because we were just looking for a cache, but it taught me a lesson in GPS usage.

The highway passed over the little canyon but the frontage road followed it, dipped down into it and climbed back up the other side. The cache was in the turn toward the bottom of the canyon. Tony stopped the van, we climbed down from it and got our bearings.

"Looks pretty straightforward to me," Tony said. "This is more like typical geocaching."

"I think it says to go this way."

"How far is it?"

"Two hundred and thirty feet."

"Okay, so we're obviously looking at a rock or bush hide. All there is around here is rocks and bushes."

I followed the direction the line pointed and I ended up on the side of the canyon in a nondescript section of land. There were no trees but plenty of rocky brushy hillside.

"Just find ground zero, then put the GPS down and use your geosenses. This is one of those where you get close and then a sharp eye will spot an irregularity in the landscape. You might have to be at just the right angle so if you think you looked in a spot look again from a different direction."

I walked around, found ground zero and I was standing in a spot of bare dirt. I looked in the bushes near the spot. I flipped over a few rocks. I looked for piles of rocks or sticks. I walked away from ground zero and then tried to find it again. This time the GPS led me to a spot about ten feet away.

"It says I am zero feet from the cache," I reported. "And it said that over there by that bush, too."

"Put it away. Use your eyes. This is supposed to be an easy one and I don't see how it can be difficult. There's no real hiding place anywhere near here."

"There sure are a lot of places that are zero feet from the cache," I said. "They must be using bigger feet than I am used to. I always thought a foot was twelve inches."

"Maybe metric would work better?" he said.

"Do the meters match real meters?"

"Just as much as the feet match real feet. Use your eyes and your hands."

"Then you take the GPS," I said. "So I'll quit depending on it."

It was his turn to follow the GPS to various spots and he came to the same conclusions I did. That ground zero moved about.

"I don't get it. The sky is clear and blue. We should get a good signal…"

He put the GPS down and began searching. I think every bush got searched and every rock got unstacked or turned over on that hillside. Twiggy picked up the GPS again.

"Oh great! Now it says a hundred fifteen feet that way."

"That's the bottom of the canyon," I said. "They wouldn't put it where water would get it."

The other side of the canyon was a rocky bluff. And when we got to the bottom of the canyon it still said the cache was twenty feet away. When we tried to walk twenty feet we hit the rock wall.

"It better not be up there," I said.

"It could be accessible from the top," he said. "It just seems strange for the GPS to lead us over there and then suddenly jump. It's not unusual for it to jump twenty or thirty feet but this is a bit much."

"It does look like there are better hiding spots up there, though."

"If we have to get to it from the top then it would be better to go back to the van and drive around. The road would take us right over there and it's nice, flat walking."

That made sense so we went back to the van and drove to the other side of the canyon. The rockier side of the canyon was fun and the view down the canyon was spectacular. After a rain the bottom probably had a stream running through it and it would be even prettier.

"How far this time?" I asked.

"Three hundred thirty-six feet."

This time we ended up walking along the top of the canyon until a trail led downward. I wasn't sure it was a man made trail, but it was wide enough to walk on. I followed Tony down the trail noticing there were more tracks from hoofed animals than people. What kind of tracks were those? Cattle? Deer? Goats? I really hadn't noticed tracks before so I could only guess. We reached a large, flat rock that hung over the canyon and this was where we reached ground zero. I stood on the rock and looked down at the spot we had been standing before.

"This is more like it," Tony said. "Lots of hidey holes for caches here. These can be tricky and the right angle is more critical in places with lots of little shadowy places. It might be completely invisible from one angle and very obvious from another. And then there's the ones that are just hard no matter how you look at it. Watch out for snakes. Sticks come in really handy in places like this. If you're uncertain about sticking your hand in, poke around with a stick first. We don't want unpleasant surprises."

I found a stick first. If there was one thing I didn't want it was unpleasant surprises, especially the slithery variety. Mice were bad enough. I definitely wanted to avoid snakes. I went from one dark, shadowy crevice to another poking the stick in and wiggling it around, then sticking my hand in to see if a container was inside. I must have looked in every hidey hole along the trail and then I heard a "found it!" from beside the flat rock.

"It was nice of them to provide a comfortable, scenic signing spot," Tony said as he carried the cache to the top of the flat rock. We sat there above the canyon sorting swag and signing the log, a gentle breeze wafting by.

"This is a pretty spot in its own way," I said.

"It sure is. That's what I like about geocaching. If a geocacher likes a spot they want to share it with other people so they hide a cache there. It's not true all the time. There are plenty of caches out there that are just there for the sake of a smiley, but I've found enough pleasant places to keep me searching for the next."

This time I had lots of swag and I really liked sorting through the swag to make sure there was something for a girl, a boy and an adult geocacher, just in case a family was out geocaching together.

"Wow, you're generous," Tony said.

"Little girls need swag, too," I said. "It might get discouraging for a kid to never find anything interesting. If you were five what would you like to see in a geocache?"

"Hot Wheels."

"Really?"

"I had this huge track setup. We used to see which cars made it the furthest down the track. So… yeah, Hot Wheels. A boy can never have too many Hot Wheels."

"I'll have to find some next time we're in a city."

"It really matters to you to restock the caches?"

"Yeah! It's like leaving a surprise present for some unknown person. It doesn't matter if I never meet them. Just knowing there was something there for them to sort through and one thing they might want to keep makes me happy."

He sat there for a minute. "That's what makes the hobby fun. A giving heart."

"If I had known where this cache was I'd have suggested a picnic on this rock."

"That would be cool," Tony admitted.

"So this is more what real geocaching is like?" I asked.

"Rural geocaching, yeah."

"Cool!"

"It's not always at an interesting spot or a view down a canyon, but you can choose to only find ones that might be at an interesting spot. There seems to be enough geocaches to keep most anybody occupied for a long, long time. One of these days I need to introduce you to geoart and power trails."

"They have geocaching art?"

"Sort of, and not exactly. Remind me next time we have the geocaching map up. It's easy enough to see what it is on the computer with the right zoom factor."

"And what's a power trail?"

"It's a whole bunch of caches spaced close together so you can find a lot at one time. They are placed mostly for the numbers. The caches are close together so the hiding places might be minimal and since there are so many of them the containers have to be easily replaced. So you end up looking for a hundred plus pill bottles all in a row. I don't like power caching. This right here, what we're doing, finding caches in pleasant surroundings, feeling the breeze and the sun and getting out away from campus, this is my idea of geocaching."

"Me, too. I think the rock dragon clan must live here. There's lots of rocky caves for them to live in."

Chapter 22

While we had a comfortable rock and a nice view we sorted through the caches on the GPS to find another one. It was very awkward trying to find an interesting cache between where we were and the lake. When we zoomed out enough to see our route we lost roads and landmarks. When we zoomed in we got more specific information, but usually not enough to base a decision on. The process was simple on a computer. We really needed that device that would make the laptop into a wifi hot spot anywhere we happened to be.

"Watch where I put it back," Tony said. "So you can see where it came from. Every hide you see in person teaches you a new way to look for the next one."

He put it back and I hopped down beside the rock to see how it was hidden. It had been hidden between two rocks in the shadows and then more rocks had been placed around it to catch the eye and distract from the container. If I hadn't been looking for a geocache I never would have spotted the hiding place, much less bothered to unstack a bunch of rocks. It amazed me how I used to just walk right past geocaches without even thinking about them being there. How many people had stood on this rock to view the canyon never knowing two feet below them and a little to the side was a box waiting to be found.

"Okay," Tony said. "I'm locking onto a cache ten miles up the road. It will at least get us closer to Belle Fourche."

"What made you pick it?"

"People write good logs for it. People don't write about caches they don't like. There must be something there to spark their creative endeavors. Let's go see what it is."

"Okay."

There was no use using up the batteries until we were five miles down the highway so I just rode along until my curiosity got the better of me and I touched a button to wake the device back up. We followed the frontage road back and got on the freeway again which put us 11 miles from the cache. When I brought the map up again we were still eight miles from the cache. I knew to just wait, and I knew seeing the map every mile was not necessary, but my curiosity would begin to grate on me and it was so easy to just touch a button and get an update.

"Eight miles," I reported needlessly.

Two miles later I was pushing the button again. I thought I better buy Tony a pack of batteries since I was the one constantly waking the GPS up. Each time I expected to get more information on the screen but it just showed the little triangle that was us on a long orange line that was the highway.

"Are you doing okay?" Tony asked.

"Yeah! Did you know watching the GPS makes miles stretch?"

He laughed, "Yeah. How far away is the cache?"

"Three point seven miles."

"How far off the road do you think it is?" He asked.

"A couple of miles."

"Good!"

"Why?"

"You're thinking."

"I thought I went on this adventure to avoid thinking."

"Sorry, kiddo, you're doing more thinking now than in class. Maybe your brain is finding the way it likes to work out here. Maybe being cooped up in a class room isn't your thing."

"I need to figure out how to make it my thing. My parents expect me to get some kind of degree and pretty soon I'm going to run out of majors and money."

"It's a little hard to get a degree when you never settle on a major."

"I know. Why don't they have a degree in studentology? I could just be a professional student."

"There are those. But I don't think you want to spend the rest of your life at the university."

"That's true. Student life might be okay for getting out from under my parent's roof, but it is not a long term solution. Oh! We need to watch for an exit, and when we find one, we need to go north. Don't you think looking for a cache called Ill Tidings is ill advised?"

"Everybody seems to like it."

"They liked Insane Asylum and The Pink Panther cache, too."

"And you did, too."

"After we survived them," I added.

"You liked them at the time, too, aside from the unexpected..."

"Turn right and then right again."

"Muggle bears and insane people," he continued.

"If we find a bear in a cache I'm going to use it for a hitchhiker and turn it into a Travel Bug named Muggle Bear."

"You're talking like you've been doing this for years."

"You're just contagious. You know how accents are contagious? I pick up a wicked Texas accent if I am around Texans. Well, I guess the same thing happens with vocabulary. What do y'all think about that?"

"I'm y'all?"

"Well, if you were in a group you would be."

"I thought that was all y'all."

"Could be. Foreign languages are so confusing."

"Since when is Texas a foreign country?"

"It's not. It just feels like it way up here in the north. Have you ever been there?"

"To Texas? No."

"We should go there someday."

"We should?"

"We… um… hm. I don't know. I'd like seeing Texas with you. They geocache there, too, right?"

"They geocache everywhere these days."

"Oh. I think we better pay attention to the GPS." I watched the little icons on the map for a minute then said, "Hmm, this road isn't matching the road to the cache. Did we miss a turn?"

"I didn't see one. Does the GPS show one?"

"Yeah, turn around and go back a little. I'll tell you when you get to it."

"Okay."

He turned around but in the spot where I thought the turn off would be there was only a wash.

"Maybe it was a road at some point in time, but it isn't anymore."

"So now what do we do?"

"How far is the cache?"

"It's still nearly a mile."

"Do you want to try hiking there?"

"I don't know. I think we should see how much water we have first. And dinner. What about dinner?"

"If we can hike two miles an hour we should be able to find the cache in a little over an hour," he pointed out.

"And we'll only be how many feet from the van?"

"We better take water, at least."

We found three bottles of water and the cheesy party mix in the back of the van.

"We'll go straight to town when we finish here. It'll be dinner time by then," Tony said.

We stuck the snack mix, the water and a couple of packages of swag into the day pack, locked up the van and off we went.

"How often is this cache found if it's a mile of cross country hiking to get to it?" I asked.

"I don't know. I read the logs but I didn't notice the dates. I guess I could do that."

We hiked as he found the logs and I wondered at the way the land had changed over the eons. The timber line was low. Trees only grew on one side of the hills. I wondered what weather came out of the other side that made life difficult for trees. I was debating if the trees grew on the south side or the north side of the hills when Tony said, "Hmm, maybe we should turn back. These logs are two years old."

"Aww, the poor cache. It's been sitting out there for two years without a single visit?"

"Yeah."

"Then we should find it. Maybe if people see it is still active they will try to find it, too."

"There might be a very good reason it hasn't been found. It might not even be there after two years."

"What could happen to it a mile from a road? Nobody's going to randomly run across that one spot in all this open land. It's lonely out there. It needs a visitor."

"Well, don't sacrifice your precious swag on a cache that might never be found again. Did you know that a cache like this really is called a Lonely Cache?"

"Aw, that's sad."

"There is a group of people who go look for the Lonely Caches. They like the challenge of finding something that's been basically out of the loop for years. If they find it they like to post about it and get it back on the radar screens of other geocachers. And if it is really gone they will see about archiving it so other people don't risk a lengthy hike for no reason at all."

"Let's go find it. Maybe we can prove it is worth the hike."

"Or maybe the title is a warning."

"Maybe a pirate hid it," I said appealing to Tony's pirate side. "And they are warning other pirates."

"Arg, then we go matey. Treasure seeking on the grand prairie. X marks the spot."

"Yeah, right. Have you *ever* found a geocache at an X?"

"Yes. Actually it isn't unusual for a geocacher to hide a cache at any X they find out of the way where it won't get muggled."

"Why do the trees only grow on one side of the hill?"

"They face the sun," he said.

"Oh."

"And the north side is colder. The snow melts slower. It's more hostile on the north side."

"I guess that makes sense. So the trees grow on the south side."

"Right."

"And if one grows on the north side it's a brave and hearty tree."

"That doesn't mind having frozen roots most of the winter," he added.

"It's hard to believe there is that much difference between the north side and the south side. I can just imagine the mama trees telling the pinecones, 'now don't fall on the north side of the hill or you'll grow up short and stunted.' Then if one did she'd warn it to watch out for deep snow and freezing wind and the poor pinecone would... pine away."

"Do you say things like that on purpose?" he asked.

"No, I just read my little speech balloon too late to avoid it."

We had a lot of uphill hiking to do and my legs got very tired of the climb. I kept telling myself that it would be downhill most of the way back.

"Do you do much hiking?" Tony asked when he saw I was tiring.

"No. Oh, I do walk places, especially during school. I don't mind walking to the mall back home, then walk the whole mall, too. So I do walk. It's just the hill that bothers me."

"We don't have to walk straight there. If it helps, follow the side of the hill and correct your path when it's convenient. The GPS will keep us on track."

"Do you want to lead?" I asked.

"I like to keep you in front. I know I walk too fast for you sometimes."

"It's okay. You're used to this cross country geocaching stuff. I'll yell if you're going too fast."

"If we just turn a little bit to the left we can follow the side of the hill until we get to that little cut over there. Then it'll be a short scramble to get up on top. It looks easier than what we are trying to do now."

How many hills can you possibly fit into a one mile hike, I thought as we topped hill after hill. Tony had the right idea walking the side of the hill. We climbed slowly that way, though we had to adjust our route when we were drawn away from the cache.

"I think," Tony said. "That there used to be a road here."

"Why?" I asked as I came up beside him and looked over the top. "Oh. How did it get all the way out here?"

"There must have been a road here at some point and this car brought Ill Tidings to its owner in a most inopportune place."

"I guess so."

"The cache is thirty-nine feet away which puts it in the vicinity of that car."

"This cache might be tougher than the fire engine one," I said. "How big is it?"

"A small."

"How'd it get upside down?"

"No telling. We don't know where the road was when it rolled."

"The car isn't that old," I said. "I remember these cars. How long does it take for a road to vanish?"

"Maybe the car was trying to fly and found out it wasn't cut out to be an airplane."

"It's a mile from the closest pavement!"

"Yeah, well, sometimes the things we discover in geocaching seem totally random."

We slid down to the car and began a quick inspection to figure out the best way to attempt to find a small container on an overturned car.

"What's the rating on this one?"

"A five/five. It looked like a pretty easy five/five so I thought it was worth the hike. Some people go their whole life without finding a five/five."

"So it's not going to be obvious."

"No."

"What does the hint say?"

"Hint after DNF only."

"Rats! We're not going to be here again so there's no point asking."

"Not necessarily. If you had a cache that hadn't been found in two years you might be a little more lenient about hints just to get it back on the found list."

"How are you going to contact them way out here?"

"Hmm, good point. That little hot spot device is looking handier all the time."

"So... no hints. I suppose they have to keep it difficult if it's a five/five. Can I read the logs?"

"Sure, I thought you would do it on the way."

"I was too focused on the map."

Since we knew where ground zero was Tony began walking around the car poking his hands into all the crevices that can open up on an overturned car that had been sitting in one place for years. The body was rusty and the car had many bullet holes through it. The tires were missing. I walked around taking occasional glances at the car as I read. The logs were lengthy compared to most cache logs I had read. All except for the last one.

"I looked for over an hour and then I realized it was staring me right in the eye," was what the log said.

"Oh!! Did you read the last one?"

"No, I just read enough to convince me it might be a fun one. Why?"

"Oh… nothing!" I said as I moved to the front of the car. It was a little difficult to get a good view of the front end because the car was upside down and crosswise in between two hillsides. I couldn't get a good look from above and when I slid down to the bottom I couldn't get the right angle to see what I thought was the hiding place.

"Grrr," I grumbled to myself.

"What?"

"Nothing. I'll figure it out."

"Figure what out?"

"How to look where I think the cache is."

"Where do you think it is?"

"In the headlight."

"It can't be."

"Okay. Then you keep looking over there, and I'll keep looking over here," I said, determined to figure this out on my own. I couldn't open the hood. How did mechanics replace headlights if not from under the hood? If a car was going to stare at me certainly it did it through its headlights. I'd seen the movies and the commercials. The headlights were always the eyes of an animated car. After several failed attempts to get in to the workings of the front end of the car I sat down to think on a rock beside the headlight. Sitting on the rock brought me eye to eye with the car and I looked into… swag. Soggy, mildewed swag. I nearly jumped with surprise even though it was what I had been trying to do all along. Now I could see why that other geocacher had written what they had. They had probably sat on the very same rock! Tony had said sometimes you have to see a cache from just the right angle. I guess this was one of those. How could I get it loose? I placed my fingers around the chrome around the headlight and jiggled gently. It didn't budge. I bent down and looked directly into the headlight and I could see a hole toward the back of the plastic housing. Then I noticed the grill was broken and a hand sized hole allowed me to reach right into the headlight. Who in the world had the tools to cut a hole in the side of a headlight without breaking it? I didn't know but I didn't question it further. This was working, though the swag was in awful shape. It was obvious that water had worked its way in and took it's time evaporating out. The log was all one solid chunk after getting wet and drying over and over. It looked like everything needed replacing. I took the log, which basically looked like a little paper pulp brick and walked over to Tony.

"Do we have any extras?" I asked as I handed him the lump.

At first he wasn't certain what it was, but there were inky spots that were obviously writing.

"Yeah! You found it?"

"Sort of. It found me. I sat on a rock and it was right in front of my face just like that last online log said. But it's a mess and anything we put in will likely get messed up from the weather."

"Where is it?" he asked excitedly.

"In the headlight. You just reach through the grill and there's a hole."

"Atta girl, partner! You did it!"

"I can't say this was my all time favorite cache, but the hide is pretty cool. Look! You have to sit on that rock."

He sat down on the rock and his eyes lit up. "Cool! I think we can even waterproof it a little. If they'd just used a container that would fit through the hole it would have survive just fine."

"Like what?" I asked.

"For the log? A mini Altoids tin and a baggie. For the swag? I need a closer look. I'm thinking a pill bottle or... larger Altoids tin or a... hmmm, there's quite a bit in here once you get it all out. We can't fit all this into a container but a container, even one that only holds tiny things, is better than all this water logged junk. Good find! It's almost unrecognizable because of all the mold. Let's see what we can do."

He pulled out all the swag and paper bits and carried them to the top, or rather the underside, of the car. He found a spot to spread it all out.

"Cache doctor at your service," he said with a smile.

We totally revamped the cache, despite the likelihood that the cache might never be seen again. Tony had a notepad that he cut in half with a tiny saw on a multi-tool. He wrote: "Replacement log Ill Tidings", on the cover then signed our names and dated the entry. He placed the half a notepad into a little, zippered, plastic bag made for jewelry, folded the top over so it just fit into a tiny tin. Then he found a spray painted pill bottle in the pack and tried it through the hole in the side of the headlight. It didn't fit so he tried an Altoids tin. That didn't fit either, so he tried the tin the log book was in. That one fit so he found another one in the pack and we tried to fit all the swag into the tin. Not much would fit in but we were able to put in a ring, a flat toy car and a keychain. The key chains were very flat and the lid just barely closed with the three things carefully positioned inside. He took a rag out of the pack and cleaned the inside of the headlight as much as he could reach. Then he placed the two tins where they could be seen.

"What do you think?" he asked.

"Looks good! I wonder if anybody will find it."

"I don't know. But I feel better about the cache anyway. It was worth the sacrifice for the five/five on our Fizzy Grid. Plus we can now post that the cache is in great shape and ready for people to flock up here to find it."

"Will they?"

"Well… no, but maybe somebody will. Good job!"

"Thanks. This calls for some snack mix."

"Yeah, I'm getting hungry. Let's go find a town and some dinner."

We felt a lot better on the hike back. We snacked on party mix and water and we were able to see downhill across the wide open land.

"Where's the van?" I asked.

"Probably behind one of those endless hills," Tony replied.

"I can't see the highway either."

"We were a ways off the highway."

We saw lots of little squirrels. They would dash away and disappear under a bush, then peek out to see if we were coming. If we got too close they ducked inside their burrow until we were gone. Fifteen minutes of walking and we still didn't see the van.

The snack mix was in dire jeopardy. We ate nearly the whole package on the hike back to the van.

"Dang, it's nearly six o'clock," Tony said.

"It can't be."

"We were at the mall at noon. Then we drove a half hour to the exit, another fifteen minutes on dirt roads. We hiked a mile, found a geocache, cleaned it up and walked nearly another hour. I guess it's possible to use up a day like that."

"Then why don't we see the van? Or the road?"

"I don't know. It might have helped to way mark it."

"How do you way mark the van?" I asked.

"You can way mark anything. We could way mark where we are right now. You just make sure to record the coordinates while you are at the van, then you can look that up later and the GPS will lead you back."

"Why didn't we do that?" I asked.

"Because it takes time and all we were doing was hiking a mile in one direction. In fact… let's see, if we walk directly away from the cache that should point us in the right direction."

When he looked at where we were in relation to the cache he said, "Oh shoot."

"What?"

"We're way off track. We need to head further this way." He adjusted his direction and set off again, but half an hour later we still didn't see the van or the road.

"How can we lose the van?" I asked. "Or the road? We went up hill to get to the cache. It should be downhill to the road."

"I suppose the GPS will lead us back to the cache. Then we can walk and keep to a certain heading to get close to the van again."

"So much for being hungry. Now we have a handful of party mix and one bottle of water."

"We'll be okay," he said. "The van can't be far. We know to head downhill. As long as we walk downhill we should reach the road. Then all we have to do is follow the road until we get to the van."

That's what I thought, too, except for one small mistake. We didn't keep an eye on the GPS and when we reached the road we looked at the GPS only to discover that it had run out of power and shut down. We stood at the road a little perplexed.

"Don't step out there yet," he said. "If there are recent tracks they could be from the van. If so we need to turn left. If we didn't cross this spot of the road we should turn right."

We looked at the road and there were fresh tracks.

"Are those van tracks or somebody else's?" I asked.

"Tire tracks look a lot alike unless you're talking mud and snow tires, which we don't have."

"But local people might," I pointed out.

"True. These are not mud and snow tires. These are normal car tires."

"So..."

"I say we go left."

"Okay," I said relieved to have that decision behind us.

We turned left and walked and walked some more. The good news was that we were tiring and so we were walking slowly. The bad news was we were walking away from the van.

After about fifteen minutes of walking I said, "I think we should stop. We need to rest our feet, check the pack and see if we can find some batteries."

"I don't think we have any, but we can look," Tony said.

We sat beside the road and I took off my shoes to let me feet breathe a little and cool off. He unzipped the pack and began taking out swag, the GPS, a handful of Ziploc bags, an extra log book, three spare geocaching containers, Morrison the Moving Moose, a rock, all the swag I'd accumulated from my trades, and down in the very bottom two batteries.

"I wonder if they are spares, or ones we used up and forgot to throw away," he said.

"There's only one way to find out."

He opened up the GPS and used the lid to pry out the dead batteries, then put the new ones in and powered on the device. It took a minute for the GPS to give us the starting menu, but it was obvious we were not going to get much use out of these batteries.

"Quick, bring up the map."

"We need to lock onto the cache. It forgot the cache when it powered off."

A few clicks and a short wait and we could see where we were and where the cache was.

"I think if we triangulate the van should be right about… here on the road," Tony said.

"Yup. Over a mile away. And it's getting dark."

"We'll be okay, now that we're pointed in the right direction."

"I wonder how far it is to town."

"I don't know."

I picked up my shoes, ready to set out.

"Aren't you going to put those on?" Tony asked.

"I will in a minute. If I walk without them for a bit, my feet will thank me for putting them on instead of complaining."

The sand was sharp on my feet but the walking was pretty easy on the road. It didn't take long for me to decide that we'd be able to walk faster if I put the shoes on so I stopped and put on my socks and shoes.

"Okay, I'm ready for a hike. Let's go find that ugly, cacheamolé van."

We verified we were closing the triangle and quickened our pace. About ten minutes later we heard tires on dirt and turned around to see a pickup truck slowly motoring down the road. We moved to the side to let him pass.

He pulled to a stop, rolled down his widow and asked Tony, "Are you kids okay?"

"Yeah," Tony said. "Though we're looking for a green van. If you didn't see it behind you we're headed in the right direction."

"I didn't see it. Hop in the back and we'll see if it's up ahead."

"Thanks."

Tony climbed into the bed of the truck and offered me a hand up.

"Ever ridden in the bed of a pickup?" he asked.

"No! It's illegal!"

"I doubt if anybody notices back here. We'll be fine. Just sit tight and hang on."

He signaled for the driver to go and the truck pulled out and picked up some speed. Riding in the back of the truck was a bit rough but if I gripped the side of the bed I did okay. I was going to be ready for a shower again after hiking and then sitting in this dusty truck bed. It was still much better than walking all that way. I don't know how we ended up over a mile in the wrong direction but the driver finally pulled up beside the van and we hopped out.

"Thanks for the ride," Tony told the driver. "Is there any way we can repay you?"

"No, kid. I was already going this way. Glad to be of help."

"How far to the next town going west?"

"Fifteen minute drive, tops."

"Good. Do they have a little motel?"

"Sure enough."

"Thanks. We can use some dinner and a good night's rest. Thanks again for the ride!"

The man tipped his baseball cap, waved to me and drove away.

"Well," Tony said. "That cache earned its five/five rating."

Chapter 23

"A bowl of soup never tasted better," I said as I dunked a grilled cheese sandwich into it.

"Anything after a day of fishing tastes like the best meal ever," Tony said.

"I've only been fishing twice."

"I bet you made your dad bait the hook," he said.

"He showed me how."

"Then you did it yourself?" he asked unbelieving.

"Yeah, but I apologized to the worms first."

"I bet you did."

"It's funny that I felt more guilty poking them with the hook than I did about feeding them to the fish. I mean, fish eat worms anyway. But worms shouldn't have to be skewered by a hook first!"

"Did you catch a fish?"

"Yeah! After losing a couple. I caught a trout. You should have seen the one that got away."

"Was it this big?" he asked as he held his hands out a couple of feet apart.

"Actually the one I caught was bigger than the ones that got away."

"Did you eat it?"

"I don't know. I was going to let it go but my dad added it to the string and we did eat them, but I don't know if I ate my fish. I bet my dad did since mine was bigger than his."

"You don't sound happy about it."

I shrugged. "I guess I'm not. I'd rather let the fish swim away."

"But you like fish."

"If I am not responsible for killing it."

"So, I guess you don't want to do any fishing on our trip across the lake tomorrow."

"If we lose our kayaks and get stuck on the island I will help you catch fish, otherwise, I'd rather not."

"Never fear. Kayaking is not difficult as long as you don't tip over."

"What makes it easy to tip over?"

"Standing."

"So how to you get in and out of you don't stand?"

"As long as you stay low, you should be fine. And even if the kayak fills with water it will float. It's very hard to sink a kayak. Stay with the kayak as long as you aren't in any danger."

"Danger?"

"We shouldn't see any rapids at all on a lake. The only thing I can think of that could be dangerous are bears, moose and rapids. So it should be a very easy paddle out to the island."

"And the cache. What's it rated?"

"Well, that's the thing. As soon as you add in extra equipment needed, like a canoe, it increases the difficulty rating. So these caches should increase your average a lot."

"My average."

"Or mine. Yours will go up easier since you have fewer numbers to average."

"I thought you didn't like to geocache by the numbers."

"Sorry, being mathematically minded, even though I disagree with the concept, I can't help but calculate it. Yes, I think finding an interesting cache is better than a rating on a chart, but in this case I think we will have the best of both worlds. Doesn't it sound cool to paddle a kayak or a canoe to an island and find the caches there?"

"It does sound like fun. I just hope my arms don't give out."

The little motel only had one room left because of a spring festival in the park across the street so we didn't find the cache in the park the next morning. We did walk around the festival and decided the cache was under craft booth number twenty-seven which sold kitchen towels with hand crocheted toppers so you could button it onto the refrigerator door. I liked the cutting boards they sold in a variety of shapes. They had boards cut in the shape of any of the nearby states as well as shapes like barns, sheep, fish and apples. If I had a kitchen to stock I might have bought one, but I didn't have a use for a cutting board no matter how much I liked them.

"Do they know they kick the cache every time they put their foot on that sprinkler head?" I asked.

"I doubt it. Hey, how did you know about fake sprinkler caches?"

"There's one outside the bookstore on campus."

"Oh, yeah. We should head to the lake. We might have a long paddle ahead of us if you've never paddled a canoe before."

"Do you think we can rent one?"

"We'll know soon enough."

"That shower was creepy," I said.

"I told them about it but they didn't seem concerned that the floor of the bathtub rose four inches when we showered."

"Yeah, and it was squishy. Somebody is going to fall through the floor of the bathtub and then they're going to have a mess on their hands."

"That's what we get for taking the very last room."

The highway was beginning to feel very long but we reached our turn off after just a short, fast drive. Tony seemed to know the way, though I think he had only seen it on the geocaching map.

"We're looking for a dock or a store or anyplace that looks like a business close to the water."

"It's hard to see any place through all the trees. It sure is pretty here!"

"Yeah, I wish the lake close to home was like this."

"I've never seen a lake that big!" I said.

"Do you see an island out there?"

"No, but I haven't gotten a good look at the lake."

"Ah, here's a turn. Let's see where this leads."

He turned toward the lake but the road ended in a neighborhood.

"I bet they know where we can rent a canoe," I said.

"We'll find it. It can't be far."

Half an hour later we were driving back to the neighborhood.

"I'll ask," I said. "If it will save your macho man image."

To prove he wasn't afraid to ask a simple question he stopped at a driveway and addressed a man getting ready to mow his lawn. I noticed most of the houses had a small boat in the driveway and this one had a boat and a motor home.

"Excuse me!" Tony called out before the man could pull the cord on his mower. "Sir? Excuse me!"

The man looked irritated to be interrupted and pleased that he could put off his lawn mowing at the same time. He walked to the end of the driveway and gave the van a disapproving glance.

"Can you tell me where we can rent a canoe?"

The man pointed down the street. "All the way down. The street will turn right. Go all the way to the end. Only, Dave doesn't have canoes. You know how to kayak?"

"Yeah."

"Dave'll fix you up."

"Thanks!"

"It's likely to get busy out there. Weekends are always crazy."

"Thanks for the warning."

"Have fun!"

"We will."

I gave Tony a, "See? What was so hard about that?" look.

Tony drove to the end of the street and turned right. The road went left, too, but it looked like it went into somebody's yard and the dog in the yard looked like he was used to cars turning the wrong way. He looked like he could take a chunk out of a tire if necessary. Trees towered over the road and even in early summer the street had a light coating of leaves and pine needles. Tony left his window down and a cool breeze blew off the lake filling the van with fresh air and driving out a little of the musty, burning smell that had threatened to take over at times.

"That white building must be Dave's," Tony said.

The store looked just like the houses, except that it had a sliding glass door and inside we could see a freezer, a rack of sunglasses and hats, and a map rack. Inside the store was packed with an odd conglomeration of groceries, fishing supplies, and camping essentials. Beside the store was what we were hoping to find, a short wooden dock and a rack holding six kayaks.

"Snacks," Tony said. "And water."

We walked around gawking at the weird assortment of stock in the store. At least I did. Tony seemed more at home in the little store.

"Can I help you find something?" a man asked.

"Dave?" Tony asked.

"Yes siree."

"We're interested in renting a kayak for the day."

I chose snacks, leaving the men to figure out the kayak deal.

"Grab some sodas," Tony called. "Fizz, geocaching, and water just seem to go together for some reason."

I took an armful of snacks and two sodas to the counter.

"Two more of these," he said indicating the sodas.

When I came back with two more bottles of soda Tony was ready for adventure. He was nearly giddy at the prospects of being out on the water.

"I just rented one kayak. That way if your arms get tired you won't get stranded."

"That's good."

"You layered like I said?"

"Yup, swim suit, regular clothes, jacket."

"Good. That lake is one big evaporative cooler. It might get chilly."

Dave pulled a kayak off the rack and carried it over his head to the end of a short dock. He set it down and went back for two paddles. Tony went to the van and retrieved our geocaching pack and GPS. He stowed the snacks and pack in the kayak.

When Dave saw the GPS he said, "Set a waypoint."

"Yeah, we just learned that the hard way," I said and Tony glared at me. Dave came back with two life vests. He handed me one and waited for Tony to input the waypoint.

"You know how this goes?"Dave asked.

"I think I can figure it out."

"Remember not to paddle further than you want to swim."

"Okay," I said, though I didn't plan on doing any swimming at all.

When Tony finished with the GPS he gave me a few pointers.

"Stay low in the kayak. Standing, reaching, anything high will throw off the balance. The paddle," he said holding the paddle across his body, "goes like this. The goal is to push water, not slice through it. You put it this way and it does no good. Keep the blades pointed up and down. Just a steady dip, dip, dip. If we need to turn just leave it to me. If we are turning slowly I'll take the time to teach you, but until then just paddle when I tell you, rest when you need to."

"Okay."

"And Gabby?"

"Yeah?"

"Have fun. I want this to be fun for you."

"It will be. I like trying new things!"

"Good. Ready?"

"I think so."

Tony and Dave lowered the kayak into the water.

"I'll hold it steady," Tony said. "Just slip into the hole and make sure your legs are pointed forward."

The kayak felt very unsteady to me. Every move made it shift in uncomfortable ways. I thought it was going to pitch me right into the lake.

"It's okay. It's not as off balance as it feels," Tony said.

"First time?" Dave asked.

"For her? Yeah."

"Good luck, man," Dave said with a grin.

"Hey, there's a first time for everything, right?"

"Right. It's just that the first time in a kayak sometimes results in some humorous stories. I've heard them all."

"Okay, Gabby," he said. "Dip, pull, dip, pull. First one side, then the other. Just alternate."

"See you later," Dave said and walked down the dock laughing quietly to himself about some other couple's story after a disastrous kayaking attempt.

I dipped and pulled and the kayak moved a few feet forward.

"Hold on. Let me get us away from the dock."

He gave the dock a shove, then paddled a little and soon we were gliding away from the dock.

"Now. Dip, stroke. Keep your paddle up and down. Dip, stroke. Other side, good. Now develop a rhythm."

Wow, it felt so graceful when the kayak was finally moving smoothly through the water! When the kayak glided toward the island and I could see open water ahead, my own excitement kicked in. I was kayaking!

"If we get water in the boat, don't worry. Even if it swamps it's designed to stay afloat."

"That's good to know. Why are you in back?"

"If I sit in back I can paddle while you rest. Plus if only one person is going to steer it works better if they are in the back. Up front is the passenger's seat."

Out across the lake we went in a straight line for a long time. Other people were out on the lake, too. We saw other people in kayaks. People in motorboats zipped past. Off in the distance we could see motorboats just sitting on the water, fisherman sitting, waiting for a bite. It only took about two minutes for my arms to get tired but I kept paddling. When Tony noticed my strokes slowing he told me to navigate. We handed off the GPS and I rested as I watched the screen and told him where to go. It was a bit like cross country hiking except that the water was so deep that we didn't have to worry about hitting things like we did on land.

"Oh! I see an island!" I said as land appeared in front of us.

"There should be three out there," he said.

"Too bad there's only one geocache," I said. "It would be fun to visit all the islands."

"Actually there are two, one on each of the bigger islands. The littlest island is barely a rock sticking up out of the lake. When the water level is low it's probably part of the island next to it. And it is too close to the larger island to make the caches 500 feet apart."

"I wish I could see the fish but they are too far down."

"Maybe you'll be able to see fish by the shore of the island."

"Is it okay if I paddle again?" I asked.

"Sure, when you want to paddle just pick it up and start paddling. I'll match my strokes to yours."

There was a bit of a hesitation when we tried to get in sync again but when we did the kayak went even faster. I wasn't sure I wanted it to, though. It was so peaceful out on the lake. I didn't want to get to there too fast or our day on the water would get cut short.

"Tell me about the cache we are looking for," I said. "I bet it's not on an old car."

"No, though it is possible. There are whole towns under the water of some lakes. The cache on the larger island is a small one. It's called Gilligan's Island and the one on the other island is The Professor's Lab."

"Great, back to school again," I joked.

"I think it's the professor from the old TV show."

"Oh, that makes sense. I wonder how often these caches are found. Not many people are willing to rent a kayak to go get them."

"In some areas paddle caching is very popular. I bet the campers who frequent the lake bring their own kayaks along so they can fish and explore. The caches on the islands better be hidden well or they'll get muggled."

"That means they'll be hard to find."

"Another reason for the five/five rating."

"After this we'll have to drive to Belle Fourche, won't we?"

"That's the plan."

"It's quite a coincidence that this contest originated in your home town," I said.

"That's how I know about it. My dad saw it in the listings and told me about it."

"That's quite a prize for a geocaching event. How could they afford to offer a prize like that?"

"I don't know. I'm not going to look the gift horse in the mouth though," he said and I didn't know if he was serious or referring to the cache we had found earlier in our trip. "Are there lake dragons?" he asked.

"Dragons live all over the place," I said. "But I have to admit I've never seen a water dragon. The dragons I imagine here live in the trees and rocks around the lake."

"An island would make a good home for a lake dragon," he said. "Uh oh! Stop paddling! Hold on! Just a sec…"

A motor boat had gone by and the wake came at us causing Tony to steer into it so it wouldn't take us broadside. He straightened the kayak and gave me the okay to begin paddling again.

"I wish we didn't have to wear these bulky life vests," I said.

"You'll keep it on or the patrol will stop us."

"There's lake police?"

"Sometimes. I admit it isn't comfortable, but I'd rather you wear it than worry about you having to swim halfway across the lake with your clothes weighing you down."

Dip, stroke, dip, stroke. It felt good working together, watching the lake shore go by and the island grow closer. Just when I was relaxing into my role a shadowy motion at the surface of the water suddenly brought me to attention with a startled jump!

"Tony! Look out! Tree! Or..." *whack!* "Tree, I think."

The nose of the kayak shot up into the air and the whole kayak settled on top of a submerged log rocking back and forth like a teeter totter.

"Well, Dave knew what he was doing buying good, sturdy, cheap plastic, tandem kayaks for beginners," Tony said. "All right, no problem. Sit still. Let's... seeee..." he wriggled in the back of the kayak trying to get the boat to slide one way or the other.

"Try leaning forward. Don't get up, just lean."

I leaned forward and the kayak teetered forward a little but there seemed to be a branch it was catching on under the water.

"Time to take pictures!" I said.

"Time to just wait."

"Aw, we need a shot of our first bit of bad luck."

"How are you going to get a picture of something directly under a plastic hull?"

"I don't know... Let's see... I stuck the camera out beside the kayak. I had no idea what I was getting a picture of, but it was all just pixels. I could erase them later. *Click.* I pulled the camera back in and looked at the shot. It only showed a bit of green plastic and murky water. I twisted around and snapped a picture of Tony in the back tilted oddly. Then I tried one more of the tree under the kayak. I leaned out a bit. A bit more...

"Uh... Gabby?"

The kayak suddenly slid sideways and I barely had a chance to jerk the camera back before the side of the kayak entered the water and dumped several gallons of water into my lap. It was so cold! But after the shock of it I realized it was no colder than swimming pool water. The kayak lurched and bobbed as it settled in the water again as I held the camera high above my head and Tony laughed at me from the back seat.

"We need two cameras!" He bellowed. "You looked so funny!"

"I did it!" I said as I looked down into the water again. It was quickly calming down after our attempt to sink our kayak. I used my paddle to push away from the tree.

"Paddles are not tools. We steer away. You push too hard with your paddle and we'll be buying a broken paddle from Dave."

"Oops, sorry."

"I didn't think we'd need a splash guard on a nice calm lake," he said.

"It's okay. It just surprised me. I'm wet, but okay."

I handed the camera back to Tony and he stowed it in the pack. He steered the kayak around the tree until we were pointed toward the island again and we were back on track.

"Ready? Dip, stroke. Keep the paddle up and down. You don't want to slice the water. There you go."

I began the rhythm again and we slowly moved away from the tree.

"How did a tree get to the middle of the lake?" I asked.

"It floated."

"But it wasn't floating."

"A waterlogged tree is still buoyant and still hard. Watch for more of those. A little sooner warning would be better."

"Okay."

We barely got away from the tree when I saw something in the water ahead.

"Slow down. I see something."

"Probably the other end of the tree," Tony said.

"No, it's little. What is it?"

We came up beside the thing in the water and I looked down to see what it was. It was gray and shaped like an S.

"I think it's a drowned snake!"

"Snakes don't drown. They are great swimmers."

"It looks dead."

"Does it have rattles?"

"No. And it doesn't have those weird diamond patterns."

"Let me see," he said.

He gave the paddle a stroke through the water and came up beside it.

"It *is* a snake. It seems harmless enough."

"We can't leave it here. It'll die!"

"You want me to save a dead snake? You hate snakes!"

"I don't want to kill them. I just don't want them near me. If we're going to the bigger island first we can drop him off there and he should be able to find stuff to eat there."

"A dead snake?"

"Well, is it stiff?"

"No," he said as he gently tapped it with his paddle.

"Then maybe he has a chance," I said.

"To be some critter's meal," he mumbled as he gingerly picked up the snake and placed it gently on the floor of the kayak.

Dip, stroke, dip, stroke. It took us nearly an hour to reach the island.

"We need to find a place where we can beach the kayak and get out to look around," Tony said. "Let me steer and we'll find a landing spot."

Tony turned the kayak and we began slowly circling the island. We were still about thirty feet away from it when I felt something on my leg. At first I thought the pack had slid down the kayak , but I remembered that it was in the back with Tony when the kayak had slid off the tree and it had no reason to shift around on the open water, so I looked down. Tony was paddling and steering as he watched for a place where we could drag the kayak out of the water. I looked down and the snake looked back at me trying to find way out.

"Tony! SNAKE! The snake! It's alive! Oh no! It's alive! It's... it's..." and this is where I lost it. I jerked my legs out of the kayak and ran, seemingly, in midair until the kayak shifted. I fell with a splash into the lake and frantically began swimming toward the island. Tony followed in case I needed help and it was a much longer swim than I had ever attempted in the past.

He kept asking me worried questions like, "are you all right? Do you want me to catch him? Can you grab the paddle?"

I just kept swimming. I did not want to get back in that boat as long as the snake was slithering around in it.

"Did it bite you?" Tony asked.

"No... it... it... just touched me... and... blinked... and stuck its tongue out," I gasped as I swam.

When Tony saw that I could stand and wade to shore he began looking for a spot to land the kayak. I followed him on shore, shoes squishing with every step. When he caught up with me he said, "Snakes don't have eyelids."

"I didn't get a very good look at him. I only saw that he considered my leg a perfectly good ladder out of the kayak. Maybe he didn't blink."

We dragged the kayak out of the water as much as we could. Tony removed the pack and we turned the kayak on its side hoping the snake would escape while we were geocaching. I took out the camera and tried to get a few pictures of the snake but he didn't cooperate and I only managed to take a picture of his back as he searched the boat for a way out.

"How far is the cache?" I asked as we turned our backs on the kayak.

"It's on the other side of the island, but this is where I thought we could leave the kayak safely."

"How big is the island? I see trees. It's big enough to have its own mini forest."

"It's not large. But it will be a little bit of a walk."

"I want to take a picture from the top. We either have to go over the top or all the way around so we might as well get the view from the top while we're here."

"If you take pictures all the way around I can stitch them together to make a panorama picture of the whole lake."

"Cool! It's a pretty lake. My parents would like that. They'd like to see I was seeing places like this instead of that icky, green cacheamolé van."

The island was a little slice of the forest. There were rocks to climb on and lovely white barked trees that quivered in the breeze and mimicked the little wavelets on the water.

"I wonder what this island is like in a storm. Wouldn't that be cool?" I asked. "I'd like to see the lightning over the forest and the trees all aflutter and the waves out on the lake beating against the shore. I wonder if people ever camp here."

"You sure wonder a lot."

"I know. But I bet you do, too. You just aren't as vocal about your wonderings."

"I bet they do camp here and have huge swimming parties. If a group of teenagers get to the island first I bet they blare loud rock music and drink and swim."

"And get arrested by the lake patrol."

"I saw house boats at some of the houses. I bet some people come out onto the lake and live in the house boat for days at a time."

"Oh! I have an idea! We have to find the cache first!"

"Why?"

"If we do the panorama picture and I'm in it holding the cache my parents will agree that this whole trip was worth it. They might even be more open to me doing it again. All I have to do is look excited and happy in this beautiful setting and they will love it!"

Finding the cache was easier said than done. It was very well hidden. And when we closed in on ground zero we found the area full of muggles. They were kids our age and they had a boat at a rocky beach. There was a path from the beach up the rocks. There was a party going on at the top of the rocks on a large flat area. The girls were all gathered around talking and the guys were daring each other to jump off the rocks into the lake below.

"Hey man! Welcome to the party!" one of the men bellowed.

"We aren't here to…" I began but Tony interrupted.

"Thanks dude!" Tony said.

"Where are you from?"

"Franklinburg. Gabby and I go to school there."

"This," the other guy said. "Is paradise *after* school. Ever taken the Cannonball Run?"

"Uh, no," Tony said.

Just then another man ran past, flung himself off the top of the rock, tucked into a ball and fell to the water below. All the men watching jumped up and down cheering their friends on. Tony and I stepped to the edge of the rock and looked down.

"How deep is it?"Tony asked.

"Deep enough."

"Did you do it?" Tony asked him.

"This is what I do," the guy answered proudly. He got in line and waited his turn. The men seemed to have no qualms about jumping off the rock. To me it looked like a long ways down, like jumping off the peak of the roof of a single story house.

"Did you bring a swim suit?" the man called from his place in line.

"Yeah," Tony admitted hesitantly.

"Hey, Grant! Quit yacking and go!"

"After me it's your turn, Mr. Franklinburg," Grant said as he began running. He jumped off the end of the rock and plummeted to the water below.

"Hey, man, don't pay any attention to Grant. He's the loud mouth of the bunch. I'm Barry, that's Duane, Aaron, Marcy, Aria, Sandra, and Kenzie."

"I'm Tony and this is Gwendolyn," Tony said. "Is it as far as it looks?"

"I think you'll live through it. We all have, dozens of times. My advice though, do it before you drink too much. You don't want to trip and go head first. Jump out away from the rock. Always give the last guy time to swim away. We've had to call 911 a time or two."

"Are you going to jump?" I asked Tony.

"I don't know."

"I tell you what. If you will, I will."

"You will?"

"Yeah!"

"You're not scared?"

"Yeah!"

"Yeah you are or yeah you're not?"

"Yeah, I am. But I've done so many other crazy things on this trip why not add this one to the list?"

"Because it's... suicidal!"

"If it wasn't safe do you think *they* would do it?"

"Yes. Everybody knows college age guys have an inborn urge to fling themselves off rocks and do foolhardy things that land them in a body cast for the rest of their summer."

"I don't think I can do a cannonball but I could jump feet first and push off the bottom," I said.

"Oh man, oh man," Tony said, clearly worried. He paced back and forth.

"You don't have to," I told him. "But if I talk myself into it take a picture and then look for the cache while everybody is distracted."

"Oh yeah. I was wondering how we were going to look."

"Can you get a look at the screen, find a beacon, and when I jump give a good hearty cheer and then go look."

"You're kidding."

"No! Do it!"

"You're going to jump?"

"They'll be so shocked to see a girl do it that you will get a good chance to look."

"That means you have to strip down to your swim suit."

"Uh, yeah."

"And you're still willing to do it?"

"Yeah. I've got my determination set to maximum."

"Wow."

I walked to the edge and looked down. The top of the rocks actually protruded out from the rocks below, so I didn't have to worry about hitting rocks on the way down. That sure looked like a long drop. It would go fast, though, I told myself. It could only take a few seconds to fall that far.

"Can a girl try it too?" I asked.

"OOOoooo," the guys said. "Yeah the girls jump, too. After they get all the gossip out of their system."

"Hey!" one of the girls said as if she had been insulted.

"Yack, yack, yack," Aaron said to the group of girls.

"So we like to talk. What's wrong with that?"

"Let her jump," Barry said.

"How do I get back up?" I asked.

"There's a big rope down there. Look."

"If somebody will show me how to climb up, I'll jump."

"Who wants to show the lady how to climb a rope?" Barry asked.

"It's my turn next anyway. I'll do it," Aaron said. He took a good, running leap, tucked and plunged out of sight. I jogged to the edge of the rock and watched him haul himself up the rock using the rope for hand holds and walking up the rock with his feet.

"It looks easy enough," I said.

Tony and I exchanged glances. "I can't let you go first," he said.

"Why?"

He looked over the crowd and I got the idea that if I went first his macho man image was in danger.

"Do you want to?" I asked.

"It doesn't matter anymore," he said.

"Okay, hand over the GPS and the camera."

He handed the gadgets to me and began stripping off his outer clothing.

"Do you go kayaking expecting to swim?" I asked.

"It's always a possibility," he said.

"Are you really going to do it?" I asked.

"No worries! Just have the right attitude and you can do anything!"

This was Tony's attitude all through school and it irked me at times, especially when he was facing an exponentially complicated, mind bogglingly long, intricately constructed, exam about some subject that I couldn't even pronounce like inversely bipolar algorithms of paranormal improbability. Then I thought that I'd even flunk a vocabulary test. While he was getting ready for his jump I glanced at the GPS screen and it pointed me to the rocks around the Cannonball Run. That was good, because it was also a good photo spot. If I stood out there I could get a shot of the run, with the group behind and the drop off in the foreground.

I was probably the only one there who could see Tony's real fear as he squared up, took a deep breath and charged to his doom. He tried not to yell on the way down, but I think he squeaked a little bit when he realized how long the fall was. I snapped the picture a tenth of a second before the jump. Then I snapped another one of him surfacing at the bottom.

"You forgot to cannonball!" Aaron shouted to Tony as he climbed the rope.

Oh yeah, the cache.

I climbed around on the rocks looking in the obvious hiding places. I couldn't imagine any cache not being muggled with all these kids crawling around on the rocks. They said they came out here often. Surely they had run across it. Was it even still here?

"Hey Gwendolyn! It's your turn!"

Mine? You mean they were going to hold me to it? Yikes!

"You can call me Gwen, or Gabby."

"Gwendolyn makes a better chant," Grant said. "Gwen-do-lyn! Gwen-do-lyn!"

"Will you switch to Gwen if I jump?" I asked.

"Gwen-do-lyn!"

"Hey," one of the girls said. "They're actually being very nice to you. For me they chanted Kenzie Kenzie Bo Benzie."

"Oh."

"Just do it and you'll earn their utmost respect."

"What if I don't care about their utmost respect?" I asked.

"It's really fun after you get used to it," she said.

I was just trying to get my foot out of the leg hole of my jeans when Tony came back. I was very grateful to him for not saying, "You have shoulders!" The other girls were nicely tanned and I was white as a college student cooped up in a dimly lit library for five months.

"You don't have to do this," he said.

"You don't want me to?"

He ran his hands up and down my arms in a slightly protective way.

"Don't let these guys intimidate you. We're here to geocache."

"Then geocache," I said as I reached down and picked up the GPS. "I'll be back in a few minutes."

I had to psyche myself up for this. It's just a natural swimming pool, I told myself. Just think of it like a swimming pool. Just jump in. When you feel the bottom, push up. That's all there is to it. Just do it!

O... kay, just do it, just do it... just... no chickening out. Just jump. Oh shoot... oh shoot. I ran, not my fastest because I was too scared to rush to my doom. I got to the edge and almost stopped but I couldn't so I leaped. And it was not at all like Wiley Coyote jumping to his doom. There was no running in place. The rocks looked closer than I ever thought possible. It looked like I could touch them. Down I fell, and fell and then the water closed over me. I shuddered from the cold. Oh, golly, it was so cold! And it was a lot deeper than I thought possible. I wished for the bottom a lot harder when I thought about catfish and my lungs started burning. I felt silt at my toes and pushed off but it was too early and I didn't get any purchase so I had to wait to reach the surface again. I had water up my nose and a cough fighting for release, but I'd done it! I jumped! And when I broke the surface again it was the most wondrous feeling! I coughed and sputtered and looked for the rope, but I did it knowing I had faced my fear and lived to find that geocache. Climbing the rope wasn't as easy as the guys made it look but I managed to pull myself up the rock until I crawled over the top again and ran over to where Tony was standing.

"I did it! I did it!" I cried as I clasped him in an excited hug. He wasn't sure what to do. He put his arms around me but it wasn't a jubilant celebratory hug. It was as if he couldn't believe he actually got a hug from me. Maybe it was the swim suit. Maybe he'd just never seen this much of me before. As far as swimsuits go it was a very conservative cut. My mom had shopped with me. "Did you take my picture?" I asked.

"Gabby... no. I was too scared. I was afraid you'd jump crooked and hit a rock or..."

"I'll do it again!"

"No! No, that's okay," he said.

"Did you find the geocache?"

"No, I haven't looked for long. I wanted to make sure you were okay first."

I thought my dad must have threatened him to within an inch of his life, or… or maybe he really did care that much.

With our jumps behind us we were accepted into the group and offered a beer.

"Oh, no thanks," I said. "We need to get going. We're just renting the kayak and we need to take it back."

"I'll take one. We've got a little time," Tony said. He took a beer and began talking with the guys about fishing. What was *he doing*? We were supposed to be geocaching and we had to have the kayak back by six o'clock. I gave him an exasperated huff before I went to look for the cache. If he was going to distract the muggles the least I could do was use the distraction to our advantage.

I found rocks, rocks and more rocks. There was a tree out on the rocky point but it was a nice, straight, attractive tree. Geocachers hardly ever used straight, healthy trees for their hides. They used old, gnarly, sickly trees with gaping hollows and loose bark. Trees that looked like they held secrets inside. This tree held no secrets. It was a young, spritely tree. A cheerful tree with brilliant green leaves quivering over the dazzling blue lake. I snapped a picture of the tree with the lake in the background. I tried not to look at the GPS very often but when I reached the spot it was directing me to there were only rocks, a few weeds and a beer bottle. I picked up the beer bottle thinking it couldn't be the cache because it was made of glass and it was too new. With the bottle eliminated I was down to rocks and spindly weeds. The weeds wouldn't hide anything. I kept walking around staring at the ground, looking to Tony to see if he was going to help. Occasionally he'd watch me but he gave me no clues. This was a five difficulty and if he thought this newbie geocacher was going to find it on her own he was mistaken. I tried broadening my search downhill, out of sight of the party.

Hmm, I thought, what would a Gilligan's Island cache look like? I had never seen the show. It was on before I was born, but I knew it was about a bunch of people stranded on an island. So what would be on the island? What kind of an island was it? A tropical island? It made sense for it to be a tropical island. They needed to live off the land. So what did they have? Coconuts? Uhh… coconuts. That's all I could come up with. I'd never been stranded on an island before. Maybe there were wild bananas? I didn't think so, though I was sure they didn't live off of coconuts alone. If I did I'd go crazy. I never did like coconut, but… if coconuts was the only thing I could think of on Gilligan's island I thought it might be what the cache owner had thought of, too. And a coconut looks very much like a rock. So oddly enough, I began looking for coconuts! And do you know what you find if you start looking for coconuts? Why… you find coconuts! Yes, the cache was in a coconut, though it was spray painted to look like a rock. But changing my thinking to include coconut shaped objects made the shape of the coconut jump out at me. It was hidden amongst the rocks. It just looked darker, rounder and hairier than the island rocks. I found it! It was under a half coconut shell. The shell had been nibbled on my animals, which led me to believe the snake might be able to find food here. I turned it over and a small, plastic jar was underneath. The jar was little enough that I could pretty much just palm it and sneak it out so I held it out of sight and climbed the hill to find a party in full swing. The girls had spread out platefuls of snacks on a plastic folding table. Music blared. They all had cans of beer in their hands and there was a small fire going in a fire pit. I found Tony sitting on the ground talking to Aaron and Grant. How could I get his attention?

It turned out I didn't have to. He was very attuned to me. As soon as I appeared his focus changed. I flashed the cache briefly and nodded in the direction of the top of the island.

The top of the island was only a short walk away. It was out of sight of the party, but trees blocked the view between the two sites. I sat down and opened the cache. I took out the log book, but Tony had the pen so I couldn't sign the log until he showed up. Under the log, though, was a shiny gold disk. A pathtag! Oh cool! I dumped the tag out of the cache container and plucked it out from the small trinkets in the cache.

"Well, would you look who's being anti social," a voice said.

I looked up and Grant stood beside a tree. I stuffed the log and the swag back into the cache and set it beside me, out of sight.

"I'm not being anti social," I said. "I just don't care for beer and loud music."

"You better be careful if you stray from the party around here. You might be asking for some… attention. So, are you and Tony… together?"

"Of course we're together. We arrived in the same boat. We'll have to leave in the same boat."

"You wouldn't have to."

"Yes, I do," I said. "We've been traveling. We need to be in Belle Fourche tomorrow evening."

"Belle Fourche? Never heard of it."

"It's in South Dakota. We've got a long drive tomorrow."

"You sure do. But you didn't answer my question. If you like, I could show you my boat. We'll be going back and forth between shore and here picking up people from the lodge parking lot. I'll buy you a drink at the lodge. Somebody else can bring the boat over. What do ya say?"

"I don't think I should do that."

He took a step closer.

"You like it quiet? We could go to my place."

I didn't know what to say. *No* wasn't in my vocabulary. I knew what he was proposing I couldn't do. It didn't fit with the plan at all and I wouldn't go with him anyway. I would only leave with Tony. But when I couldn't bring myself to just say *no* then I had to come with an effective substitute and an effective substitute required explanations and Grant didn't look like he wanted explanations.

"I think I should find Tony," I said.

I grabbed the cache, hiding it from view again and stood but when I did I realized Tony was standing right behind Grant.

"I suggest you go back to the party," Tony said.

"Okay," I answered.

"Not you. Him," he said. "We'll be on our way soon."

"Hey man, you can't blame a guy for trying!" Grant said.

Tony just glared at Grant. I'd never seen Tony truly serious about anything and he made quite a striking figure. I sure wouldn't argue with him, especially after hearing what he did to that mugger.

"We all come out here," Grant said. "Everybody's friends, you know? We all know each other from town. We all know who's taken, who's not. A new girl shows up, she can expect some attention around here."

"We're not from around here," Tony said flatly. "And I do know where you're coming from. And I'm telling you. Gabby is taken, unless she doesn't want to be."

"So darlin', what do you say?" Grant asked.

"I think we should leave," I said to Tony.

"Good idea," he said.

Grant slunk back to the party. He stopped a few times to say something, changed his mind, and continued on.

"We only have one problem," I said after Grant left.

"What?"

I showed him the cache.

"You found it?"

"Yeah, but it was out on that rocky point. How are we going to put it back now?"

"Well, first things first. Did you sign the log?"

"No. I got interrupted."

"Okay, well, sign the log. I'll take it back."

"You don't know where it goes."

"Where *does* it go?"

"Under the coconut."

"How did you find a coconut in a place like this?"

"I started thinking about the TV show and coconuts came to mind so I started looking for coconuts and I found one! Once I was thinking about round hairy things it was easier to spot. It looks like a hairy rock."

I opened the cache and pulled out the log. He handed me the pen, so I handed the container to Tony. He dumped the contents into the palm of his hand. I signed the log and handed it back to him. He showed me the swag.

"We seem to be having excellent pathtag luck," he said.

"Why?"

"We've been looking for some really cool caches. People are more likely to leave a pathtag in a cache they award a favorite point to. The last person to find the cache must have enjoyed the hunt and the hiding place."

The pathtag had a green sea turtle on it and a hibiscus flower and the word KonaCachers.

"Why are we getting geocachers from California and Hawaii way up here?" I asked.

"I don't know. If we go to Hawaii or California let's make a pathtag so they can ask why people from South Dakota would be all the way down there."

"It's not the same. They get tourists from up north all the time."

"Maybe they come here to see what snow looks like."

"Maybe."

I added all the swag the little bottle would hold in trade for the pathtag. I didn't know why the little disks appealed to me, but I thought, since they were specially made, that they deserved as much of a trade as I could afford.

"It was under a coconut?" Tony asked.

"Yeah."

"How far from ground zero?"

"Let me see the GPS."

I zoomed in on the little screen until I could only see the cache and the shoreline.

"Here's ground zero," I said pointing to the little cache icon. "The hiding spot was about half way between ground zero and the water. Right... about... here." I pointed to the spot I thought the coconut resided.

We heard the sound of a boat motor and saw a pontoon boat closing in on Cannonball Run.

"There's no way we can put this back unobserved," Tony said. "I say we go find the other one. On our way back we can look for a landing spot on this side of the island. Maybe I can climb up and replace it without being seen."

"We can do that? Just take the cache? What if we can't put it back?"

"Then we try again tomorrow."

"Rent the kayak twice?"

"Let's give these people some space."

"Okay."

Tony had to go back to the party to get the pack and our clothes. When he came back he was scowling. We skipped the panorama picture at the top of the island and hiked to the kayak. We shoved the kayak back into the water and Tony tossed in the pack. He held the kayak steady and I waded out and attempted to climb in. I was glad I was used to the water temperature, because it wasn't easy to clamber into the kayak while it was freely floating. It kept trying to tilt. It would have been even more awkward if I wasn't already wet.

"Just in case you run into that problem again," Tony said. "You're welcome to tell guys anything you want. I'll back you."

"Are we locked onto the next cache?" I asked.

"Locked and ready," he said handing the GPS across to me. After we paddled out to open water it was obvious where the other island was. As we paddled towards it a boat pulled away from Cannonball Run. It looked as if it was going to cross the lake but then it turned sending a large wake straight towards us.

"That son of a..." Tony said as the wake hit us broadside. Tony tried to keep the kayak from flipping but we didn't have enough time to react. The water closed over my head and I struggled to extricate myself from the kayak.

"Let go of the paddle!" Tony yelled as he tread water beside me. "It'll float!"

That was good to hear. Without the paddle I could better use my hands so I was able to pull my legs out and twist around.

"Are you okay?" Tony asked.

"Are there catfish in this lake?" I whined as my hair dripped into the lake and I snuffled water out my nose.

"No, but they wouldn't hurt you anyway. Let's turn this thing over."

"Did we lose the pack?"

"I don't think so. I heard it rattling around inside. Where's the GPS?"

"Around my neck," I said. "I wanted my hands free to paddle."

"I hope it's as water resistant as they claim."

Tony rolled the kayak over and instructed me to hang on one side of it while he hung on the other. Then he told me to climb in. I thought I should take Kayaking 101 if we were going to do anymore paddle caching. Climbing in was difficult.

"Try to keep the kayak balanced while I climb up," he said. He didn't climb into his seat, though. He straddled the kayak and inched forward until he was right behind me. "Don't let me near that guy again. I'm likely to do something I'd be sorry for later." Then he hugged my shoulders. "He can pick on me, but if he hurts you he's asking for it."

"I'm okay. No catfish got my toes," I assured him.

"Is the GPS still functional?"

"Yeah, but I don't have a paddle."

"Okay, hang on," he said as he scooted back into position. "We'll get the paddle."

He steered the kayak around and eased up next to the paddle floating a short distance away, then used his paddle to pull it right beside my seat so I could grab it.

"If Gilligan's Island was hidden in a coconut I wonder what The Professor's Cache is hidden in," I said as I took up my paddle.

"I don't know. Let's go look."

The other island was little bigger than my bedroom back home but it had its own little forest of trees on top. We stopped when we got close.

"It looks like the cache is on the left where that dead tree is," I said.

"Oh boy, what fun. A hide over the water."

"We could leave the kayak on the island and climb to the middle of the tree from on land," I suggested.

"Except I don't see any place to beach a kayak."

"Let's go around. Maybe there is a place and we can't see it."

We paddled around the little island and there seemed to be no place to safely leave the kayak.

"Okay, I say we paddle directly under the tree and see if we can reach it from the kayak," Tony said.

"The tree? Or the cache?"

"Yeah."

"I thought we weren't supposed to stand up in the kayak."

"We aren't. Oh, it won't hurt the kayak to stand up but it balances better the lower you stay. So if you do stand up in it you're risking a dunking."

"We got the dunking over with twice, thanks to Grant."

"We just want to take our dunkings under controlled circumstances," he said. "Under a fallen tree is not a safe place to go overboard."

The tip of the kayak fell into shadows as it passed under the fallen tree. The tree was still alive, because part of its roots remained in the soil of the island. But the side of it was embedded in the bottom of the lake. I imagined it dying a slow death, the part under water slowly rotting away, while the leaves and the roots functioned above.

"The Professor would never have hidden a geocache here," I said when we sat squarely beneath the trunk of the tree. I saw nests in the branches above. It felt incongruous to have fresh green leaves and baby birds growing up in a dying tree. There were plenty of trees on top of the island that surely made a better nesting place, but then when I saw the multitude of bugs in the shade of the tree I understood why it might make a good nesting place. It was like living in a birdie cafeteria.

"Do you see it?" Tony asked.

"No," I said as I craned my neck to see directly above me.

"They would put it within reach, but out of the water."

"Well, that rules out half the tree. The bottom half is too high to reach. The top is lower and has more hiding places, too."

"Is there a hint?"

"I don't know. I'll check."

Several clicks later I said, "It just says U-P-O-S."

"Oh! Well, that helps a lot," Tony said.

"What's a U-P-O-S?"

"Do you remember what a UPOR is?"

"Yeah…"

"Well, UPOS is an Unnatural Pile of Sticks."

"A tree is all sticks."

"Look for unnatural sticks."

"Is this like organic produce?"

"Sort of. It will look like sticks but placed in an unnatural way."

My mom was a health food nut except when it came to foods that were unhealthy that she liked. However, she insisted organic foods were better, whereas I could not see any difference. A carrot was a carrot. I didn't really care where my carrots were grown. They came from the ground. The ground was dirty. So I had a choice between dirty carrots or dirty carrots. As long as my mom did the cooking I wasn't going to complain about where the food came from. So I didn't really see the point of natural versus unnatural sticks. Until…

"I think I might see it."

"Where?"

"Riiiight… there! Do you see it?"

"Is it sticks?"

"Uh… yeah, sort of, held up with some wirey… wire."

"Let me get where you are."

He paddled the kayak forward until he was sitting in the same spot.

"Oh! Chicken wire! Good catch! I wonder if I can… reach it…" He shakily stood up and reached over his head. The kayak quivered with his foot movements. It reminded me of the tension on a tightrope when the tightrope walker is trying frantically to balance. He knelt down again to lower his center of gravity. "I don't think that's it. But I'll give it one more try."

"Can't we climb up that big branch right there?" I asked.

"I tell you what. You try the branch while I try to reach it from below. Then I won't have to worry about tossing you overboard again and you can try looking from above."

"Okay."

"Let me put you in line with the branch."

It was rather tricky and very shaky to climb out of the kayak and onto the branch. There was nothing to push against. If I pushed against the kayak it moved more than I did. I was just about to pull myself up onto the rough bark of the branch when the motorboat went by making the kayak buck under my feet and both feet slipped off. I landed on my bottom on the front end of the kayak launching Tony's end up into the air. I grabbed a branch to keep from falling into the lake and the branch came loose, sending me head first into the water. The GPS sank quickly and when I struggled to swim it snagged on a piece of the tree deep under the water. I was trapped! I couldn't get up for air! There was thrashing about all around me and everything was confusing to me with too many arms, legs, branches and currents swishing around as I tugged and pulled, trying frantically to free myself! I felt a hand on my shoulder and a steadying hand, then a yank to cause the safety buckle on the back of the lanyard to release. I hit Tony's hand in my panic causing him to drop the lanyard. I came up spitting and sputtering, coughing and crying. Tony made sure I was able to keep myself above water before he dove to search for the GPS.

"I lost it!" I cried. "I'm sorry, Tony! I lost it!"

I tried diving and feeling around for the lanyard, but I couldn't find it. I surfaced again and found Tony glaring at the lake behind him. He was so mad and I was so sorry. I knew how expensive a new GPS was and it was his link to his favorite hobby. I dove again. I didn't know if I was crying from fright or sorrow. I just had to find it!

"Gabby, stop, stop for just a second," Tony said. When I stopped my hysterics he said, "Are you all right?"

"I... I think so. But I lost it. It sank and I couldn't grab it. I'm sorry! I'll get you a new one!"

He just put his head in his hands and said to himself, "Thank God." He was almost in tears himself. "Gabby, if it ever comes to a choice. A GPS or a car or a kayak or... I don't know what... let it go. Things can be replaced. You cannot. Oh Lord, I wish we were on land so I could hug you and never let go." When he looked up he had tears in his eyes and I realized he wasn't worried about the GPS. He was worried about... me.

The Professor's Cache was hidden in an old transistor radio. The battery compartment opened to reveal a bison tube and inside the bison tube was a log sheet. Of course getting back to the kayak I found an easier way to get to the cache. There was a space between two branches where we could have wedged the kayak, but we didn't see it in time.

"Do you remember the way back to the store?" I asked.
"We'll get there. But first we need to replace the Gilligan's Island cache."
"Are you sure we should? You might run into Grant up there."
"I might," he admitted grimly. "I might kick his sorry butt, too."
"No, don't."
"We'll go scope it out. Maybe I will, maybe I won't."

When we reached the bigger island again we could easily tell that the party had doubled in size. Cannonball Run was surrounded by guys and gals laughing and partying, the music carrying out across the water. Every couple of minutes somebody would run and jump off the rocks and the crowd would cheer.

"I see where the cache goes," I said as we sat in the distance. "I think I can get up there from this side. Sneak in close and I'll swim in and climb the rock."
"No way."
"Then what are we going to do?"
"I'll do it. You can give me signals to show me which way to go."
"No way. If Grant sees you there's going to be a fight. He won't hurt me. He'll just talk."
"Won't hurt you? He nearly drowned you!"
"He didn't mean to. He was just being mean."

It's hard to have a stare down when you cannot face your opponent, but that's what we did and I knew he wasn't going to let me go.

He paddled in as quietly and closely as he dared. He pulled his feet up out of the hole in the kayak and straddled the boat. I'd have to remember that it was a stable way to extricate myself. I handed him the cache before he swam to shore and climbed up onto the nearest rocks. He glanced upwards to make sure the coast was clear. He had to put the cache in his pocket to climb but he scaled the rock quickly and skillfully, glancing my way occasionally. When he got closer to the coconut I began signaling for him to move to his right and up. We had to play a quick game of colder/hotter until he finally saw the coconut. He stuck the cache into the crack between the rocks, covered it with the coconut and stacked rocks around to make the coconut blend in. I signaled an okay sign to him to let him know it was hidden well enough.

A group of men appeared at the top of the rock. Grant! I wanted to signal to Tony to come down as fast as he could but they saw me out in the kayak and if I signaled to Tony it would draw attention to him. All I could do was hope the two men wouldn't see each other until it was too late.

Hurry, oh Tony, hurry. Where is that geocacher stealth you told me about? I wished I could do something but anything I did would only make matters worse! All I could do was sit.

The men waved and I waved back. Grant's wave wasn't as friendly as the others. I was guessing the other two men didn't know who I was or how I was connected to the group. I wanted to keep it that way. When I waved Tony looked up but I don't know how much of the group he could see from his angle. They didn't seem to spot him until he had swam half way back to the kayak and then they exclaimed and pointed. Grant looked angry and stalked away.

I never paddled harder than I did going back to the store, but it wasn't fast enough. Grant badgered us all the way until one of those infamous lake patrol boats came on the scene. When the officer saw him skimming past us just to try and tip the kayak the blue light came on and I breathed a sigh of relief.

We were not on the dock for a minute before Tony clasped me in a hug, life vest and all. He tied the kayak to the dock, dropped in his life vest and helped me out of mine.

"Life vests don't help a whole lot when you're tied to the bottom of the lake," I said.

When my life vest was in the kayak with his he tried another hug, but it was chilly and damp. He put his arm around my shoulders and we went back into the store to tell Dave his kayak was back safe and sound.

"Maybe kayaking isn't our thing yet," he told Dave.

"Oh?"

"Yeah. And if Grant comes looking for me tell him I'm out of town. Permanently."

"Are those kids out there again?" Dave asked.

"Yeah, jumping off Cannonball Run," Tony said.

"Foolhardy kids. But I have to admit I did the same thing. Lucky I lived through it. Don't you go and do crazy stuff like that."

"Okay, we won't."

Chapter 24

"We won't do anything foolhardy, will we Gabby?" Tony asked as we climbed into the van.

"No," I said sadly. "Not without the GPS. I'm still sorry, Tony."

"Don't be. It's as much my fault as it is yours. We'll stop in Grand Rapids and get another one."

"But I know you can't afford it any more than I can."

"Nonsense. If a GPS is what we need to find more adventures I'll work at the golf course all summer to pay it off."

"But you shouldn't have to.."

He almost put the van into *reverse* but he stopped when he knew he had to make a point.

"Gabby, look at me," he said. "If we were strangers and you harmed something of mine, I'd expect you to make it right, just because that's what we do when we damage something. Like the van. We tore it up. We made it right. Ned will never know what this van has been through."

"Unless he reads his new bumper stickers."

"But Gabby, I know you can't afford a new GPS. And hopefully our... friendship goes beyond that. I was kind of wishing I could get a newer model anyway. Maybe now I can instead of holding onto the old one."

"But... it's not just the GPS. It brought us to so many places. I'll get a new one. Stop in a city and I'll find you a new one. I've got a card. I can pay my parents back."

"No." Something was bugging him and he turned off the van. "Take a walk with me."

He got out of the van, so I opened my door and got out, too. We walked to the end of the dock and then sat with our feet in the water.

"The GPS means nothing to me," he said. "You. You mean more to me than anything I could ever think of. If you let that dumb gadget take you from me I'd never get over it. Do you understand what I'm saying?"

"Of course. I'd hope any person would put their life above a personal possession."

He sighed, as if I didn't understand.

"Name anything. Anything you can think of. Name the thing that means the most to you in the whole wide world."

"It isn't things that mean the most to me. It's the times."

"And the times are made special by the people we experience them with."

"Uh huh."

"And Gabby… Gwendolyn, there is nothing, nobody, no time I treasure more than the time I've spent with you. That GPS is just junk compared to the times we've had. We'll get another one, just so that we'll have it to lead us on more adventures. But it's not your responsibility to buy it."

"Find a store where they sell them. Let's see what they have. We have to find the event, too, you know."

Dave was cleaning out the kayak. I think his ears picked up the possibility of a sale. A big sale.

"GPS units?" he asked.

"Yeah, but not just any GPSr," Tony said. "We need one for geocaching."

"I've got a few. Let's take a look."

In the back corner of the cluttered store was a little glass case. In the case was a conglomeration of expensive fishing reels, fifty dollar sunglasses, scopes for rifles, digital cameras and… four GPS units. One Tony ruled out immediately because it was for use on a boat. Another was for hiking but not geocaching. That left two units.

"Can we try them out?" Tony asked.

"I don't see why not," Dave said.

I guess you can get more of a demonstration in a little town with only one store and no customers. Dave found some batteries in a drawer and we put them in the GPSrs, then took them outside so they could find a satellite. Tony found our location on the map, but there were no caches loaded into the device. Still, he was able to see how readable the screen was and zoom in and out and see all the features listed in the menus.

"Do you have wifi?" Tony asked Dave.

"If it'll help make a sale," Dave replied.

When the guys went into a high tech huddle I decided it was time to check out the snacks again. They got out the laptop and rigged up the GPSrs and Tony showed Dave the geocaching site and explained the hobby to him.

"We've had a few geocachers in here," Dave said. "I've got an account but it's only so I can own the two caches out on the islands. Somebody told me I could rent a few kayaks if there were geocaches out there."

"Well, it worked. You rented one to us," Tony told him.

When Tony could see the nearby caches he was able to judge the two units capabilities.

"Gabby, would you go see if I left my wallet in the van?" he asked.

I am so gullible. I went to the van to look for Tony's wallet and of course I didn't find it because he was inside paying for the GPSr. When I reappeared without the wallet he held the GPS unit and the bag of snacks up triumphantly.

"You tricked me," I said.

"No, I didn't. Gabby, I just want to be right here beside you. Finding adventures. Let's go find a motel. Tomorrow we'll find that event. I wonder how we'll measure up."

As we were climbing back into the van Dave went back to the kayak to hose it off and add it to the rack. Instead he knelt down.

"How did you get in there?" he asked the snake. "You're lucky that girl didn't spot you." Then he gently caught the snake and let it go into the woods.

Chapter 25

It was hard to believe that our trip was nearly over. We had a long drive ahead of us to reach Belle Fourche but we drove part of it after leaving the lake. We splurged a bit on a better motel and it was worth it because the shower was nicer and the beds had foam toppers and luxurious comforters. There was a coffee maker in the bathroom, but we didn't use it to make coffee in the morning. We had seen a coffee shop on our way into town and went back to it. We brought the laptop and the GPS in and loaded up the caches on the highway we were to travel that day. Then we only stopped to stretch our legs where there were geocaches. The closer we got to Belle Fourche the slower Tony seemed to drive. He seemed thoughtful, which was unusual for him. Usually he was very extroverted, never keeping things to himself. When I saw the Belle Fourche city limits sign I understood how he felt. Our trip was almost over and when it was over… I had to go home. I was beginning to see how Sarah felt at the end of school. I didn't want to leave Tony here. Even if it was his home town, the end of our adventures saddened me. When I thought of the noise and commotion I'd find at home with siblings coming and going and vying for attention, the quiet of running from an angry man in a speed boat seemed peaceful. Hiding from bears and listening to stories about cannibalistic demons seemed like fun. A Sweet Sixteen party full of teenagers was going to drive me crazy. Maybe I could hole up in my room and call Tony and let him hear what he was missing.

"Time to turn on the GPS," Tony said. "And find the event. It's at a pizza joint. We don't have to find ground zero. We only need to find the place, but the coordinates will still help."

I was excited, even in my melancholy state. I had never been to a geocaching event before. It seemed strange that I looked forward to hearing geocaching stories and the chatter about FTFs and DNFs and hides. He stopped on the way so I could stand at the geographical center of the United States and find the cache nearby. We read the sign and talked about visiting Kansas where the other center of the US was located.

"All right, the event," he finally said. "Are you tired of pizza?"

"No, I'm a college student," I said. "Pizza is my middle name."

Twiggy pulled up outside the pizza place. He said events are almost always at restaurants because geocachers like to eat, or at parks because they like the outdoors and geocaching. Events at parks sometimes had games.

This one was at a pizza parlor and so it was termed a meet and greet. I hoped I had enough money for a Hawaiian pizza as I slid out of the van.

I expected to be able to figure out easily who the geocachers were but they blended in with the regular pizza lunch crowd. Only a simple sign that said RESERVED and a fat box with Travel Bugs in it tipped me off that this was a geocaching event. A man walked up to Tony. He was tall and spry with eyes squinted a bit from being out in the sun a lot. He was tanned darker than his gray hair, but he didn't look old. He looked comfortable with himself, confident but mild mannered. I thought he was one person you better not double dog dare to do anything because he had probably already done it and knew more about it than you did.

"You made it!" he said with a broad grin.

"I told you I would. Gabby, this is my dad. Dad, this is the Gwendolyn."

"I've heard a lot about you," Tony's dad said. "You can call me Greg, or The Devious Cachester. Most of these people shorten it to Cachester."

"You geocache, too?" I asked.

"We got into it together," Tony said. "It was an activity father and son could do together when mom was out of the picture."

"Did you do it?" Greg asked his son.

"I... no, Dad, I didn't. But we're getting there."

Greg Yancy looked disappointed.

"What were you supposed to do?" I asked Tony.

He looked a bit uncomfortable and then suggested we should meet the other geocachers. We walked around to talk to the other attendees and it seemed Tony knew most of the people there. They called him by name and then he introduced me. There were not many of them and they seemed to be a tight group unused to outsiders, but they were all friendly and glad to see Tony had brought a friend. The time for the start of the event came and went but pizza began arriving so we settled down to eat. Twenty minutes later most of the geocachers had slowed down and the pizza pans were half empty.

"Hey Cachester!" a man called across the assembly. "We're all waiting expectantly down here!"

"Sorry, Skeeter," he said, then he stood up. "It looks like the normal crowd is here. The Carters are on vacation, hopefully finding the lowest cache in the US. You're all waiting for the big announcement, but it appears Dad's Caddy has lost his bet with the Cachester."

"Awww, why?" half the geocachers asked Tony. The other half were glaring at me.

"Why? What's going on?" I asked Tony.

He hesitated and stared at his feet for a few seconds before explaining, "Gwen, the contest we were in was a bet I had with my dad. I asked him how I could break the ice and get to know you better."

"Break the ice? What ice? We're best friends!"

"He said spending time doing something together, like geocaching, would either bring us together or break us up. And… so…he said if I could… get you to marry me, that he'd pay for the honeymoon. We just picked the Bahamas because it sounded exotic."

"There was no contest?"

"A bet is a contest of sorts," he said.

"I got shot at and rained on and slept in a van with you. I climbed mountains and almost got struck by lightning just so you could win *a bet with your dad*?" I was mad. "I almost got arrested! And we're lucky nobody found that knife! If somebody took it you'd be in jail right now!" The anger came from several sources. He had lied to me. He'd tricked me into his scheme and his bed. I had fallen for it hook, line and sinker. I felt humiliated and embarrassed. There was a room full of people expecting me to be a happily engaged woman and I sat there being a shocked, angry, mess of emotions.

"A door prize! We have a door prize!" Tony's dad announced, hoping that changing the subject would diffuse the situation. It sure did. I headed for the door.

"Gwen don't! You don't have a ride home!" Tony said as he knocked his chair over in his haste to stop me.

"I'll figure something out!" I cried and ran out the door. I stumbled out into the parking lot and a car screeched to halt to avoid hitting me.

"Gwendolyn! I'm sorry!"

I just kept walking. I needed activity to burn off the tears. I might have been at the center of the United States but I was so far off course that I didn't know how I was going to get back. I had no money, no car, no plan.

"Gwen, please don't leave," Tony said when he caught up to me.

"You lied. I can't believe I went along with your crazy scheme for two weeks! You could have told me! I'm going home. I don't know how but don't worry about me. I'll find a way. Go… have fun with your geocaching friends. I'm out of here."

"I'll take you home."

"I don't think so. I'm so mad… you're lucky I'm able to talk to you at all!"

"I won't leave you out here."

"And you can't come with me," I said and walked miserably away.

I decided a plan had to come first. What could I do without money? This business about growing up was not for sissies. It was even more humiliating when I had to call my parents for help.

"Hello?"

"Hi, Mom, it's me."

"Gwendolyn! How are you?"

"I'm... I'm okay. But... I got myself into a mess and I think I'll be okay."

"What kind of a mess?"

"It's a long story. Is there any way I could borrow enough money to rent a car?"

"Where's your car?"

"In Franklinburg. In storage."

"And where are you?"

"Belle Fourche."

"Where is Belle Fourche and how did you get there?"

"I rode with Twiggy. But... Mom, if you don't want to help just say no and I'll figure something else out."

"Something's wrong. I'm a mother and mothers sense these things."

"Everything will be fine, as soon as I get a car."

"You've got a card. Put it on that."

"You said it was for emergencies."

"It's for legitimate needs."

"I'm not sure what a legitimate need is."

"You need to come home."

"Okay, I'll come home."

I'd never rented a car before. I just handed over what they asked for and signed what they told me to. I felt like a little kid in a big, adult world and now I was by myself on top of everything else. I passed a little book store and stopped to see if they had a road atlas. They had atlases but not one that would show me the way home.

"Try the gas station five blocks down," the bookstore owner advised. "They probably have a state map."

"I need more than a state map, but it's a start. Maybe I'll pass a truck stop along the way."

It didn't help much that Twiggy called every hour or so.

The car was really cool. It had a super stereo system and I cranked up the satellite radio and sang for mile after mile. After a while the singing made me sad, because Twiggy and I had sung some great duets along with the radio.

I didn't drive very far before darkness set in and I thought I better stop in the next town. I looked at the map and figured the next town big enough to have a motel was fifty plus miles. I stopped at the first motel I came to and then realized I hadn't eaten dinner. I was still very hurt. My heart ached worse than any hunger pangs could. My phone continued to ring off and on and I answered it before I turned it off.

"Hello?"

"Gwen."

"I don't want to talk yet."

"Where are you? Are you okay?"

"I'm going home. I rented a car."

"Come back."

"I can't. I told my mom I'd be home tomorrow."

"When will I see you?"

"I don't know."

"When *can* I see you?"

"Twig... I don't know."

"When school..."

I had to hang up before I cried again, then I cried anyway. I turned the phone off and went to bed still in my clothes, hungry, sad, and lonely. The bed felt empty. Beds shouldn't feel empty. I hugged the other pillow. I wondered if there was a geocache nearby, then realized I didn't have a GPS. I turned on the light and found my phone again. Maybe I could turn my phone into a GPS. It was midnight before I figured out that I not only had a GPS but after I downloaded an app, I could even bring up nearby caches! At least I could in my motel room. There was one on the next street over. I turned off my phone again glad to have that one piece of normalcy back in place. Just knowing I wasn't cut off from finding those silly boxes was a comfort to me. My link to the wonders of anyplace-I-happened-to-be was still connected.

In the morning I realized I'd walked away from all my possessions. All I had were the clothes on my back and what was in my pockets. So I had thirty four dollars, my phone, fourteen cents in change, a pen, and the pathtag. I fingered the little metal disk and wondered who the geocacher was who had it made. I thought Twiggy needed a pathtag to drop into caches. Maybe I'd save up my pennies over the summer and... maybe I wouldn't. I skipped the shower, since I didn't have a hair brush, and smoothed down my hair as much as I could.

I bought a ninety-nine cent breakfast burrito at the nearest fast food place, then drove to the nearest geocache. I stopped beside a little ditch. A short rock wall framed a metal culvert. I felt around the edge of the culvert checking for magnetic micros. I scanned the rocks of the wall for any nooks or crannies. There was a fence running along one side of the ditch and I found the cache in the first post. It was a hollow victory, though. There was nobody there to celebrate with.

I sat in the car planning my route and my phone rang again. Twiggy.

I pulled into my hometown in the mid afternoon but I had to turn in the rental car to avoid added expense. It was a two mile walk to my parents' house but I was so used to walking that I didn't think to call for a ride. I just pointed myself in the right direction and started hiking. The house was locked when I got home. I knocked and my sister answered the door.

"Gwen! You're home!" Meredith said with a big hug.

"Yeah, I'm home," I said wearily.

"Where were you? Mom was so worried!"

"She was?"

"Well yeah, DUH."

"Do I still have a bedroom?"

"Nothing has changed."

"Okay."

I started up the stairs but Meredith was impossible. She had to know everything!

"You mean you went camping... WITH A GUY?"

"Yeah. We're just friends." I wished I could edit speech balloons. I missed Tony so much. We were not just friends. Something had happened, something that erased the just in just friends. Something had happened and we had gone beyond friends we were... I didn't know what we were. But I was miserable.

"So what was IT like?"

"I don't know. We didn't do IT. But he's a good kisser."

I had to explain it all again when my mom got off work.

"You did *what?*" my mom asked.

"I know. I'm in big trouble."

"Honey, do you have *any idea at all* what *could* have happened?" she asked.

"Of course."

"And... did it?"

"No! It could have but it didn't. He was a gentleman every step of the way."

This drew a skeptical look. "If he managed to spend a week in the same bed with you and he controlled himself that well he deserves a medal of honor."

I was so naïve. I asked, "why?"

When she explained it all to me, about how powerful sexual urges could be, I felt guilty for putting Tony through that. No wonder I found him sleeping by himself in the van. He did it to avoid hurting me.

"But, Mom, what makes this all even worse is… I miss him like crazy. I don't want to spend the summer without him. I…"

"You love him."

"I do?"

"Do you?"

"I don't know. I don't know what real love feels like."

"Love is what makes you miserable when things aren't right. And it's what gives you the most joy when they are."

"But he put me up in front of all those people and happily admitted he lied to me!"

"And you're miserable, because you love him and he disappointed you."

"Yes! I mean no!"

"Have you forgiven him?"

"If forgiveness is a feeling? No."

"What if forgiveness is a decision that will eventually erase the feelings you hold against him?"

"Then… yes, I think so."

"Then call him."

"What about Meredith's birthday?"

"Just do what you need to."

"Can I rent another car?"

"No, but I'll drive you to your car."

"What would you have done?" I asked.

"I don't know. Your reaction seemed to be pretty normal."

"But I don't even have any clothes!"

"Gwen, I'm shocked that you were able to handle this as well as you have. I just wish you hadn't put yourself in such a precarious position. But your whole future sits in your hands. You either continue in school like you were before you met Twiggy…"

"Tony. The nickname is silly. I can't think of him as Twiggy anymore."

"You either go back to school as if you never met Tony, or you go make up and see how it goes. You can even bring him home for Meredith's birthday party! I'm sure the girls would love to have a college guy attend."

"You mean, I'm not in trouble?"

"Honey, you're just growing up. You know what you did wrong. Now let's try to right it."

I had to buy a couple of outfits. It was kind of fun trying to think of what Tony would like. When I saw him again I wanted it to be like in the books. I wanted there to be joy and forgiveness and sexiness and friendliness all wrapped up into one moment. I knew it was a childish wish and it was unlikely to happen that way, so I only hoped without putting a lot of my heart into the hoping. It took a whole morning to go get my car.

"Now I trust you to know right from wrong," Mom said before she left. "Go follow your heart. If he'll come visit over the summer please try to bring him home."

"I'll try."

All the lonely nights in motels were contrasting sharply with the warm, friendly nights I had spent with Tony. Every lonely moment wiped away a touch of bitterness. I stopped at a rest area and called him when I was about an hour's drive away.

"Hello?"

"Tony? It's me."

"Gwen! How are you?"

"Miserable. Would it be okay if I stopped by…"

"Yes!"

"I don't know what I'm doing. I just had to see you."

There was a long emotion filled silence.

"That would be awesome."

"Okay, I'll call when I get there."

I saw the outskirts of Belle Fourche in the distance so I watched for a large pull out, then I did a search for the closest geocache. Then I did a search to see if there were any caches hidden by The Devious Cachester or Dad's Caddy. Tony only had two that I assumed were maintained by Greg while Tony was in school. I chose the one that sounded the most interesting and then navigated to within six hundred feet of it. It was a pleasant hike, precisely the kind of geocaches Tony liked to look for. But the last fifty feet was waist high brush that had probably grown up after they hid the cache. I bullied my way through and found ground zero to be a twisted old tree. Tony always had liked what he called "trees with personality."

The phone rang once.

"Gwen? Don't hang up! Please don't hang up."

"I'm not."

"Where are you? I'll be right there!"

I thought for a moment, then I read the coordinates off the GPS in my hand.

"I'll be right there! Don't go away." He was so insistent, so hopeful. I couldn't leave. It was a long wait, as I knew it would be, but I passed the time searching for the cache, signing the log, going through the swag, removing old dirty swag and replacing it with swag from my pack. I rehid the cache and sat on the ground reading the descriptions of the nearby caches. Finally, I heard what sounded like an elephant barreling through the brush. And it was Tony! The brush was thick. I knew that because I bushwhacked my way in. "You waited! Oh Gwen, it's so good to see you. I thought I'd ruined everything. I thought you'd never forgive me and I couldn't imagine next semester without you. I couldn't even think about *tomorrow* without you. Don't go. Please don't go away."

He clasped me tightly in a hug. I never felt a hug so urgently needed and I haven't since then, either. I felt a lump in my throat and I willed myself not to cry but it didn't work.

"You're crying. Why are you crying?" he asked as he wiped a tear away.

"I missed you. I reacted badly and acted like a little kid and... once I got on the road reality set in. Reality looked awful bleak without you. But I didn't know how to come back."

"I told you how to get back. Just follow your heart."

"My mom sent me back."

"*Your* mom?" he asked.

"Uh huh. She even took me to retrieve my car."

"Is she all right?"

"Tony... she knew even before I did... I love you. The contest might have been a sick joke, but it worked. It showed us we can depend on each other through thick and thin."

"Let's get out of here. Have you had dinner?"

"No."

"Let's pick up Dad from work... no, let's not. Let's find a place where we can be alone. I have some apologizing to do."

"No, let's find a geocache placed by each of those people at the meet and greet and log that we're back."

"Really?"

It took us all the rest of the day to find one cache for each family and it wasn't really as interesting as the contest had been, but Tony's dad began receiving congratulatory phone calls. I spent the night in Tony's room complete with Fatheads on the wall and team pennants hanging from the ceiling. He slept on the couch. The bed felt empty, so I dragged a blanket down to the living room and we spent an uncomfortable night sleeping sitting up, shoulder to shoulder, on the couch.

"I have to go home," I said the next day. "Mom and Dad would like to meet you. You can see what happens at one of Mom's stuffy birthday parties."

"Do you have to?"

"I should. You're welcome to come along. Oh, and I need my clothes. I had to buy a couple of outfits just to come retrieve the boxes."

"You have to stay," he insisted.

"Tony... the party can't be postponed. The invitations were sent months ago."

"When is the party?"

"Two days, but I had to spend the night in a motel on the way here."

"Stay until tomorrow. I'll make sure you get back on time."

"And how are we going to do that? Fly?"

"One day, just one."

I couldn't imagine what could be so important that it would keep me from Meredith's party. He knew I had promised to be there weeks ago.

That night I found out what it was he was waiting on. We were once again snuggled up on the couch, this time spooning sideways, when his phone made a strange noise. *Briiiiiinggggg!* it said.

"They did it!" he said excitedly out of a sound sleep. "Get some sleep. We need to get up really early to beat the FTF hounds."

"I stayed overnight for a geocache?" I mumbled half asleep.

He kissed the back of my head and squeezed tighter.

"Get a room," his dad joked when he walked into the living room the next day.

"Yikes! Gwen! Wake up!" Tony said as he climbed over me to get to the shower. "Use the one in the hall!" he said to me as he dashed away.

"Coffee," I mumbled as I followed him down the hall.

The shower helped a little. I only had one more outfit that I had bought for the trip so I put it on.

"You need coffee," Tony said when he saw me walking down the hall.

"Am I that bad? You saw me worse. Is it worse than that?"

"No, you just still have the tags on your clothes."

"Oh. Scissors?"

"Scissors, then coffee and a muffin. We'll need the van."

I don't know what he was so excited about. A geocache to be certain. But he already admitted he wasn't an FTF hound.

I removed the tags and Tony grabbed the geocaching gear.

"Aren't we going to read the description and hint?"

"I already did," he said. "It's a regular size. The hint is 'a little higher than pond scum'."

"What's that supposed to mean?" I said as I followed him to the van.

"I'll see you later!" his dad said as we hurried past.

We drove through and got coffee and cheese Danishes.

"Here, you navigate," he said.

"I got the geocaching app on my phone now!" I said.

"Uh oh, you're hooked. You were geocaching deprived enough to download an app?"

"Yeah. But it wasn't the same. There wasn't a lot of celebrating making a solo find."

"I know how it felt. I did a lot of that after I left to go back to school. I'd been geocaching with my dad and then in school I just seemed to be playing the numbers game. Just adding smileys to my list. It wasn't until I took you with me that I really enjoyed it again."

"You could have told me that. We could have done a lot more geocaching during the school year if I knew you liked it so much."

"It's okay. I enjoyed those midnight coffee shop conversations."

"Okay, I think I got it. This is highway 212?"

"It is."

"Okay. I'll tell you when to turn. It looks like we'll be turning left. Hey, there's a big lake out there."

"I know. I've fished there many times. Is the cache near the lake?"

"Yeah. Kind of."

He just grinned as he kept his eyes on the road.

"Okay, the turn is about half a mile ahead. Be watching for a left turn."

There was a sign that said Belle Fourche Reservoir and Rocky Point Recreation Area.

"Okay, turn where the sign says to turn. Oh, look! It *is* a big lake! There's going to be another left."

He turned and followed the road around the lake. I wanted to get out and walk the shoreline but I waited to find the cache first. I saw a little group of trees beside the road and told him I thought the cache was in those trees. We came to a little pullout on the left side of the road but he drove slowly past the trees.

"It is! It's in those trees!"

He drove back and parked the van in the pullout. I handed him the GPS but he said, "No, I want to see you do it."

I hopped out of the van.

"It's a pretty lake," I said. "It could use a few more trees than this."

"Sometimes Dad and I came up here and fished for hours without so much as a nibble. It was a great day if we came home with enough fish for dinner. Dad can cook up a mean fish."

"The fish were mean?"

"I mean he knew a lot of good ways to cook fish."

"I know that. I think the cache is this way. Come on! I didn't see any other cars so maybe we have a chance. I've never gotten an FTF before. Have you?"

"Yeah, though it was a matter of chance. I just happened to be in the area with nothing to do when it got published."

"It's a regular sized one so maybe they put some good stuff in there."

He smiled and followed, then he watched while I looked in all the little hidey holes.

"You could help a little," I said.

He began looking around, mostly looking in the places I had already looked.

"There's one disadvantage to being FTF," I said. "There are no helpful logs to read."

"What's it rated?"

"A one and a half/one and a half. It should be simple."

"Maybe the coordinates are off. Try further out from ground zero."

"Oh! A dragon house! Look! A dragon house!"

It was a little cave carved out of the base of a tree, surrounded by rocks and sheltered from the rain by the tree above. I found a stick and poked it into the hole. I was rewarded by a hollow thump.

"I think I found it!" I knelt in the dirt and looked into the hole. There was the olive green of an ammo can deep inside the hole. "I found it! I found it! Look!"

"Pull it out."

I pulled it out, noting the bright green geocaching sticker on the side.

"Why is it called Eating Crow?"

"Let's see what's inside."

We found a flat spot to sit down and look through the contents. The lid was stiff, but Tony didn't try to take it from me. He just watched as I hopefully tugged and pulled.

"Use the wire on the front to hold it steady, then pull firmly up."

"I am!"

"Pretend you're a soldier. They do this all the time," he joked.

"Private Gwendolyn doesn't quite sound right. Oh, I guess they'd use my last name. Private Brody sounds better."

When the lid finally gave way I nearly fell over backwards. I went straight to the bottom of the can.

"A pathtag! And a Travel Bug! Look! A goofy Pez container."

"Aren't you going to see if we were FTF?"

"Oh, here, you look," I said as I handed him the log book. "And there's a plastic dragon, and a box, and a pair of toe socks. This is a weird cache."

"What's in the box?"

"It's probably just a box. They never put real jewelry in a geocache."

I opened the box.

"See?" I said as I tipped what I thought was an empty box for Tony to see, but as I did it a flash of gold caught my eye. I jerked it back. "Wow! It is a ring, a real ring! Who would do that?"

"Why don't you read the log book and see?"

He handed me the log book and I flipped it open. There was no note of the name of the cache and a place to sign it. Instead, the cover of the notebook had a short letter hand printed inside.

"One day I did a terrible thing. I lied to the one person I swore I would never hurt. I thought I'd ruined my life. I thought I'd never be forgiven and I could spend the rest of my life lonely, wishing I could go back in time and change something. I ate crow. I spent a day up here at the reservoir fishing, thinking, and the next day I did some shopping and hid this cache with the one hope that it would be found some day by a very special person who means the world to me."

I had to turn the page.

"Gwendolyn Amelia Brody, would you forgive me, marry me and make me the happiest man in the world?"

I was speechless. My heart wanted me to leap to my feet and say, "Yes! Yes!" But as a realist I couldn't.

"Follow your heart."

A tear fell.

"Gwen, I'm sorry."

"I want to say yes. I really do. But the future…"

"Will take care of itself as long as we face it together."

"We don't have jobs."

"Gwen, there will always be reasons to put it off. Or we can overcome all those reasons. All I ask is the chance to face all those stumbling blocks with you. Hey, if we can face bears and crazy shot gun wielding farmers we can graduate, find jobs and deal with our parents."

He reached into the cache and pulled out the box. He opened it plucked the ring out and knelt down on one knee.

"Gwendolyn, will you marry me?"

"I... I... Yes! Yes, I will."

It was like the sunshine breaking through after a storm. That hug beside the lake was long and emotion filled. And this time the kiss was genuine, breaking down the walls I didn't know were there.

"I would have said yes, even if there wasn't a ring."

"That's good to know but I wanted you to have it."

"What are we going to do?"

"Don't worry. You worry too much. First, let's go tell your parents."

"Uh oh."

"No, no uhoh's."

"My dad would want to talk to you first."

"So? I'll talk to him."

"You will?"

"Yeah! Probably lots of times. Don't worry."

"Have you ever heard a banshee?"

"No, I can't say that I have."

"Well, when my sisters find out cover your ears."

"Gwen..."

"What?"

"Let's pack up here. We have some miles to travel today."

"I need to sign the log."

"Oh, yeah. Should I leave the cache here?"

"Sure! Why not?"

"Well, because everything in it I placed with you in mind. Look, here's a little dragon. This shotgun shell is to remind you of Insane Asylum. Here's a rock from under the bridge."

We probably added another half hour to our trip to the lake as we took out each thing and he explained how it was connected to some memory from school, or our geocaching adventures.

"What about these silly socks?"

"You had been looking for silly socks for some dorm event but you didn't have time or money to go searching. I had a pair of blue and a pair of brown argyle socks so you borrowed those and wore them mismatched to the event."

"Did you ever get your socks back?"

"I don't know. It doesn't matter. I mostly wear sports socks anyway."

"Let's take pictures of it all and leave it so other people can enjoy our story and this spot. There's lots of stuff in it. I can choose a couple of favorite ones and we'll leave the rest for the other geocachers."

So that's what we did. I kept the pathtag and we took the Travel Bug so we could find a cache back home to drop it into. It wasn't until much later that I noticed the pathtag looked like a golf ball and had Cachester written across it. At the last second I took the little purple dragon, too. In the log I wrote, "She said YES!" and signed my name. I still didn't have a permanent geocaching name.

"I think you should call yourself Engaging One."

I laughed because I thought it would make me sound too conceited, but I understood his pun.

"Or Bahama Bound."

"My hot Bahama Mama."

We laughed all the way to the van.

Chapter 26

We drove to Tony's house and packed up. I hauled my boxes to the car and Tony threw some clothes into an old suitcase. Tony drove all day and all night to get me home in time for Meredith's party. We pulled up to the house and I hesitated.

"What do you think your dad will say?" he asked.

"You can expect all the... expected questions."

"But do you think he'll approve?"

"Give him time. He doesn't know you. I didn't even know you when the semester ended. He'll come around, just like I did. Mom's already convinced you're a saint."

"Gee, thanks."

"Just be friendly, have a plan in mind, and ask him if his laptop is working better."

"He's really a nice guy," he said.

"He is. He just cares a whole lot. And he's never done this before."

The front door bumped open and Meredith bounced down the steps.

"Traditional house," Tony said. "It even has a porch swing."

"Yes, and it's wonderful on cool nights."

"Gwendolyn! You're home!" Meredith said as soon as she reached the car window.

"Traditional," Tony said of Meredith's greeting. "I enter the realm of... THE TRADITIONAL."

"You can lose the alien voice."

"Okay."

"You must be Tony!" Meredith said.

"And you must be Meredith."

Meredith blushed. "Gwendolyn told me about you."

"Happy Sweet Sixteen!" Tony said and gave Meredith a shoulder hug.

"Gwen, will you do my hair?"

And I stepped back into the realm of the traditional. I styled Meredith's hair for the big event. She was so lucky. She had long bouncy hair and big blue eyes. Her dress fit her wonderfully and made her look like a young woman.

Dad was quite taken aback by Tony's hair and cargo shorts, but when Tony spoke intelligently of computers and geocaching and companies that were looking for aspiring programmers Dad fell into the traditional role of the father figure. Tony played soccer with my brother. He even sat through all of an animated movie about an enchanted princess who had to find a serum before her mother died of some horrible curse. And my mother did her best to show Tony what a real mother was like. She doted on him as if he was royalty. She was amazed at the party when Tony knew how to do the twist. I think some of his spontaneousness rubbed off on my family and he was able to see that a traditional family wasn't quite as rigid as he had come to believe.

We were married the summer after that fateful contest. It was a traditional wedding. I wore an elegant white gown and Tony wore a tux... with black and white basketball shoes. At the reception Tony showed a movie he had made of our geocaching adventures. My brother thought the bears were cool. My sister thought the asylum was creepy. Picture after picture moved across the screen and I found myself on the edge of my seat.
"How many mice did you count?" I whispered to Tony.
"Four, but I'm sure there were more."
"Yeah, like the one in my pants," I whispered.

I never did find a college major I wanted to stick to. Tony continued his Computer Science studies and I spent many evenings in the library reading and studying Anything 101. We found over a thousand geocaches, my biggest achievement of the whole school year. I saw shady lanes and rushing rivers, the insides of fence posts, guard rails and lamp post skirts. And all along the way I grew in my wonder of the world around me, thanks to little hidden containers and the people who hide them in places they hope other people will enjoy. In fact, I know of a little grotto that isn't too far from parking. We discovered it while geocaching but there wasn't a cache there. I think I'll hide a cache there.

www.ingramcontent.com/pod-product-compliance
Lightning Source LLC
Chambersburg PA
CBHW020828260626
47169CB00003B/878